ON THE WINGS OF WAR

SOULBOUND V

HAILEY TURNER

Cover design by AngstyG LLC.
Professional Beta Reading by Leslie Copeland: lcopelandwrites@gmail.com
Edited by One Love Editing
Proofing by Lori Parks: lp.nerdproblems@gmail.com
Proofing by Jenni Lea at LesCourt Author Services

Don't miss out on sneak peeks, exciting news, and more!
Sign up for Hailey Turner's newsletter
to stay up to date on her upcoming books.

WELCOME TO THE WORLDS OF HAILEY TURNER

Urban Fantasy
Soulbound

Science Fiction Romance
Metahuman Files

Steampunk-inspired Epic Fantasy
Infernal War Saga

To Leslie Copeland
Because I literally could not do any of this without you.
Thank you for being such a supportive and wonderful friend.

1

SPECIAL AGENT PATRICK COLLINS WASN'T FOND OF WASHINGTON, DC. He had a feeling the people he'd been dealing with for the past three days weren't fond of him either. Patrick hadn't missed the heat, humidity, fake smiles, or the political maneuverings. There was a reason he'd been part of the Rapid Response Division of the Supernatural Operations Agency before being transferred to New York City for a permanent posting—it got him out of this goddamn city.

Patrick was a special agent and not a politician for a reason.

"I hate ties," Patrick said, tugging at the one wrapped around his neck. "I hate suits. Why couldn't I have done all of these meetings remotely?"

"Because you've done enough property damage earlier this year that it's best to remind people you aren't the enemy," SOA Director Setsuna Abuku replied without looking at him as they continued down a corridor in the Pentagon. The military aide escorting them was doing a fine job of pretending not to hear a word they said.

"Chicago was not my fault."

Setsuna finally deigned to look at him, arching one eyebrow. "The people of Chicago beg to differ."

"It was months ago. They should be over it by now."

Setsuna twisted her wrist so her cane smacked him in the shin, never breaking stride. "You know a city doesn't easily recover from an attack like that."

Patrick scowled, knowing she was right. Niflheim had nearly burst through the veil after Yggdrasil had taken root in Grant Park, drawn by Odin's near sacrifice and Hel's sinister power. The mess that had happened in Chicago hadn't been easy to clean up and contain politically. Spring had seen a host of congressional hearings arguing over the threat the Dominion Sect was to the country. The political talking heads in the media had kept the story alive, much to Patrick's annoyance.

As the head of a federal government agency, Setsuna had her finger on the pulse of politics targeting magic users and the preternatural communities across the country. She'd also spent considerable time and clout keeping Patrick in a job and out of the media spotlight over the past four years. Spring had seen her cashing in favors left and right to keep him from testifying in public, but he couldn't get out of closed-door hearings. Patrick would probably be more grateful if it was anyone else looking out for him.

They had a history and they had their differences, two things which ensured Patrick would never completely trust her. The gods had tasked Setsuna with keeping him hidden since he was eight years old. That entailed an identity change, ten years spent at an Academy, and nearly a decade honing his skills as a combat mage with the Mage Corps after graduating from the Citadel. She'd shepherded him down the only road he was allowed to walk with all the gentleness of a drill sergeant under orders.

Setsuna had never been a mother figure to him; neither had she been a friend. She'd done her best, in her own way, to help keep him alive during the years she cleaned house in the SOA. Maybe someday Patrick would be grateful about that, but he carried a soul debt that dictated his life, and he would always feel, in some small way, that Setsuna was complicit in it.

At the moment, Setsuna was still cleaning house. Last summer's betrayal by Rachel Andrita had proven that Setsuna's efforts to remove the Dominion Sect's hidden influence from the SOA hadn't been enough. That failure was why this meeting with those in charge of the joint task force concerning the Morrígan's staff was happening at the Pentagon, after hours, and not written down on anyone's itinerary.

Patrick's reason for returning to Washington, DC, was to meet with Setsuna and separately brief a select group of senators sitting on the Committee for Magical Enforcement, as well as the Joint Chiefs of Staff for the president. SOA Deputy Director Priya Kohli had joined him in those meetings, helping to bring everyone up to speed on the threat the Dominion Sect posed to the United States.

Ethan Greene had been on everyone's radar since it came to light he was the mastermind behind the Thirty-Day War. What most people didn't know—or didn't want to believe—was his true goal. Turning himself into a god was a lifelong mission of Ethan's that had come with setbacks and successes over the years. He was getting closer to a reality none of them would survive if they didn't stop him.

Despite magic being accessible to roughly a quarter of the world's population, humanity living beside the preternatural community, and dealing with monsters and demons, believing in gods was a step too far for most people. Myths still existed as stories people read about. Those who worshipped the gods that had come before the ones currently staking claim to humanity's cumulative hearts and souls weren't nearly as numerous as they once were.

Religion, in all its varied forms, created blinders that many were happy to never remove. Politics aided that tunnel vision. Sometimes the ignorance of men was useful. Sometimes it was a fucking headache.

Patrick's ties to Ethan were buried deep in sealed court records and a past that was as much a nightmare as it was his reality. Stopping his father meant fulfilling his soul debt to Persephone, but the cost of doing so left Patrick waking up from nightmares more and more these days.

The military aide escorting them through the Pentagon veered left, stopping in front of a door with wards etched in the center of it. He touched a finger to the middle of the concentric circles, waited for the flash of magic to subside, then pushed open the door.

"The SOA director, sir," the aide said before waving them inside.

The layers of silence wards were a weight that pressed against Patrick's shields as they entered the heavily protected conference room. The static of white noise buzzed in his ears for a few seconds before it faded to a background hum to his senses. The aide closed the door behind them, leaving them within the SCIF conference room.

"Gentlemen," Setsuna said, giving a perfunctory nod to the two people seated at the long table.

"Director," General Noah Reed rumbled. "Collins."

The three-star Army general looked to be in his midfifties, though he was far, far older than that. A dragon hiding in human form who oversaw the US Department of the Preternatural, Reed had been the drive behind the formation of the joint task force. He was short and barrel-chested in appearance, salt-and-pepper hair cut to regulation length, and had a chain-smoking habit he used as a cover. Reed had no need for cigarettes and cigars when fire burned inside him. Patrick got a whiff of smoke coming off Reed as he pulled out a chair, the smell of sulfur impossible to miss in the small room.

Preternatural Intelligence Agency Director Cornell Franklin was in his late forties, a tall African American man with close-cropped hair going white at the temples. A sorcerer who had come up in the PIA ranks over the years, Franklin had a no-nonsense demeanor that rivaled Setsuna's. It was a trait that should've united them, but as with all federal agencies these days, they were rivals first and allies second when it came to intelligence. The SOA's track record with Dominion Sect interference meant every other agency treated them with inherent suspicion and high walls.

That wariness left the country vulnerable in a way no one liked. What had happened within the last year in New York City and Chicago was proof the status quo in the intelligence community could not continue. The Dominion Sect, and Ethan Greene's desire for godhood, couldn't be fought piecemeal anymore.

The four of them were the only ones attending this meeting. Those others who'd been read into the mission were scattered around the country and the world, unable to join in, or barred from attending if they worked out of the national headquarters in the tristate area. Since Patrick was directly tied to this whole mess, Setsuna and Reed had wanted him present for the meeting. Franklin hadn't fought his inclusion, but Patrick knew he wasn't the other director's favorite person, not after the tough spot he'd put PIA Special Agent Nadine Mulroney in a year ago.

They'd declined an aide for record-keeping purposes because enough leaks had happened over the years that they couldn't risk another one. Patrick figured it was for deniability purposes as well. The leaks issue was also the reason none of the others assigned to the joint task force had called in or scryed in—magical and electronic hacks were still a problem, and they couldn't afford for this plan to get out.

It's why Setsuna kept cycling through burner numbers, and why Patrick's own cell phone went through encrypted security checks every month. Precautions were expensive but necessary.

Setsuna settled into her chosen seat, leaning her intricately carved rosewood cane that doubled as an artifact against the chair beside her. "It appears we are running out of time."

Reed leaned back in his chair and scratched at the edge of his jaw. "Indeed."

"We need to make a decision tonight on who best to sign over the invitation to. If we wait any longer, we'll lose our window of opportunity."

Patrick chewed on his bottom lip, thinking about the invitation he'd left Chicago with back in February. It was technically evidence in a criminal case concerning the Westberg family, but also a vital clue to finding the Morrígan's staff. The spelled invitation was their access to a black market auction the joint task force had finally managed to pinpoint a tentative location for. The break found through signals intelligence indicated it would go down in London within the month.

Patrick was trying very hard not to think about traveling to his partner's birthplace. When Jonothon de Vere had left London because of what Marek Taylor had promised him, the god pack there had exiled him. The pack politics involved in going back was enough to give Patrick an ulcer.

Being separated by half a country back in February hadn't been easy on the soulbond tying them together. Patrick didn't want to know what going across the Atlantic Ocean would do to them if he had to go alone, but it was becoming glaringly obvious they would find out soon.

"We need someone with criminal bona fides who won't be questioned in the black market community," Franklin said. "Forgive me, but your agent isn't going to work."

"Neither will yours," Setsuna replied.

"I have a deep-cover agent who has the background needed to get this job done."

Patrick tried not to wince at the icy way both of them discarded him and Nadine as possibilities. "Special Agent Mulroney and I may not be able to go undercover, but we should still be on the field for this."

Franklin ignored him and turned to look at Reed. "General?"

Reed's brown-eyed gaze moved from Franklin to Patrick, impossible to read. Patrick instinctively sat up a little straighter. Four years out of the Mage Corps meant he might have lost the urge to salute, but he'd probably never give up the urge to stand at attention before his former commanding officer.

"Collins is correct in that we need him on the field. He fought Ethan Greene at the end of the Thirty-Day War and knows how to counter that mage better than anyone in your agency, director," Reed said to Franklin.

Franklin raised a single finger, not looking at their side of the table. "He seems to be in the midst of every problem we've had with the Dominion Sect and Ethan Greene lately."

The unspoken accusation made Patrick clench his hands into fists beneath the table, but he kept his face expressionless. He knew the rumors that dogged him these days in the SOA about his track record with the Dominion Sect. They were starting to outpace the ones that followed him due to his ability to hunt demons and monsters because of a damaged soul.

He'd been at ground zero for the past two attacks against the veil on domestic soil. That was a fact Patrick couldn't escape, not when it was written down in the case files he'd handled. It wasn't a surprise some people looked upon those incidents with suspicion. He ran his cases by the book when he could, but he couldn't say no to the gods when they came around. What the gods wanted didn't always mesh with his job.

"I have the utmost faith in Collins," Reed said, pulling a pack of cigarettes out of the inner pocket of his jacket. He tapped out a cigarette and a lighter that had been stuffed inside.

Franklin's disapproval was writ clear across his face. "The Pentagon has a no-smoking policy, General."

"I know." Reed lit his cigarette before offering Patrick the pack. "Cigarette?"

Patrick eyed the pack for a moment before he shook his head. "I quit last year."

Reed arched an eyebrow before chuckling, a curl of smoke escaping his lips. "At least one of us has."

It had taken boxes of nicotine patches, Jono's unwavering support, and complaining to his VA assigned therapist about the lack of a crutch until he learned to not want it anymore. Patrick handled stress in better ways these days, usually at the hands of Jono while in bed.

Patrick got up to get an empty glass from the credenza and set it near Reed to use as an ashtray. Franklin sighed deeply but didn't say another word about Reed smoking in the conference room.

"My agent is our only option," Franklin said.

"Can you be certain their deep cover will be believed amidst the criminals who will be at the auction?" Setsuna asked.

"My agency knows how to do its job."

The silence that followed was filled with the implication the SOA did not. Patrick shifted in his seat and cleared his throat. "Is your agent someone who is known in the criminal underworld, with enough clout and money at their disposal, and who won't be viewed as a plant or outright killed?"

"We built them an identity they've inhabited for nearly a decade now. It will hold up," Franklin said coolly.

"They may hold up for your agency's needs, but your agent is not going to work for this mission," Setsuna said.

"Then what, pray tell, is your suggestion?"

"It's mine, actually," Patrick said.

Franklin and Reed both looked at him. Reed took a hit off his cigarette before flicking ash into the glass.

"Go on," Reed said, waving his hand holding the cigarette at Patrick.

"A deep-cover agent isn't going to work here, no matter what identity you build. These are the kinds of people who will assume anyone they or their contemporaries don't know is a threat. We risk them issuing new invites and rescheduling the auction if we send in an agent."

"What makes you think they haven't done so already?" Franklin asked.

"If they have, and your agency has no intelligence on that, then we're back at square one," Setsuna said mildly.

Franklin leaned back in his seat and eyed her with a faint grimace. "Don't place your mistakes in my house."

"I'm cleaning up what was in mine when I took over the directorship."

"And your agent is here by the grace of nepotism."

He wasn't wrong, in a way, but it still rankled. Patrick swallowed against the knee-jerk response he wanted to spit out and forced himself to abide by the one Setsuna expected him to give.

"I'm here because I have a job to do, and I get it done," Patrick got out after unclenching his teeth. "Agents won't work, even with a deep cover. Not for this. You need someone who has lived their entire life in the shadows, preferably a couple of centuries, at least."

"You think we haven't vetted any of those options?" Franklin asked.

"I'm pretty damn sure you don't have the person I'm thinking of who will get us into that auction and get us a chance at taking back the staff."

"Then enlighten us."

Patrick dug his fingers into his thighs. "Lucien."

Franklin leaned forward and jabbed his finger in Patrick's direction. "Not on my fucking watch."

"It's all our watch, and I stand by this choice," Setsuna said.

"Your choices haven't been the best," Franklin snapped. "You want to let a mass murderer, one of the world's most wanted monsters across more than a hundred countries, get unfettered access to an auction filled with artifacts? He'll run off with anything he can get, including the staff."

"He won't," Patrick said.

"You don't know that."

Except Patrick did, because Lucien, the master vampire of the

Manhattan Night Court and head of a worldwide criminal empire, owed him a promise of safety, one bound by Lucien's oath to the mother of all vampires. If saving the world from the creation of a new god and a new hell didn't fulfill that promise, Patrick didn't know what would.

"If we make it worth his while, he won't," Reed mused, blowing smoke out of his nose that was thicker than cigarettes alone could account for. "We've done it before."

Franklin leaned back in his chair, brows furrowed. "When?"

"During the Thirty-Day War."

"I thought news of the vampires aiding our side were rumors at the time."

"They weren't, but the classification level involved with that information meant the rumors could never be acknowledged as fact in a public setting." Reed smiled thinly, but his gaze was hard when he looked at Franklin. "Lucien and his Night Court were one of the first to partner with us and our allies at the time. For whatever reason, the vampires have no love of the Dominion Sect."

"They can't eat the dead or demons. Letting the Dominion Sect win means they'd starve," Patrick said.

Some days, he didn't think that would be a bad thing if Lucien went first.

"Do you honestly believe the president will let us strike a bargain with an international criminal?" Franklin asked.

"She did it before and it didn't cost her winning reelection. She'll have nothing to lose this time if we ask," Reed said.

"Do you even know where Lucien is?"

"The SOA has a way of contacting him," Setsuna said.

Franklin snorted, eyeing Patrick. "Through your agent, I presume?"

"I fought with Lucien during the Thirty-Day War. Under General Reed's orders, if you were curious," Patrick said evenly. "I know how to get in touch with him."

"He won't help for free. Monsters never do."

"Paying whatever price he wants will be cheap compared to the Dominion Sect getting control of the Morrígan's staff," Setsuna said.

"We need someone with black market criminal bona fides. Lucien fits that criteria," Patrick added.

Franklin grimaced at that reminder. "And if he says no?"

Patrick shook his head. "He won't."

"You seem pretty damn sure about that. You don't even know what price he'd demand in exchange for helping us. What if we can't pay it?"

"Then we try it your way," Setsuna said.

"You're still trying it my way, because one of my agents will work with yours on this. The PIA refuses to be left out."

Patrick knew the PIA, for all their skill at handling clandestine missions, didn't have an agent with a strong enough identity that would be believed at the Auction of Curiosities and Exceptional Items. But everyone who was anyone in the worldwide criminal underworld knew who Lucien was.

Now all Patrick had to do was get Lucien to agree.

"There's whiskey and scotch in the wet bar," Setsuna said.

Patrick undid the knot on his tie and yanked it off. "You don't drink."

Setsuna set her cane on top of the coffee table in the downstairs living room. "Others who come here do. Some prefer alcohol over water for hospitality purposes."

The home in Dupont Circle that Setsuna had lived in long before Patrick was dropped into her life had belonged to her parents before they passed it on to her. He remembered coming here on school breaks from the Academy he'd boarded in and the two of them not knowing how to live in each other's spaces.

Setsuna hadn't been a mother. Patrick hadn't been her son.

He'd been her ward though, and she'd done her best to make sure he got the training he needed to survive. The gods had required it of her, and Patrick had always felt like an obligation to her. But that was in the past, and neither of them could change the events that had brought them together.

Patrick took in the living room with its drawn curtains, leather couch, and years-old television set. An old-fashioned record player sat on a table beside a bookcase filled with a collection of records. They were dusty, which spoke of long days in the office for her.

There was no hint of his time lived in this house anywhere within its walls. The threshold still remembered him though, and it was an easy weight against his shields as he made his way over to the wet bar. He came to a halt beside it, staring at the small altar Setsuna had set up on a wall shelf above it.

Setsuna was a powerful witch and member of a diminished family coven. She prayed to ancestral kami and the sun goddess Amaterasu in her home, not to the goddess enshrined on the shelf before him. As an only child, with no children of her own, when Setsuna died, her kami would die with her, and her coven would cease to exist.

All covens worshipped spirits, ancestors, or even gods, depending on what they were formed around. Some covens were better about growing, but the ones that remained within families sometimes died out as people found other ways to worship, or ceased worshipping at all. Their altars were all different, where and when they prayed dependent on their individual traditions, but Setsuna had never prayed outside her coven in all the time he'd known her.

This altar was not dedicated to her kami.

Scattered bits of bone shards surrounded a tiny white dish coated in old blood that had built up on the bottom. Two gold rings sat beside the dish, and a white candle was half-burned behind it. It looked similar to the altar Patrick had set up in his apartment in New York City, but he hadn't expected Setsuna to have one as well.

"You pray to her," Patrick said, running his thumb against the edge of a bone shard, wondering if it was human or animal.

Probably human.

"It seemed only fair, considering the bargain you struck with Lucien," Setsuna said.

Patrick set the bone back on the altar. "I don't know what our prayers are worth. Ashanti is dead, and the only people who have ever worshipped her before now have been vampires and their human servants."

There weren't millions of vampires in the world to bring her back the way Santa Muerte's worshippers had prayed her into life. The mother of all vampires might have been loved by her children, but love had never saved anyone before. Patrick had carried Ashanti's ashes off the battlefield beneath his fingernails after the Thirty-Day War was over. She'd died a sacrifice beneath the desert sun, lost to magic and hellish heat, only existing in memory now.

And memory was a fickle beast, easily lost and forgotten.

Lucien did his best to keep the memory of his mother alive. His price back in February to aid their god pack with an alliance of every Night Court in the five boroughs had seemed insignificant at the time. Setting up altars in every home of the packs under their protection had taken a week to finalize, but everyone prayed to a lost goddess now. Looking at the small altar in Setsuna's home, Patrick wondered what Lucien hoped to gain from it.

Patrick poured himself a glass of whiskey, carrying it with him back to the couch. He sat beside Setsuna and took a sip, not saying anything for a long few minutes. The silence that settled over them wasn't easy, but he wasn't going to break it.

"Ashanti is worth whatever we give her," Setsuna finally said, sounding tired. "She always will be."

Setsuna and Ashanti hadn't been enemies during his formative years, when everything they each stood for meant they should be.

Patrick had learned different lessons from each of them, but a few of Ashanti's had cut deeper than all the others, sticking with him through the years. She'd been in favor of war over peace with humanity, but that was just the way of her making.

The mother of all vampires had been a goddess born in West Africa long before borders drawn on a map were even a concept. She'd taken the form of an Asanbosam vampire, and that was the skin she'd lived in, walking the earth on bone hooks sheathed in iron caps and smiling with iron teeth. Her final steps had taken her to Patrick, and she'd died in sunlight that had never burned her until that day.

He swallowed more whiskey, trying to stop thinking about one of his worst failures and the regret that came with it. It wasn't the sort of prayer he wanted to place before the altar in Setsuna's home.

"Director Franklin doesn't seem thrilled about giving the invitation to Lucien," Patrick said.

"Neither am I, but Lucien already has a vested interest in stopping Ethan and the Dominion Sect. I don't trust Lucien, but I trust he'll undermine Ethan first before he tries to undermine us."

"The enemy of my enemy is my friend?"

Setsuna smiled slightly. "In this instance, yes."

Patrick knew Setsuna wasn't above getting her hands dirty if it meant the job got done. She'd done it last year when she'd given up whatever favors she owed Lucien to bring him to New York City. He hadn't left Manhattan after dragging Patrick's ass out of the fire, choosing instead to hide out in the shadows and steer clear of the authorities while raking in money at his club in Chelsea.

Despite the litigation the other New York City god pack was neck-deep in these days, they hadn't yet disclosed to government officials the identity of the master vampire heading up the Manhattan Night Court. Patrick figured Estelle Walker and Youssef Khan were as good as dead if they ever opened their mouths on that subject. Some leverage wasn't worth dying for.

Setsuna sighed and leaned back on the couch. Patrick glanced at the old grandfather clock in the corner, noting how late it was. The military aide who had driven them to Setsuna's home was still parked out front, waiting to take Patrick back to his hotel.

"You need to fly out tomorrow," Setsuna said.

Patrick frowned at her. "I still have a couple of meetings with senators scheduled. You set them up, remember?"

"Eloise Patterson is appearing before a subcommittee tomorrow to advocate for a stronger defense against the Dominion Sect." Setsuna turned her head to look him in the eye. "You cannot be here."

Patrick's fingers tightened on his glass before he dropped his gaze, staring into the amber-colored liquid. After a moment, he nodded silently to that order.

Eloise Patterson was his grandmother on his mother's side, and the high priestess of the Salem Coven. He only had dim memories of her from when he was a child, but he could never make any more. His ties to that side of his family had died in the basement of his childhood home, along with his mother, Clara Patterson.

To stay alive and free from the Dominion Sect's grasp as he grew up under a different name meant Patrick could not reach back into his past and reconnect with what family he had left. Patrick had, for all intents and purposes, become an orphan after the courts sealed away his true identity and granted him a name change to ensure his protection.

No one in the Salem Coven knew he was alive. No one who had the power to interfere in his job as an SOA special agent knew he was Ethan's son.

That secret had to remain buried if he was going to pay back his soul debt.

"Go home," Setsuna said. "Get Lucien to agree to take the invitation on our behalf. I'll make your excuses here."

Patrick ran a hand down his face before bringing the glass of whiskey to his mouth and tipping its contents down his throat. It burned all the way to his stomach. He set the glass on the coffee table with a steady hand. "You don't ask for much."

Setsuna said nothing to that, merely got to her feet when he did. She didn't reach for her cane because she didn't need it for balance. The artifact was a weapon she could set aside behind the threshold of her home.

Setsuna walked Patrick to the front door, holding it open as he stepped outside onto the dark porch. "Patrick."

He half turned to look back at her as the military aide in the town car on the street started the engine. "Yeah?"

"Good luck."

They were outside the barriers of the silence ward and threshold wrapped around the walls of her home. Setsuna would never warn him to be careful of the threats dogging his heels, not out in the open like this. Patrick was thirty now, and had lived a life full of secrets and lies for the past twenty-two years. He'd learned to read between words spoken and stretched silences that were a language all their own.

"Let's not tempt the Fates," Patrick said, facing the street again and heading for the car. "They hate me enough as it is."

2

One of the things that had changed for Patrick since moving to New York City was someone from his pack was always there to greet him at the airport. It was a marked difference from the years of always finding his own way home to an empty apartment or a hotel room after finishing up a case and moving on to the next, or taking some much needed R&R back when he was with the Mage Corps.

Jono was easy to spot in the crowd of people waiting to greet arriving passengers in LaGuardia. The tall Brit looked good in a pair of dark jeans, white T-shirt, and aviator sunglasses that hid his wolf-bright blue eyes, a trait that pegged him as a god pack alpha werewolf. Unlike many of the people around them, Jono wasn't sweating through his shirt from the June heat beyond the sliding doors.

"I checked my luggage. We need to grab it," Patrick said in greeting.

Jono leaned down and kissed him on the mouth. "That's fine. Welcome back."

Patrick sighed against his lips. "Thanks for coming to get me."

"Always." Jono pulled back, a smile tugging at his mouth. "Let's get your things and be off."

Patrick's carry-on consisted of his backpack that held his MacBook and the lockbox for his agency-issued semiautomatic HK USP 9mm tactical pistol. As a special agent, he was permitted to bring his gun onto the plane, but the only weapon he always carried on hand with him while traveling was his gods-given dagger. The look-away ward embedded in the leather sheath meant no one spared a second glance for the weapon strapped to his right thigh.

The dagger was a powerful weapon that could break high-level magic in ways no magic user alone ever could. Patrick had used it in Chicago to save Odin, disrupting the spell Ethan and Hel had tied the Allfather to. Odin's godhead had returned to him at the edge of the Bifröst between worlds, bringing life back to the immortal's body.

While they hadn't lost Odin, they'd lost his spear to Loki. Gungnir wasn't a weapon they could afford the other side to have, but the choice between saving Odin or stealing back the spear during the fight on Navy Pier had been an easy one to make. As far as Patrick knew, Thor was searching for Loki, but since the Norse trickster god could shapeshift, he had a feeling that hunt could take years, and that was time none of them had.

"How'd everything go?" Jono asked.

Patrick made a face. "We'll talk about it in the car."

Jono nodded, and Patrick led the way to the baggage claim. Patrick's time in DC had been stressful, but standing beside Jono as they waited for his luggage to arrive was enough to loosen his shoulders. He always felt better when Jono was close by, and that steadiness had nothing to do with the soulbond tying them together. Jono was Patrick's safe harbor in the storm that was his life, one he never knew he needed. That would never change.

Jono grabbed Patrick's luggage when it finally appeared and led the way back to the Mustang. He'd parked in the hourly lot, and even though he probably hadn't been waiting long, the interior was like a sauna in the summer heat. Patrick got in and immediately switched on the air-conditioning to full blast as soon as Jono started the engine. The air blowing out of the vents was hot, but it cooled off eventually.

Patrick waited until they were past the pay gate to set a silence ward within the frame of the car. The wash of static drowned out the sound of traffic around them as Jono headed for Manhattan.

"Any trouble while I was gone?" Patrick asked.

"Bit of a scuffle in Brooklyn, but it got sorted before I arrived," Jono said.

"Werecreatures or hunters?"

"Rival pack. I haven't seen any hint of hunters for at least a week."

Patrick frowned, thinking about the date night that had gotten interrupted because a pair of Krossed Knights looking to gain respect from their fellow hunters had tried to ambush them. *Tried* being the operative word, because the two hadn't been prepared for a mage who could sense the demons from hell riding their souls and a werewolf who had no problem permanently taking out a threat.

Estelle Walker and Youssef Khan were the alphas of the rival New York City god pack. Over the years, the pair had made horrific bargains with an old master vampire who'd been murdered by Lucien. Their latest bargain was with the Krossed Knights. The pair had placed a bounty on Jono's head in February while Patrick had been in Chicago chasing a lead on the Morrígan's staff.

If Estelle and Youssef thought Jono and his pack would be easy prey, they had severely miscalculated. Jono, with Fenrir's help and without consulting Patrick first, had made a bargain with Lucien. The alliance with the Night Courts meant Estelle and Youssef had been forced to reassess their position after Jono officially staked his claim on New York City.

But neither side was backing down.

So far, they were fighting block by block for territory that was expanding wider and wider with every pack that defected from Estelle and Youssef and came to them asking for protection. The bounty on Jono's head from the Krossed Knights hadn't gone away, and the packs they were responsible for were still in danger. Alliances with the fae and vampires gave them some breathing room, but Patrick had a feeling things would get worse before they got better.

Cities never fared well when two god packs fought over territory. The NYPD's Preternatural Crimes Bureau was aware of the burgeoning civil war, and Chief Giovanni Casale wasn't happy about any of the fighting going on. Patrick had heard from Casale personally about the problem and the NYPD's concern, which were never fun phone calls to take.

It put Patrick in an uncomfortable position. As a federal agent, he wasn't supposed to have any overt biases that could impact his cases. Being the co-leader of a god pack—and not having informed anyone other than Setsuna of that fact—was going to be a problem at some point. Patrick risked all the cases he'd worked on for the past year being scrutinized and tossed out when word broke of his pack leadership, but he didn't have a choice. This was the path the gods had told him to walk, and they didn't believe in the rule of mortal law, only their own.

"What about you?" Jono asked, reaching out to settle his hand on Patrick's thigh. "What happened with your meetings? I thought you weren't coming home until tomorrow?"

Patrick curled his fingers around Jono's and propped his right elbow against the edge of the window so he could rest his head against his fist. "Setsuna ordered me back early."

"Why?"

"My grandmother is speaking to some members of Congress today. I had to leave."

Jono tightened his fingers a little before relaxing his grip. "They still need to think you're dead?"

Patrick grimaced, staring out the windshield. "Yeah."

"Do you want to reach out to them?"

"I can't."

"But do you want to?"

Patrick opened his mouth to respond, but the words were jumbled in his head. He snapped his mouth shut and stared at the traffic ahead of them on the highway.

"Want is a meaningless desire. That was one of the first things Ashanti ever taught me," Patrick said slowly.

Jono shook his head. "That's a load of bollocks."

"It doesn't matter. Letting my mother's side of the family know I'm alive would be a messy distraction I can't afford right now. We have bigger problems."

"Like what?"

Patrick straightened up enough that he could dig his cell phone out of his pocket. "Like we need to have a meeting with Lucien before we go home. The government needs his help."

Jono made an aggravated sound. "Must we? I had plans. They involved you naked and under me."

Patrick sighed wistfully even as he dialed the latest burner number to reach Carmen. "I'll let you fuck me after we deal with Lucien."

"This is why Sage always says you're terrible at bargains. We should probably have her come with us and do the talking instead of you."

"You think you're funny, but you're not." Patrick pressed the phone to his ear, listening to it ring. "We can have a pack meeting after Lucien pisses me off."

The line picked up and Carmen's sultry voice drifted into his ear. The succubus was Lucien's partner in all ways, and the face of his business ventures in daylight hours. While Lucien could walk in sunlight without burning—a gift courtesy of Ashanti—he didn't like to advertise that particularly rare vampire trait.

"How was DC?" Carmen asked.

Patrick made a face even though she couldn't see it. "Spying on me again?"

"It would be lax of us not to have eyes and ears in the governing bodies of every country we work in."

"Right. Because you're on the same scummy level as lobbyists. I need a meeting with Lucien."

"He's resting."

"Then wake him up."

Carmen's voice became flat, the protectiveness she felt for Lucien evident in her tone. "He does not answer to you."

"He can answer to the United States government, who I represent. Tell him General Reed sent me. There's an offer on the table, and we need to know what he wants in exchange for helping us. We'll meet you at Ginnungagap in an hour."

Carmen hummed thoughtfully before ending the call without a word. Patrick pulled his phone away from his ear and scowled at it.

"What's the offer?" Jono asked.

"We need Lucien to carry the invitation to the auction and buy the Morrígan's staff," Patrick said.

"He'll run off with it."

"Maybe not."

"Why can't you do it?"

"Because I don't have the background necessary to pull something like that off. There's a strong possibility Ethan may have warned whoever is running the auction about me, and to be on the lookout for government agents in general."

Jono sighed. "All right. Where is the auction taking place?"

Patrick glanced over at Jono. "London."

The way Jono's grip tightened on the steering wheel said as much as the silence that settled between them. It lasted until they were halfway to the Queens Midtown Tunnel, but Patrick didn't try to get Jono to talk until he was ready.

"London," Jono finally said, voice empty of all emotion.

"Yeah. Our intelligence indicates the auction is being held there. Whoever is Medb's intermediary, they're selling it in the black market equivalent of Sotheby's or some shit."

"Do you have to go?"

"Probably. Lucien needs oversight."

Jono looked at Patrick over the rims of his sunglasses. "You're the last person he'd ever obey."

Patrick snorted. "We're gonna have to make it worth his while."

"What's it going to cost?"

"Not my soul."

Jono pulled his hand free to smack Patrick lightly on the chest. "You aren't funny."

"You love my sense of humor."

"I love you, even when you're a right arsehole."

Patrick didn't fight the smile that came to his face. Jono's love was something he didn't ever want to take for granted, even if he couldn't bring himself to voice the same words back. A year of being together and Patrick could arguably say he'd found the man he wanted to spend the rest of his life with—if he managed to survive.

"You know, we missed our anniversary dinner because I was in DC," Patrick said.

Jono turned his attention back on the road. "I thought we agreed it was after summer solstice?"

"Okay, so we missed our pre-anniversary dinner. I still think the first night we met needs to be celebrated."

They could do without fighting a soultaker, but Patrick wouldn't be averse to some wall sex.

"We could be celebrating it soon if we didn't have to go see Lucien."

Patrick groaned. "Stop reminding me about how much my job sucks."

It was a means to an end on some days. Paid the bills on others.

He was a pawn no matter how one looked at it, and when Jono finally turned down the alley that ran the length of Ginnungagap in Chelsea, Patrick was tired of the overtime already. A familiar motorcycle was parked by the side door ahead of them, which meant Lucien had arrived before them.

"Tell Fenrir not to interfere," Patrick said as they got out of the car, the summer heat a heavy blanket of mugginess in the air around them.

"Might have better luck with you not having a row with Lucien," Jono mused.

Patrick shoved him, but Jono barely moved. "Hilarious. Of the two of us, you tend to threaten to tear out Lucien's throat more than me."

"Because I have the teeth and claws to do it." Jono flipped his sunglasses on top of his head, revealing his wolf-bright eyes. "Let's get this over with."

The side door was unlocked, the brass plate detailing out the name Ginnungagap gleaming in the sunlight. What lived in the building's walls was a heavy pressure against Patrick's shields as they crossed the threshold into a muffled silence that always echoed strangely in his ears. Ginnungagap, the yawning abyss, was a primordial void whose unearthly power reached through the veil to settle here.

Ashanti had made a deal with the Norse pantheon for its use, or so the story went, and out of all her children, she'd left control of it to Lucien. Whether or not he could do anything with it outside of making a club that brought in humans for food and kept out most magic users due to the unsettling feeling Ginnungagap produced in people was up in the air.

Patrick was able to grit his teeth and stand within these walls because he had to. Fenrir was birthed out of the void, and from what Jono had told him, the god considered it a home away from home.

The club lights had all been turned on, chasing away the shadows. The air-conditioning had not. Patrick was sweating by the time they made it over to the bar on the first floor. Carmen sat perched on a stool, wearing jean shorts cut high over her hips, a lacy bandeau, and heeled sandals the same patent leather red as her lipstick and the pupils of her eyes. Her thick, black curly hair was pulled off her neck in a high ponytail, the curled horns of her kind twisted back over her skull. Despite the skimpy outfit, she wasn't lacking in the weapons department.

The sexual desire all her kind exuded hung in the air like perfume around her. Patrick strengthened his shields against her power and ignored the smirk Carmen directed his way. Naheed, Lucien's favorite human servant who doubled as Carmen's bodyguard during daylight hours, stood behind the bar, sipping at a glass of water. The necklace of bite scars circling her throat were courtesy of Lucien's teeth. The pistol that sat on the wooden counter within easy reach was an extension of her hand whenever she held it.

The master vampire in question still had blood on his lips from feeding off her. Lucien stared at them with black eyes like holes in his pale face, no sclera showing. The black jeans he wore were torn over the knees, and the shirt beneath his leather jacket was more gray than white. His dark hair was messy from the motorcycle helmet sitting on the bar counter.

Lucien had been sired by Ashanti directly, the last child she'd ever made. He was almost a thousand years old, born in the time of William the Conqueror, and better at changing with the times than any of his brethren. Patrick always thought Lucien's desire for murder stemmed from his stint in that ancient army as much as the hunger for blood that drove him these days.

"I hear Reed can't get the job done again," Lucien said from where he lounged against the bar.

"General Reed has always gotten the job done, no thanks to you," Patrick retorted.

"The battle at Cairo would have ended differently without help from us vampires. Your history books tend to gloss over that fact." Lucien smiled, revealing sharp, jagged teeth. Vampire teeth weren't pretty, despite what Hollywood showed on the big screen. "I'm curious what your government wants from me this time."

Patrick and Jono came to a stop a couple of feet from Lucien. Patrick kept his hands loose by his side, his dagger and magic within easy reach. Despite the alliance they'd brokered with Lucien, Patrick would never trust him.

"We have a lead on the Morrígan's staff. There's an auction happening in London. Black market, deep pockets, and run by people like you," Patrick said.

"There is no one like me."

"Maybe, but everyone who got invited are all arrogant fucks like you, so you'll fit right in."

Lucien didn't move for several seconds; his chest didn't rise and fall because the undead had no need to breathe save to speak. When he finally did, he sounded viciously amused. "You want to use my name."

Patrick nodded. "They'll see me coming a mile off. Anyone the PIA tries to send in will get made, probably killed, and I'd bet good money the police would find their body dumped in the Thames. People who run in those kinds of circles know each other. They don't trust outsiders."

"And you think they will know me?"

"Everyone who matters in the shadows of the preternatural world knows you. If you walk into that auction carrying the invitation, they won't question it. You're a believable buyer."

"All I hear is a job. I'm not hearing an offer."

Patrick grimaced. "Price isn't an issue. Whatever you want, the government will pay."

Lucien didn't react, but Carmen sat up straighter, a slow smile curving her mouth. "Carte blanche is a dangerous offer. Your president must be desperate."

"The government believes Ethan getting control of the Morrígan's staff is a worse situation than whatever threat your Night Court poses," Patrick said.

"You don't know what I'd demand in payment," Lucien said.

"If it is within the government's ability to pay, then they will pay it."

Carmen slid off the barstool and sauntered closer to Lucien. She wrapped an arm around his waist and rested her head on his shoulder. "We won't be asking for money."

"Got enough dosh?" Jono asked. "That's a first. I thought you were the greedy sort?"

Lucien blinked slowly, a sleepy-eyed predator hunting for prey. "Money is useful, and I have a lot of it. What I don't have is the legal freedom to walk upon these shores."

Patrick stared at Lucien before shaking his head. "I thought you didn't care about pieces of paper that confer rights on a person?"

Lucien draped one arm around Carmen's shoulders. "I don't, but you humans do."

"I'm pretty sure the government would draw the line at handing over a state or two for you to rule. Us Americans are allergic to monarchies in this country."

"If your government wants my help, then it will let me and my Night Court remain in the United States without being arrested or spied on. I'll take that guarantee in writing." Lucien smirked. "Consider it diplomatic immunity."

"So you want the government to just look the other way every time you break the law?" Patrick asked incredulously.

"It can't be a difficult task," Carmen said. "They do it for you."

Patrick wanted to argue that wasn't true, but he'd be lying if he did. Setsuna did her best to cover for him while he followed the gods' orders, but even she had limits. So far, his ability to get the job done despite the property destruction was enough of a defense against the resentment he ran into. He knew that wouldn't hold up forever.

"Diplomatic immunity. Right. I'll pass it along," Patrick said.

"You have twenty-four hours," Lucien said.

Patrick scowled. "That's not enough time to make the government agree on anything."

Lucien smiled, fangs pricking his pale lips, all the blood licked clean. "Twenty-four hours. If my terms aren't met, then the deal is off the table and you lose the staff."

"You lose your food if the Dominion Sect turns Earth into a brand-new hell," Jono shot back.

"Then consider the deadline an incentive to get shit done."

Patrick dug out his cell phone and dialed Setsuna's latest burner phone number. The signal wasn't the best inside Ginnungagap, but it eventually connected. When the line rang, he hung up. He repeated the action two more times before calling a fourth time and staying on the line. It picked up after the fifth ring.

"I'm about to leave for a hearing. Make it quick," Setsuna said.

"My criminal informant will agree to show up if we give them diplomatic immunity. The deal is on the table for twenty-four hours," Patrick said, giving the news in the bland descriptions like they'd agreed on. They were risking a phone call now because they didn't have time for Patrick to fly back and forth as a courier.

Setsuna sucked in a sharp breath. "Understood. I'll relay the terms."

She hung up and Patrick shoved his phone back into his pocket. He raised an eyebrow at Lucien. "Happy?"

"We'll let our lawyer take a look at whatever contract the government comes up with," Carmen said.

"You have a lawyer on retainer?"

"Don't sound so shocked. Anyone can be bought for the right price."

"We're buying you," Lucien pointed out.

"The hell you're buying me. I've been off the market since I was eight," Patrick said.

Lucien slipped free of Carmen's arms, sauntering toward them. Jono took a step forward, not getting in the way of Patrick's line of sight, but making his presence known nonetheless. Jono and Lucien had gone toe-to-toe several times in the past, both of them fighting to a draw.

"Twenty-four hours," Lucien said, keeping his attention on Patrick. "Now get out of my fucking club."

Patrick turned his back on Lucien when smarter people never did. He knew Jono would keep him safe. He also knew Lucien was bound by a promise he'd made to his mother to keep Patrick alive in the fight against the Dominion Sect.

Patrick still expected to be stabbed in the back one day.

Jono's footsteps behind him drew closer until they were walking side by side. They left Ginnungagap for the muggy heat outside, city noises rushing back into his ears once they crossed the threshold. Patrick pulled the collar of his T-shirt away from his scarred chest, trying to get some air flowing against his skin.

"We should get everyone together for a pack meeting," Patrick said.

Jono beeped the alarm off and opened the driver's-side door while Patrick looped around to the other side. Jono looked over the top of the car at him. "Do you want to call them, or should I?"

"You drive. I'll call."

"Where are we meeting them?"

"Marek's place. It won't be as crowded."

Their two-bedroom apartment in a Chelsea brownstone could handle their close group of friends, but Patrick had been cooped up in committee rooms and airplanes for the past week. He wanted space, and Marek owned an entire Art Deco building in the Upper East Side. Pack meetings were easier to conduct there when they needed to include people other than the four that made up their god pack.

"Everyone's working," Jono reminded him.

"Not anymore."

Sometimes pack business had to come first.

3

Jono looked up when Wade Espinoza came barreling through the front door, arms laden down with plastic shopping bags nearly overflowing with snacks. The nineteen-year-old fledgling fire dragon hopped on one foot while trying to keep his balance as he kicked the door shut behind him.

"Am I late?" Wade wanted to know.

"Did you clean out a bodega?" Jono asked.

Wade sniffed haughtily as he came over to where everyone lounged in the living room of the apartment Marek and his fiancée, Sage Beacot, called home. "'Course not. I left the vegetables."

"Just for that, we're making you eat double portions of vegetables tonight," Patrick said, not looking up from his mobile.

Wade flopped down onto an empty armchair and immediately started digging into his bags. "Gross. I'm allergic to vegetables."

"You're allergic to actual food, mate," Jono said, raising an eyebrow at the candy bars and bags of crisps spilling into his lap.

Wade ignored them both, sorting through his hoard of snacks

with a happy look on his face. Jono opted not to argue about the merits of real food over processed junk food and looked over at Sage. Their pack's dire was furiously tapping away on her laptop, a slight frown marring her pretty face. Her thick black hair was pulled back in a chignon to get most of it off her neck in the hot weather, and she hadn't bothered to change out of the pantsuit she'd gone to work in. She had kicked off her high heels though, and the Louboutins were tucked under the coffee table.

"Okay, I've emailed Tiarnán about needing time off. I don't think it will be a problem," Sage said.

She set her laptop on the coffee table, her diamond engagement ring catching the light. Sage was a partner at Gentry & Thyme, a fae-owned and -run law firm whose managing partner was their contact for the Seelie Court. Tiarnán had helped broker their alliance with the fae and followed through whenever they needed assistance. Jono was always uncomfortably aware at how easy it would be to owe the fae beyond the terms of their alliance, so they tended to let Sage do the talking.

Their dire could play word games as well as any fae, but it was her steely resolve and calmness in the face of adversity that made Sage the rock he and Patrick leaned on every day. Luckily, Tiarnán knew what was at stake, and his firm was more than willing to cover Sage's cases when she needed to be with them.

"We had cake tasting planned for this weekend," Marek said with a mournful sigh from where he lounged beside Sage on the smaller sofa.

Wade's head snapped up. "Cake?"

"Wedding cake decision, and no, you don't get to come," Sage told him.

"But Sage, it's *cake.*"

"You have enough Twinkies in your bags that you basically have a full cake," Leon Hernandez said as he came back from the kitchen with a beer.

Wade looked Leon dead in the eye while digging out a packet of Twinkies and opening it slowly. He shoved the entire snack into his mouth and chewed with bulging cheeks. "Doesn't taste like wedding cake."

"Don't talk with your mouth full, Wade," Sage told him while Leon laughed.

Leon and his partner, Emma Zhang, were the co-leaders of the Tempest pack, some of Jono's closest friends, and the ones who handled access to Jono's time with other packs when Sage was busy. Their bar that Jono managed was neutral territory for his god pack, but a target where Estelle and Youssef were concerned. Packs went there to socialize and work out problems between each other, but it had been the site of attempted vandalism lately that was as much a warning as a threat. Luckily, the wards Marek had paid a lot of money for were holding.

"How big is this cake going to be?" Patrick asked.

"Big enough to feed me," Wade said.

"It's our wedding, not yours," Sage reminded him.

Wade turned a pleading look on her. "Can I have my own cake?"

"Sure. Next year on your birthday."

Wade groaned dramatically before opening a bag of Cheetos and shoving a handful of the neon orange crunchies into his mouth. Jono shared a look with Sage before shaking his head.

"I hope this latest mess won't disrupt your wedding plans," Jono said.

"Everything is on track," Sage said with the firmness of someone who was ready to go to war and win to ensure she got married on her chosen date.

Marek had proposed to Sage last year, and the wedding was scheduled for this August. Jono hadn't been involved much in the preparations except to agree to walk Sage down the aisle.

Patrick looked up from his phone and gave Jono a half grimace, green-eyed gaze steady. Jono couldn't stop himself from reaching out to smooth back some of Patrick's wayward dark red hair.

"No news yet on what the task force has decided, but we should plan accordingly," Patrick said.

"That doesn't sound ominous at all," Emma drawled.

Patrick slouched on the sofa until he was resting most of his weight against Jono. The silent request for contact had Jono shifting until he could wrap an arm around Patrick's shoulders and hold him close. It was a public sort of comfort Patrick only allowed amidst their group of friends, and Jono knew none of them took that trust for granted.

"The Auction of Curiosities and Exceptional Items is going to be held somewhere in London this month," Patrick said.

"How soon?" Sage asked.

"We won't have an actual date, time, and precise location until the spell written into the invitation recognizes the owner. But the invitation is starting to get spelled ink lines in the instruction section. They haven't formed words yet. I'm betting the words will show up within a week or so though, which is why the joint task force is finally making a decision about everything."

Jono looked over at Marek, and he wasn't the only one. As a seer, Marek's ability to see the future came with a price—blindness, madness, and then death, usually by way of suicide. For the past year, his visions had become few and far between, mainly because of Patrick and the fight against the Dominion Sect. With various Fates working for the heavens and the hells, the future was ever-changing. No single Fate had a monopoly on a future set in stone, and Marek's patrons had been curiously silent for months. It meant less migraines for Marek, less risk of losing color and bits of his sanity, but they all knew this break wouldn't last forever.

"I haven't seen anything," Marek said, hazel eyes staring into the far distance.

Sage reached up to curl her fingers over his chin and turn his face toward her. "Don't look if the Norns haven't given you a reason to."

Marek blinked and smiled wanly at her. Jono wasn't sure how many shades of color Marek had lost since last summer, but he still felt guilty about every hint of gray seeping into his friend's vision.

"Can you really trust Lucien to take this invitation to the auction?" Leon asked as he sat on the armrest of the chair Emma had claimed. He draped an arm over her shoulder, tangling his fingers in her fishtail plait. She didn't seem to mind him messing up her hair.

Jono snorted. "Nah, mate. That's why we'd have to go."

"One of us needs to stay here," Patrick said, tipping his head back a little to look at Jono. "We can't cede New York City to Estelle and Youssef. I left for Chicago and they sent hunters after you. I don't want to know what they'd use this time to claim back what territory they've lost if I go to another country."

"I'm not letting you go to London alone."

"You were exiled from that city."

"Sage can talk our way into pass-through rights."

Sage rolled her eyes. "No pressure."

Patrick grew tense beside him, and Jono gently rubbed his fingers against Patrick's arm. "We'll work it out."

Patrick said nothing to that promise.

"If you're all going, then I'm going," Wade said right before he burped.

"That leaves us without our god pack," Emma pointed out. She didn't look worried, but Jono could smell it on her, the sudden spike that cut through her scent. "None of us can afford that, not with the Krossed Knights still stalking the streets."

"We have the fae and the Night Courts to aid us," Leon reminded her.

"That aid was brokered through Patrick and Jono. Will it still hold if they don't have a presence here?"

Jono frowned. "I don't know."

God packs always required a sustained presence in the cities they claimed territory in. If the entire pack left, that essentially gave up the city. But the idea of Patrick going off to Europe alone was unthinkable to him, and not just because of the soulbond.

London was an ache Jono would always carry with him—a home that had never wanted him before or after he was infected with the werevirus. Growing up in a council estate in Tottenham was worlds away from the wealthy parts of London he'd traipsed through as a lad. He was always made to feel like an outsider as a child because he and his family had been poor.

Once he was infected with the god strain of the werevirus, things got worse. The London god pack hadn't wanted anything to do with him—either because he brought nothing to the pack, or his anger back then had been a problem. Jono never got an answer from the alphas at the time, and while he'd been allowed to stay in London, he hadn't made many friends. He didn't get a pack until moving here, and Jono wasn't willing to lose his family *or* his territory.

"What if we have a proxy?" Jono asked slowly. "If we bring others into our god pack who don't carry the god strain and designate them with the authority to lead in our absence, would that still keep our foothold in New York?"

Sage frowned thoughtfully. "I honestly don't know if that's been done before. There's no precedent for something like that."

"Emma and Leon took Marek into their pack."

"The Tempest pack isn't god pack, and no one is going to argue with the Fates."

"Patrick does," Wade muttered.

"Don't be like Patrick."

"The only one with the god strain of the werevirus in our pack is Jono. I know that gives us some legitimacy, but the rest of us don't meet any criteria people expect of a god pack," Patrick said.

"And we've been fighting for acknowledgment since day one because of that," Sage reminded him.

"Then if you think a proxy alpha won't work, a dire will," Jono said.

Sage glared at him. "I am not staying behind while you two destroy any and all political avenue of god pack alliances."

Jono winced. "I'm gutted at your lack of faith."

"And I prefer no headaches."

"I'm not asking you to give up your title and rank. I'm saying what if we appoint a second dire?"

"There is only ever one person who holds that pack title and rank."

"Yes, but if you're with us, we need someone *here* to keep hold of our territory. If Estelle and Youssef get to call in hunters and no one in their pack will call them on their bollocks, then we can change up the rules on them." Jono looked over the top of Patrick's head at Emma and Leon. Both his friends were staring back at him with unblinking eyes and steady heartbeats. "Emma? If we take you into our god pack as our proxy dire, you can watch over our territory here."

He'd already taken them and their Tempest pack under his protection last year. They might not have the god strain of the werevirus running through their veins, might not have the bright amber eyes that designated them god pack here on this continent, but Jono would trust Emma, Leon, and their Tempest pack over any of the other god pack members currently residing in New York City.

"Estelle and Youssef won't see me as god pack," Emma warned.

"The packs under our protection and the god packs who acknowledge our place will."

"I'm up for pissing them off if you are," Leon said, tugging on Emma's plait.

Emma looked up at her partner, giving him a slight smile. "I'd never pass that up, but if we do this, our entire pack will lose what's left of their anonymity. If I'm dire, even temporarily, that's a lot of public scrutiny."

God packs existed to take society's punches so other packs could live normal lives. The Tempest pack could blend in with mundane humans, but Jono couldn't hide. He wouldn't want them to go through what he did on a daily basis when out in public, but holding their territory was important.

"We can find a different way," Patrick said.

Jono shook his head. "I don't think we can."

"Forcing Emma to give up her autonomy isn't fair."

"If our entire pack is going to London, we need someone else to represent us here in New York. We can't just abandon our territory."

"Then maybe you should stay."

Jono fought back a scowl. "I'm not letting you fly to another country without me, Pat."

Patrick eased away from Jono a little. "And I think forcing Emma into a corner is being a shitty friend."

A tense silence followed Patrick's statement. It was broken only by Emma clearing her throat. When Jono looked over at her, he couldn't see any hint of accusation in her gaze, and she smelled calm to his senses.

"We've been heading toward more scrutiny for months already. It's not a surprise, it's just not ideal, but it's also something I wouldn't ever say no to," Emma said.

Leon smoothed his hand over her shoulder in a comforting manner. "Em."

She reached up to slide their fingers together. "We both lead for a reason, Leon. If I act as dire here for Jono's pack while they're gone, you can still keep our pack safe because Tempest will still have an alpha."

"I don't want you to stand alone."

"She won't be alone," Patrick promised before Jono could speak up. "If this is what's being decided, then she'll have the backing of our alliances. I'll see if maybe Brynhildr and her valkyries might want to spend some time in New York while we're gone. They can keep Emma company when she's doing proxy work for us outside your guys' pack."

"Isn't that asking the gods to interfere when they're technically not supposed to?" Marek wanted to know.

Patrick snorted. "They make up and break their own rules all the damn time. The valkyries liked New York when they were here in February. Just let them drink for free at the bar."

Emma got a pained look on her face. "We went through double our weekly inventory last time they were here. That mead they sell is damn good though."

"I'll adjust the order when I go in tonight," Jono said.

Patrick wouldn't look at him. "You're still working?"

"Not much else I can do, not until you hear back from your director. Friday nights are always busy anyway. My workers can use an extra hand."

"Right. Enjoy that."

Jono raised an eyebrow at Patrick's terse words. The anger coming off Patrick was subtle, but there. He didn't think it was just about asking Emma to act as their proxy dire.

"You all right?" Jono asked.

"Fine."

The shortness of Patrick's reply had Jono reevaluating his schedule for the rest of the day. The bar would keep for a while longer until after he'd driven Patrick home and talked through whatever had suddenly put Patrick in a strop.

"I'll take you home. You can't have the conversation you'll need to with the government at the bar."

Patrick said nothing to that. Emma got gracefully to her feet and padded over to where they sat on the sofa. She settled on the coffee table in front of Jono, head tilted to show off the line of her throat. Jono placed his hand against her throat, feeling her pulse beneath his fingers. The scent of Emma's pack was strong in Jono's nose as he pressed his own scent into her skin. She might not carry his strain of the werevirus in her veins, but she'd carry the proxy mantle of a god pack dire against Estelle and Youssef with all the righteousness of a mean right hook.

"I'll keep watch over New York City," Emma promised.

"We all will," Leon added.

"I know," Jono said.

Because that was what pack did.

4

———

LUCK SEEMED TO BE WITH THEM WHEN THEY ARRIVED HOME AND A parking spot had opened up in front of their brownstone. Jono claimed it before anyone else could, locking the car doors once they were out and the luggage had been removed from the boot.

The teeth-shivering sound of stone grinding against stone had Jono glancing up at the roof of the five-story brownstone. Lined up on the edge were the half-dozen gargoyles the fae had convinced to take up residence on the property back in February. They'd started off with three, but once the gargoyles became aware of Patrick's presence, three more had joined the group.

Jono thought they'd done it to annoy Patrick, who wasn't overly fond of gargoyles and tolerated them at best because he had no choice. Gargoyles were great home guardians, added value to a property, but they certainly made a mess everywhere. The amount of pigeon feathers that drifted onto the stoop these days was annoying, and their grinding chatter could get loud on occasion.

Jono carried Patrick's luggage up the flights of stairs to their flat, depositing it in their bedroom. He came back out to find Patrick in the kitchen, pulling a beer from the refrigerator. The air-conditioning had kicked into higher gear, cooling off the flat to a degree Patrick preferred in the face of the summer heat outside.

"Grab me one?" Jono asked.

Patrick silently got out a second beer, opened both, then left the kitchen to hand one to Jono. He would've kept walking if Jono didn't curl an arm around his waist, keeping him there. Patrick took an angry swallow of his beer but didn't try to break free.

Jono frowned at him. "Why are you angry?"

"You shouldn't come."

"To London?"

"Yes."

Jono shook his head. "I'm not letting you go off on your own. I already told you we're doing this together."

Patrick finally pulled away, glaring up at Jono. The anger in his scent was strong, but worry cut deeper. Jono wished he could soothe it all way. "The London god pack exiled you."

"That doesn't change the fact I'm going with you."

"You coming with me is a good way to piss them off and get hurt."

"None of us are safe anywhere. You know that. Stay, go, it doesn't matter. Someone is always out to get us these days."

Whether gods, hunters, mercenary magic users, or rival god packs, they had giant targets painted on their backs. If Patrick couldn't see they were stronger and safer together, Jono would have to argue with him until he did.

"We risk losing too much if we all leave New York. Even with Emma as a secondary and proxy dire, that doesn't fix the problem of us not being here," Patrick said flatly.

"I risk everything I care about by letting you fight alone. We tried that with Chicago, and look how things went pear-shaped."

The strain put on the soulbond by the distance between them had been hard, but being separated was worse. Not knowing what was happening with Patrick had been stressful. Jono didn't regret the choices he'd made in Patrick's absence, but he regretted the hurt it had caused the other man. Jono wasn't willing to go through that again.

Patrick's mouth twisted, lips going white from the pressure. Jono reached up and pressed his fingers to the seam of them.

"We're a pack, remember?" Jono said softly. "I'm not leaving you."

"I'd come back," Patrick said, breath ghosting over Jono's fingers.

He said that more these days—a promise that was *I love you* in sound, if not the right syllables. Jono had yet to hear those three words come out of Patrick's mouth, but he didn't miss them. He knew where they stood, and he wouldn't change what they had.

Sometimes, though, he wished Patrick wasn't so bloody *thick*.

Jono pulled his hand away, fitting it over Patrick's hip and stepping closer so they stood chest to chest. "I know. But you have a tendency to try to martyr yourself, and I'm tired of watching you break yourself into pieces in order to stay alive."

Some of the anger faded from Patrick's scent as he heaved out a sigh. "I just don't want *you* to get hurt."

"I know London better than you, Pat."

"It's been years since you left. Things have probably changed. With our luck, it's probably not good changes."

"We'll sort it out when we get there. If we have to, I can track down some old mates. They might be able to help us get in touch with the London god pack on our terms." Jono paused. "Or they'll ignore us and warn everyone else I'm back."

Patrick took another sip of his beer, shifting beneath Jono's touch but not pulling away. "Are you sure reaching out is a good idea?"

Jono raised an eyebrow. "We can't ignore the London god pack like you did the Chicago one."

"Hey, everything worked out in the end."

"We were lucky Naomi and Alejandro hated Estelle and Youssef more than our transgressions into their territory. The

London god pack won't care either way if we don't ask for pass-through rights. They may deny us outright because of me."

"What's the punishment for you going back after you were exiled?"

Jono wasn't going to lie to Patrick, but he wished Patrick had asked that question after their airplane tickets were bought. "The alphas at the time were adamant they'd kill me if I returned. They considered me abandoning them a betrayal."

Patrick scowled. "That's bullshit. You were a fucking independent werecreature for the entire time you were there. You didn't owe them shit back then. If they want any piece of you, they'll need to go through me, and good fucking luck with that."

"I know."

Fenrir's presence uncoiled in the back of Jono's mind, clawing at his soul. *They will not get the chance to harm you.*

A god's promise was fickle, as Jono had come to learn through Patrick. They weren't to be trusted, even if they owned your soul or lived in it.

"We'll make it work," Jono promised in a gruff voice. "Emma will keep hold of our territory, and we'll do what the gods require in London."

Patrick slumped forward and rested his forehead against Jono's shoulder. "No chance I could convince you to stay behind?"

"No."

"Not even with a blowjob?"

Jono squeezed his hip. "Wouldn't say no to that, but you need a kip and I need to get to work."

Patrick sighed heavily but didn't move. "I want you safe."

"I'm safest right by your side. We're better together. You know that."

Jono shifted a little, forcing Patrick to lift his head. Jono tipped Patrick's chin up, leaning down to kiss him slow and deep, tasting the beer on his lips. If the gods wanted them to fight, then they would fight—together. Patrick needed to accept this was one argument he would never win.

"You're knackered. Go to bed and I'll see you tonight," Jono said after he broke the kiss.

Patrick licked his lips. "You sure you don't want that blowjob?"

"No."

"Fine."

He sounded so grumpy that Jono could only laugh, despite everything going on. "I'll see you tonight."

"Yeah. Leave me the car in case I need to go into the office."

Jono nodded, and Patrick tugged him down for one last kiss. He no longer smelled of anger, but the worry remained. Jono doubted it would ever go away.

It was close to dawn on Saturday, last call fifteen minutes away, when the door to Tempest was pushed open and a familiar heartbeat filtered through Jono's hearing. He looked up from drying a glass, watching as Patrick came his way. The only people in the bar besides them were the werewolf acting as a bouncer at the door and a group of witches who'd been consoling a member of their coven going through a breakup. Most of them weren't capable of driving, and if they weren't going to call a taxi or an Uber to get home, Jono would do it for them.

"Hey," Patrick said.

His blank expression was all the hint Jono needed to know that Patrick had heard back from Setsuna. Jono nodded over at the only occupied table. "Let me get them sorted, and then we'll chat."

It took upward of fifteen minutes to close out their tabs and get them a taxi with the help of their only sober friend. She tipped him well enough, and Jono handed the twenty dollars to his employee watching the door.

"Head home. I'm closing up shop early," Jono said.

The werewolf didn't argue, just took the money and left. On a hot night like this, no one had to grab any jackets from the employees-only room. Jono closed the door and locked it. The protective wards etched into the doorframe flared up brightly for a split second before the magic embedded in them faded away. When he turned around, Patrick was behind the bar, pulling a bottle of Macallan 12 Year whiskey off the shelf.

"Did you drive?" Jono asked.

"Parked out front in Marek's spot," Patrick said.

When Marek had bankrolled the bar for Emma and Leon some years back, he'd bought rights to the parking spot directly out front on the street. It was convenient on nights like this.

"If you're drinking, then I'm driving."

Patrick pulled down two glasses. "We're both drinking."

Jono scanned the dirty bar, mentally cataloguing everything that needed to be cleaned up before he left for the night, and opted to take a break. "All right."

Patrick placed both glasses on the bar counter and then wrote out a silence ward between them. The sigil glowed softly, the pale blue color of Patrick's magic a familiar sight. Patrick's bitter scent —a hint at the damage to his soul and magic—settled around them, telling Jono he'd lowered his shields. Beneath the bitterness was a tangle of sharper scents that always spoke of stress.

"What did the government say?" Jono asked.

Patrick took a sip of his whiskey before answering, looking out of place behind the bar. "They've agreed to Lucien's terms. Mostly."

"Is mostly going to be enough?"

"Probably? Setsuna told me the lawyers are arguing over the details right now. Lucien will take the invitation to help us retrieve the Morrígan's staff in exchange for one hundred years of free passage through the United States' borders and diplomatic immunity."

Jono winced. "He's going to make a mess of things."

"Yeah, but we'll be dead and gone when the agreement comes to an end."

"Your president is okay with making a deal like this?" Patrick shrugged, hunching his shoulders a little. Jono reached for his free hand so he could slide their fingers together. "Your name isn't on that agreement. History won't blame you for it."

"The decision is classified for national security reasons, but that won't stop people from finding out the truth in the future."

"Not our problem. Not yet."

Patrick took another long swallow of his drink, putting a dent in what he'd already poured. Jono hoped he wouldn't have a second glass. Patrick had given up smoking last year, but drinking away his stress was sometimes the choice he made when he could afford to. Old habits and vices were sometimes difficult to unlearn. For all the years that Jono had worked in pubs and bars to make ends meet, watching people drown their problems in drink was a common occurrence, and never the answer to anything.

Jono didn't much care for that habit, and he liked it even less when the man he loved gave in to it. If they were home, he'd do his best to distract Patrick with sex, but that wasn't an option here.

"Setsuna said it'll be finalized by Lucien's deadline. They've got the legal departments of two agencies and a military branch reviewing the agreement and parsing every single word. PIA Director Franklin is appointing one of his agents to meet me in London," Patrick said.

"Nadine?"

Jono liked Patrick's best friend. Nadine Mulroney was a lovely person with a spine of steel and got on well with the pack.

Patrick shrugged. "I won't know until I get to London. Reed has already ordered the invitation to be extracted from the Repository and escorted to DC for the handoff."

Jono raised an eyebrow. "That soon? When does Lucien leave?"

"For DC? After sunset tonight. They want to brief him before dawn on Sunday, and he won't go without Einar. Lucien has to at least pretend the sun is a problem for him."

"What about London?"

"He leaves for that city on Monday." Patrick drew in a breath. "Same day I do."

Jono tightened his grip. "*We* do."

Patrick made a face. "Yeah, all right. We already fought over that."

"Don't be stroppy."

"I'm not." Patrick took another sip of whiskey. "Could the British government stop you from entering the country?"

"I don't think so. I still have British citizenship. The London god pack was able to exile me from the city, but they didn't have the political connections necessary to revoke anything else."

Patrick nodded slowly. "We can't hide what you are, but I'll tell Marek to reach out to his government handlers, and I'll give Setsuna a heads-up. He can let them know you need clearance. Maybe that will help our chances on the other side of the Atlantic."

"Lying about his visions is a federal crime."

"Who's going to question him?"

Jono snorted and let go of Patrick's hand to join him behind the bar. He cupped Patrick's jaw with one hand, smoothing his thumb over a lightly freckled cheek. Patrick met his gaze without blinking, and Jono didn't hesitate to kiss him, slow and sweet, sharing the breath between them.

"We'll figure it out," Jono murmured against his lips. "We always do."

"One of these days our luck will run out."

Jono squeezed Patrick's hip with his other hand, holding him close. "Luck has nothing to do with any of this."

If anything, it was the Fates, but Jono had come to terms with what Patrick meant to him months ago. He loved Patrick because he could, because *he* wanted to, and no god would ever tell him otherwise.

"London's calling," Jono said. "We better answer."

Patrick rolled his eyes and pulled Jono down for another kiss. "At least you have decent taste in music."

Jono laughed against Patrick's mouth, refusing to give in to the worry eating at the back of his mind. They'd find out soon enough what problems waited for them across the pond.

5

THE LAST TIME JONO HAD WALKED THROUGH LONDON HEATHROW, he'd been on the Departures level, leaving with a rucksack, a carry-on, and the bitter memory of being unwanted following him to the States. Heathrow was the same sort of hamster maze Jono remembered from years ago, but at least this time he wasn't fighting the crowds alone.

Jono reached out and hooked a finger over the collar of Wade's T-shirt, hauling the teenager away from the direction of the Costa stand just outside the passport control area.

"No," Jono said in a firm voice. "You ate on the plane."

"But I'm *hungry*. It feels like it should be dinner, not lunch," Wade grumbled.

"If he has coffee, he'll stay up until tonight, and that will help with the jet lag," Sage said as she tucked her passport into the oversized Louis Vuitton tote bag she'd traveled with.

Wade scowled. "Jet lag is for the *weak*."

Jono let Wade go, reaching up to shove his sunglasses higher on his nose. Getting through Customs had taken longer for Jono than the other two, but not nearly as long as Patrick. While the agent overseeing his queue had pulled Jono aside for further questioning, he at least hadn't been escorted to a private room like Patrick had been.

Having Patrick out of his sight didn't help the tension in Jono's shoulders. He couldn't blame the tightness on shit sleep for the overnight flight, not when Sage had booked them all first-class tickets since those were the only ones available last minute. No, his anxiety had everything to do with the proverbial English soil he was standing on for the first time in years.

Sage grabbed the handle of her carry-on and nodded at the sign indicating the location of the car hire desk. "We need to get a car."

"The Tube is the easiest way around London," Jono said.

"But not the quickest on short notice. Patrick is going to need a car, and so will we."

"Do I get one?" Wade asked.

"No," Jono and Sage said in unison.

Wade rolled his eyes. "Whatever. I'm getting coffee."

He ran off before Jono could tell him to stick close. Sage shook her head at Jono. "Let him have the coffee."

"He's going to be bouncing off the bloody walls," Jono said with an irritated sigh.

"When isn't he?"

Wade made it back to them with coffee in one hand and a bag of pastries in the other well before Patrick finally escaped Customs. Patrick's dark red hair was easy to spot in the sea of people he cut through to get to them once he was finally cleared.

"What took you so long?" Wade asked.

Patrick scowled. "They needed to double-check my credentials and the paperwork for my dagger. Long blades are restricted in this country."

He'd left his gun at home, because the UK's Department for Witchcraft and Supernatural Affairs had refused to clear any firearms for the SOA. The WSA had argued that Patrick was a mage and his magic would be enough within the country's borders. Jono had listened to Patrick whinge about how magic wasn't always the answer on the entire drive to JFK Airport yesterday. It wasn't new information. Patrick defaulted to his sidearm or dagger as often as he used his magic in a fight.

"Let's get our cars and get out of here," Patrick said.

"Do you even know how to drive on the wrong side of the road?" Wade asked.

"Shut it," Jono said. "You Yanks are the ones who do everything backward."

Wade arched an eyebrow in supreme teenaged judgment. "Mr. Green Card over here doesn't think he's a Yank."

"Have you heard his accent?" Patrick asked.

"I'm *surrounded* by his accent now."

Jono shoved Wade toward the car hire counter. "Let's go. We need to get the cars and our luggage, and then head for the hotel."

"We could've stayed at the Dorchester," Sage said with a deep sigh.

"The government doesn't pay for comfort," Patrick reminded her.

The rest of them *could* have stayed at the Dorchester, but the pack was sticking together, and since Patrick's job dictated their movements in terms of lodging, they'd gone with the Sanderson London.

Getting there took time. They had to confirm their car reservations, get their luggage, and then go retrieve their rentals at the offsite lot. Jono had spent years driving an automatic in New York when he got behind the steering wheel at all. Having to drive a manual again required dredging up the skill from the back of his mind. When he inevitably ground the gears together, Patrick gave him a sidelong look.

"Should I drive?" Patrick asked.

Jono rolled his eyes. "No."

It came back to him—the manual driving, the city streets, and the people who sounded like he did. Driving into London after years of being away was a shock to the system that left Jono at a loss for words for miles on end.

"Are you all right?" Patrick asked when they were some distance down the M4.

"I will be," Jono said, refusing to lie.

Patrick reached over and settled his hand on Jono's left thigh, his touch familiar in a way London hadn't been at the end.

"I won't let anyone hurt you," Patrick promised.

Jono smiled tightly, teeth clenched together. "This isn't your jurisdiction. Don't do anything that might get you arrested."

"I'll have some legal authority with whoever I end up working with out of the WSA."

"Your badge isn't going to get you out of trouble like it does in the States."

"The gods will."

"Let's not rely on those arseholes, yeah?"

Jono glanced at the rearview mirror, seeing Sage's car behind them, refusing to let anyone merge between them. She was a deft hand at driving a manual, a knack Sage had probably picked up from some of the expensive sports cars she and Marek shared.

"I have a feeling we won't get a say in that." Patrick scraped his fingernails gently over Jono's jeans-clad thigh. "If you got the chance to come back here and stay free and clear, would you?"

"I'm not leaving you."

"That wasn't my question."

"You're my home, Pat. The only pack I've ever had. London doesn't have anything for me. Not anymore."

He'd wanted it to, when he was younger, but he'd learned over time that a city couldn't care for you—you needed a pack for that.

But the memories came back to him on the drive into the city center: the years growing up in Tottenham, falling in and out of the wrong crowds that could never seem to fully leave the council estates behind. Living on the outskirts of all the packs in London, barely scraping by with jobs in pubs and construction work. He'd left nothing behind and was returning with everything he'd ever wanted, found on another shore.

Jono wasn't willing to lose any of it.

He knew Emma would hold the line back in New York while they chased after the Morrígan's staff. Jono hoped all the precautions they'd scrambled to set up wouldn't fall apart, and that everyone they'd left behind would be safe.

"When will Lucien ring you?" Jono asked.

Patrick shrugged. "Whenever he gets settled. I'm assuming he chartered a private flight over here for himself and whoever he ordered along."

"He's not taking his entire Night Court?"

"No. He's making sure the government back home won't go back on its word. Lucien doesn't trust any authority but his own."

"Arrogant wanker."

Patrick huffed out a laugh. "Yeah."

They took the Chiswick Roundabout onto the A406, turning onto the A40 and taking it all the way to the Fitzrovia District in central London. The Sanderson London was a street or two up from Oxford Street, taking up half the block in a slightly dated-looking building, but the interior, once they made it inside, had a modern vibe to it. Sage, unlike he and Patrick, was greeted by the manager on duty the second she walked through the doors ahead of them.

"Ms. Beacot, a pleasure," the man said with a professional smile. "The penthouse suite is ready for you and your guests."

Sage smiled back politely, handing off her luggage to the porter with an absentminded ease that spoke of wealth in a way Jono didn't think he'd ever be able to emulate. "Thank you. It's been a long trip."

They left Sage and Wade to the capable hands of the hotel's staff and headed for the receptionist counter so Patrick could check in. He needed a separate room to keep the government from learning about the pack. If he left London without a hotel invoice, too many questions would be asked.

"Two people?" the receptionist helping them asked, glancing over at Jono, who still had his sunglasses on.

"One," Patrick corrected. "But I'll take two keys."

Patrick had booked a standard room with a queen-sized bed, and Jono must have been in the States for too long, because he thought it looked positively tiny when they entered it. The third-story street view wasn't much to look at, and the room smelled like cleaning solutions and bleach from the white sheets and duvet. Jono's lip curled a bit before he dialed down his sense of smell.

Patrick tipped his luggage over onto the floor in the bathroom, since that's where the wardrobe was located, and started to unpack. He'd checked a bag, because apparently he'd had to bring along a couple of suits for the times he'd need to work out of the WSA. Jono had honestly been a little surprised he'd owned any. Jono left his luggage by the bed, choosing to unpack later, and waited for Patrick to finish up.

"At least we won't have to fight Wade over the bed," Jono said when Patrick came out of the bathroom.

Patrick rolled his eyes. "I'd have let Sage get him his own room if we weren't in foreign pack territory."

They'd all agreed to pair up as much as possible while in London, though they all knew Patrick would have to work alone some of the time. Jono didn't like that, but the nature of Patrick's job made it inevitable, and CCTV made it difficult to wait around government buildings without looking suspicious.

Familiar footsteps in the hallway caught Jono's ears seconds before someone banged on the hotel door.

"Hey!" Wade called out. "You better be dressed. Sage wants us upstairs."

"If he has air freshener, I'm confiscating it and spraying his bed," Patrick decided.

"I heard that!"

Jono laughed and got to his feet. He followed Patrick out of the room, finding Wade waiting for them in the hallway, eating from a bag of Walkers cheese-and-onion crisps. He shoved another handful into his mouth, then jerked his thumb over his shoulder.

"You can't get to the penthouse without my key card, but Sage has some upstairs for you guys," Wade said.

"Let's be off," Jono said.

Wade left a crumb trail to the lift. They rode it back down to the lobby so they could switch over to the private lift that would take them to the penthouse suite. Wade waved his keycard in front of the sensor pad with greasy fingers, gaining access. The lift took them to the top floor, opening up onto a small foyer.

They followed Wade into the suite, the spacious open-plan area bright with early afternoon sunlight streaming through the windows. The curtains had all been opened, offering up a distant view of the London Eye on the south side of the Thames. Jono paused, taking in the sight.

"Someone with a long gun wouldn't even need to work hard to take out anyone up here," Patrick said.

He conjured up a mageglobe, still muttering about sightlines. Jono left Patrick to ward the penthouse while he went in search of Sage. He couldn't track her by scent, but the two-bedroom suite was only so large. The turquoise pendant filled with fae magic that masked her scent completely and hid her status as a weretiger had been latched firmly around her throat before she even stepped foot outside her home yesterday.

Jono found her unpacking her luggage, an open bottle of sparkling water within easy reach. She flashed him a quick smile as she hung up a summer dress in the wardrobe.

"Wade has raided the minibar for snacks already," Jono said.

"We can afford it," Sage replied.

Beyond the tithes he and Patrick received from the packs under their protection, Marek was a billionaire and had given Sage access to all his accounts years ago. He had no problem fronting costs for their pack. Jono had long since gotten over the awkward-ness of needing and asking for money for pack needs, and receiving it with no strings attached.

Sage had changed out of her linen trousers and loose blouse that had been her travel outfit. Her skinny jeans and fitted shirt were trendy enough that she wouldn't look out of place in the city.

"We need to meet with the London god pack alphas. Those overtures aren't something we can afford to ignore," Sage reminded him.

Jono sat down on the bed. "Were you able to get any contact information on them?"

Sage shook her head and pulled another dress out of her luggage, this one protected in a garment bag. She'd come prepared to dress for any manner of events or meetings that might be thrown in their path.

"Other than one of the alphas who had exiled you having lost her position in a challenge ring some time ago, no. I'm hoping Patrick might be able to get what information we need from the WSA."

"Jessamine was forced out?" Jono asked, unable to keep the surprise out of his voice.

Sage glanced at him. "You didn't know?"

Jono shook his head slowly, thinking about the older god pack alpha who had passed judgment on him years ago. "Anyone I was mates with that I left behind risked punishment if it was found out we kept in contact. We cut ties because we had to. Once I was in the States, I didn't care about what happened in London."

He'd wanted to in the beginning—had tried to keep up to date on what was happening in the werecreature community he'd left behind. But the distance and lack of communication made it diffi-cult until he'd come to the bitter conclusion it didn't matter anymore. None of the people he'd left behind had wanted him in the first place, while Emma, Leon, Marek, and Sage had been more than willing to fill that void at the time.

"Patrick doesn't meet with the WSA until tomorrow. I don't think we can afford to wait that long to announce our presence here. Do you have a way we can try to get information?" Sage asked.

"Might do," Jono said slowly. "We'd need to go to Hackney for it."

Sage frowned slightly, looking at him with concern in her brown eyes. "Are you sure?"

"Sure about what?" Patrick asked as he wandered into the bedroom. "I've warded your suite."

"We need to find a way to contact the London god pack."

Patrick made a face. "Do we really need to do that today?"

"I don't know if we'll be asked to meet, but we need to call. Jono thinks he can get us their number."

Patrick sighed, looking over at Jono. "So where are we going?"

"We can try the last place I used to work. There might be someone in the old neighborhood there who will have information," Jono said.

"Will there be somewhere we can eat? Wade is decimating the minibar."

"Yeah."

"Then let's go."

<hr>

JONO'S PREFERENCE would've been to take the Tube, but if they needed a quick getaway, a car was more useful. They took Patrick's rental instead of dividing up into two vehicles. Jono drove, needing the GPS app on his mobile to show him the way. He wasn't a black cab driver with the Knowledge, and he hadn't owned a car while living in London. He'd relied on his mates if he needed a ride, and his memories of London's streets were best mapped through the Tube and bus stops.

"I'm hungry," Wade whined from the back seat.

"Shut it. We're almost there," Jono said.

"Do you even know where you're going? It feels like we've been driving forever."

Jono ignored him, taking the next left. Midafternoon meant the street traffic wasn't terrible. While many people took the trains in, Jono doubted the evening rush hour had gotten any better since he'd left London. Finding parking was the hardest part. There wasn't a public car park to pull into, and they had to wait for a metered spot to open up one street over from their destination.

City blocks in London were nothing like those of a city built on a grid. And unlike central London, the area of Hackney they were heading to was a poorer section of the neighborhood, with many of its buildings run-down compared to the wealthier parts of the city. It meant their rental stood out a little, but Jono figured Patrick's magic would help it blend in.

They got out, Jono's sunglasses firmly on his nose as he took a deep breath, getting the scent of the place. The city smells mixed with a particular one that meant *pack*, but beneath it was a faint hint of smoke that was embedded in the concrete in this area. He couldn't smell Patrick or Sage at all, and Wade smelled as human as he could be these days.

"I thought we were going to a pub? One with food?" Wade said accusingly.

"We will be, but we need to pop into the kebab shop first," Jono said.

Wade perked up at that, grinning widely. "Gyros?"

"Kebabs."

"Whatever. It's a tasty food wrap, and I want ten of them."

"You think the same person still owns the shop?" Patrick asked as they walked down the street.

Jono shrugged. "I'm out of the loop with everything here. The shop might not even be there anymore. In which case, we'll go to the Black Knight where I used to work."

"Oh, hey! They have snacks," Wade said, pointing at the corner shop across the street.

"We'll get you lunch in a few minutes," Sage said.

"But the gyros place won't have chocolate."

The light changed and they crossed the street. Jono was unsurprised when Wade darted into the corner shop. Sage sighed loudly before turning to follow him. "Order me a mixed doner kebab. We'll be there as soon as I can pry Wade out of the candy aisle."

"Good luck with that," Patrick said.

The kebab shop was several shop fronts down, and the smell of greasy meat and chips hung heavy on the air outside it. The door was propped open, and a couple of people were eating at the counter by the window. They stepped inside, and Jono was glad to see that Ahmed was still working behind the counter.

The djinn hadn't cared about his status as an independent werecreature when he lived here. All Ahmed cared about was Jono's ability to pay for food. They'd been friendly in their interactions, but they weren't mates.

"Huh," Patrick said from beside him, the quiet curiosity in the tone easy enough for Jono to decipher.

"He's not like the bloke in Chicago," Jono said.

"I'll be the judge of that."

Ahmed was looking at them through narrowed eyes, smelling a bit uneasy to Jono's nose. The djinn still looked exactly the same as he had years ago on the night Jono and Marek had eaten dinner and had a chat about his future. Jono stepped up to the till and shoved his sunglasses up on top of his head.

Ahmed's eyes went wide. "Never thought I'd see you walk through my doors again, Jono. I thought you'd left for the States?"

"I did. I'm back temporarily," Jono replied. "I was hoping we could chat."

Ahmed pointed at the sign bolted over the food prep counter, listing out the kebab shop's menu with corresponding pictures. "Better feed yourself first."

Food in exchange for information was a cheap price to pay. "All right. Two fish and chips, one mixed doner kebab, and ten doner kebabs."

Ahmed didn't blink. "That's a lot of food for just the two of you."

"It'll get eaten."

Ahmed placed the order in the tablet, and Jono stuck his card in the reader on the counter. The total wasn't terrible because the prices were cheap enough. While the cook on duty started filling their order, Ahmed crossed his arms over his chest and studied Jono with dark brown eyes in an expressionless face.

"Last I heard, you were exiled," Ahmed said in a low voice.

"Still am," Jono admitted.

"And still a bit thick, are you? What are you doing here?"

"Been out of touch with everyone. I don't know how to reach the god pack alphas here to ask for pass-through rights for my pack. I figured you might be able to point me in the right direction."

Ahmed's thick eyebrows crept toward his hairline. "Your pack?"

"Yeah. My pack."

Ahmed's wary gaze flicked over to Patrick for a second before returning to Jono. "He's not a werecreature."

"We're a tad unconventional."

"If you want gossip, you won't find it here. You'd have better luck ringing up your old crew for that." Ahmed nodded at the windows. "They're still about. The lot of them spend time at the Crossed Arms. I don't see them much here."

"They aren't welcome?" Jono asked. That was a surprise, as Ahmed had been one of the few shop owners who had done business with Jono and his mates back then without hassling them.

Ahmed gave him a thin-lipped smile that looked forced. "London runs on crazy these days, mate. Especially amongst the werecreature community."

Before Jono could question that remark, Wade's loud cackle

echoed through the air. Jono half turned, watching as Wade came into the kebab shop carrying a shopping bag bulging with crisps and biscuits. He held a familiar-looking box in one hand, using his other to pry a Jaffa Cake free of its plastic wrap and shove it into his mouth.

"Jono, these are *amazing*," Wade got out around a mouthful of food. "I think I might like them better than Pop-Tarts."

Patrick shook his head. "That's a first."

Wade dug out another Jaffa Cake and held it up for them to see. "Look! Chocolatey cake goodness."

"We bought you ten kebabs for lunch."

Wade beamed at them. "Don't worry, I'm still hungry."

"Chew with your mouth closed," Sage said as she came inside.

"I am!"

"No, you aren't," Jono told him.

Wade shoved the Jaffa Cake into his mouth, staring past Jono. "Are those my gyros?"

Jono turned around again, eyeing the multiple takeaway bags the cook was setting on the counter for pickup. Then he noticed Ahmed had gone a little pale in the face, his gaze riveted on Wade.

"Ahmed?" Jono asked.

The djinn's brown eyes flashed with an inner light—a hint of fire burning within his black pupils. "That one is—"

"Pack," Sage interrupted calmly as she stepped up to the counter to retrieve the takeaway bags. "As am I."

Ahmed blinked, and the fire in his eyes was gone, though the acrid scent that now surrounded him couldn't be explained away by the cooking meat behind him. He stared at Jono in silence for a couple of seconds before shaking his head.

"Are they who the seer promised you?" Ahmed asked.

Jono thought about that night years ago when he and Marek had come here to discuss his future, and Marek had promised him a pack he'd never find in London.

"Yeah," Jono said, refusing to lie about the people he cared about.

Ahmed nodded slowly. "Is the young one with you of his own free will?"

"Duh," Wade muttered before digging out another Jaffa Cake.

Jono rolled his eyes and rapped his knuckles on the counter. "Cheers."

He led the way out of the kebab shop. It might have been years since he'd walked these streets, but he knew where the Crossed Arms was. He'd drunk enough pints there to never be able to forget it.

"What now?" Sage asked as she passed Wade a bag of kebabs.

"We see who's up for a chat," Jono said.

6

The Crossed Arms was a shitty pub—always had been, always would be. But that's the way its regulars liked it.

Unlike Tempest, the Crossed Arms was an utter mess, the floor sticky underneath their feet from spilled pints and spirits when they walked in. Jono's nose twitched at the smell of stale beer and worse messes that permeated the air. The walls were scribbled over with graffiti from decades of people staking their claim in this space. Jono's name was somewhere on the wall, probably buried under someone else's ink by now.

The pub was dimly lit and not overly full on a Tuesday afternoon. People were still at work, after all, but some of the locals were around. The bartender laughed at something one of his patrons had said but cut himself off when a dark-haired man abruptly stood from the table at the far end. Jono recognized him by scent alone, despite the long years since their last meeting.

"Oi!" Tom Milner called out in a Scouse accent that had never faded in all the years he'd lived in London. "What do you want?"

"Is that any way to greet an old mate, Tom?" Jono asked.

His memory of Tom had grown fuzzy over the years. Standing

across from him now sharpened in Jono's mind all the times he'd stood in this same pub, hanging out with the lads who hadn't always been human. Tom was the sort of bloke who was shit at hiding what he was, but luckily, most of the people who came to the Crossed Arms didn't care. He was short and barrel-chested, carrying less of a paunch than he had some years ago, but still easily pissed off, judging by his greeting.

Tom's ruddy face went through a complicated rush of emotion, as did his scent. "*Jono?*"

"Yeah, mate. I'm back in town for a bit."

Jono took his sunglasses off, and Sage discreetly palmed them from him, tucking them into her purse. Wade veered away from them to go sit at the bar, dropping all of his bags on the counter and claiming a chair. He rifled through the containers, took out a kebab, and started eating.

"What the bloody fuck?" Tom came forward, staring at Jono in shock. "Since when? I haven't seen you in *years*."

"You know why."

"Fuck me, bruv. I can't believe you're back."

Tom gripped Jono's hand and pulled him into a back-slapping hug that Jono accepted without a second thought. Of all the people in London who might want to stab him in the back, Tom was at the bottom of the list.

"Good to see you," Jono said when they separated.

"Who's this?" Patrick asked with the particular shade of curiosity in his voice that always told Jono someone was about to get hurt.

"Old mate of mine who didn't care much that I was an independent werecreature when I lived here."

"Who's the Yank?" Tom asked, eyeing Patrick with the bristling annoyance he'd always had with new people.

Jono ignored the question. "Got a table we can have a chat at?"

Tom hesitated, gaze flickering back to Jono's face. After a

moment, he gave a sharp nod and gestured for them to follow him. "Can't chat long. You know why."

Jono's mouth twisted. "Yeah."

Jono, Patrick, and Sage followed Tom to the rear of the pub, bypassing the table filled with three other werecreatures, who watched them intently. Tom waved at them. "It's all right. I'll handle it. Don't ring no one yet."

Jono didn't recognize any of them, so he made sure to put his back to the wall when they sat at the table. Sage sat beside him while Patrick dragged another chair over rather than put his back to the room at large. He spun the chair around and sat on it backward, resting his arms on top of it. Tom raised an eyebrow at their show of solidarity but gamely took a seat across from them.

"Want a pint?" Tom asked.

"No, we're good," Jono said.

Tom studied him for a long minute before letting out a quiet, disbelieving chuckle. "Never thought I'd see your face again, bruv. Not here in London, at least."

"Found better options in New York City. That's part of the reason I'm here to chat with you. I need the contact information for the London god pack."

"You know where they live. You could've gone there rather than here."

Jono shook his head. "That's their personal territory, and I can't enter it."

"You can't enter *London*, bruv, but here you are." Tom smiled tightly at him, his scent worried—whether for Jono or himself, Jono couldn't tell. "You know the terms of your exile."

"You haven't tried to kill me yet," Jono said, aiming for lightness.

Tom barked out a heavy laugh and waved off the words. "You'd rip out my throat before I even got halfway through my shift. I'll leave it to others to try."

"Some friend you are," Patrick said.

Tom scowled at him. "Shut it, arsehole."

"Yeah, not happening."

"Pat," Jono said, glancing over at him. "Don't hurt him, yeah?"

Patrick rolled his eyes. "I'll leave him alive so long as he doesn't try to kill you."

"What the fuck do you think you could do to me?" Tom snapped.

Patrick stared at Tom without fear in his eyes and smiled mockingly. "Nothing you'd remember because you'd be in a grave."

"Tom," Jono said sharply, the tone in his voice stopping Tom halfway out of his seat. "He's my pack. They all are."

Tom sat with a heavy thump, staring at Jono with a gobsmacked look on his face. "They're your *what?*"

"We're the New York City god pack, which is why we need to speak to the London god pack about pass-through rights. Entering their personal territory isn't something we can do without permission. Can you give us a contact number or name? I'm Jono's dire, and I'll be initiating outreach," Sage said calmly.

Tom outright laughed, his casual dismissiveness making Jono grind his teeth. He hadn't minded Tom's attitude when he was younger, but Jono didn't much care for it today. "You made a god pack with mundane humans? What the fuck kind of joke is this, Jono?"

"It's not," Jono stated flatly. "We're here on pack business."

Tom's mirth faded in seconds, and he stared Jono in the eye. "You really got a pack?"

Jono nodded slowly. "It's why I left."

"A *god* pack though?"

"It's the only sort I can make with these eyes of mine."

"You don't have any other werecreatures with you. That's not a pack."

Jono figured Patrick's shields and Sage's fae pendant were doing their job if Tom's nose hadn't picked out what they really were. Wade was still at the bar eating, no one paying him any mind, but he appeared human to Jono's senses.

"Pack is what you make of it, and I made mine."

This time the silence lasted longer, and Jono waited Tom out with a patience he hadn't had when he was younger. Eventually, Tom blew out a heavy breath and leaned forward. "It's a shit time for you to return, bruv. Things are a mess, and your exile still stands, even with Jessamine gone."

"I'd heard. What happened?"

Tom shrugged. "She got challenged and lost."

He said it with a finality that could only mean Jessamine's body was buried in an unmarked grave somewhere on the land the god pack owned outside of London proper. It's where the challenge ring had moved some generations back, between two world wars. The god pack still held territory in the city, but the ancestral grounds had expanded in a bid for privacy they didn't always get from the government and the London streets saturated with CCTV.

"And Finley?"

"Still alpha. Cressida co-leads with him, but she's...not someone you want to cross. You go before them and they might kill you for knocking on their door."

Jono shared a look with Sage, who immediately pulled out her mobile and accessed a saved article that came with a face and name in less than a minute.

"Cressida Moore. Gained the alpha rank three years ago," Sage said.

Patrick extended his arm at her. "Let me see."

Jono passed the mobile over so Patrick could review the article. Jono would take a look at it later. Tom watched the interplay with a curious look in his eyes.

"Pack, huh?" he said after a moment.

"Yeah," Jono replied.

Tom leaned back in his seat, rubbing at his mouth. "Well. I'm chuffed you found one finally, but I can't pretend I never saw you here. I'll need to ring my alpha so he can report to the god pack and let them know you're in town."

"If you give us a number, we'll do the announcing for you."

Tom smiled tightly. "Doesn't work that way. You know that. But I'll still give you Devin's number anyway."

"Is he the dire or your alpha?" Sage asked as Patrick passed back her mobile.

"Dire."

"Excellent. As I'm our god pack's dire, I'll handle communication."

Tom seemed amused in a condescending way, but his amusement withered beneath Sage's steely eyed stare down. He dug out his mobile and scrolled through his contacts before reaching the one he wanted. He showed the number to Sage, who saved it to her mobile.

"Things are different from the last time you were here," Tom warned Jono as he put his mobile away.

"I wasn't liked then, doubt I'll be liked now. Not that different," Jono said with a shrug.

"You weren't the only one to leave London, you get me?"

That warning hung heavy in the air between them before Patrick stood, the wooden chair creaking under the motion. "We're not strangers to pack infighting."

Tom said nothing to that statement, merely got to his feet with the rest of them. "Glad to see you're still alive, Jono. Try to stay that way, yeah?"

Despite the underlying warning, Jono still reached out to knock their fists together, just like old times. "Don't worry about me, mate. Do what you have to, all right?"

It was the same words he'd spoken years ago before leaving. He hadn't blamed Tom then, and couldn't blame the other man now for looking out for his own skin. Pack law was brutal, and nothing good ever came of disobedience.

"Are we leaving?" Wade asked from the counter.

Jono looked over to see the mound of wrappers on the bar counter in front of the teenager, the last kebab in his hand and half-eaten. "We are. Don't leave your mess."

Wade rolled his eyes and started stuffing the rubbish into the takeaway bag. The bartender came over and offered to take the bag, which Wade gladly handed over. They exited the bar, none of them saying a word on the long walk back to the car. Wade finished his kebab before they arrived, meaning Jono didn't have to warn him about messing up the upholstery. Only when they were inside the vehicle and Patrick had cast a silence ward did Sage break the silence.

"Are we going to have to worry about werecreatures hunting you as opposed to actual hunters in this city?" Sage asked from the back seat.

Jono grimaced. "Possibly."

"Then I guess we'll have to strike a bargain with the London god pack to keep you alive. Neither of you are arguing that case."

"Wouldn't dream of it," Patrick said dryly. "How long do you think Tom will wait before he notifies his alpha?"

"Not long. He probably rang them once we were out of earshot," Jono said.

"Then let's get back to the hotel before anyone thinks to follow us."

Jono didn't hesitate to pull onto the road. They were halfway to the hotel when Patrick's mobile rang with an unknown number flashing over the screen. The area code was local, but Patrick didn't seem to recognize it. He answered after the second ring anyway, and Jono dialed up his hearing to listen in.

"Special Agent Patrick Collins. Line and location are secure," Patrick said.

"We're in London," Carmen said, sounding bored. "We'll expect you after sunset tonight."

"Where? A hotel?"

"How plebian. We own a penthouse in Knightsbridge."

She rattled off the address before ending the call.

"Plebian my fucking ass," Patrick muttered.

"Knightsbridge?" Jono mused. "Lucien really is a posh blood-sucking arsehole."

"That asshole better do the job we're paying him for."

Personally, Jono thought one hundred years of freedom to cause an unending amount of trouble was a bit much, but no one had asked him.

"How will the Night Courts here handle Lucien's presence?" Sage asked.

Patrick shrugged. "Probably how the Night Courts in the five boroughs handled it—by not getting in his way."

"Suppose that's our job," Jono said.

Sage sighed. "Wonderful."

Wade cackled loudly before opening up a box of Jaffa Cakes and shoving one into his mouth.

WELLINGTON COURT in Knightsbridge was the sort of neighborhood Jono would never be comfortable in, much less welcomed. The streets and buildings were too posh, to say nothing of the people inhabiting them. Those who lived in Knightsbridge would probably have a heart attack if they knew Lucien was their neighbor and driving down their property values by his sheer presence alone.

Sometimes the monsters in the shadows found their way into the light, and humanity had to learn how to play nice. Jono knew there was no playing nice with Lucien.

The rental they drove stuck out on the street, but Jono didn't care. He got out, staring up at the grand, red-bricked and white building taking up space across from One Hyde Park. The soft glow of the streetlamps provided more than enough illumination to the front entrance of the massive residential building. Night in London was a cacophony of noise and scents and light pollution that he used to love. Strangely, Jono found himself missing New York.

"Place overlooks Hyde Park and has a mess of windows. Makes no sense for a vampire to live here," Jono said.

"Real estate is a money sink Lucien has been investing in for centuries," Patrick said.

"He should invest in a crypt. Might be more to his liking."

Patrick laughed, though his eyes held no humor in them. "Let's go."

They headed for the front entrance, and Jono was unsurprised to see the inside lobby manned by a concierge. The man on duty wore a dark suit and looked down his nose at them.

"Are you lost?" he asked with all the enunciation of an old-school BBC presenter.

"Do we look lost?" Patrick shot back. "We're guests of the penthouse owners. We should be on their approved visitor list. Look for Patrick Collins."

The man didn't blink as his gaze cut away to his computer. Jono knew the second their names popped up, because the man's expression smoothed out into one of fawning cheerfulness. Jono rolled his eyes behind his sunglasses. It was well past sunset, and he knew it was ridiculous to wear them, but he hadn't wanted to tip off anyone here about what he was.

"Of course. Ms. Foscari is expecting you. I'll scan you into the lift."

He escorted them to a private lift, using a key card to give them access. The doors closed on his smiling face, and the lift started to move. Jono took off his sunglasses and gave them to Sage.

"Foscari?" Jono asked.

"It's an alias." Patrick paused. "I think."

"You think?"

"If you want to interrogate Carmen about her name, be my guest."

"You'll do no such thing," Sage said.

"Spoilsport," Wade muttered.

The lift doors opened onto a private foyer done in black marble shot through with gold. The crystal chandelier smelled like magic, and not the nice sort. None of them walked beneath it on their way to the penthouse apartment's closed front door.

Patrick knocked loudly on the door, and moments later it was opened by Naheed. She smiled at them, her large blue-green eyes ringed in kohl. A fresh bite mark was scabbed over on her throat, but Jono didn't think being down a pint or two of blood would stop her from taking out a threat. Jono had learned over the past year of dealing with Lucien that the master vampire only brought highly skilled vampires and human servants into his Night Court —the sort who would rather kill first and worry about questions later.

"Hospitality first," Naheed said in her quiet voice.

Jono looked at Patrick, who made a face. "Fine."

They stepped inside the penthouse and went no farther than that until after they ate the bits of bread Naheed offered and sipped on the water she passed to each of them. A heavy weight that Jono hadn't immediately noticed seemed to slide off his shoulders. Beside him, Patrick's own shoulders twitched.

"Who'd you pay to put that much power into your threshold?" Patrick wanted to know, looking across the living area at where Lucien had suddenly appeared.

"A dead man," Lucien said.

Jono eyed Lucien, the master vampire looking none the worse for wear after a cross-Atlantic flight to another country. "Who did you bring with you?"

Lucien flashed his fangs at Jono. "Unlike you, I know better than to uproot my entire Night Court when I need to hold territory."

"Einar and a couple of others are resting here with a handful of our human servants," Carmen said as she sauntered out of the hallway that led to the rest of the penthouse. She wore a silk robe that skimmed the top of her thighs and did nothing to hide the outline of her full breasts, the belt tied loosely around her waist. She'd dropped her glamour for them, appearing as the succubus she was.

"How did you even get them here while the sun was out?" Patrick asked.

"You don't need to know how. It's not part of our bargain."

"Speaking of that bargain, did you activate the ownership spell on the invitation?"

"Yes," Lucien said.

"I want to see it."

"It's not yours to do with as you want. It's mine."

"Only because the United States government struck a bargain with you. I go into the WSA tomorrow. I need some intelligence to give them about the auction location."

"You can tell them not to get in my way."

Jono followed Patrick over to the group of sofas situated in the middle of the living room. The large space was accessed by several doors but had no windows. Jono assumed the view of Hyde Park was found elsewhere in the penthouse and Lucien wasn't willing to show it off.

"I'm not telling the British government I brought you into their country. It was difficult enough getting them to agree to allow the joint task force to operate on their soil. If they knew we were working with you, they'd question every open back channel they have with us," Patrick retorted.

"That's not my problem."

"It's all our problem," Jono said.

Lucien's black-eyed gaze slid his way. "The bargain was get you access to the staff in exchange for diplomatic immunity for me and my Night Court."

"I thought the bargain was you bring us the staff?" Sage asked.

Carmen's smile was more of a smirk as she came to stand beside Lucien. "Our attorney argued for more general language. Your government agreed to it."

Patrick rolled his eyes. "Because you backed them into a corner."

"This is your mess, not ours," Lucien said.

"It's all our mess. The SOA put me in charge as your handler. I know you find that idea distasteful, but we need to work together. There's too much at stake not to."

"We've kept our side of the bargain between us," Jono said, staring Lucien down. "Altars for your mother in every pack home with prayers to feed them every night. You're getting more than you deserve with payment from the government. Abiding by the rules they set won't hurt you."

"You talk as if I care about what you have to say," Lucien said.

Patrick made an annoyed sound in the back of his throat and extended his hand. "Let me see the fucking invitation."

Lucien stared him down. "No. The magic is tied to me. You can't afford for it to be tainted."

Patrick closed his hand into a fist before dropping his arm with a frustrated sigh. "Where is the auction being held?"

"The spell indicates the final location will be revealed on Sunday, on the day the auction is set to take place. Until then, you have as much information as we do," Carmen said.

"Doubtful," Sage replied.

Carmen's smile was full of secrets Jono didn't care for. "Keep our names out of any conversation you have with government officials here."

"That was the plan to begin with," Patrick said.

"Then abide by it."

"Soon as you show me the invitation." Patrick raised a hand before Lucien or Carmen could argue. "I won't touch it, but I need to know what it says. You owe me that."

Lucien's eyes narrowed, and Jono took a step closer to Patrick. He didn't trust Lucien at all, and anytime Patrick brought up the promise Lucien had made to Ashanti, it always ended with someone getting bruised.

"Careful with your words," Lucien hissed.

Patrick was as defiant as ever in the face of the master vampire's wrath. His willingness to run his mouth and worry about the bruises and broken bones later was a stress Jono could honestly do without.

"You were the one who called us here. If it wasn't to chat about the auction, then why?" Jono asked.

"We've been in contact with some of the groups we've done business with in the past. The auction is popular," Carmen said.

"I can't imagine why."

Carmen tilted her head, staring at Patrick. "It is popular with the Orthodox Church of the Dead. The Patriarch of Souls is very, very interested in what the auction is selling this time."

Patrick went still, and Jono frowned at him. "Come again?"

"Necromancy, with a side of cult-level madness," Patrick said.

"The use of church in its name is a misnomer, and that group is anathema to all religions. If I recall correctly, they were run out of Odessa and have been banned by every country," Sage said slowly.

"Laws mean nothing to those of us who do business in the shadows. Your government better be willing to pay whatever price the buyer sets for the Morrígan's staff. The Patriarch of Souls has deep pockets," Lucien said.

Patrick ground his teeth so hard Jono could hear the enamel scraping together. "I'll be sure to ask my counterparts at the WSA about them. Setsuna already set up an open-ended wire transfer for the buy. It will cover whatever your bid price is."

"Good."

"Is the Orthodox Church of the Dead in contact with the Dominion Sect?"

Lucien gave him a scornful look "What do you think?"

Which was answer enough.

Patrick let out a heavy sigh. "We'll be in touch before Sunday. You aren't going to the auction alone. Play by the fucking rules the lawyers hashed out or the deal's off. Got it?"

Lucien didn't argue, but the way he smirked in response hinted at his opinion of that order. Patrick turned on his heels and headed for the door. Sage and Wade followed after him, but Jono didn't immediately move.

Looking at Lucien, knowing full well what sort of games the master vampire liked to play, Jono smiled in a way that was as far from friendly as one could get. "If you betray us, I'll let Fenrir hunt you down and enjoy the mess he'll make."

"I don't fear your god," Lucien said.

"*You should.*"

It wasn't Jono's voice that came out of his mouth, but Fenrir's, the harsh tones of his animal-god patron scraping at his throat. Lucien acknowledged the god's presence with a hard smile that drove the color from his lips.

"The only god I fear is my mother. You will never hear my prayers."

"Maybe you should auction off a bit of your hubris," Jono said as he turned his back on Lucien and headed for the door where Patrick impatiently waited. "Could probably pay off this flat's mortgage with the funds."

He left the penthouse for the foyer, skirting the chandelier with its tangle of magic. Patrick was holding open the lift doors, and Jono stepped past him into the car.

"Why's everyone so worried about some church?" Wade asked as the lift doors closed and it started to descend.

"Because it's a church founded and run by necromancers," Sage said.

"It's a cult," Patrick corrected.

"It's a problem."

"Yeah, I know."

Wade opened his mouth to ask another question, but the lift came to a stop and the doors slid open. He stayed quiet until they made it back to the car.

"Do you think they'll outbid us for the staff?" Wade asked.

"They'll try," Patrick said.

Jono started the engine and worked the gears as he drove onto the street. "Think Lucien can pull it off?"

Patrick's face appeared as if it were carved from stone when Jono glanced at him, the streetlights they passed washing him out. His shields were still locked down, and Jono couldn't get anything off him.

"Lucien loves his bottom line too much not to."

"That's not a ringing endorsement."

"It wasn't meant to be."

"If we can't rely on Lucien, then what do we do?"

Patrick's right hand strayed toward his dagger. "Whatever we have to."

Jono bloody well hated that plan.

7

The UK's Department for Witchcraft and Supernatural Affairs was located at One Horse Guards Road. The gray stone building took up what passed as a city block in the City of Westminster. On a Wednesday morning, the streets were full of cars ferrying government officials to work, but the sidewalks were just as bad with commuters exiting the Tube. The business of government never really stopped, but mornings were usually the busiest.

Patrick drove down Parliament Street, left hand resting on the gearshift as he kept an eye on the traffic. Jono had offered to drive him, but Patrick had no trouble handling a manual vehicle, and he hadn't wanted any British officials to know they were working together in London. They couldn't do anything about CCTV, but they could steer clear of being together near government buildings.

He changed lanes a couple of buildings from the turnoff, eventually pulling into a short narrow drive leading to the Triple-Arched Bridge entrance. The wards written into the stone pillars and the arches burned hot to his senses, the magic old, layered, and powerful. Patrick braked to a stop between two of the pillars, rolling down his window so he could speak to the security guard on duty.

"Special Agent Patrick Collins," he said, holding out his SOA badge for the man to review. "I'm here for a meeting."

"Right, then. Let me check your credentials."

The security guard took Patrick's badge into the tiny guard station built inside one of the pillars. Patrick waited, engine idling, until the man returned and handed back his badge. The yellow arm of the security gate ahead of him raised for passage.

"You're cleared through. Turn left up ahead into the courtyard."

Patrick drove forward and turned where directed, pulling into a wide circular courtyard ringed by the building's walls. He took the first available parking spot that didn't look reserved. He was getting out of the car, tugging his suit jacket into place around the lower back sheath that held his dagger, when a crisp female voice called out to him.

"Special Agent Patrick Collins, I presume?"

He shut the door, remote locked the car, and turned to face whoever had come down to be his minder for the day. The blonde woman standing at the nearby entrance wasn't shielded, and Patrick got a sense of her magic through his own—sorceress. She matched him in height in the high heels she wore, navy blue sheath dress skimming the top of her knees. Her gaze was frankly curious as she sized him up.

"That's me," Patrick said.

"You're late."

Patrick shrugged. "Traffic."

She pursed her lips, nose wrinkling slightly, most likely from the feel of his magic. He hadn't completely locked down his shields, and the taint in his soul and magic seeped through his aura. She still extended her hand in greeting, and Patrick accepted the firm handshake.

"I'm Leighton Northcott. I'm a WSA intelligence officer and the liaison for your case."

"Great. I was told I'd be meeting with you and a couple other people this morning."

"Yes. We're waiting on you."

Patrick raised an eyebrow at that subtle dig. "Then lead the way."

"Put this on first."

She handed him a visitor's badge, the charm cast on it making his fingertips itch. If it was anything like the badges the SOA handed out, Patrick figured it would set off a magical alarm if he went where he wasn't supposed to. He clipped it to the lapel of his suit jacket.

"You are not to go anywhere without an escort," she informed him. "Now stay close."

Leighton spun neatly on her heels, which was impressive, since they looked to be about four inches in height. Patrick's feet ached just looking at them. He followed her through a heavy wooden door warded as strongly as the entrance he'd driven through a few minutes ago. The threshold buried deep in the building would never be as strong as a home since it was public space, but the defensive magic laid down around it more than made up for its lack.

Patrick tightened his shields even more as they entered an atrium. People hurried back and forth, ignoring them. The main staircase was a switchback near the main entrance, and Leighton cut through everyone to reach it. Patrick followed in her wake, dodging neatly around anyone who got between them.

"We're meeting with my superior. Operations Officer Albert Lee is lead on this matter."

Patrick committed the name to memory. "Understood."

Leighton took the stairs to the second floor, and from there it was a maze of hallways until she reached a warded door. She touched the handle, and the metal glowed briefly from whatever magic was embedded in it. Pushing it open, she waved Patrick inside.

"SOA Special Agent Patrick Collins, sir," Leighton announced to the room at large.

Patrick's gaze swept over the space, taking in the multiple desk terminals all facing the front wall dominated by a large screen. A couple of people looked up at their arrival before returning their attention to the task at hand.

A gray-haired sorcerer stood at the front of the room, studying the information on the large screen. He turned around at Leighton's announcement, staring at them over the heads of everyone working. The woman standing beside him was familiar, welcome, and someone Patrick hadn't seen since December.

PIA Special Agent Nadine Mulroney wore a dove gray pantsuit, a white blouse, and her heels were just as high as Leighton's. The cut of her clothes told Patrick she wasn't carrying a gun, but that didn't mean she was unarmed. An ex-combat mage like he was, Nadine's affinity for defensive magic was matched by no one. She was his closest friend, despite living and working out of Paris the past couple of years.

He hadn't known who PIA Director Franklin had been going to appoint as the agency's representative for this mission, but Patrick was glad it was someone he knew.

"Collins," Nadine said with a faint smile on her face.

"Mulroney," Patrick replied in a friendly tone.

Albert eyed Patrick as he and Leighton approached. "I take it you two know each other?"

"We fought together from time to time in the Mage Corps," Nadine said.

"This is London, not a battlefield, Mulroney."

Patrick wondered if his reputation had somehow crossed the Atlantic ahead of him. Nadine said nothing to that warning though, and Patrick followed her lead by keeping quiet.

Albert turned to face the large screen. Someone had uploaded a set of grainy photographs taken with a long-lens camera. Ethan's face was familiar in a way Patrick wished it weren't. The other two men were unknown to him.

"Your government asked for assistance in locating and apprehending these three targets. INTERPOL has a long-standing Red Notice for Ethan Greene, though we haven't flagged him inside the UK's borders as of yet," Albert said.

"Have they flagged him in any other country in Europe?" Nadine asked.

"No. Considering his criminal connections and background, we're operating on the assumption that if Greene has business inside a country, he'll find a way through the border in question with no one the wiser."

"And the other two?"

"Targets your government asked us to keep an eye on. The first one is Dillon Rossiter. He's Irish, and that's about as much as we've got on him."

Patrick studied the sharp-featured man in the photograph, wondering if his eyes were truly silver or if it was a shadow effect from being photographed. His hair was a riot of curls on top, shorn along the sides, revealing ears that were a shade too pointed at the tips to be fully human.

Patrick and Nadine shared a glance, but they didn't say a word. Patrick knew he wasn't the only one thinking about how the fight in the Gap of Dunloe against Medb's Unseelie Court had ended.

"He's got fae blood in him," Patrick said.

"That's the WSA's assessment as well. We've been trying to track down his lineage, but no luck. The fae have been stonewalling us."

Patrick crossed his arms over his chest, staring at the photograph of Rossiter. No telling which Court he was from, but if Patrick had to guess, he'd bet all his money on the Unseelie Court.

"He's your auctioneer," Leighton said, coming over to their small group with a stack of folders in her hands. She gave one to Patrick and Nadine before offering one to Albert. "He's known for facilitating the sale of hard to find objects and people of power."

"People?" Patrick asked sharply.

"The Auction of Curiosities and Exceptional Items consists of anything and everything for sale. To the ones looking to buy from him, people are as much an object as an artifact."

"Slave trading is abhorrent," Nadine said as she flipped open the file.

"We've never cared for Rossiter's sort of business ventures. Parliament is adamant we put a stop to the auction before a single sale goes forward," Albert said.

"That will risk us losing the item we're searching for."

Albert eyed them both. "It would be helpful if you told us what, exactly, you're searching for. Your country's liaisons haven't been forthcoming."

"Our superiors will have to be the ones to answer that for you," Patrick said.

Albert appeared unsurprised at that answer, even if he seemed annoyed. "We are under no obligation to allow the auction to go forward."

Nadine offered him a thin smile. "It is my understanding that high-level talks have happened on both sides of our governments concerning this auction. What Rossiter is selling is something the Dominion Sect is very interested in. You know their history, and why that group can't get their hands on what they desire. Attempting to interfere with the auction and cause the item in question to fall into the wrong hands helps no one."

Albert and Nadine stared each other down in a bid for dominance Patrick knew his friend would never back down from. Rather than spend hours sniping at each other, he tried to move along the meeting because he had plenty more on his schedule for the day if the update texts on his phone from Sage were anything to go by that morning.

Patrick flipped through the folder until he came to an

INTERPOL Red Notice page for the other wanted man. "Who is Ilya Nazarov?"

"The latest Patriarch of Souls," Nadine said.

Patrick studied the printout, taking in the man's dirty-blond hair, light eyes, and tall frame. Judging by his name and appearance, Patrick assumed he was Russian, even if the storefront behind him on the picture had a sign in French. The sheet listed out his identifying information, and while his date of birth put him a decade older than Patrick, he looked a little gaunt in the face, making him appear older.

"Necromancer?"

Albert nodded. "All signs point to yes. The UK government doesn't want him within our borders. He will be tracked down and arrested if chatter indicates he is, no matter your country's needs."

Necromancy was a form of magic no country in the world wholeheartedly approved of. Messing with a person's soul was illegal, doubly so after someone had died. It was a capital crime in the United States, and one of the many reasons Patrick and Jono had to keep their soulbond a secret. The United States government sanctioned and employed a handful of magic users whose magic dealt specifically with necromancy, souls, and the dead.

Necromancers were heavily regulated in some countries, and outright killed in others. The subtle differences in that form of magic wasn't worth it to most governments to grant life to those magic users. Not all necromancers were bad or a threat though, but the general public would never see the good they could provide for the living.

"We have intelligence that the auction will happen next week. Our analysts are working on uncovering the location it will occur at," Albert said.

Patrick kept his face expressionless at that information—it was different from what Lucien had told them. Patrick trusted the invitation's timeline over intelligence guesses at this point. He trusted in Nadine as well, and let her take the lead for the rest of the meeting since this was more her purview than his.

"Why is it whenever I see you these days, it's always in preparation for a fight?" Nadine asked.

Patrick glanced over at her as they walked through St. James's Park in the early afternoon. The silence ward Nadine had cast covered their immediate area in a bubble of silence. It left Patrick's ears muffled, the sounds of the city absent from his hearing.

The trees surrounding them were in full greenery, giving the illusion they weren't in the middle of London. On a sunny Wednesday, the park was filled with office and government workers on their lunch breaks, along with tourists and locals alike taking advantage of the sun. The heat had Patrick wishing he wasn't wearing a suit.

"Because Setsuna still hasn't let me take a vacation," Patrick said.

"That's a travesty."

Nadine's high heels clicked against the asphalt of the park pathway they walked down, the only sound Patrick could hear beyond their breathing.

"I didn't think Franklin would allow us to work together again. What changed his mind?"

Nadine shrugged lightly. "I think Reed demanded it. Honestly, there are a limited number of agents assigned to the joint task force. There were only so many people he could've picked from, but it didn't make sense for him to send someone from the States when I'm working out of Paris."

Her location had been helpful last December when Patrick, his pack, and the Hellraisers had been in a tight spot in Ireland. Nadine had flown out on an emergency basis to act as backup they desperately needed.

"Have you worked with the team here before?" Patrick asked.

"I've worked with people out of the WSA before, though not these particular officers. The WSA tends to share information a little easier than the French do."

"I guess the special relationship between our countries comes in handy."

"Sometimes." Nadine peered at him through her designer sunglasses. "What did you want to talk about that you couldn't say in there?"

Patrick automatically cased the area, wondering if they had a tail or not. Trust only went so far between foreign intelligence agencies, especially when magic was in the mix. "Albert is wrong about the timing of the auction."

"Do tell."

"The invitation says it's happening this Sunday."

Nadine nodded, the expression on her face remaining blank. "Location?"

"We won't know until this weekend." Patrick chewed on his bottom lip for another second before continuing with "I don't think we should share that information, especially if Nazarov is onsite."

"They'd expect us to."

"Doesn't mean we have to, especially if their necromancy laws would put them at odds with our needs. We can't risk the WSA ruining the meet-up. We need the auction to go forward."

"That's going to cause problems down the road."

"I don't have a choice. You know why."

She did, which put Nadine in a small category of people who knew about his past and the soul debt that dictated his life.

"Anything else I should know?" Nadine asked.

Patrick scratched at an itch on his jaw that stemmed from shaving that morning. "We're trying to get a meeting with the London god pack to clear us for pass-through rights. I think things are going to get messy."

"How so?"

"Apparently Jono's exile came with a death sentence over here. A fact he never told me about until the other day."

"Doesn't he already have hunters after him?"

"Yeah. I don't know if any operating over here are chasing the same bounty. Think you could find out for us?"

"I'll see what I can do, but you might have more luck contacting the SOA's permanent liaison officer in MI5 directly."

"I can't leave an evidence trail about my pack."

"Then I'll reach out to the PIA's permanent liaison officer in MI6 and hope for the best. I might have something for you by tonight, but I can't guarantee it."

"I'll take anything you can give me."

"Anything else I should know?"

Patrick ran a hand through his hair. "We went to one of Jono's old neighborhoods yesterday and ran into one of his old friends. The guy didn't come right out and say it, but there's discord happening within the London god pack and probably the packs in this country in general. If we're walking into the midst of a civil war within the werecreature community here, I want to know."

Nadine frowned as they approached a fork in the path, opting to veer left. "Aren't you in the midst of your own civil war? Now you're going to deal with two?"

"Yes, but I only started one of them."

Nadine snorted. "I'd say don't start any, but this is you we're talking about."

Patrick would've argued, but he figured she had a point. "We're staying at the Sanderson if you need to find us."

"Mobility?"

"Two cars. It's me, Jono, Sage, and Wade."

"Isn't that your whole pack?"

"We left a proxy dire holding the line back in New York, and the valkyries agreed to come guard her. The fae and the Night Courts should help with any gaps in the defense of our territory."

"Was that wise?"

"Doesn't matter. We had no choice. The Morrígan's staff needs to be found."

Nadine hummed thoughtfully, mouth twisting a little as she processed the information. Patrick had seen that exact look of concentration on her face plenty of times before.

"My superiors out of Paris won't like the sleight of hand we'll be pulling on the WSA, but I'll let Franklin deal with them. Count me in for whatever your plan is."

"Right now—"

Patrick cut himself off as recognition burned through his magic, the particular sting of *werecreature* making him skim the area. The hair on the back of his neck stood on end as his magic coalesced on the warning coming from behind them.

"What is it?" Nadine asked, keeping her stride even. Despite her high heels, Patrick knew she'd kick them off in an instant to fight, then moan about their loss later. "Soultaker?"

"Werecreature," Patrick said.

"And me without my silver bullets. Should I shield?"

"No. Let's loop around and head back to the WSA."

"If we stay on this path, it'll take us back to the street."

Patrick nodded and let her lead the way back to the WSA. The werecreature at their back never retreated, and Patrick resisted the urge to turn around and confront them. He couldn't risk interacting with werecreatures so close to a government building.

They dropped the wards once they reached the street. The bubble of silence popped, and the sound of city traffic rushed back into Patrick's ears. They walked in silence back to the WSA, keeping their pace even and unhurried. When they reached the main entrance to the building, Patrick pulled his visitor's badge out of his pocket and clipped it to his lapel again. Nadine dug hers out of her purse and clipped it to the collar of her sheath dress. The werecreature couldn't follow them inside, but Patrick almost wished they would try.

"Let me get the door for you," Patrick said.

He knew Nadine was perfectly capable of opening her own doors, but he used the opportunity to look behind them, catching a glimpse of a blond-haired man in dark jeans and a polo shirt, sunglasses perched firmly on his nose to hide his eyes. Patrick committed his face to memory before they entered the building, wondering how the London god pack had found him so quickly.

Nadine took off her sunglasses and tucked them into her purse, the questions in her eyes going unanswered for now. The WSA might be their country's allies, but some secrets could only be shared between the two of them.

Patrick's phone buzzed in his pocket as they climbed the main staircase. He took it out and unlocked it, reading the text that had come through. The words on the screen made him want to scowl. Jono's update was succinct and annoying.

MEETING TONIGHT WITH THE LONDON GOD PACK. CHALLENGE RING A POSSIBILITY.

"Everything all right?" Nadine asked.

"Situation normal," Patrick muttered.

Nadine's smile was knife-sharp and too-knowing from shared experiences. "All fucked-up."

8

"How the fuck is the Savoy neutral ground?" Patrick asked as Jono navigated the car through evening London traffic. Patrick had swapped out his suit for his usual jeans, T-shirt, and leather jacket with its cold charms activated instead of heat. He had a feeling his outfit wouldn't pass muster with hotel staff.

"Why are you asking me? I haven't been in London for years," Jono said.

"Conducting pack business isn't usually done so publicly, but the London god pack alphas were adamant about meeting at the Beaufort Bar," Sage said from the back seat.

Patrick rested his elbow against the window to prop up his head. "That's a lot of literal human shields they could end up using if things go bad."

"Do you think things will?" Wade asked. He had a box of Jaffa Cakes in hand, another in his lap, and was steadily eating his way through them. The sound of him chewing hadn't stopped since they got in the car.

Sage's expression became grim in the rearview mirror. "It's a possibility we have to accept. Their dire wasn't pleased about being forced to agree to the meeting. I think it's safe to say his alphas will feel the same way."

Patrick's gaze drifted over the winding view of the Thames at night and the way some of the more well-known London landmarks glowed against the night sky. It was just the four of them for the meeting, with Nadine handling the needs of the WSA while Patrick turned his attention toward his pack. He trusted her to keep the WSA from asking too many questions about his absence, but knew he'd have to face them all again tomorrow.

Showing up bruised would definitely have them asking questions.

"Tom didn't know what you three were when we met with him at the pub yesterday," Jono said.

Patrick turned his head fractionally to look at him. "Meaning?"

"He thinks you're human. Depending on what the god pack has heard about New York, they may not know you're a mage, Sage is a weretiger, and Wade is a dragon."

"We aren't giving up Wade's form unless we're backed into a corner."

"Didn't you tell me not to shift mass while we were in London?" Wade asked.

"We'll make an exception if it looks like we're losing the fight."

"We won't lose," Jono said, sounding way too confident for Patrick's liking.

Patrick snorted. "Let's operate under the assumption they know everything public about us and we don't know jack shit about them. If we're going in blind, let's be prepared for anything."

Sage leaned forward between the seats. "If they demand a fight in the challenge ring, will you agree to it?"

Patrick opened his mouth to say *no* when Jono beat him to it with the wrong fucking answer.

"Yes," Jono said, sounding calm even if the steering wheel creaked beneath his grip.

Patrick jerked his head around to stare at Jono. "Excuse me?"

"If things are as messy as we think they are, then refusing to fight won't get us very far. We need the right to stay in London." Jono turned his head to glance at Patrick, his wolf-bright blue eyes flashing from reflected streetlights. "*You* need that right, Pat."

Sage sat back with a sigh. "He's not wrong."

Patrick stared at Jono. "You aren't fighting them."

Jono turned his attention back to the road. "Neither are you."

"*I* will be fighting them if they insist on deciding things in the challenge ring. That's my responsibility as dire," Sage said.

While Patrick knew Sage could hold her own in a fight, he didn't like anyone fighting if he could do it for them. Judging by Jono's expression, he didn't like it much either, but he didn't try to argue with Sage about her demand.

Patrick sighed heavily. "Is this some pack rule I don't instinctively know because I'm not a werecreature?"

"Dires handle everything except a direct challenge. We fight for our god pack alphas."

"I'm more than capable of fighting my own damn fights."

"Fighting, sure. Winning is another thing entirely," Jono muttered.

Patrick scowled at him. "Oh, fuck you."

Jono ignored him and flicked on the blinker, veering right and away from the Thames. The lit-up London Eye disappeared behind trees and buildings as they went farther into the dense city. London wasn't built on a grid, and Patrick missed Manhattan's setup. The twisted route they were taking to the Savoy was as far from a straight line as one could get.

Despite the hour, there were lots of cars on the street, as well as numerous double-decker red transit buses. Patrick kept his attention on the road and intersections in case of any unexpected trouble. London wasn't a city he knew well, and he didn't know what to expect while they were here without approval for pass-through rights.

"United front?" Patrick said as Jono switched lanes and the GPS map on his phone announced their destination was on the left.

"Always," Jono said.

"You take lead, I'll follow. But if they go for your throat, I'll cut open theirs."

Patrick had his dagger strapped to his right thigh where it belonged. He traced a look-away ward over the sheath even as he locked down his personal shields as tight as they would go. His bones ached for a few seconds, joints flaring with heat as the magical anchors Persephone had burned into his skeleton held up his defensive magic.

"Can't smell you," Jono said, sounding vaguely annoyed.

"Good. That's the whole fucking point of shields."

Coming across as human was a skill Patrick leaned into hard when dealing with the preternatural world. If the London god pack alphas hadn't done their due diligence on Patrick's pack, then oh fucking well.

They turned left, driving down a short narrow street to the main entrance of the Savoy. The high-end luxury cars they passed shined from the white lights above. Their rental looked completely out of place. The valet who came to collect their keys managed to hide his distaste once he got a good look at Jono's eyes, even if he couldn't hide the fear in his scent.

"We're here for a meeting," Jono said, handing over the keys. "We won't be staying the night."

"Very well," the man said, passing over a numbered ticket. "Myself or another can retrieve your car when you're finished."

They passed by a fountain and between gold and black pillars on their way into the luxury hotel's lobby. Inside, it was brightly lit, the black-and-white floor tiles clean of any scuff marks, with white pillars stretching up to a high ceiling. Wooden panels lined the wall but didn't reach the ceiling, broken up by antique-style wallpaper with hearth wards woven into the design. As much as the Savoy was a luxury hotel, someone had paid lots of money to treat it as a home as best they could where magic was concerned.

The effort was wasted. Public space could never carry a threshold or be a place where hearth magic could settle.

"This way," Sage said, taking the lead. Her high heels clicked softly against the tile as she walked, black dress swirling around her knees. Out of all of them, only she looked like she belonged in the hotel.

"I take it you've been here before?" Patrick asked.

"Marek prefers the Savoy when we come to London. I prefer the Dorchester."

Jono glanced at her. "I thought you owned an estate in London?"

"We do. Sometimes it's easier to abide by pack laws by staying in transient places though."

Patrick smirked at her. "Meaning you don't have to ask for pass-through rights."

"It wasn't worth the hassle when I was an independent or even after when Emma took me into the Tempest pack. It's worth it now."

Unspoken went her reason—her pack. Sage had become family, and her fierce protective streak and incredibly sharp mind had saved their collective asses multiple times in the past. Patrick had a feeling she'd do it again if tonight went as shitty as he thought it would.

The guests they passed at the Savoy came from money—new, old, it didn't matter, but every last one of them forgot their manners and stared when Jono passed them by. Patrick knew it was his eyes and what they represented that made people look twice. Most werecreatures tried to hide what they were from the public. God pack members didn't have that luxury.

Sage led them through the hotel to the stately red double door etched in gold at the edges that led to the Beaufort Bar. The hotel hostess situated in the nearby alcove was fighting through nerves and hiding it well enough that she didn't look like she was about to have a panic attack. Patrick figured the sooner the god pack were-wolf standing between her and the entrance left, the happier she'd be.

Patrick eyed the familiar-looking man waiting for them outside the bar—the same man who'd followed him and Nadine in St. James's Park earlier that afternoon. This time Patrick could make out the wolf-bright blue eyes that were eerily similar to Jono's. Up close, he was handsome and dressed like he knew it, but his taste in designer clothes was overkill.

Jono's stride hitched slightly, and it was enough of a tell for Patrick to look at him sharply. The surprise on his face told Patrick he knew the guy. The way the blond guy raked his gaze up and down Jono's body hungrily made Patrick want to stab him.

"Bryson," Jono said slowly.

Bryson smiled at Jono, ignoring the rest of them. "Mate. It's been bloody forever."

"You know why."

Bryson's oil-slick smile never left his face. "I would've rung you, but my alphas laid down the law, yeah? You know how it is."

Jono said nothing to that. Sage neatly stepped between him and Bryson, forcing Bryson to look at her. "We're here to meet your alphas."

Bryson's wolf-bright, blue-eyed gaze flicked to her then back to Jono. "Who's the bird?"

"Our dire," Patrick answered flatly, throttling his anger and glad his shields were locked down tight so Bryson wouldn't smell it. "Sage Beacot. Address her by her name or title, or don't fucking talk to her at all, got it?"

Bryson finally looked at him, some of the easiness in his gaze disappearing, replaced with a cold annoyance Patrick didn't give one goddamn fuck about. "I'd say humans aren't allowed tonight, but you aren't that human, are you?"

"Pat?" Jono asked, not looking at him.

"Dickface here tried to tail me today. He wasn't very good at it," Patrick said.

"You need to learn some fucking manners," Bryson snarled.

Patrick smiled at him, baring his teeth. "Take us to your alphas. Now."

Bryson glared at Patrick before looking over at Jono. "Bit of a pissant, that one. You let him order you about like this, Jono?"

"Patrick is my god pack's co-leader. We lead together," Jono stated flatly. "Show us to your alphas, Bryson. That's why we're here."

Bryson arched an eyebrow at him. "You can still call me Bry, you know that, right?"

It was Jono's turn to smile, and his teeth were sharper than Patrick's ever could be. "Your alphas. *Now.*"

Whatever sort of camaraderie Bryson hoped to start up again with Jono, Patrick was pleased to see it die a withering death outside the Beaufort Bar.

"You know, I did miss you when you left," Bryson said, turning toward the door.

Patrick had *so many* questions for Jono right about then, and maybe he would've asked them if he wasn't fantasizing about stabbing Bryson in the back. He'd never thought of himself as the jealous type, but apparently he was finding new depths about himself within the pack.

"Friend of yours?" Patrick asked, going for curious and coming off murderous.

"We'll chat later," Jono said, not bothering to keep his voice low.

"Damn right we will."

They went from bright lights to the low lighting inside the jet-black and gold bar. A single chandelier hung from the ceiling in the center of the room, while sconces and lamps lined the wood-paneled walls broken up in intervals by square marble pillars. Black tables and chairs were situated so there was plenty of room between them to ensure a cozy, almost private space. A pair of low couches turned back-to-back between two tables offered up a different kind of seat for guests to claim.

The bar itself was set against the wall to the right on a low antique stage. Light flowed through a frosted base, and only a few high seats were spaced in front so as to not overcrowd the bar. Dozens of liquor bottles sat on glass shelves and inside recessed spaces, the light shining down and from behind making everything glitter like it was crystal. A single bartender was working on some drinks for a pair of glamorously dressed women.

Three recessed booths on the side wall were painted a deep gold, the black couches in front embroidered with gold stitching as well. Two of the booths were empty. The far left one in the corner was full, as were the tables nearest it. The people there were all looking back at them, their wolf-bright blue eyes glittering in the dim bar light.

Recognition punched through Patrick's magic behind his shields—werecreatures, but something else. Something malevolent and insidious, a warning he only ever experienced when faced with demons. Patrick swallowed, tasting a hint of sulfur in the very back of his throat. Either the London god pack here tonight knew about the demon in their midst and they didn't care—or they were unaware, which meant the demon was powerful.

Shit.

Wade made a surprised noise behind him. Patrick wrenched his attention away from the London god pack when Wade grabbed his arm, looking into the teenager's wide brown eyes, not seeing any hint of gold.

"Patrick—"

Patrick shook his head sharply, cutting Wade off. Wade snapped his mouth shut, chewing on his bottom lip as he stared at Patrick. He let Patrick go and stayed close, knowing better than to speak about pack things in public, especially in front of the enemy. Wade was practically vibrating from tension though, and Patrick wanted badly to calm him down, but he didn't have the time.

Bryson led them to the corner table, and Patrick took a quick head count, coming up with twelve, including Jono's terrible past taste in men. All but one of the seats were taken at a table, and no one seemed inclined to offer them any. Bryson claimed that seat, trying to look unconcerned, but the stiff way he held himself proved it was a lie.

The people who mattered for these negotiations sat on the couch in the recessed golden space, and Patrick's gaze went immediately to the woman who carried a hint of the hells to his magic.

Cressida Moore was a slim woman with a riot of blonde curls that fell to her shoulders and framed a delicately featured face. Her impossibly wolf-bright blue eyes dominated her face, ringed by false eyelashes, thick eyeliner, and eyeshadow that matched the silky rose-gold tank top she wore.

Whatever skin she wore, what lived in her soul wasn't human. Patrick's magic was sounding a warning that lifted the hair on the back of his neck, and he wanted desperately to get his pack out of there. He'd faced hunters who carried demons in their souls many times before, but none of them had ever made him feel like running away was the only option. All Patrick could think of was Shakespeare's apt warning as they came to a stop near the group.

Hell is empty and all the devils are here.

The man sitting beside Cressida on the couch was only a werecreature. Taller than her even while sitting down, his brown hair was slicked back, face clean-shaven, and he dressed about ten years younger than he looked.

"You've some bollocks on you to come crawling back to London, Jonothon," Finley Harris said. His accent was a more refined version of Jono's, but still a far cry from upper class speech.

"Do you see me crawling?" Jono said coolly.

Finley reached for his drink, the cut crystal glass filled with a deep amber liquid. "You're here, aren't you?"

"I'm here as the alpha of the New York City god pack. Under pack law, you're obligated to negotiate with me as equals."

Finley threw back his head and laughed, causing a wave of chuckles to echo in the pack members around him. "Bollocks. You've never been my equal."

"You're right," Patrick said. "He's always been better than you."

Finley's laughter cut off, and he set his glass back on the table with a heavy smack. "What the fuck do you think you know about pack when you aren't part of our community?"

"I'm the co-leader of ours, so let's go with everything that matters."

"How adorable," Cressida drawled, tapping one manicured nail against the edge of her cocktail glass. "The human thinks he's one of us."

More laughter made Patrick want to clench his hands into fists, but he didn't give in to the urge. Physical tells were as much a give-away as scent in a situation like this, and he didn't want to give them the satisfaction of knowing they were pissing him off.

Cressida leaned forward, the tank top she wore shifting to show off more of her ample cleavage. She smiled, teeth sharp in her mouth. "I hear you have magic, which means you can never be part of our community, much less pack."

"Do I smell like I have magic?" Patrick asked.

"Bryson saw you at the WSA today. You were walking with a witch."

Bryson's nose was way off if he thought Nadine was a witch. "Not everyone who works at a place like that is a magic user."

"You don't work there at all."

Patrick shrugged, never taking his eyes off her. "I thought that was obvious?"

"I called your dire on behalf of my alphas for a parley over pass-through rights. You're obligated under pack law to come to the table and speak. That holds true no matter what continent you stand on," Sage said.

"That holds true for a *real* pack, which you aren't," Finley said.

"The packs under our protection in New York City say otherwise, as does the Chicago god pack and the San Francisco god pack. The Night Courts and the fae in New York acknowledge our standing. That's more than enough validation by anyone's count," Jono stated flatly. "More than the support I hear you've lost lately, yeah?"

Finley scowled at them, unable to deny that fact. Sage's research had come up with a lot of London gossip concerning the werecreature community here. Marek had trawled PreterWorld posts for hints of discord that Sage had run with by doing a deep dive into media articles. What they'd uncovered didn't paint a pretty picture—and the probable cause of the mess here in London was staring right at Patrick with the eyes of a god pack alpha werecreature and the soul of a demon.

"My understanding is you fled our country because you couldn't be arsed to listen to any of the alphas heading up the packs in London," Cressida said.

"There was only one pack I should've belonged to. Neither Jessamine nor Finley allowed me to join the London god pack. That's not on me, but on them."

"That wasn't my decision since I wasn't here at the time, but I understand their order was a death sentence for you if you returned. I'm absolutely willing to adhere to my predecessor's judgment."

Patrick tilted his head to the side, falling into that focused frame of mind as he readied himself for a fight. Werecreatures shifted in their seats, tension thrumming through the group, but Sage cut everyone off at the metaphorical knees before anyone could start flipping tables.

"Then we'll settle this disagreement in the challenge ring. You'll grant us pass-through rights and pardon Jono when we win," Sage said evenly.

"*When* you lose, we take your lives, is that it, love?" Finley sneered.

Sage stared him down, refusing to show throat. "You're welcome to try."

A tall, lanky black man stretched out his legs and leaned an elbow on the table. "Won't need to try very hard for that."

Sage casually turned around, putting her back to the group in a show of disdain that wasn't taken well by any of the London god pack. Patrick kept his eyes on everyone he considered the enemy while Jono and Sage handled pack politics.

"Dire to dire?" Sage asked Jono.

Patrick would've rather it be alpha to alpha—with him fighting, not Jono. Sage was their expert on pack law though, and this was the confrontation she'd thought would be the best chance to get what they needed—freedom to move about London without being hassled or attacked.

Jono nodded. "Dire to dire."

"As you will it."

The words sounded way too formal to be anything but tradition handed down through the years. More shifting of bodies on chairs had Patrick moving his right hand closer to his dagger. Cressida's gaze followed the motion of his hand, and he watched her eyes narrow fractionally. Her expression didn't change, neither did the way she held herself, but when she looked at Patrick again, the mockery from before was gone.

"Our challenge ring is outside London. You'll meet us there in an hour and a half," Cressida said.

"Bryson will escort you to our territory," Finley said.

"He rides in his own car," Patrick said.

"That's not how things are done here in London. You get an escort. This isn't your city."

"And he's riding in his own fucking car. If he tries to ride with us, I'll leave a body behind."

Someone laughed, and Finley grinned like he thought Patrick was amusing. Which was fine by Patrick. He didn't care if the

London god pack underestimated him—their arrogance only meant they'd never see him coming when it truly mattered.

He preferred those odds over the ones where all his secrets were laid bare.

Jono brushed the back of his hand against Patrick's arm in a subtle show of support. Patrick scraped his fingernails against the leather sheath of his dagger and tried not to think about the trouble he'd be in if he committed murder on foreign soil.

"We'll see you in Farningham," Jono said.

Sage headed for the exit, and Wade hurried after her. Patrick didn't take his eyes off the table of werecreatures, not even when Bryson stood. "I'll escort you lot."

"Patrick?" Jono said.

"Go. I've got your six," Patrick said.

He wanted himself and his magic between everyone at the table and his pack. For once, Jono didn't argue. Bryson smirked as he moved to follow Jono, but Patrick put himself right in the other man's way.

Patrick glared at him. "Back the fuck off."

"And what are you going to do if I don't?" Bryson asked, reaching for him.

Warmth pressed against Patrick's back, the familiar scent of Jono's cologne washing over him as Jono reached around him to grab Bryson's wrist.

"He'd kill you," Jono said in a low, dangerous voice from behind Patrick. "And I'll be the one listening to him whinge about the loads of paperwork he'll have to fill out to justify your murder. So don't fucking touch him, or I'll go for your throat myself."

"I'll bitch about paperwork if I want to," Patrick muttered.

"I know you will."

Bryson wrenched his wrist out of Jono's grip, staring at him with an unreadable look in his matching eyes. "So it's like that between the two of you?"

"What Patrick and I are isn't your business. You and I aren't pack, Bryson. We never were."

"We were mates."

"Yeah. Don't make me regret that."

Jono tugged on Patrick's shoulder, and he allowed himself to be turned around. He let Jono get ahead of him, all his formidable attention focused on the threat behind them he couldn't see. But instincts honed by war would ensure Patrick kept his pack safe. He spared a glance over his shoulder only once, seeing Bryson staring at them before the other man finally started to follow.

"If you kill him and make a mess of the hotel carpet, Sage will never forgive us for getting her banned from the Savoy," Jono warned without turning around.

"No promises," Patrick said as they left the Beaufort Bar.

9

London was behind them, the A2 bracketed by the smaller towns making up Greater London. Patrick drummed his fingers against his thigh, staring straight ahead at the taillights stretched down the length of the highway. The silence ward lining the frame of the rental car was a bubble of quiet surrounding them.

"We have many. You need to be more specific," Sage said from the back seat.

"One of their alphas is a demon. Is that specific enough? Because I don't know what kind, but it smelled gross," Wade said.

Jono jerked the steering wheel a little before he got himself under control. "*What?*"

Patrick nodded stiffly. "There's a demon in Cressida's soul. My magic picked up traces of its presence."

Wade leaned forward between their seats. "She smelled like rotten eggs. Like the hunters in New York."

"I didn't smell anything," Jono said.

"Neither did I," Sage added.

Patrick shrugged. "Then that means it's either a *powerful* demon riding Cressida's soul, or *she* is a demon."

"Hunter?"

Jono shook his head. "She's a werecreature. I smelled *that*."

"That doesn't preclude her from being a hunter."

"They hate our kind."

"We'll argue about it later," Patrick interrupted. "Jono, do you know this Devin guy?"

Jono frowned. "He wasn't dire when I lived in London, but he was god pack. Didn't ever run with him. He was more interested in climbing the ranks, and hanging out with me wasn't going to help him reach his goals. He never struck me as dire material though."

"Do you know what his fighting habits were like at least? Dirty and underhanded, or dirty and underhanded on steroids?"

Sage snorted. "When you're a dire, you fight to win, no matter what."

"Oh, good. So you should be able to take him no problem since you're a lawyer."

Sage kicked the back of his seat. "Hey now."

"He's a werewolf, Sage," Jono said, keeping his eyes on the road. "Not as big as me, but still fast."

"No one is as big as you," Patrick said, thinking of more than just Jono's wolf form.

Wade made a gagging sound from the back seat. "Gross."

Sage sighed loudly. "Get your mind out of the gutter, Wade."

"Patrick was there first!"

"Eat your Jaffa Cakes and let us work out our plan of attack," Jono said with a straight face.

"I could always eat the furry bastards," Wade grumbled while ripping open another packet of his latest snack.

Patrick looked over his shoulder at Wade. "No eating the enemy tonight. We don't need that spotlight in this country."

"Is the entire London god pack made up of werewolves?" Sage asked, driving the conversation back on track.

"They were when I was last here. Don't know about now. Devin is one, if that's what has you worried," Jono replied.

"So they won't expect my animal form."

"Not many do in the western hemisphere."

"In that case, do you want their dire dead or for him to show throat?"

"Make him show throat. Pat is right. The less bodies we have to explain, the better."

"Murder inside the challenge ring is legal."

"I know, but we aren't looking to take over the London god pack. We just need pass-through rights."

"Fine."

Sage sounded annoyed they weren't going to let her kill the guy, and Patrick snorted. Then he turned his head to stare at Jono's profile. "Who's Bryson?"

Jono blinked, but that was the only glimmer of reaction he let slip through. "An old mate of mine."

"Did you fuck him?"

Jono rolled his eyes. "A long time ago."

"He seems to want to pick up where you left off."

"We didn't even date, we just shagged. I don't want anything to do with Bryson like that. Stop being jealous."

"I'm not jealous."

Jono glanced at him, arching an eyebrow. "If I could smell you, you'd smell like jealousy."

"No, I wouldn't."

"That's a bloody lie." Jono reached over to squeeze Patrick's right knee. "You've nothing to worry about, Pat. Only person I love is you."

Patrick knew that, he did, but that still didn't stop him from wanting to punch Bryson in the face. "He comes near you again, I'm stabbing him."

"So much for no bodies," Wade muttered.

"Eat your snacks." Patrick shifted his gaze from Jono to the car in front of them, the one Bryson was driving. "If anyone tries anything outside whatever rules they lay down, I'm not holding back."

"I wouldn't ask you to," Jono said.

They lapsed into silence for the rest of the drive to Farningham, a village off the A20 surrounded by dark pastures. Patrick studied the map on his phone, noting the tiny nature reserve that buttressed the village.

"Nice place to bury some bodies," Patrick mused.

Jono hummed thoughtfully at that. "Where?"

"The nearby group of trees by the property."

"Yeah. The god pack owns it."

"Is that where the challenge ring is?"

"No. It's in the field before the reserve."

"How many bodies are buried in the fields?" Sage asked.

Jono was silent for another mile before he answered. "The London god pack has owned that land for decades."

Patrick leaned his head back and grimaced, wondering how many graves they'd be walking over tonight. In the States, god packs could legally kill each other inside the challenge ring. He knew from Jono they could do the same in the United Kingdom. Legal murder was never a good look for any community, but sometimes it was the only way for werecreatures to handle their issues and differences.

That didn't mean he liked the thought of Sage stepping into the challenge ring.

Bryson's car eventually pulled off the highway onto a less busy road. They followed him down the road, across an overpass, to a three-story country house that had seen better days. It wasn't on par with any of the estates the peerage would own despite the land it sat on, but it was bigger than any other house they'd passed by.

A lot of cars were already parked in the driveway, forcing them to park closer to the road than the house after Bryson braked to a stop. They got out, the breeze warm despite the late hour. Patrick kept his leather jacket on, flexing his fingers. The urge to call up his magic was difficult to push aside.

"Jono, are you sure about this?" Bryson asked as they approached him.

Wade snorted scornfully. "You're the enemy. Aren't you supposed to not talk us out of a fight?"

Bryson ignored him, focusing only on Jono with a habit Patrick wanted him to break, preferably yesterday. "I don't want to see you end up dead, mate."

"That's not going to happen. Lead on, yeah? We've a challenge to win," Jono said.

Bryson glanced at Sage before shaking his head. "Right, then. This way."

He didn't lead them into the house, but around it, cutting between the main building and the detached garage. Patrick couldn't see all that well in the dark, unlike the others, and wasn't willing to cast some witchlights. He hoped everyone continued thinking he didn't have magic, or if they believed he did, that he was a low-level magic user.

Maybe the gods of luck were on their side this time.

Then they cleared the buildings and came upon the crowd of werecreatures milling around a large circular space made up of flagstones pressed into the ground. Tiki torches shoved into the dirt were lit, providing flickering illumination that was more than enough light for everyone to see by. He sighed irritably.

Scratch that. The gods of luck were definitely not on their side tonight.

"Someone clearly doesn't have a need for speed," Patrick muttered as he attempted to count how many people were in the audience. "Did you do a mass group text and threaten murder if anyone was late to get them out of London and here tonight before we arrived?"

"This isn't everyone," Bryson retorted.

"This is enough," Sage said calmly as they approached the challenge ring. "You have your witnesses, and I have mine."

As they drew closer, the London god pack shifted, drawing back until they were grouped around half the challenge ring. Bryson went to join his pack, lines clearly drawn. Patrick, Jono and Wade spaced themselves along the curved stone, not needing to fight for elbow space. Sage had left her purse in the car, but had kept her shoes on. Her high heels clacked sharply against the flagstones as she stepped over the raised edge and into the challenge ring.

Patrick clenched his hands into fists and bit his tongue so he didn't argue about taking her spot. He'd seen the end results of some challenges over the years—messy, bloody, with bodies usually in pieces no matter if they were human or animal—but he wasn't familiar with the traditions surrounding how they started. The underlying rules were the same, but how god packs executed their law varied by country.

Devin was already standing inside the challenge ring, barefoot and stripped down to his jeans. He was joking with a few other pack members standing beyond the flagstones, laughing and shoving each other in mirth. When he finally turned to face them, his sharp teeth were a line of bright white against his black skin.

Behind him, Cressida stood on the slightly raised stone barrier, the height of it making her almost even with Finely. Her skintight white jeans came to a stop above the top of her rose-gold strappy heels. The feel of hell scraped against Patrick's soul and magic as he stared at her and whatever demon rode her soul.

Cressida had one hand cocked on her hip, chin raised high, blue eyes reflecting the light in flashes. It was strange being surrounded by people with eyes like Jono. Most god packs in the United States had bright amber-colored eyes, and Patrick had gotten used to seeing that coloring in a person's face.

"You wouldn't normally be worth our time except to hunt you

down for the kill, but you requested a challenge. Who am I to deny us a fight?" Cressida asked.

Some members of her god pack cheered; there were just as many who didn't. Patrick couldn't smell a goddamn thing other than grass and pollen that made him want to sneeze. He hoped Jono was reading everyone's scent because Patrick was focusing on body language. Maybe it was the flickering firelight from the tiki torches, but some people didn't seem thrilled about being there.

"Dire," Sage said as she methodically started removing her diamond earrings.

Devin smirked at her as he started undoing his jeans. "You could always walk away, love."

"Don't call me love." Sage handed Jono her earrings before slipping out of her Louboutins and handing them over as well. Her engagement ring was safe in Marek's hands back in New York. "Say again the terms, dire."

Devin kicked aside his jeans and underwear, standing naked in the firelight. "When you die, the rest of your pack is forfeit."

"And when I put you on your knees to show throat, we'll earn pass-through rights and Jono's pardon." Without looking away from Devin, she lifted her platinum necklace with its turquoise pendant wrapped in fae magic away from her throat and passed it to Patrick. "Hold my necklace."

Patrick tangled his fingers around the warm metal chain, listening as a quiet murmur rose up from the London god pack. Devin's smile faded, and Cressida looked positively murderous.

"This was werecreature against human. Magic is forbidden in the challenge ring during a fight," Finley snapped.

"Which is why Sage removed her necklace," Jono said as Sage unzipped her dress and let it fall off her shoulders and slip down her body. Wade reached down to pick it up and shake it clean. "We agreed on dire against dire, not human against werecreature. Not our fault your sense of smell is shit."

"You thought I was human. Your lack of due diligence is your failing, not ours," Sage said calmly as she removed her bra and underwear and passed those over to Jono as well. "The challenge was called and I am here to answer."

Across the challenge ring, Cressida's face contorted in a way that wasn't human. Patrick couldn't be sure it was even a shift of skin, because the expression looked too monstrous for it to be anything but demonic. Then it was gone, replaced by a fury fueled by hate that was just as ugly in its own way.

"*Kill her,*" Cressida snarled.

Devin shifted fast, but Sage was faster. The months of training and fighting and learning to shift fast in order to survive meant she had all four paws on the flagstones before he did. Sage was massive in her weretiger form, a ferocious beast that looked nothing like the tigers in the wild. She was all dull orange-and-black fur, defined muscles, articulated limbs, and teeth that reminded Patrick more of a saber-toothed cat's than anything else. The only werecreature Patrick had seen who was larger than her was Jono.

Despite her size, she was quick on all four legs, lunging across the challenge ring for Devin in a blur Patrick could barely track. The werewolf dodged, but couldn't escape the swipe from her claws, and got raked across his side for his efforts. Sage's claws were larger than his, wickedly curved, and cut deep. Blood spurted from the wound as Devin twisted out of range with a pained snarl, sliding across the flagstones.

Sage followed him with an agility that looked bone-breaking, twisting her body into a charge Devin had no other choice but to meet. This was supposed to be a fight, and he couldn't win it by running away.

Devin went low, aiming for her throat, but Sage had a longer reach with her front legs. She slashed at his face, forcing him back again or risk losing an eye for the rest of the fight. It would grow back with the shift to human, but no one wanted to be half-blind in the challenge ring.

One minute into the fight and Patrick realized Sage was playing with Devin. He'd seen her fight for her life before in other battles, seen her rip the head off a soultaker after werewolves drove the ever-hungry demon to the ground. Alone or with their pack, Sage was a force to be reckoned with that most other packs never saw coming.

Devin might have fought his way into being dire for the London god pack, but he hadn't been fighting against gods and the Dominion Sect. Sage was prepared for underhandedness—Devin wasn't prepared for the sheer ruthless brutality Sage brought to the fight with her size and strength and cunning mind that outclassed his.

Werewolves made up the majority of werecreatures in the world. People infected by the werevirus gleaned from wildcats or bears were rarer on certain continents or countries, but they tended to be the hardest to take down in a fight. Sage was used to fighting werewolves. It became immediately apparent Devin was not used to fighting against someone larger and stronger than he was.

Patrick took his eyes off the fighters in the challenge ring and scanned the crowd of god pack members on the other side. Some people looked surprised while others appeared grimly worried. One or two had a vicious smile on their faces, and Patrick figured Devin maybe wasn't the most popular dire around.

When his gaze passed over Cressida and Finley, Patrick found only one of them staring back at him. Cressida wasn't watching the fight; he couldn't be sure she even seemed interested in it. Despite the distance separating them, Patrick could see the way her lips were pulled back in a snarl, the shadows brought on by flickering tiki torches not enough to hide the sharpness of her teeth.

The grating feel of hell grew sharper against his shields, digging past his magic and into the damaged parts of his soul that always seemed to know where to find bits of hell in the world these days. No one else bearing witness to the fight seemed aware of the hellish taint—or if they were, they were used to it.

Neither option was a good one.

Patrick's fingers twitched as he resisted the urge to touch his dagger and draw attention to it. The magic and prayers that resided inside its matte-black blade came and went as it pleased, but when faced with a threat from the hells, it always answered the call. The last thing he wanted to do was tip off a demon about his ace in the hole.

"Damn, I'm out of Jaffa Cakes," Wade grumbled, shaking the box upside down to prove he had nothing left. "Sage! I'm hungry. Can you hurry up?"

"Wade," Jono ground out. "Not the time."

"But I'm hungry!"

Sage let out a roar that sounded less like pain and more like annoyance as she slashed at Devin. Wade crossed his arms over his chest and scowled mulishly. Patrick watched as she faked a dodge and twisted sharply on her hind legs to leap onto Devin's back and drive him to the ground. He let out a howl that was abruptly cut off when Sage clamped her jaws around the back of his neck, sharp curved fangs digging through fur to latch onto skin, spilling blood.

If she wrenched her head to either side, she'd break Devin's neck and kill him.

Patrick almost wished she would.

Devin went rigid beneath her, his panting the only sound lingering in the silence around them. Sage growled a warning deep in her throat, the noise vibrating through the air, causing more than one London god pack member to take a step back.

Cressida appeared incandescent with rage, practically vibrating with it, while Finley's face was wiped clean of emotions. Other pack members around them seemed just as stunned by what had happened, but there were a few who were doing a bad job of hiding their relief.

Sage growled again, the sound harsher, more of a demand as she pressed the claws of one rear paw against Devin's flank. He stayed stiff for several more seconds before going absolutely limp beneath her.

Someone on the other side of the challenge ring gasped loudly. Patrick never took his eyes off Sage as she lifted her jaws away from Devin's neck and backed away, having gotten him to submit and show throat. Her striped tail lashed the air in quick motions.

"Fight's over," Jono said.

Cressida's vicious growl said more than words ever could as she stepped into the challenge ring and stalked over to where Devin still lay on the flagstones. He tried to scramble away, but she was on him in a second, still human, but with preternatural strength backed by hellish power behind her. She kicked him so hard in the head even Patrick could hear the bone break.

Devin's wolf head snapped around, the side that had taken the blow appearing dented in the firelight. He collapsed, wolf body lying limply between Cressida and Sage, blood beginning to trickle out of his muzzle. Then Cressida turned her attention on Sage.

Instinct had Patrick reacting, and a mageglobe formed in his hand without him needing to think about it, the command trigger seeping through his thoughts and into his soul. He let the mageglobe fly, arcing it over Sage as she retreated to give him room. Patrick's magic exploded between them, forming a shield that arced over the London god pack.

Cressida skidded to a halt before hitting the shield, one heel snapping off her shoe as her right ankle bent in an awkward way she didn't seem to feel. She straightened in a fluid motion, not caring about her damaged shoe.

"We won the fight and it's fucking *over*," Patrick snapped, conjuring up another mageglobe, filling it with an offensive spell instead of a defensive ward. "Back the fuck off."

Someone touched the glittering pale blue barrier and yelped from the backlash. Patrick ignored them, keeping his attention on Cressida and the way she smiled at them when none of her god pack could see—like something else moved beneath her skin, and it wasn't the wolf she could shift into.

"Mage," Cressida snarled. "It's illegal for your kind to interfere in our challenges. Magic is forbidden in the challenge ring."

Jono stepped into the ring as Sage shifted back to human, both of them safe outside the shield encasing everyone else. "Patrick is the co-leader of our pack. He acted when you went after our dire unprovoked."

Sage was fully human now, comfortable in her nudity as she wiped blood off her lips and chin. She flicked it off her fingers in a sharp gesture. "Patrick's magic never entered the ring until *after* the fight was over and your dire had already showed throat to me. The terms were met. Grant us the pass-through rights and Jono's pardon."

"Perhaps I'll find another dire and issue a rematch," Cressida said.

Sage met her glare calmly, standing tall and proud beneath everyone's attention. "Jono asked for leniency this round. If we go again, I will leave your new dire's spine at your feet."

Cressida threw back her head and laughed, her curls bouncing with the motion. "Such confidence you have. Perhaps I should offer *you* the job."

"You couldn't afford me."

Jono handed Sage her clothes, and she dressed with easy motions. He passed over her high heels, and only when she was fully clothed and cared for did he face Cressida.

"We'll cross London when and how we like. We aren't here for your territory," he told her.

Cressida pressed both hands against Patrick's shield, ignoring the way her skin sizzled at the touch. "You may walk London, but it will never be your home."

Patrick wanted to stab her in the gut with his dagger for that remark, but he figured that wouldn't go down well with the other side. He consoled himself with keeping the shield up so everyone couldn't follow them back to their car.

"And his pardon?" Sage pressed.

"Granted," Finley called out.

Cressida hissed, half turning to look over at her co-leader. "Fin."

Finley wouldn't look at her, but he had no trouble meeting Jono's gaze. "The order we handed down when you left years ago is rescinded. No one will kill you."

Cressida scowled, and while Finley didn't flinch, Patrick had the distinct impression the other man wasn't going to get through the night unscathed. Whatever was going on amongst them was worse than the relationship between Estelle and Youssef. They at least worked together for the power they craved. These two seemed willing to break each other and their pack rather than abide by pack law unless their hand was forced.

Jono and Sage turned their backs on the London god pack and returned to their side of the challenge ring. Jono wrapped an arm around Sage's shoulders, pulling her close in a friendly hug as they walked.

Wade poked at the mageglobe hovering near Patrick's shoulder, unburned and unbothered by the magic. "Are we done?"

"We're done," Jono said. "Let's be off. Wade, stop touching his magic."

Wade pulled his finger back just enough to be clear of the glow. "I'm not touching it."

Sage smacked him lightly on the arm as they came within reach. "Get to the car."

"Ugh. Fine."

Patrick let everyone else go ahead of him before taking up the rearguard position. He didn't want to turn his back on Cressida, but he wasn't going to give her the satisfaction of looking over his shoulder at her.

Despite the warm summer night, Patrick felt chilled down to

the bone, and he couldn't blame it on the anchors burned into his skeleton by Persephone's hand.

That chill of winter in the midst of summer came from something straight out of hell.

Patrick didn't drop the shield he'd constructed around the challenge ring until they were in the car, engine running hot, with the country house shrinking in the rearview mirror. Only then did he distantly recall his magic, feeling the power seep back into his soul when they were already on the road.

"Could've gone worse," Jono said, staring straight ahead.

"Next time, let Sage have the kill," Patrick said.

Jono's mouth twisted, but it was telling he didn't argue.

"You're still mad."

Patrick looked up from undoing the straps that secured his dagger to his thigh. Jono sat on the bed, undoing the laces on his Chukka boots before toeing them off. Patrick pulled his dagger, sheath and all, free of his belt and thigh to set it on the small glass table beside the bed.

"What gave you that idea?" Patrick asked.

"I know when you're angry, even if I can't smell you. Is this about the fight or Bryson?"

Patrick made a face at the asshole's name. "What do you think?"

Jono rested his elbows on his knees, watching Patrick with unblinking eyes. "Pat. Drop your shields."

A small part of him didn't want to, because even now Patrick struggled with opening up to people. Jono had taught him over the past year that leaning on someone else wasn't a bad thing. Patrick had kept too many secrets over the course of his life because he had to. He'd learned never to keep the truth from Jono, because things always ended badly when he tried, and that meant he dropped his shields.

Jono drew in a breath, taking in Patrick's scent and whatever truth he could pull from it. Patrick would never know how to read someone like that since he couldn't get infected by the werevirus. Time was he'd have hated being read and known and understood in such a base way. But this was Jono, the man he'd faced down hell for, had killed for. The person he was learning to live for.

It never felt like giving in, more like shoring each other up.

Patrick went to Jono, crawling onto his lap and hooking one arm over his shoulder. He framed Jono's face with his other hand, staring into those eyes that were out of place in New York but looked like they belonged in London.

"Just tell me he didn't mean anything to you," Patrick said.

It was stupid, he knew, to be jealous of someone he'd never met or known about until now. But he hadn't liked how Bryson had looked at Jono, at the familiarity he attempted to impose. Jono wasn't Bryson's, and the sooner that asshole understood that, the less homicidal Patrick might feel.

Or not.

Jono's hands curved over his ass, tugging him closer. Patrick shifted his weight, letting himself be manhandled until there was barely an inch of space between their chests.

"I told you, love. He doesn't mean anything to me. Not how you think. He never did," Jono said in a deep, low voice that went straight to Patrick's cock.

"You never told me about him."

They'd talked about past relationships last summer, when they'd gotten to know each other more after the mess surrounding summer solstice. Patrick hadn't had any to disclose, and Jono's handful had happened when he was younger. Patrick was annoyed with himself that he hadn't asked about fuck buddies.

Jono turned his head briefly to press a kiss to Patrick's palm. "There was nothing to tell."

Patrick stroked his hand over Jono's cheek, feeling the faint scratch of a beard beginning to come up. "You were friends."

"Back then, yeah, and we shagged. It doesn't mean we're anything close to being mates right now because of it. He had a pack when we lived in London, and I didn't." Jono leaned closer, lips brushing over Patrick's. "You're my pack. You're all I need."

Patrick opened his mouth, drawing Jono in like air, needing him like a heartbeat. He'd get over the jealousy—he *would*—but right now all Patrick wanted to do was mark Jono in such a way that Bryson and anyone else would know Jono was *his*. That they were each other's, and that would never change, no matter what piece of ass walked on by trying to catch Jono's eye.

Jono laughed against his mouth, whatever he was smelling coming off Patrick amusing him. Patrick bit Jono's bottom lip in retaliation, but it didn't stop him from laughing. Jono squeezed his ass with strong fingers.

Patrick pulled back, breathing a little heavily, jeans starting to get a little tight. "Get on the bed."

"I am on the bed," Jono said with a wicked smile.

Patrick rolled his eyes before sliding off Jono's lap. "Lie down on it."

Jono trailed his hand up Patrick's inner thigh to cup his cock through his jeans. The way his fingers moved had Patrick rocking into the touch. "Bossy tonight, aren't you?"

Patrick shoved at Jono's shoulder. "Get on the bed so I can ride you, or I'll go take a shower. *Alone.*"

Jono smirked at him, and the way his eyes darkened told Patrick showering alone wasn't ever going to be an option. "Lube's in my luggage."

Patrick pushed him again, and Jono let himself fall back on his elbows. "*Bed.*"

Jono laughed, the sound ringing through the hotel room, the same way it rang through their bedroom back home. Sex for Patrick used to be quick fucks while on leave—fast and meaningless and hidden in the dark so his scars wouldn't show. With Jono there was always laughter, and Patrick hadn't known what he was missing until Jono showed him.

Jono got out of his clothes before Patrick located the bottle of lube. He tossed it at Jono's head, but it never found its target. Jono caught it with a smirk before he uncapped it and proceeded to put on a show for Patrick. The way he stroked his cock while never looking away from Patrick was positively illegal.

"If you're getting yourself ready, you might as well do the same for me," Patrick said once he was naked and crawling back onto Jono's lap.

Jono pulled him in for a kiss, slick fingers sliding over Patrick's ass. "I'll give you whatever you need, Pat."

Patrick shivered, less from the finger sliding inside him than from the heavy promise in Jono's words. Because need was different than want, and Jono seemed to have some sixth sense when it came to Patrick.

He rolled his hips down onto Jono's finger, the stretch in his body a slight burn. Jono stroked their cocks together using his other hand, and the slow friction was enough to drive Patrick mad. He gripped Jono's shoulders, digging his fingers into warm skin. He was always so much warmer than Patrick, and even though Patrick would never be able to smell him and the pack scent that lingered between them, the warmth of his body was a comfort.

Jono was a comfort he never wanted to give up.

A second finger slid inside him as Jono kissed a line down Patrick's throat to his collarbone, nipping at the threads of scar tissue there. The damaged skin and nerves on his chest were an ugly reminder of his childhood that Jono soothed with lips and tongue as Patrick rode his fingers.

"Only person I want is you," Jono murmured as he pressed his thumb teasingly beneath the head of Patrick's cock.

Patrick's breath stuttered from the touch and the way his nerves were set on fire. He chased after Jono's mouth, undulating between Jono's warm touch, always wanting more. Jono never stopped touching him, and Patrick could feel the soulbond humming between them, a barrier and balm to the damage already present in Patrick's soul.

He pulled at Jono's shoulders, dragging his lips over the curve of Jono's jaw as he yanked a pillow out from behind Jono. He tossed it aside, giving Jono more room to lie back. Patrick lifted off Jono's fingers and grabbed the lube, shoving Jono down into the position he preferred. Jono sank against the last two remaining pillows, lifting one arm to tuck a hand behind his head. He stroked slick fingers over Patrick's hip, watching him with half-lidded eyes.

"Need help?" Jono asked with a smirk.

Patrick moved forward on his knees and reached around to grab Jono's cock. "Does it look like I need your help?"

Jono's grip tightened as Patrick sank onto his cock with steady rolls of his hips. The pressure of being filled made Patrick swallow hard as he opened up on that cock, sinking lower. The way Jono's pupils dilated, how he licked his lips and never looked away made Patrick groan when he finally bottomed out.

"Fuck," Jono growled, thrusting up lightly and forcing Patrick to move.

The slide of Jono's cock deep inside him had Patrick digging his fingernails into the skin over Jono's chest. He used Jono to brace himself as he rose up on his knees before sinking back down, shivering at the thick fullness inside him.

Patrick fucked himself on Jono's cock at whatever pace he wanted. Jono met him halfway, thrusting up into him with a focused intensity that made Patrick moan. The only sound between them was their breathing and the steady slap of skin on skin as Patrick chased his release. When Jono wrapped his hand around Patrick's cock and started to jerk him off, Patrick tossed his head back, mouth falling open on a stuttering gasp.

"*Jono*," he bit out, cock throbbing, the burn in his thighs an ache he didn't mind.

Jono moved his hand to grab Patrick's ass, hauling him up higher on his knees. Jono moved beneath him, and Patrick had to use both hands to brace himself on Jono's chest. Then Jono got his feet underneath him and started fucking Patrick in earnest. The whine that fell unbidden from Patrick's mouth only spurred him on faster.

The bed creaked beneath them, and Patrick tried to meet each hard thrust halfway. He bent his elbows, leaning down to kiss Jono on the mouth, only to miss as his body shook through a particularly deep thrust.

He bit at the edge of Jono's jaw, moaning loudly as Jono fucked him with a single-minded intensity Patrick would never complain about.

"Come on, fuck me harder," Patrick got out against Jono's skin. "Fuck me like you mean it. Like I'm yours."

Jono let out a growl that vibrated between them. Patrick swore when Jono slid out of him, but before he could protest, he was rolled onto his side as Jono moved out from underneath him. Patrick got up on his elbows, but that was as far as he got before Jono slid back inside him, pinning him face-first to the bed and fucking him so hard starbursts of light exploded on the back of his eyelids.

"This what you want?" Jono growled into his ear. "Me fucking you so everyone will know you belong to me?"

Patrick spread his knees as wide as he could and got one hand wrapped around his cock, stroking himself off, so close to the edge he could practically taste it. "I want them to know you're *mine*. That you're the only one who gets to fuck me like this."

Jono swore, his fingers digging into Patrick's hips with bruising strength he knew would leave a mark. Patrick came like that, held down and fucked nearly breathless, Jono's cock deep inside him and the pack scent he could never smell buried in his skin.

Jono collapsed on top of Patrick, forcing his cock deeper as he came, hips grinding against his ass. Patrick could only shake through it, overwarm and refusing to move. Jono ran his hands over Patrick's body before leaning down to leave a lingering kiss on his shoulder.

"You're so bloody thick if you think I'll ever look at anyone else when I have you," Jono murmured.

Patrick clenched down on Jono's softening cock, sighing softly. They were messy and sticky, but Patrick didn't care, not when Jono was tracing promises into his skin with warm fingers.

10

A LOUD KNOCK ON THEIR HOTEL ROOM DOOR HAD JONO OPENING IT after Patrick dropped his wards and indicated it was okay. Wade wrinkled his nose in greeting, then held up a stolen bottle of air freshener.

"I came prepared," Wade said, brandishing the bottle at him.

Jono rolled his eyes. "Don't be rude to housekeeping. Put that back where you found it."

"I need it more than they do right now."

"You spray our room, I'm dumping all your snacks in the trash," Patrick threatened as he finished knotting his tie.

Wade gasped loudly before narrowing his eyes. "You wouldn't."

Jono snagged the bottle of air freshener from him. "Where's Sage?"

"We were gonna wait for you guys downstairs, but she sent me back up because there's an asshole waiting for you."

Jono tossed the bottle of air freshener into the hotel room, not caring where it landed. "Who?"

"That Bryson guy."

Patrick swore and went to grab his suit jacket from the wardrobe. "What the fuck does he want now?"

"Uh, breakfast? Like me? Sage said our table is ready, and I'm hungry."

Patrick looked fit to murder someone, but he didn't raise his shields. Jono could still smell him—the underlying bitterness that was Patrick's own scent, along with the scent of them together and the pack on its own. The mix was better than any cologne on the market as far as Jono was concerned.

"Let's go," Patrick ordered.

Jono let him leave first, enjoying the view of Patrick from behind. The suit was decently tailored and fit him well, and it wasn't every day Jono got to see him clean up nice. Jono figured Nadine probably had a hand in it at some point since it was reasonably on trend.

He let the door close and latch behind him before hurrying after Patrick and Wade. They took the lift down, exiting into the lobby. Sage stood near one of the chaise lounges, dressed casually, with a tote bag on her shoulder. Bryson stood a meter away from her, hands at his sides, not showing throat but not looking like he wanted to fight.

They strode across the lobby, and Jono watched as Bryson turned his head to look at them, eyes hidden behind sunglasses. Beyond the hotel's sliding glass front doors, it looked as if the sun from yesterday had been swallowed by clouds.

"Give me one good reason I shouldn't knock your ass into the street?" Patrick demanded in a low voice once they got within arm's reach, mindful of the front desk workers nearby.

"Because it would go against pass-through rights when I'm not here to fight," Bryson drawled. He sniffed unsubtly, jaw twitching a little from whatever he was picking up from Patrick.

"Your attitude leaves much to be desired. How many of you have been ordered to spy on us?" Sage said.

Bryson's mouth twisted a little before he shook his head. "I came by for a chat and to check up on you lot."

"You mean you came to spy."

Bryson shrugged expansively, the smile on his face brittle. "Are you surprised? You left an impression."

"We could leave another one," Patrick said, one hand in a fist.

Bryson didn't snap back with an insult this time, and Jono wondered if it was because he knew what Patrick was now. Jono caught Sage's eye and jerked his head in the direction of the restaurant where breakfast was being served.

"Think they'll up our table from four to five?" Jono asked.

Sage nodded. "They'll do whatever I ask."

"Then let's eat."

"*Yes*," Wade said feelingly, already walking away. "Because I'm starving and I wanna try a full English breakfast."

Sage followed after him, but Patrick didn't move, staring Bryson down. Jono nudged him in the side to get Patrick walking before gesturing at Bryson. "Come on. Breakfast is on us."

"He can pay his own way," Patrick muttered.

"Be nice, Pat."

"Blow me."

"Later, if you're good."

Humor laced through Patrick's scent for a second or two before fading. The three of them caught up with Sage and Wade, the hostess listening attentively to Sage's request. Changing a table from four to five was a simple matter, and they were led to the central courtyard dining area rather than the long tables inside.

The weather was cool, the sky above overcast, which meant they were only one of two groups eating in the area. A server had already pushed three of the small marble tables together. Sage and Wade opted for the bench, while Jono, Patrick, and Bryson claimed the chairs. Jono made sure to take the seat between the two men as a precaution against Patrick stabbing Bryson over his morning coffee.

The small garden beyond the long bench was in high summer bloom, and the greenery was a nice touch. Their server returned before they even had a chance to look at the menu, appearing far too awake and perky for the early hour.

"Tea for the table?" she asked brightly.

"Coffee for me," Patrick corrected.

"I want both," Wade said.

Sage gave the young woman an easy smile. "Tea for the rest of us, thank you."

The server left, and Patrick slipped his hand beneath the table. The static of a silence ward washed over them, and Jono's ears popped as the bubble of magic surrounded them. Bryson's head jerked up.

"What the fuck?" he said.

"In case you brought any friends, I don't want them listening in," Patrick said coldly.

Bryson smelled uneasy to Jono's nose, even if he didn't look it. He rallied well enough though, plastering on a smile when the server came back with their drinks and to take their orders. Between the five of them, they ordered enough to feed ten.

Patrick reached for his coffee and glared around Jono at Bryson after the server left. "Start talking. I want to know what you're here for."

"We all do," Jono agreed.

Sage poured a tiny bit of milk into her mug. "If it requires further negotiations between dires, Devin has my number."

Bryson grimaced. "Devin is dead. Cressida killed him."

Considering what Patrick had told them about what lived in Cressida's soul, Jono wasn't surprised. "From the kick to the head?"

"After." Bryson stared down at his tea, his sunglasses sliding down his nose a little. "We had to watch."

Jono didn't care for the scent coming off Bryson. Despair

always left a sickly taste in the back of his throat and ruined his meal.

"Does she replace her dires often?" Jono asked.

"More than Jessamine ever did."

Jono shared a look with Sage across the table. She cleared her throat, taking up the questioning. "I expected a longer fight with Devin. He seemed ill-prepared."

Bryson's mouth quirked at the corners. "I think any of us would've been ill-prepared to face your weretiger form."

"He was a dire. Our job is to be prepared when it comes to challenges."

"Devin should've never had the job to begin with. Isn't that right, Jono?"

Bryson looked at him, and Jono reluctantly nodded. "There were plenty others more fit for the job when I lived in London."

"That was then," Bryson muttered darkly before sipping at his tea.

Jono wondered how many of the people who were dire material had either fled the god pack or been killed like Devin. Dires were usually some of the strongest pack members outside the alphas. Some god packs chose them to keep them close and in line. Others opted for loyalty over paranoia. The fact that Cressida was running through dires the way a drunk demolished pints worried Jono.

"Who is your dire now?" Sage asked.

Bryson shrugged. "They haven't decided yet."

"That means we have to deal directly with your alphas." Sage glanced at Jono, frowning thoughtfully. "The absence of a dire removes me from direct communication."

"The fuck it does," Patrick said.

Jono shook his head. "She's right. If there's no dire appointed yet, communication between our packs falls to us."

"It's a shame the UK doesn't allow guns."

"Pat."

Patrick looked him dead in the eye. "The London god pack has a bigger problem than we do, and that's saying something."

Jono wished he were wrong.

Sage cleared her throat and passed the sugar over to Wade, who happily started to empty it into his tea and coffee. "I don't believe they have a civil war problem."

"*Yet*," Patrick bit out. Sage lifted her mug in a silent toast of agreement at him before sipping at her tea.

"Is Sage right?" Jono asked, turning his head to look at Bryson.

Bryson looked up from his tea, blinking at Jono through his sunglasses. "You left. Things changed."

"I didn't have a choice."

"You could've stayed."

Jono thought about Marek's promise back then and his future sitting on the other side of him now, angrily sipping coffee. "There was no chance of me staying."

The other man sighed, leaning back in his chair. "Probably for the best, mate. I shouldn't be telling you this, what with you being a rival pack now and all, but the London god pack is a right mess."

"So we've been told."

"So we've seen," Wade muttered into his coffee mug.

Patrick raised his coffee mug in Wade's direction. "Cheers to that."

"Cressida wasn't part of the god pack when I was here. I know she arrived a few years ago, but from where? What's her background?" Jono asked.

Bryson shook his head. "You know we never care about shit like that. She has the god strain of the werevirus running through her veins. That's all that matters."

"Maybe that's your problem right there. You let almost anyone be pack without doing a background check," Patrick said.

"Cressida isn't an exception. You are."

"I'm still pack. I've proven my loyalty to them just like all of us have. I'd take our pack over yours any day of the fucking week."

The hint of jealousy that hit Jono's nose came from Bryson, not Patrick. He shifted on his seat, settling his right hand on Patrick's thigh, giving it a gentle squeeze. Patrick's scent momentarily spiked with pleasure at the touch.

"If you aren't happy, you can always leave," Jono said.

Bryson laughed bitterly. "And what? Become an independent? That might've worked out for you in the end, but it's not what I want."

"And living in a pack run by a tyrant is?"

Bryson snapped his mouth shut, his silence ringing in Jono's ears. No one spoke. The silence lasted long enough for the server to return with another co-worker, trays in hand and laden down with plates.

They were served breakfast, the amount of food completely covering the pushed together tables. The smell of proper bacon, not the thin strips of fatty nothing sold in the States, made Jono's stomach growl. He dug into his full English, glad he'd ordered two.

Wade reached across the table for the butter, snatching up the dish before anyone else could get some. "Okay, I gotta ask. What is up with you Brits and beans?"

"Beans and toast are a staple," Jono said mildly.

"Says you."

"And the rest of this country."

"You're all wrong."

"Eat your food and stop complaining," Sage ordered as she cut into her omelet.

Jono managed to taste everything on his plate at least once before Bryson started talking again.

"Things weren't so terrible before Cressida became alpha," Bryson said.

Considering what she was, Jono could believe it. "And now?"

Bryson scraped his fork over his plate, pushing around his baked beans. "Now she's the root of all our problems. And I could be killed for saying that."

Jono stabbed at a piece of sausage and popped it into his mouth, chewing slowly. Thinking of the big picture was something he'd only seriously been doing since last summer. It wasn't something he'd had to do while living in London or after he'd moved to New York City. But knowing what Patrick had found out about Cressida and seeing the discord in the pack last night made Jono acutely aware of the poison seeping through the London god pack.

He could see how it would play out—the infighting in London causing fractures in all of the UK packs over time, if it hadn't already. London was where all the packs looked toward for stability, and if the god pack there was broken, there would be a leadership void when it came to representing themselves to international packs.

A void demons would have no problem filling.

It was a mess Jono couldn't clean up. He had his own problems back in New York, fighting over territory with Estelle and Youssef. London wasn't his responsibility. What's more, he didn't know who he could trust within the London god pack to warn them about the demon in their midst.

He could see the moment Sage must have reached the same conclusion, because her face shut down and her scent went icy from tension rather than fear. Jono only got grim resignation from Patrick, which proved he'd probably hit on that problem before they even left the Farningham country house.

"We can't help you," Jono said after a moment.

Bryson shook his head and kept cutting up the omelet on his second plate. "Not asking you to. Our pack problems aren't yours."

Patrick snorted his opinion on that but thankfully didn't argue, merely shoveled a bite of potatoes into his mouth.

They ate in stilted silence for the rest of the meal. Time was Jono and Bryson would've filled the quiet with pack gossip and friendly insults. But that was then, and this was now. They were on opposite sides despite having the same eyes and the same god strain of the werevirus running through their veins. Time healed and time changed and time made it clear their separate paths would never cross again.

"I'll pay for my meal," Bryson said at the end.

"Don't bother. We'll cover it." Jono stood, nodding at the restaurant exit. "I'll walk you out."

Patrick hooked an arm over the back of his chair and leaned back, balancing it on two legs. "Stay within eyesight."

Bryson arched an eyebrow over the rim of his sunglasses as he looked at Patrick. "Don't trust me?"

Patrick twisted his wrist of the hand dangling over the chair, calling up a tiny mageglobe that fit snug against his palm in warning. "Fuck no."

Bryson smirked, but he smelled wary to Jono. They headed for the exit, and Jono was mindful not to go where his pack couldn't see.

"How many werecreatures did Cressida assign to watch us?" Jono asked.

Bryson raked a hand through his blond hair. "You know I can't tell you that."

Jono decided not to point out Bryson had just confirmed Cressida *had* ordered werecreatures to watch and follow his pack. Being treated like the enemy was nothing new, but it meant they'd have to continue to pair up, which wasn't easy when Patrick had to go to work at the WSA.

"I'm chuffed for you, mate," Bryson said after an awkward pause. "I know how much you wanted a pack. Now you've found it."

"Yeah."

If things had been different, their reunion wouldn't have gone so terribly, and maybe Jono could've kept believing Bryson was still his mate. But everyone he'd left behind in London couldn't be trusted, even when they stood before him smelling like regret.

"Never thought you'd be shagging a mage though. Thought you didn't trust magic users?"

"I trust Patrick."

"Yeah. I can bloody well smell that." Bryson half turned, mobile in hand. "Ta for breakfast. Give me a ring before you flee the country again."

Jono didn't promise anything. "Cheers."

He watched Bryson walk away, knowing the other man would be ringing his alphas the second he was out of earshot. A familiar scent hit his nose as Patrick came to a stop beside him on quiet feet.

"I still don't like him," Patrick said.

Jono sighed. "I know you don't."

"He's an asshole."

"So are you, Pat."

"Yeah, but I'm a *likeable* asshole, and you love my ass."

Jono looked over at him, laughing a little. "That was never in doubt."

"Sage put the meal on her room account. We're heading back up to the penthouse."

"Don't you need to go to work?"

Jono watched as Patrick's smile faded into a flat line, the grim look in his green eyes erasing all humor. "Pack meeting first."

Jono's humor faded as well. "All right."

Sage and Wade approached, with Wade unabashedly biting into a makeshift sandwich made out of everyone's leftovers from the plates. The four of them headed back to the private elevator, taking it up to the penthouse. Patrick warded the suite for silence once the door shut behind them.

"What's the emergency?" Wade asked as he flung himself onto the sofa.

"Don't get crumbs everywhere," Sage warned.

Wade shoved the rest of the sandwich into his mouth and chewed, cheeks bulging. He pointed at his face, then gestured widely to prove he hadn't gotten crumbs anywhere.

"We need backup," Patrick said bluntly.

"You already pulled Lucien into this mess," Jono said, not believing those words were coming out of his mouth.

"Lucien won't be any help against a demon old enough to hide what it is from preternatural senses while living in a pack."

"We agreed to leave everyone else back in New York," Sage reminded him.

Patrick shook his head as he pulled out his mobile. "I'm not talking about Emma's pack, or even the fae. If we're going up against demons and necromancers, we need someone who can break that kind of magic."

"Another necromancer?"

"No. Not exactly. He's an old friend of mine. He sometimes fought with us Hellraisers in the Mage Corps." Patrick hesitated before meeting Jono's eyes. "If the PIA sends him out here, he'll take one look at us and know about the soulbond. Shields never mattered to him for shit like that."

Jono crossed his arms over his chest, shoving down his worry. "Do you trust him?"

"Yeah."

"Then so will we."

Patrick bit his lip before nodding. "Right. I'm going to call Setsuna before I head out. Anything else?"

"If Devin really is dead, it sounds like Cressida is using the dire position to get rid of personal enemies or anyone who would risk challenging her and maybe winning," Sage said.

Jono nodded slowly. "I think you're right. Devin always wanted a higher rank in the god pack, but he never struck me as dire material, even when I lived here."

Sage made a face. "It's an ugly precedent. Even Estelle and Youssef never went that far."

"They might get ideas from this," Patrick said over his shoulder as he headed for the bedroom to take his call.

Jono rolled his eyes. "Then we'll take in more packs if they do."

"Hey, can we go see the London Eye today?" Wade asked,

looking at his mobile. "Ooh, no, I changed my mind. I wanna see the Tower of London."

Sage poked Jono in the side. "You're the native Brit. Time to play tour guide. We can see who the god pack sends to watch after us."

"I'd rather we lose them in the Tube. Parking over by the Tower is nonexistent," Jono said.

Wade pumped his fist in the air. "Yes! I can't wait to see the Crown Jewels."

"No stealing," Jono and Sage said in unison.

Wade scowled and gave them a sulky look. "*Fine.*"

Jono had a feeling the monarchy would lose a diamond or two if they didn't pat Wade down before leaving the Tower.

11

"You're late," Nadine said by way of greeting when she slid into his car.

Patrick waited long enough for her to shut the door before hitting the gas pedal and clutch, pulling away from the pickup area in front of the Waldorf Hilton. "I texted you why."

He'd done it in code he knew she'd understand. Patrick did his best not to leave an electronic trail about his personal life with other government agents, even ones he trusted with his life. Patrick just didn't trust the government.

He also didn't trust nosy werewolves, which was why he'd told Nadine he was going to be an hour late to give him time to lose anyone following him.

"You could've requested breakfast to go." Nadine gave him a sidelong look as she buckled up.

"Had to eat with my pack this morning." Patrick smacked his hand against the roof, filling the car with a silence ward. Static washed through the vehicle, providing privacy. "We have a problem."

"That's the general nature of our jobs."

"My pack ended up having to fight the London god pack last night to get pass-through rights. Sage won, not like there was any doubt, but one of the alphas killed their dire because he lost." Patrick switched lanes, glancing at his phone and the GPS map there. He could drive in London just fine, but not getting lost was another matter entirely. "That alpha has a demon riding her soul, and no one in the pack seemed to know."

Nadine turned her head to stare at him. "Please tell me you're joking?"

"Wish I was."

"How does a pack of *werecreatures* not know they have a demon in their midst?"

"I think it's old, and it's good at hiding."

In Patrick's experience, the older a demon was, the harder it was to banish or kill. He hated working those kinds of cases.

"Fuck." Nadine stretched out her legs, shifting to straighten out the skirt of her sheath dress. "Any idea which hell it belongs to?"

"No. But it has to be powerful if it can hide itself from werecreatures."

"Is it hiding itself from its host?"

Patrick thought about how Cressida had acted last night—comfortable in her skin, with no hint of distress about her. "Pretty sure Cressida accepted it willingly."

"Gods fucking damn it. You can't get sucked into pack politics right now."

"I *know*, but that doesn't mean I can ignore whatever the fuck is going on. We needed the pass-through rights so I could work without drawing attention to us. The WSA doesn't need to know I have a pack."

"We need to focus on the auction. Pack politics are not the mission."

"I am aware of that, but what are the fucking odds that Estelle and Youssef hire a bunch of hunters to come after us and the packs under our protection earlier this year, and the London god pack has been infiltrated by one?"

Nadine scowled out the windshield. "It could be coincidence."

"Coincidence doesn't fucking happen in my life when the Fates are looking over my shoulder."

"You can't fix the London god pack."

"I'm not gonna fucking try. But I still have to deal with them, and if they're being led by a demon, like hell am I going against them alone. We're already dealing with a bunch of necromancers, demons just make it worse."

"You can't tell the WSA about the London god pack. They'll want to know how you learned that information."

"I know. We aren't telling them anything, same way we aren't telling them the location and date of the auction. But we still need help."

"Gerard?"

"No. I asked Setsuna to have your director put Spencer on a plane."

Nadine groaned. "Patrick."

"He was read into the joint task force back in December. It'll be fine."

"He *ruined* my Alexander McQueen dress the last time we were all together!"

"Technically, the zombie ruined it."

Nadine smacked Patrick in the arm without looking. "He owes me a new dress."

"Then you can tell him to pay up in person. He flies out tonight and gets into London tomorrow."

PIA Special Agent Spencer Bailey had fought with them on occasion in the Mage Corps. Like Nadine, he'd never been assigned permanently to a team or a base, but moved around on an as-needed basis. Spencer was a soulbreaker with an affinity for the dead. If they were going up against the Orthodox Church of the Dead and a demon-led god pack, Patrick wanted someone on their side who could put the dead to rest and exorcise demons.

The three of them were friendly even though they never got to see each other very much. Patrick used to fly across the country for cases while Nadine was stationed out of Paris, and Spencer called San Francisco home whenever he was stateside. Patrick didn't know what Spencer's job entailed in the nitty-gritty, just that his magic was in high demand.

"Is he coming on official orders or no?" Nadine asked.

"The orders are official, but Reed doesn't want his presence announced to the WSA or anyone else outside the joint task force." Patrick glanced at her. "You know how people get about his kind of magic."

"That's going to be a headache trying to keep Spencer off the grid. Is he traveling on an alias?"

Patrick shrugged, switching lanes again. "Your guess is as good as mine. He'll tell us his cover if he has one when he gets here."

"Let's hope they have decent coffee at the meeting. I need something stronger than tea this morning," Nadine said, rubbing at her forehead.

"You and me both."

They weren't heading to the WSA headquarters, but to Winfield House, the place where they had been ordered to meet with the PIA's permanent liaison officer. Patrick knew they could be tracked on the CCTV that saturated London, but there was no getting around that, especially when it came to diplomatic property.

Magic made spying a hell of a lot more difficult though, even with modern tools at hand. They'd meet with their WSA counterparts in the afternoon, but right now they had to focus on their own country's needs. International cooperation only extended so far, and PIA Special Agent Gael Santiago's loyalty was to the United States of America first, no one else second.

Patrick followed the GPS route to Regent's Park where

Winfield House was located. The residence was home to the Ambassador of the United States of America, which offered up a space for diplomatic protection for their meeting.

They were stopped at iron gates that towered over the narrow road, the wards etched into iron scratching at Patrick's shields. The tips on every other spiked rod were coated in silver, and he could sense the building's foundational wards stretching through the acres of greenery between the walls surrounding it.

A pair of armed guards exited the guardhouse beyond the closed gates. Patrick looked around the area, spotting several discreetly placed security cameras that probably didn't account for all of them. They'd most likely been tracked half a mile out.

One of the guards stayed in position ahead of them as the other guard opened one side of the gate. Patrick rolled down his window as the woman came over to his side of the car, a no-nonsense look on her face.

"Identification?" she demanded.

Nadine passed over her PIA badge, and Patrick offered up his SOA one. The guard compared their faces to the photos printed on the badges before walking back to the guardhouse to further confirm their identities. They waited patiently, car idling, before the guard returned with their badges.

"Permission to enter has been granted."

Patrick could feel it in the wards, the way the magic embedded in the brick and iron and dirt eased back from his senses. He let out a heavy breath as he pressed the button to roll up the window.

"Ambassador homes take some getting used to," Nadine said as the guard opened the other half of the iron gate to give them clear passage through.

"And I thought the Pentagon was bad," Patrick muttered as he drove forward.

They made their way up the drive to the Neo-Georgian town house. Up ahead, the red-and-white brick façade stood out against the sleekly mowed green lawn and trees thick with leaves. To the left was a stretch of cultivated gardens that ran up against the house.

It was difficult to see London beyond the treetops, and the city noise was lessened by the greenery, but not by much. Patrick parked out front of the main entrance. As they got out of the car, a staff member exited the front door, giving them a polite nod in greeting.

"Special Agents Collins and Mulroney," the woman said, her American accent a little jarring after days of being surrounded by British ones. "You're late."

"We were held up by a case matter," Patrick said easily.

She didn't seem impressed with that excuse. "Special Agent Santiago is waiting."

Patrick shared a look with Nadine before following their escort inside Winfield House. The second Patrick crossed the threshold, a shock of magic ran through him, cutting across his shields. The searching spell wasn't subtle, and he rolled his shoulders to shake off the tingles skittering through his nerves.

"Apologies about the threshold, but it's for our protection," the woman said, not sounding sorry at all. She waved them over to a small side table situated between the women's bathroom and a small office in a foyer lit by a crystal chandelier. "Hospitality first."

"Really?" Patrick couldn't help but ask.

The woman held up a small plate filled with miniature pastries and gestured at the two glasses of water for their use. "Hospitality, if you please."

Nadine nudged him in the side with a subtle jab of her elbow as she approached the table. Patrick rolled his eyes but joined her. They took the food and drink on offer beneath the woman's watchful gaze.

"Be welcome in the ambassador's home," she said.

The pressure against his shields eased but didn't completely fade away. The magic was decades old, layers upon layers set into the building's foundation, and about as subtle as a missile strike.

The woman smiled at them once they weren't struck from the earth and led them out of the foyer into the cream-and-red-themed Reception Room. Everything looked a little vintage in that museum-quality way that always made Patrick want to leave fingerprints everywhere just to spite the owners—in this case, the United States government.

They veered right into the Garden Room, and Patrick was overwhelmed by the amount of green in the room. Not just the plants, but the antique Chinese wallpaper, the upholstery on half the furniture, and a good portion of the artwork.

"It looks like a jungle threw up in here," Patrick said.

Nadine shot him a quelling look he pretended not to see. Their escort cleared her throat, and the middle-aged man in the dark suit seated on a vintage-looking couch raised his head. The vague annoyance on his face didn't clear once he saw them. Recognition hit Patrick's magic with a subtle scrape of power—warlock, and shielded tight.

"Thank you," Special Agent Gael Santiago said in a crisp voice that hinted at a Texas drawl. "That will be all."

Their escort left, but privacy was difficult to come by in a building Patrick knew was always targeted by foreign intelligence organizations. The heavy thresholds and wards surrounding the town house made sense even if they were uncomfortable.

Gael got to his feet, and Nadine closed the distance between them, Patrick on her heels. Gael extended his hand in greeting, grip firm when he shook Patrick's hand.

"You're late," Gael said.

"Something came up," Nadine replied smoothly.

"Hopefully not mission critical."

Nadine shrugged one shoulder. "Critical enough."

Gael took his seat again and waved at all the empty ones around them. "Sit. Mulroney, cast a silence ward."

Patrick ground his teeth against the desire to mouth off at Gael's casual demand. The guy outranked them both, but his attitude annoyed Patrick. Nadine still did as she was ordered, and wrote out the silence ward onto the low table in the center of the conversation circle. Her magic glowed a soft violet before fading away, static washing around them in a bubble of quiet.

Patrick ignored the way his ears popped in favor of studying an agent he'd never met before and could've gone the rest of his life without meeting. Gael was tall and broad-shouldered, filling out a Hugo Boss suit that would've looked better on Jono. His black hair was that particular black men sported when they refused to cop to dyeing it.

At forty-six, Gael had the start of crow's feet at the corner of his eyes, and a sternness to his face that spoke of little humor in his life. Patrick knew some people lived for their job, and he used to be like that until Jono showed him a better way. It was advice he wasn't going to give Gael.

"I understand the WSA believes the auction is happening next week. What does the invitation say?" Gael said.

Patrick blinked, staring at him. "How much of the mission were you read in on?"

Gael smiled thinly. "Enough that I know about the invitation."

"Do you know what we're after?" At Gael's silence, Patrick shook his head. "And the CI? Did anyone tell you about them?"

More people knew about the invitation than he was comfortable with, but that decision wasn't his to make. Judging by Gael's reactions, Patrick could hope that Setsuna and the rest of the powers that be had locked down everything else to Eyes Only.

"Ah." Gael leaned back and gestured at nothing with one hand. "Our director refused to disclose the identity of your CI or what you are after."

He sounded indifferent about that, but Patrick knew it was all a lie. When your entire job was learning secrets, not knowing something rankled. While Patrick knew they were supposedly all on the same side, the betrayal he'd dealt with in the SOA just last summer had him not appreciating Gael's attitude, and trust was a long way off in a situation like this.

"If you weren't read in, then what are the parameters of your orders?" Patrick asked.

Gael's expression was impossible to read. "Whatever Director Franklin needs."

Patrick bit his tongue. He fucking hated politics and all the ways a person could say nothing at all. "Need isn't the same thing as permission."

"We're all on the same side here, Collins."

Patrick kept stubbornly silent at that remark. Gael studied him in a way Patrick disliked, but he refused to break eye contact.

"If I'm to help throw up distractions with our allies so we can claim whatever it is you're after at the auction, I need information," Gael said evenly.

"So do we, and that's why we're here. Mulroney asked for a status update on the London god pack. Do you have it or not?"

Gael glanced from Patrick to Nadine. "It was an odd request, considering they haven't been flagged as a problem."

"Did you find anything?" Nadine asked.

Gael picked up a sleek briefcase from the floor near his feet and set it on the table. He withdrew a folder from within and flipped it open, passing over a copy of a photograph. Patrick took it with a cold knot in his stomach.

The picture was taken with a long lens, blown up and pixelated at the edges, but the two people fucking in the apartment bed were still identifiable. Cressida's profile was familiar as she rode Dillon Rossiter, who looked like he was enjoying himself as much as she was despite the blood streaked between them.

"Did they murder someone, or is that just how they like sex?" Patrick asked.

"Dublin has quite a few unsolved missing person cases. If there was a body, it was disposed of." Gael shook his head. "I had an analyst do a review of case files the PIA has handled in the last five years for the werecreature communities in the British Isles and that came up. Offshoot evidence of a potions trafficking ring, but no evidence stuck to them."

"Rossiter is fae. He'd claim diplomatic immunity, no matter how thin his blood ties."

"Cressida Moore can't." Gael glanced at Nadine, raising an eyebrow. "You wanted to know if the London god pack was up to anything beyond the usual. Her ties to Rossiter could become a problem with the upcoming auction. I'm curious what made you ask in the first place."

"Our CI wanted assurances they wouldn't be hassled while in London," Patrick answered before Nadine could. "They've had run-ins with the New York City god pack and didn't want the same kind of problems here."

More like Lucien had torn up all bargains and treaties when he took over the Manhattan Night Court. These days, the rest of the Night Courts in the five boroughs toed his line while Estelle and Youssef's god pack had lost territory on all fronts. Lucien wasn't a good neighbor unless people wanted a war. In which case, he'd happily bring it to their doorsteps.

"You can tell your CI that Cressida has previous ties to the auctioneer. Whether or not those ties are still viable is inconclusive at this time, but I'd counsel toward yes."

"Thank you," Nadine said. "Do you have anything else for us?"

"No." Gael retrieved the photograph and called up a spark of fire with his magic to burn it to ash. Patrick hoped it wouldn't set off the sprinklers. "I'll do what Director Franklin wants, but if you require backup, reach out. I'm sure you can always use an extra set of hands and some decent magic, Mulroney."

Patrick ignored the veiled insult to his diminished magic and rank, used to the subtle disdain that colored his professional interactions.

"If those in charge clear you, sure," Patrick replied lightly with a sharp smile.

The PIA wasn't his agency, and he was playing nice for Nadine's sake. But Patrick's instructions came from the SOA as much as the gods, and Gael wasn't close to the clearance level needed for him to be read in on the nitty-gritty details of the hunt for the Morrígan's staff. Reed had been firm regarding the restrictions surrounding the joint task force. Not everyone was permitted to know everything surrounding the Morrígan's staff. That Gael kept pushing to know made Patrick want to deny him even the most mundane detail.

"Thank you for the update," Nadine said as she stood.

"The WSA won't like being lied to. I hope this mission is worth the fallout," Gael said.

Considering the only option was the world getting turned into a hell, Patrick thought the exchange was worth it even if politicians and the intelligence communities never would.

Gael got to his feet and shook their hands. He didn't offer to show them out. "Don't forget that we're all in this together."

"Some more than others," Patrick replied before heading for the doorway that led back to the Reception Room.

Nadine followed a few seconds later, and neither of them spoke until they were back in the car and driving away from Winfield House.

"One of these days you'll need to remember not everyone is the enemy," Nadine said when they were stopped at a red light on their way to the WSA headquarters.

"I have scars that prove practically everyone is," Patrick retorted, watching as a handful of people crossed the road ahead of them in the crosswalk.

"You have a reputation. It's not always good."

"I don't care."

"Sometimes you need to if only so we get what we want. Grease the wheels. You know how this game is played."

Patrick grimaced, drumming his fingers against the steering wheel. "I play it with gods. Humans are different."

Nadine slanted him a look. "Easier to manipulate?"

"No."

When it came down to it, humans were their own worst enemies and the monsters in the shadows no one ever saw until it was too late. For Patrick, gods were straightforward in their enmity and machinations and eternal grievances. Immortals never cared about mortal politics, only their own. Humanity lived to tear each other down, bury the bones, and rewrite history to suit their own needs.

"Harder to survive," Patrick finally said, thinking of Ethan and Hannah, and the glass-sharp connection in his soul that tied him to his twin.

For the first time in months, he let himself think about the niece or nephew Hannah was carrying, the quiet horror of that nightmare washing over him.

They were thirty years old and Hannah had spent twenty-two of them as a prisoner beneath Ethan's cruel desires. Chicago had been many things, but above all, it had been a further degradation of Hannah's lack of agency and the right to her own body and soul. Ethan had stolen everything from her, but the fertility rite had added a new layer of horrific fuckery to his actions.

Patrick refused to think about who the father might be.

If he did, he might throw up in his rental, and he didn't want to deal with the cleaning fee for that.

"All right." Nadine sighed. "We'll do it your way."

"Secrets and lies it is," Patrick said, wishing he were joking.

12

Jono looked up from the electric kettle as Patrick came out of the bathroom Friday morning dressed in jeans and a T-shirt, scrubbing a hand through his damp hair.

"No suit today?" Jono asked.

Patrick scowled. "One of us needs to pick up Spencer from the airport. Nadine already has a working relationship with the WSA. She's better suited at taking lead in that area than I am at the moment."

"So you're skiving off whilst she does all the work?"

Patrick smacked Jono on the ass as he went to grab his combat boots. "No. We're going to drive around and see who comes out of the woodwork."

The kettle clicked off. Jono picked it up to pour hot water into his mug. "That's a waste of money on the congestion charge."

"We're billing the government."

"You're hunting for the auction location, is what you're doing. Lucien said the spell on the invitation would show the address this weekend. What do you hope to find out there today?"

Patrick sat on the chair and shoved his feet into his combat boots. "I told you last night Cressida fucked Rossiter. If Cressida's demon is also in contact with the Dominion Sect, then they'll know we're in London."

"You want to play bait."

"No." At Jono's disbelieving stare, Patrick rolled his eyes. "Yes. Nadine called while you were in the shower. The WSA thinks they got a hit on Rossiter on the CCTV in Tottenham. I want to case the area, see if I can't track him with my magic."

Jono carefully set his mug down on the glass table. "Tottenham."

Patrick's gaze softened a little. He finished lacing up his boots before getting to his feet and closing the distance between them. Jono tilted his head down to look him in the eye.

"I can take Sage with me, if you want," Patrick said quietly. "You don't have to come."

"I'm not letting either of you go there without me. You both stand out too much."

"So will you. Just because we're in London doesn't mean you need to go everywhere with us. I told her if you didn't want to come you could take Wade to do some more touristy shit. He was saying something about the Victoria and Albert Museum last night."

"They've a jewelry gallery," Jono said absently, staring past Patrick. "He probably wants to nick some."

Cool hands framed his face, Patrick's thumbs bracketing his mouth. Jono blinked, refocusing on him. This close and Jono could see the freckles scattered over Patrick's nose and cheeks, darker lately from summer sunlight and long hours working cases in the field.

"I don't want you to go back there if the memories are going to hurt," Patrick said.

"You getting hurt would be worse."

"Jono."

"I'm going, Pat."

He didn't say *home*, because it wasn't, not anymore. Tottenham and the council estate he'd grown up on before getting kicked out after being infected with the werevirus hadn't been home for years. His family hadn't wanted him, neither had his old mates, and Jono had done what he'd had to so he could survive.

It had meant shady jobs, under-the-table payments in cash, skirting the edges of local gangs, all with a target on his back. He'd had no pack, no territory to call his own, no support, and dealt with discrimination every day because of the telltale color of his eyes. What relationships he'd made were thin at best after his family disowned him. He hadn't seen a quid of the settlement amount from the court suit against the hospital that had given him the bad blood transfusion. His family had kept it all, and he'd been left out in the cold.

You couldn't change the past, but you could change your family, and he'd done that.

He wouldn't let anyone make him feel less because of it.

Jono shook his head. "Sage can keep an eye on Wade today. You and I will drive up to Tottenham, though it's in the complete opposite direction as Heathrow. Traffic is going to be bloody terrible."

"If we're late, Spencer can take the Tube in. We can pick him up from a station or something."

"That's a bit rude if you already told him we'd pick him up from Heathrow."

Patrick patted Jono's cheek with one hand before pulling away. "He and Fatima can fend for themselves. Trust me on that."

Jono had never met PIA Special Agent Spencer Bailey, but Patrick had been explicitly clear they'd never dated. Jono figured Patrick was making a point, but rather than get jealous, Jono had only shrugged and proceeded to distract Patrick in bed. All he knew was that Spencer used to be in the Mage Corps, and now he wasn't, and that the joint task force was bringing him over on an unofficial basis.

Jono had a feeling the *unofficial* bit would make things messy in the end, but diplomatic niceties weren't his forte. He left those to Sage.

"Let's get the car and be off. I'll text Sage she's on her own with Wade today," Jono said.

"All right."

Patrick wandered off to finish getting ready, and Jono tried to mentally steady his nerves. He didn't even know if his family lived in the council estate anymore. Last he'd heard years ago, they'd been talking about buying a home and moving out. Jono didn't know if they had, and he'd never bothered to find out.

They'd washed their hands of him, and he'd done the same.

Definitely going to need a pint after today.

Somehow, he didn't think Patrick would mind keeping him company if he did.

Patrick didn't take long, and before Jono knew it, he was seated behind the steering wheel of their rental, driving north, following a route he'd never thought he'd ever take again. Time was he'd ride the Tube, but the drive wasn't unfamiliar. He used to borrow Tom's car back in the day, had actually learned to drive in it, but that hadn't been his regular mode of transportation.

"How will you even know if Rossiter is around?" Jono asked.

Patrick didn't lift his head away from where he had it leaned against the window. "Same way I know when demons are around. My magic will tell me."

"What does it feel like?"

"Like I need to gargle with alcohol to get the taste of hell out of my mouth. Why?"

"Just curious."

If Patrick was shielded, Jono couldn't tell when Patrick was using his magic unless he used the soulbond to tap a ley line. The connection between them wasn't always open, but it was tighter than it had been last summer. Part of it was due to the torn open hole in Patrick's soul and the deeply buried connection he had with Hannah. The soulbond had spread deeper into their souls to block that connection since Chicago, but Patrick hadn't figured out how to sever his tie to Hannah yet.

Some days, Jono wasn't sure Patrick even wanted to.

Patrick had a lot of guilt where his sister was concerned. Jono hadn't raised the issue about the connection tying the twins together and what to do about it because that was a minefield he had no map for.

"So we're just burning petrol whilst you"—Jono lifted a hand off the steering wheel and wiggled his fingers—"go abracadabra?"

Patrick smacked Jono in the shoulder, but he was laughing as he did so. "Fuck you, that's not what I'm doing."

"Could've fooled me."

"You're lucky you're cute." Patrick's mobile beeped with an incoming message. He lifted his hips to pull it from his pocket and check it. "Hey, is there a grocery store or butcher shop somewhere we can get a bone?"

Jono glanced at him, not sure what to make of that question. "A bone?"

"Yeah. Spencer reminded me I owe Fatima a bone."

"Isn't he on the plane? Shouldn't he be sleeping?"

Patrick shrugged, typing away at the screen. "Who knows with him, but Fatima isn't one I'd like to piss off."

"His partner?"

"His psychopomp."

Jono returned his attention to the road. "Ah."

"Don't worry, she's harmless." Patrick paused. "Mostly."

"Mostly," Jono repeated dryly.

Patrick lowered his mobile but didn't put it back into his pocket. He reached up with his other hand to set a silence ward in the car, static buzzing Jono's ears. "There's something I wanted to tell you."

"Sounds serious."

"It's about Spencer's kind of magic. It's within the family of necromancy."

"You told me that already. I said I don't mind."

"He cleaves souls apart. I think he could maybe undo the soul-bond if that's something you wanted."

Jono drew in a sharp breath, jerking his head to the side despite the traffic on the road. He stared at Patrick's profile for a second before wrenching his gaze back around. "What the bloody fuck gave you the idea that's something I want?"

"Because you didn't have a choice—"

"I'm going to stop you right there," Jono interrupted. "We've been over this. What's done is done, and I don't regret what ties us together."

"I'm offering you a possible way out."

"I don't want it." Jono swallowed, fingers tightening on the steering wheel. "Unless you do?"

"No," Patrick admitted, and the utter honesty in his scent put Jono at ease. "But it's something I had to offer you, knowing what I know about Spencer and his magic. He'll know about the soulbond the moment he sees us."

"Then tell him to keep his gob shut, and we'll be fine."

Patrick cracked a smile, but it appeared strained when Jono glanced at him. "He knows how to keep a secret."

"Good." Jono reached over and settled his hand on top of Patrick's, sliding their fingers together. "I don't know how to make it more clear, Pat. You're all I want, soulbond or not. I love you. That's never going to change."

Patrick lifted their linked hands so he could kiss the back of Jono's. He didn't say anything, but he didn't need to. Jono could smell the tangle of emotion on him that settled into something pleased and relieved, and that was all that mattered.

***

"So, it's like our Section Eight housing?" Patrick asked, squinting against the dull sunlight peeking through the clouds.

"The British government is better at housing people overall," Jono said.

"If you say so."

Jono looked out at the drab gray concrete building of intersecting wings that rose like a prison amidst the homes surrounding the area. Rainriver was a council estate in Tottenham that had never seen better days. The block was high-density social housing that served a needed purpose but didn't do it well in Jono's opinion.

The playground between them and the first wing of the complex was filled with half a dozen women in abayas and hijabs who were watching young children climbing about the slide and swing set. Music echoed in the air from quite a few flats, and he could see a group of teenagers congregating around a couple of cars down the street having a smoke.

It was exactly how he remembered, and yet, it wasn't. The building was the same, but the people were different, and the stressful bitterness had long since disappeared. Staring at the place he'd grown up, Jono realized, for maybe the first time in years, that his past didn't matter anymore. This was where he'd come from, but it was the present with his pack that needed his attention.

"Did you want to take a look inside the grounds for old times' sake?" Patrick asked.

Jono shook his head. "Don't need to. There's nothing here for me."

Patrick nodded, not bothering with platitudes others might've given voice to. "We're still within the vicinity where the WSA caught Rossiter on CCTV. Let's take a walk, see if we can't find anything."

"The car would be quicker."

"A car isn't as maneuverable as you think it is in a chase unless it comes with a mounted machine gun. In which case, then it's a tank, and while I wouldn't mind that on occasion, it's not street legal."

"You just want a gun."

Patrick rolled his eyes. "Magic isn't the answer to everything."

"I've listened to you whinge about that enough already. No need to start again."

Patrick laughed but didn't offer up more complaints. They'd parked some streets over and done a bit of wandering before angling back toward Rainriver. Patrick had been following whatever traces of magic Jono couldn't scent, and he didn't seem in a hurry to leave.

They started walking, heading down the street at an easy pace. Jono could feel eyes on them, could smell the wary curiosity on the air, but he didn't take any of it as a threat. They weren't local, didn't really look like they belonged, and Patrick definitely didn't sound English. Jono dialed up his hearing, keeping an ear out around them.

"Think Rossiter and his ilk will be about?" Jono asked.

"Who the fuck knows. I'm just checking for black magic."

Jono couldn't smell him anymore. Patrick had locked down his magic before leaving the car, and he smelled human to Jono's nose. He looked it, too; they both did—coming across as out-of-place, easy marks. Maybe that was why the teenagers they passed started following them.

"Oi!" one of them yelled from close behind. "Bit lost, are you?"

Patrick sighed loudly. "What's the law here on punching idiots?"

"Could still get arrested," Jono said mildly as they both stopped at a corner and turned around to face the group of five teenagers.

"I'll take my chances."

"Oh, one of them's a *Yank*. Did you wander too far from your tour group and get lost? Could help you on your way, but it'll cost you," a tall youth jeered.

The five drew closer, one on a bicycle, going so far as to ride directly at them, fully expecting them to move. Except neither Jono nor Patrick jumped aside, and the youth's smirk was wiped clean off his face when Jono grabbed the handlebars. He halted the bicycle's forward momentum with preternatural strength, grabbing it with one hand while using the other to snatch the teen out of midair as he went flying forward from unchecked momentum.

Jono let go of the bicycle and swung the teen around, holding him off the ground by the collar of his polo shirt. Fabric tore, but Jono didn't let go. The kid gripped Jono's hand with both of his, trying to pry himself free, eyes gone wide in surprise.

"What the fuck, mate! That was my bike!" the teen yelled.

He stank of anger, bravado, and fear, but the fear overrode everything else when Jono removed his sunglasses.

"Oh shit, oh *fuck*, didn't mean nothing by it, bruv," the teen got out, eyes wide in his suddenly pale face, feet kicking but getting nowhere close to Jono.

"Seems like you did," Jono said, shooting an annoyed glance at the other four, who looked like they were going to come to their mate's rescue, then thought better of it once they saw Jono's eyes. "I don't see anyone else trying to run me and my mate down."

"I swear, we wouldn't have done it if we knew what you were!"

The teen's voice had gone up an octave, and his group of mates were jostling each other as they backed up. Their attempts at trying to run away weren't subtle.

"But if we were human, you'd see us as fair game, is that it?" Patrick asked.

"Please let me go," the teenager begged, eyes wide and stinking up the whole area with his fear. "Don't—don't bring the god pack around here."

Jono opened his mouth to respond when Patrick swore and moved past him, a mageglobe sparking into existence at shoulder height.

"Jono," Patrick snapped.

He looked in the direction Patrick was headed, down the cross street that cut deeper into Rainriver and became a car park. The tiered wing of the council estate they were near came with patios, and a group of creatures were flinging themselves down the building one level at a time with a swiftness Jono knew meant trouble.

They looked *wrong*, stretched out limbs and torsos giving the human bodies an almost animalistic appearance. As the creatures threw themselves off the building and drew closer, Jono realized their heads were larger than their bodies. The sluggish breeze was blowing in the opposite direction, which was why Jono hadn't smelled them.

He unclenched his fingers from the teenager's shirt. The teen stumbled when his feet hit the ground, falling on his bum. Jono paid him only enough attention to growl, "Get the fuck inside."

The teenagers scattered. Patrick was already racing toward the threat. Jono followed, closing the distance between them in half a second.

"What are they?"

"Drekavac," Patrick said, dagger already in hand.

"In English, mate."

Patrick's mageglobe multiplied, and Jono knew that wasn't a good sign. "A type of undead."

Jono flexed his hands, fingertips splitting around the beginnings of claws. "Zombies?"

"Close enough."

"Think that necromancer summoned them?"

"Someone did." Patrick shot him a look, green eyes reflecting the pale blue light of his mageglobes. "Don't shift."

Jono gestured angrily at the small horde of demonic-looking zombies running toward them. "You want me to stay human whilst we face off against those bloody things? Not on your fucking life."

"For once, could you just listen?" Patrick shot back before he snagged one of his mageglobes and threw it at the oncoming drekavacs.

Raw magic exploded in the middle of the group, but the

fuckers were fast, and all but one escaped the blast radius. Black asphalt rose into the air before coming down on the surrounding parked vehicles, crashing through numerous windows and denting metal.

The drekavacs screamed a warning, the shrill sound enough to shatter a couple more windows. Jono resisted the urge to cover his ears, dialing down his hearing for a couple of seconds to save it before risking sound again.

"What are they? Part banshee?" Jono asked.

Patrick didn't answer, too busy flinging a magical strike at the undead while digging out his mobile. He tossed it to Jono, who caught it with one hand.

"Call Nadine. Tell her what's going on," Patrick said before flinging another mageglobe at the drekavacs, which the lanky bastards dodged with preternatural speed. "She needs to get the WSA to get eyes on CCTV around this place, and then you need to get the hell out of here."

"I'm not fucking leaving you."

"The WSA *can't* know about you. The only way they won't know is if you get the fuck away."

Jono unlocked Patrick's mobile and speed-dialed Nadine. "Sorry, you're speaking *idiot* again. There's CCTV all around. It doesn't matter if I stay or go, they'll see me anyway, so piss off with your suggestion that I walk away."

Patrick snarled wordlessly, irritation in the curl of his lips. Jono ignored him and his stupid bloody idea of standing his ground alone.

"Did you find anything, Collins?" Nadine said in lieu of a hello.

"Sorry, not Pat. He's a bit tied up at the moment with some zombies," Jono said.

Nadine swore. "Where?"

"Tottenham. Rainriver council estate."

"Tell him not to blow anything up. I'll notify the WSA and local police."

She ended the call, and Jono shoved the mobile into his pocket. "Nadine knows."

"Great," Patrick grunted, magic sparking at his fingertips.

"She said not to blow shit up."

"Too late."

A mageglobe exploded, managing to catch one more drekavac in the blast range. Its body was torn apart, blood and meaty bits arcing through the air to splatter around them. They hit various cars and Patrick's shield, the curve of it flickering pale blue for a second.

Jono scanned the area, studying how the drekavacs moved. They stayed close, hunting like a pack, though he doubted they'd have a problem attacking one-on-one. He counted nine of the bastards left, and they moved too quick for Patrick to contain them in a shield.

"I'll shift," Jono said.

"*Don't*," Patrick snapped.

Jono ignored him. "I brought a change of clothes in the car."

Patrick conjured up another mageglobe, the sphere losing its shape to a shocking amount of fire that Jono could feel from a meter away. Then the soulbond snapped between them, opening deep in Jono's soul. The oncoming rush of magic pouring through him from somewhere else momentarily made his teeth ache and his skin go hot.

The pain was manageable. Jono's years of shifting from human to wolf and the training he and Patrick had done together helped him to push past it all and focus on the fight. The magic was only passing through his soul to Patrick's, its power something Jono would never be able to use. Patrick could, and did, creating what could only be called an inferno in the parking lot when he let the spell loose.

The magefire was hot enough to scorch paint off the cars, damage the framework, and liquify the asphalt. Burning through the undead was child's play. The drekavacs couldn't run fast enough to escape the fire. Patrick's magic burned them down to bone, but they didn't go quietly. Even with his hearing dialed down and hands over his ears, Jono could hear how loud they screamed.

Glass from shattered windows from the flats above them rained down onto Patrick's shield, clattering to the pavement. The fire died down to nothing, and Patrick's mageglobes faded away. He still held his dagger, the matte-black blade lined with white fire.

"Was that spell legal?" Jono asked, eyeing the half-melted cars nearby.

"For this country?"

"In general."

"Outside of a war zone, not really."

"Then why use it?"

"Fire breaks all kinds of magic. It's one of the few things that can stop zombies, but it's risky, and you need to hit a particular heat level."

Jono stared at the crispy mounds of what used to be drekavacs and now were little more than piles of charred bone. "What now?"

Patrick sheathed his dagger and started toward the bodies. "I wait for Nadine and our WSA counterparts to arrive."

Jono could make out the sound of sirens in the distance, the tone different from the ones he'd been hearing for the last few years on the streets of New York. "Police will get here first."

"Then you need to go."

Jono didn't want to, but he knew it was the better option. He knew he'd probably show up on CCTV with Patrick whenever the government pulled the security feed. He'd leave Patrick to make up whatever story he thought would work to keep people from digging into Jono's identity. It wouldn't stop anyone from asking, but Patrick could stonewall with the best of them, and if push came to shove, the gods owed them.

"I'll take the Tube back to the hotel," Jono said, pulling out

Patrick's mobile and tossing it back to him. "Ring me when you can."

"Spencer will probably get to the hotel before I do. I'll text him your number so you can tell him where to go."

"All right. Be safe."

Patrick nodded, most of his attention already on the mess in the car park. Jono wanted badly to kiss him but didn't want to risk getting any sort of familiarity on camera. So he turned on his feet and hurried off, trying to look like a civilian running away from a threat rather than someone getting mixed up in trouble.

He'd done it as a lad, and the reminder wasn't lost on him as he headed for the nearest Underground station. While Jono might have changed over time, London's streets and its Underground hadn't, and his feet took him down the route he'd walked growing up as easily as breathing.

13

"THE BRITISH GOVERNMENT ISN'T PLEASED WITH YOUR ACTIONS," Setsuna said over the phone.

Patrick rolled his eyes even though she couldn't see it, too tired and annoyed to care. "Would they have preferred a horde of drekavacs running rampant through dense social housing and feasting on their tenants?"

"There were only ten. That's not a big enough hoard to justify the incineration spell you used."

"If someone had died, the British government would be bitching about why I *didn't* use the spell."

"Since that didn't happen, we're stuck smoothing over your actions. Again."

"There's a goddamn necromancer running around London. Just because the British government is pissed they can't find the fucker doesn't mean they need to blame us."

"Your attitude and decisions make diplomacy harder."

"We're lying to our allies on the president's authority. Don't blame me when the commander-in-chief okayed the damn mission."

"Then do *better*," Setsuna snapped. "Too much is at stake for you to run roughshod through another city, much less a foreign one."

Patrick ground his teeth, staring at the car stopped ahead of them at the intersection. Nadine was driving them back to the Sanderson after spending hours stepping on diplomatic landmines with the WSA. He was hungry, tired, and not in the mood for the dressing down Setsuna was giving him.

"I'm doing what I was ordered to do by *everyone*. What else do you want from me?"

"To not risk the mission."

"Sure thing," he said acidly. "I'll just risk my life instead."

He ended the call, too angry to continue the conversation without saying something he'd regret. Patrick gripped his phone so tight the edge dug into the big muscle near his thumb, making it throb.

"Doesn't sound like that went well," Nadine said as she kept her eyes on the road.

"You think?"

"Don't get pissed at me. I just spent hours trying to smooth things over with Albert on your behalf. You know better than to use an incineration spell within city limits. I didn't think you could even cast that spell anymore."

Patrick unclenched his teeth, jaw aching from the release of pressure. "I tapped a ley line through Jono."

Nadine frowned, her voice sounding worried rather than accusatory. "Should you have done that?"

"Would you rather have bodies for the Met's morgue to handle?"

"Drekavac victims we can explain. You being able to do higher-level spells again is a little harder to ignore."

"We'll say the SOA issued me an artifact with the spell embedded in it. If the WSA asks for it, we'll deny them. If someone sends a request up the chain of command, Setsuna will cover for me."

"You are making my job so much harder."

Patrick kept his mouth shut, not wanting to take his anger out on her. She'd had her hands full since appearing on the scene at Rainriver earlier in the day. Nadine had expended a lot of personal political capital to soothe all the ruffled feathers at the WSA that Patrick's actions had caused.

Nadine sighed. "What's done is done. Let's get to the hotel and bring Spencer up to speed."

Patrick loosened his grip on his phone, watching the cars around them. Friday night in London was busy, especially on Oxford Street. The upscale shopping district was clogged with vehicles and people, the stores brightly lit beyond the sidewalks. Nadine had taken him shopping in the area once years ago, some months after they were both discharged from the Mage Corps. If there was an Olympic sport for shopping, she'd win a gold medal.

By the time Nadine turned off Oxford Street and made it to the Sanderson, Patrick was ready for the entire fucking day to be over with. Except he knew what waited for him upstairs in Sage's penthouse, and when they entered the suite, Patrick got an earful despite the silence ward embedded in the walls.

"You fucking asshole," Spencer said from where he was sprawled on one of the two white couches, not bothering to lift his head at their arrival. "You go and get yourself soulbound to a god pack werewolf and you don't even have the courtesy to *tell* me?"

A streak of tawny gold and black darted across the penthouse. Patrick barely had time to brace himself before Fatima flung her twenty-five-pound body at his legs, paws planted firmly on his left thigh. He stared down at the psychopomp, watching her tail lash back and forth, golden eyes unblinking. She'd taken the shape of an ocelot when she chose to work with Spencer, though the intelligence in her gaze was one no animal would ever have.

"Shit," Patrick said. "I forgot your bone."

Fatima growled deep in her throat before swatting at his stomach in a reprimand. She shoved herself away from him and pranced over to where Wade sat on the other couch, Jaffa Cake boxes scattered around him, and a look of pure adoration on his face as he held out one of the treats to Fatima.

"You can't keep her," Patrick warned Wade.

"But she's *cute*," Wade cooed, watching as Fatima demolished the Jaffa Cake, getting crumbs everywhere.

"She's a spirit guide and belongs to Spencer."

"The fledgling can have her. She was annoying the entire flight over. That's the last time I fly economy with only one seat," Spencer said.

Fatima yowled at him and flicked her tail in disdain. Spencer ignored her.

"Sit up," Nadine told him as Jono and Sage came out of her bedroom. "You go to sleep now and you'll be a mess tomorrow. You know that."

Spencer flapped his hand at her before heaving a loud sigh and reluctantly sitting up. He blinked tired blue eyes at them, the small Band-Aid over the bridge of his nose not doing much to hide the bruised cut there. The circles under his eyes could've doubled as bruises, and his dark blond hair resembled a rats' nest. He stretched out his long legs, digging his socked feet into the trendy rug beneath the coffee table.

"What have we told you about kissing the ground with your face?" Patrick asked.

Spencer raised both middle fingers at him. "Like you have room to talk. When's the last time you've taken a case and come away with no bruises?"

"He hasn't," Sage said calmly as she crossed the space to greet Nadine with a hug and an air kiss on each cheek. "Good to see you again."

"Wish it was under better circumstances," Nadine said.

"If only."

Jono came to a stop between both couches and crossed his arms, raising an eyebrow at Patrick. "How did the meeting go?"

"It went," Patrick said.

Sage turned to face Patrick, tilting her head in Spencer's direction. "You were right. Spencer took one look at Jono when he arrived and asked about the soulbond."

Patrick shrugged. "He's a soulbreaker."

"Can he be trusted?"

"Hey!" Spencer protested.

"He's one of the few who knows about Ethan, so yeah, he can be trusted," Patrick said.

"Apparently not enough that you'd tell me you got a pack."

"When do I ever see you? You live on the West Coast."

Spencer made a face. "You could visit me."

"Setsuna still owes me a trip to Maui. You're a flyover state when it comes to my vacation time."

"Just for that, you owe Fatima two bones now."

"She's a spirit guide. She doesn't even need to eat."

"Tell her that when she's growling across the Atlantic Ocean because she's hungry and won't eat airplane food. I got no sleep on the flight over."

"That's your fault for not packing her food." Patrick watched as Spencer stood, raising his arms over his head to stretch. His spine cracked loudly, and Patrick winced at the noise. "That doesn't sound comfortable."

"Economy seats aren't comfortable." Spencer ran a hand through his hair, ruining it even more. Paired with his bruised but healing face, worn jeans, and wrinkled T-shirt, he definitely looked as if he'd seen better days. "So when did all this happen?"

"When what happened?"

Spencer gestured widely. "Don't be dense."

"The soulbond mess happened last June. The rest of it all came after. Right now, our focus needs to be on the Orthodox Church of the Dead. The WSA is certain the Patriarch of Souls was the one who summoned the drekavacs today even though he wasn't caught on CCTV," Nadine said.

Spencer made a face. "I hate those things."

"They're why we called you in."

"Yeah, but I can still hate them."

Patrick crossed over to where Jono stood, ignoring Fatima's growl directed at him. Jono reached out and curled a finger through Patrick's belt loop, tugging him closer.

"Is he the only one who can see the soulbond?" Jono asked.

"Spencer?" Patrick glanced over at his friend and arched an eyebrow in a silent question. Spencer waved at him before shuffling over to the minibar with its decimated snacks. "He breaks souls. He knows when one's been messed around with."

"If you're worried about another magic user being able to read your auras, don't be," Spencer said as he came back with a bag of chips in his hand. "Patrick's specialty is hunting monsters and demons. Mine is sending them back to where they came from. I peel souls apart when I do that, so I know what a pieced together soul looks like. I've seen soulbonds before, but never one as cleanly placed as yours."

"The gods did it," Jono said.

"Yeah. That would explain it." Spencer popped a chip in his mouth, chewed once, then made a *hurk* noise before swallowing quickly. He turned the bag around in his hands and groaned. "Aww, chips, no. Who thought ketchup was a good flavor?"

"Dinner should be here soon. I ordered us room service," Sage said.

Jono tugged pointedly on Patrick's jeans. "Lucien rang. Sage and I were chatting with him before you arrived."

"What did that bastard want?" Patrick asked.

"He saw the news about what happened in Tottenham. Said you're too recognizable for the auction."

"My name didn't even make the news."

"Doesn't matter. Lucien doesn't want any of us to go with him to the auction."

"Oh, fuck that. He's not going alone. He's getting oversight whether he likes it or not, because that was in the bargain we made. I'll call him."

"Wait," Spencer said, blinking at them. "*Wait.* Lucien is here in London?"

"Weren't you read in to this mission?" Nadine asked exasperatedly.

"I was briefed about the Morrígan's staff, just not the specifics of this mission. The director put me on a plane and said go to London." Spencer wheeled around to face her, clutching the chips bag to his chest. "You didn't tell me Lucien was here. *No one* told me Lucien was here."

"He's getting us the Morrígan's staff." Nadine narrowed her eyes. "You are not fucking him."

Wade paused in opening up another box of Jaffa Cakes. "*Ew.* Lucien? Really?"

Patrick left Nadine to deal with Spencer and grabbed Jono's wrist, hauling the other man with him into Sage's bedroom. He closed the door, muffling the beginnings of the argument out in the living area.

"Is he really attracted to Lucien?" Jono asked, wrinkling his nose.

"Vampires have no souls, so Spencer's magic doesn't work on them. It's a danger kink with him, I think. He's always had shitty taste in men and women the entire time I've known him." Patrick paused before shaking his head. "Except for Nadine. She's been his only good choice."

"She looks ready to throttle him, the poor sod."

"Well, he owes her a really expensive dress and he's bunking with her, so they'll either end up arguing all night, or fucking all night. Either way, their neighbors won't be happy."

Patrick pulled out his phone and dialed Lucien's latest burner number from memory. It rang a total of ten times before the master vampire picked up.

"What?" Lucien demanded.

"We're going with you to the auction. The government doesn't trust you, and *I* don't trust you. One rule of the bargain was you get oversight, and I'm your fucking oversight," Patrick said.

"Buyers with business ties to the Dominion Sect have been warned you're in town. The auction doesn't happen if you walk in with me. If you want that staff, you'll do things my way."

"What makes you think Ethan hasn't ratted you out to them as well?"

"Because I play any and every side when it suits me, and everyone knows that. Denying me entrance won't go over well for their future financial base."

Patrick supposed if someone owned a criminal empire as vast as Lucien's, they could issue a threat that would make everyone think twice about cutting them out.

"Spencer and I will go. Everyone else will stay outside the venue but ready to come help if needed."

"You called in the soulbreaker?" Lucien asked, sounding interested in a way Patrick didn't like.

"Ethan and whoever is at the auction won't recognize Spencer. I'll figure out a way to hide myself."

"The protective wards that secure these kinds of locations will strip you of your magic. You don't have any spell that can keep you hidden."

"You aren't going alone. That's not happening."

"I get diplomatic immunity to move freely in the United States whether or not you get the staff. My terms were based on aid, and your government agreed. If you lose the staff because you couldn't hide your face, that's not my problem."

Lucien ended the call, and the silence in Patrick's ear made him scowl. Jono frowned, brows drawn together worriedly, having obviously listened in to the conversation. "What now? I hate to agree with that fucker, but he has a point. You and your ginger hair are a bit too recognizable."

Patrick glared down at his phone. "Spencer will still be unrecognizable. He fought in the Thirty-Day War, but never with the Hellraisers. The Mage Corps needed his help against the soultakers and zombies. I don't think Ethan has any current information on him."

"You can't be sure."

Patrick sighed, scrolling through his contacts. "I know."

"So what's the plan?"

"Rossiter is fae. If he's setting the wards, then we'll need fae magic to get us through."

"What if someone else is setting the spells?"

"We'll still need a strong defense." Patrick's thumb paused over the name Smooth Dog in his contacts, and he pressed the icon. Holding the phone to his ear, he listened to it ring a couple of times before it picked up. "It's Collins. Line and location are secure."

"Line and location are secure," Captain Gerard Breckenridge echoed in turn. Patrick's old team captain sounded on high alert, but if he was answering the phone, then it was safe to do so.

"Are you on leave?"

"Forty-eight hours R and R. I hear you're in London."

"Not the vacation I wanted. They sent us Spencer."

"Dead Boy got the call up?"

"We're dealing with the Orthodox Church of the Dead. I wanted decent backup."

"Fair enough. I haven't received new orders, so why are you calling?"

"Lucien is carrying the invitation to the auction. The Dominion Sect knows I'm in town, which means Lucien's criminal contemporaries probably know as well. The auctioneer is fae, and I was hoping you or Órlaith had some artifacts with glamour we could use."

Gerard made a thoughtful sound in the back of his throat. "Órlaith is in Dublin. I'll see what we can do."

"Dublin?" Patrick asked, sounding surprised. "She's not with you?"

"Cernunnos asked for her aid in a rite during Beltane. She opted to stay through summer."

Patrick's mouth twisted. "Is she preparing for your return?"

Gerard sighed. "Something like that."

Gerard wasn't his real name. As the immortal Cú Chulainn, he lived under a human alias far from Ireland's shores. He'd made a promise to the Cailleach Bheur to return to his ancestral home once the Morrígan's staff was found and bring with him the prayers and stories that sustained him. The fae hoped he could spearhead their resurgence, but Patrick knew Gerard only hoped to keep their memory alive in these modern times.

Some days, that was all you could do.

"If I have to fly to Dublin, we have time. The auction is scheduled to take place Sunday."

"I'll call Órlaith and tell her to reach out to you."

"Thanks."

"Stay safe. Stab Lucien in the back for me."

"I'd do it for myself first."

"That's the spirit."

Gerard ended the call, and Patrick shoved his phone into his pocket. "Now we wait."

"I like his idea," Jono said.

"Having Órlaith call us rather than go through him?"

"No. Stab Lucien."

Patrick laughed, allowing himself to be reeled in for a kiss. Jono tasted like the beer he must have been drinking before Patrick arrived. When they broke apart, Jono reached up to press his wrist against Patrick's throat, rubbing their pack scent into his skin.

"Did the WSA ask about me?" Jono wanted to know.

"Unfortunately, yeah. They got your identity off the CCTV, but Nadine made it seem like you were our criminal informant we brought along, which was why we were together."

"Can't be much of an informant if I've been gone for years."

"That's what Albert said. It's still the story we're sticking to."

Jono nodded. "All right."

Wade leaned into the room, holding himself up by gripping the doorframe. "Room service is here. Come quick or I'm eating your dinner."

He disappeared, but Patrick knew that wasn't an idle threat. Patrick slipped his hand into Jono's. "Let's go eat."

A quiet dinner in was something they all needed. Patrick had a feeling the weekend wasn't going to be easy.

THE EMBASSY OF THE SEELIE COURT WAS LOCATED ACROSS FROM Kensington Gardens, near the Lancaster Gate Underground Station. On a dreary Saturday morning, Patrick opted to take the Underground rather than drive, leaving the car behind for Jono's use if he needed it.

Hiding his presence on a semi-crowded train was easier than weaving through traffic. The werecreatures Cressida had parked outside their hotel hadn't been aware of his departure, but they would've been if he'd had to wait for the valet to bring the car around. If anyone had managed to follow him, Patrick hoped he'd lost them in Oxford Circus.

Still, Patrick was on high alert as the train rattled toward its destination, the automated computer announcing *"The next station is Lancaster Gate. This is a Central Line train to Ealing Broadway via Nottingham Hill Gate."*

The train rolled into the station with a squeal of brakes and the echoing rumble of the engine, the Underground's ancient protective wards flashing at the corners of Patrick's eyes through the windows. Patrick stood, grabbing hold of the railing overhead as he swayed with the motion of the train car. It braked to a stop, and the doors opened. He exited with everyone else, following the weekend summer crowd to the elevators that were the only way out if one didn't want to ascend twenty-six staircases.

It took a couple of minutes to make it onto the elevator and then out of the station, stepping back into weak sunlight. The weather was mildly warm, and his leather jacket was enough without needing to activate either the heat or cold charms embedded in it. He tucked his hands into his jacket pockets and turned right, walking down Bayswater Road.

The embassy was centrally located between the Lancaster Gate and Queensway station. The walk there was shaded by an abundance of trees, with cars and buses driving past him on the left. The numerous white row houses were eventually broken up by a single building separated by a brick wall with steel spikes set into the top. The open gate Patrick approached wasn't made of iron, but steel, the metalwork of it twisted into wards he wasn't familiar with.

The magic around him had a different feel to it, nothing like a human's. The fae guards on duty might've been wearing suits, but the halberds in their hands had probably taken more negotiation than Patrick's dagger to be allowed in London—or they just didn't give a fuck and had brought them anyway.

It was probably the latter.

The fae guards watched his approach and didn't bar him from entering. Patrick gave them a polite nod on his way up to the embassy's entrance. He hauled the heavily warded door open and stepped inside a building that was like all the other government-type buildings in London. The only difference was the number of plants in the place.

Ivy covered the wood paneling from planters that had over-whelmed free-floating shelves nailed to the wall. Potted trees and flowers took up space in the lobby. Patrick fought back a sneeze, eyes watering, as he approached the receptionist desk. The woman seated there wore modern clothes, her hair done in trendy waves, though the pointed ears peeking through them and the yellow eyes the shade of a buttercup proved she wasn't human.

"You're expected," the fae said before Patrick could even open his mouth. "Please follow your escort."

Patrick looked up at where she pointed. A pair of colorful wings pried itself off the ceiling, coalescing into the tiny figure of a pixie who fluttered down to their level. The giggling fae darted around Patrick's head, making him almost cross-eyed from its antics. He just hoped it wouldn't bite him.

"This way," the pixie said in a soft, tinkling voice.

The pixie flew off, and Patrick followed after it. The inner workings of the fae embassy would remain a mystery, as every door he passed was shut tight. He couldn't hear anything but his own footsteps on the hardwood, the sound muffled by the forest grown out of pots and vases in every hallway he was led down.

Eventually, they came to an intricately carved door on the third level, guarded by a pair of fae in armor rather than three-piece suits. The pixie flew off, leaving Patrick standing awkwardly outside. He watched it go before returning his attention to the door and the guards, wondering if he was supposed to knock. Before he could try, the door opened, and the person blocking the way greeted him with a smirk.

"What," Patrick bit out, "the *fuck* are you wearing?"

Hermes reached up to pat the ugly white wig perched on top of his head, a couple of dyed green curls peeking out from beneath it. "When in Rome, as they say."

"We're in London."

"Then god save the queen."

"Someone needs to save you from your shitty taste in clothes."

Instead of jeans and a T-shirt, Hermes wore royal purple velvet breeches and matching coat and vest, with silver stockings and a white dress shirt that wouldn't look too out of place in today's business world. Hermes looked like he had walked out of a painting depicting court life in the 1770s, except no artist would ever be able to capture the unearthly look in his gold-brown eyes.

"I'm not here to meet with you," Patrick said.

Hermes smiled. "You are now."

"This is Seelie Court territory, so long as I stand here. Mind your place, Hermes," Órlaith said as she pushed the door open wider. She graced Patrick with a smile that lit up her whole face. "Hello, Patrick."

The Summer Lady of the Seelie Court was as gorgeous as Patrick remembered, and her laughter had a joy to it that had been missing on the Skellig Islands back in December.

"Órlaith." Patrick extended his hand for a shake before it was batted aside so she could hug him. "Oof."

She smelled like summer flowers blooming after a rainstorm. Her slim frame belied the otherworldly strength he could feel in her arms. Patrick pulled away after a moment, taking her in, from the mass of her long, wavy red-orange hair to her pale blue sundress and the trendy white sneakers she wore. A thin gold circlet was twisted through her hair, the glittering leaves and flowers there made out of jewels any collector would kill to own. Her eyes were summer-sky blue shot through with gold, inhuman in color, but the kindness in her gaze put him at ease.

"What are you doing hanging out with the likes of him?" Patrick asked, jerking his head in Hermes' direction.

"Diplomacy."

"Shame."

"I'm beside myself with grief at our severed friendship," Hermes drawled, wig sitting askew on his head.

"We aren't friends," Patrick retorted.

"Gentlemen," Órlaith warned before gesturing at the huge sunlit office behind her. "Come, there's tea."

Patrick sighed. "Great. More tea."

Órlaith smiled at him, eyes bright with a fondness Patrick

didn't think he deserved, not after what Ethan had put her through over winter. "We're in England, therefore, we drink tea."

"I'm American. We tossed it into the harbor."

"Heathen," Hermes coughed under his breath.

Patrick flipped him off. "Fuck off."

Órlaith shot them both a quelling look that seemed to channel her grandmother enough that Hermes kept his mouth shut. Patrick followed her into a palatial office that could've doubled as a throne room if someone—Wade—stole the pair of seats out of Buckingham Palace. Thankfully, the Staterooms weren't open to tour yet.

"How was your flight?" Patrick asked.

Órlaith shrugged. "It was fine. I brought what you requested over with me."

She went to sit on the love seat by the windows overlooking Kensington Gardens. The low table there was set for tea, and a rosewood box sat near the teapot. A platter of cookies and one of small sandwiches were arranged within arm's reach.

"I hope you didn't declare it for Customs," Patrick said as he took a seat beside her. Hermes sprawled on the armchair opposite them, slinging one leg over the armrest.

"I arrived through diplomatic channels."

"Handy."

"I hear Lucien asked for a similar sort of protection."

Patrick made a face. "The government agreed to the bargain."

"Compromise is never easy, but needed in a situation like this. We all do what we must."

"Patrick knows all about our needs," Hermes drawled.

Patrick glared at the messenger god, watching as the centuries-old clothing melted away into the modern-day outfit Hermes usually preferred—ripped jeans, a well-worn band T-shirt, and a battered pair of Doc Martens.

Órlaith reached for the teapot and poured out three cups, doctoring hers with milk and sugar. Patrick did the same, breathing in the scent of Earl Grey. It wasn't coffee, but it would do. Hermes twirled his finger in the air and his teacup rose off the table and floated to him. He plucked it out of the air and sat up far enough to sip at it.

"Hospitality?" Patrick asked.

"Not for you." Órlaith smiled, lips curving up without any of the malice Patrick was used to seeing in some of her people's faces. "Never for you."

"If you're sure."

"Cú Chulainn is rarely wrong about the people who fight beside him. You and yours have already proven your loyalty. We would not have the alliance with you if that wasn't the case."

Patrick knew better than to say *thank you* to the fae, even one who would one day marry his friend. He inclined his head in a silent acknowledgment of her statement instead. "So what did you bring me?"

"Something to save your ass since you can't do it yourself," Hermes said, stealing a cookie off the platter and eating it in two bites.

Órlaith rolled her eyes while the other god pretended not to see. "Ignore him."

"I've tried. He's like a cockroach that won't go away," Patrick said.

Órlaith laughed. "True."

"I'm just here to ensure you do your job, Pattycakes," Hermes said.

Patrick flipped him off. "I don't need your help for that."

"Seems like you do. I hear the Orthodox Church of the Dead wants the Morrígan's staff. Their Patriarch of Souls has loud prayers."

Patrick frowned. "Do they pray to you?"

Hermes snapped his fingers, and another cookie appeared between them. He dipped it in his tea before popping it in his mouth to chew. "I guide the dead, but I'm not the only one who does so. Those prayers the Patriarch of Souls shepherds aren't for me."

"Then who are they for?"

"Peklabog."

It was one thing to know a necromancer wanted the Morrígan's staff, quite another to realize the human was only a proxy for a god of the Slavic underworld.

"Peklabog has to know we would go to war in his realm to retrieve the staff," Órlaith said.

Hermes shrugged and sat up, swinging his leg back around to put both feet on the floor. "Medb is selling the staff for money instead of prayers. She isn't the only one looking to make a killing off it."

"Do you think he's in London?" Patrick asked.

"Hard to say. Peklabog goes where he likes, much as I do." Hermes set his teacup on the table and stood, bowing extravagantly to Órlaith. "Until we meet again."

Hermes left through the veil, taking all the cookies on the platter with him. Patrick looked at the empty platter and sighed. "I'd say he's worse than Wade, but no one is worse than Wade when it comes to stealing cookies."

"The fledgling is sweet," Órlaith said.

"The fledgling is a walking bottomless pit for a stomach." Patrick gulped down some more tea, wishing it was coffee. "What do you have for me?"

"Rings. Two of them. Brigid placed the glamour, and we will want them returned after use. These are artifacts we do not want mortals to have."

"I'll make sure they get back to you."

"Good."

Órlaith set her teacup down and reached for the box, placing it between them on the love seat. Opening it revealed a pair of silver filigree rings that burned with magic to Patrick's senses.

"May I?" Patrick asked.

At Órlaith's nod, he picked one up, the spark of recognition in his magic hot in his soul. He turned the ring around, studying the knotwork and flowers carved with incredible precision into something so small.

"They will size to fit whoever wears them. The magic will mask itself once worn, and the glamour will give you a new face," Órlaith said.

"The auctioneer is fae. Do you think he'll be able to sense the magic?"

Órlaith frowned. "Who is the auctioneer?"

"Dillon Rossiter."

"The name is not familiar."

Patrick put the ring back in the box and pulled out his cell phone, unlocking it and swiping through to get to the encrypted folder stored on it. He pulled up a picture of Rossiter and showed it to her. Órlaith's eyes narrowed thoughtfully as she studied the image.

"I do not know him, but that is not to say he isn't fae. He could be from either court," she said.

"Could it be a glamour?"

"We fae are not always what we seem when you meet us."

Patrick nodded, thinking of Gerard. "But the rings will work?"

"My grandmother's power can connect Tír na nÓg to the mortal world if she so wishes. The rings will work." Órlaith reached for one of the tea sandwiches. "Let's finish our tea, and you can tell me how your pack is doing."

As much as Patrick wanted to take the rings and leave to get ready for tonight, he knew the polite thing to do was to stay. He didn't know Órlaith well, not how he did Gerard, but sipping tea for another hour and making small talk wasn't the worst way to spend a Saturday morning.

"I DON'T LIKE IT," Jono said, watching as Patrick finished lacing up his combat boots.

"So you've said. Doesn't change that we have a plan and we're sticking to it," Patrick said.

He double knotted the laces and stood, automatically checking the security of the straps connecting the dagger sheath to his belt. It was the only physical weapon he was bringing with him, but he still wanted his gun.

"I wish I could go in with you."

Patrick looked over at where Jono sat on the bed, dressed in dark clothes, a backpack with an extra set of clothes resting beside him in case he needed to shift later. Sage and Wade would do the same.

Patrick and Spencer were set to be picked up by Lucien and his Night Court in less than ten minutes. The rings with their inlaid glamour were still in their warded box on the table. Jono and the others would follow in a rental, and Nadine would keep them hidden from prying eyes.

The Auction of Curiosities and Exceptional Items was taking place at Smithfield Market, the location having finally come through the invitation at noon. The place had apparently been a meat market at one point before being turned into a museum, but everyone still called the building the Smithfield Market, according to Jono.

When Lucien had notified them of the updated location, Patrick and Nadine had in turn notified their individual directors. Neither of them had notified the WSA, though Special Agent Santiago was on standby to aid them. Gael hadn't been made aware of the auction location, a fact he'd bristled at but which neither Patrick nor Nadine would budge on. The decision concerning the WSA was one Patrick was glad he wasn't responsible for explaining when this was all over.

His phone rang, and Patrick ignored Jono's frown in favor of whoever was calling. He wasn't surprised to hear Carmen's voice on the other side of the line.

"We're two minutes away. Be ready out front," she ordered.

"We'll be there," Patrick said.

She ended the call and Patrick shot a text message off to Spencer to meet him downstairs in the lobby. Then he went to stand between Jono's legs, framing the other man's face with both hands. The scrape of a beard coming through pricked his skin, but Patrick didn't care. He still kissed Jono as hard as he could, relishing in the heat of Jono's hands that gripped him by the waist and held him tight.

"No matter what magic they have wrapped around that place, you can still feel me. You can still find me," Patrick murmured against his lips.

Jono chased after his mouth. "Always."

They kissed for a few seconds more before Patrick reluctantly stepped back. Jono stood and hauled the backpack onto one shoulder while Patrick pocketed the rings. They left the hotel room for the lobby, finding everyone else waiting for them by the front doors.

Sage and Wade were dressed in comfortable clothes they wouldn't miss if they shifted. Nadine wore a casual outfit with boots, no weapon in sight, but Patrick could see the outline of her badge in her back pocket. She and Spencer had come over earlier for the pickup. Spencer was dressed like Patrick—in durable clothes that would hopefully survive a fight.

Patrick's shields were locked down so tight his joints ached a little. It would keep his damaged magic from being recognized, and he'd come across as human to anyone casting invasive spells at the auction, but he could do without the encroaching headache. He hoped the rings Órlaith had given them would work as they should and hide them both in a seamless glamour.

"Ready?" Spencer asked, looking less bruised and more awake

than he had the other night. Nadine must have forced a healing potion down his throat.

"Let's go," Patrick said.

They made it outside in time to see Lucien's caravan of luxury SUVs pull up in the valet parking area, tinted windows making it impossible to see who was inside. The side passenger door on the middle SUV opened, and Patrick caught of glimpse of Carmen in a crimson red dress he wasn't sure was lingerie or not. One never knew with Carmen.

Patrick climbed into the far back after Spencer while Carmen closed the door behind them. She looked over her shoulder at them, the rubies and diamonds wrapped around her throat sparkling even through the tinted windows. As he watched, her personal glamour sloughed off, revealing her red-pupiled eyes and the curled horns of her kind.

"Your face is still your own," Carmen said.

"Not for long," Patrick said as he dug out the rings. "The London god pack assigned some of their people to watch us. We may be followed."

"We came prepared. The London Night Court is handling escort duties tonight."

"Did Lucien order them to, or did they do it out of the goodness of their cold, undead hearts?"

"What do you think?"

"Obedience through threats means we can't trust them to watch our six."

"Get rid of your face, Patrick."

"Yeah, yeah."

Patrick handed one of the silver filigree rings to Spencer and slipped the other onto his right middle finger. The ring seemed too big for a second before the filigree twisted tighter, creating a snug fit.

Cool magic crawled down to his fingertips and up his arm, spanning across his body. It slid over his skin and shields, adhering itself to his body and aura with a tenacity that made him want a shower. Patrick shoved aside that desire and looked up from his hand to meet Carmen's shrewd gaze.

"Curious toy. Where did you get it?" Carmen asked.

"Does it matter? Just tell me we look like someone else," Patrick said.

"You sound like someone else as well."

"That's the point of glamour."

"You'll pass as someone else so long as you stay shielded and don't use your magic. I can't see your true form beneath it." Carmen's gaze slid toward Spencer, and her smile widened ever so slightly. "Spencer. Where is your companion?"

"Around," Spencer replied vaguely. "Fatima will meet us at the auction. Where's Lucien?"

Carmen chuckled throatily. "Around."

Patrick elbowed Spencer in the side and looked at him, surprised to see the face of a dark-haired man who could have walked a fashion runway in lieu of Spencer's familiar features.

"Don't take this the wrong way, but you make a terrible blond," Spencer said, eyeing Patrick.

He rolled his eyes. "Thanks."

"You remember your roles?" Carmen asked.

"Favored human servants."

"Don't forget your place. Be silent. Be adoring. Don't interfere."

The idea of needing to get up close and personal with some vampires and pretend they were everything Patrick could ever want wasn't how he wanted to spend his evening. But he'd gone through worse to get the job done before, and it wasn't like Lucien was demanding he take shine. Some things would be a deal breaker, but pretending he liked the master vampire for a mission wasn't one.

Patrick couldn't orient himself on London's twisted streets, but the GPS on his phone told him they were driving east. The lights of bars and restaurants flashed by as they drove, traffic still heavy despite the late hour.

Patrick sensed the magic before they got within view of Smithfield Market. The undercurrent of black magic was subtle, difficult to detect if one wasn't searching for it. Patrick's soul and magic honed in on the taint even through his shields. He swallowed against the bitterness that erupted in the back of his throat, grimacing at the taste. Not sure what they were driving into, he cast a silence ward through the frame of the car. Carmen glanced at him over her shoulder but didn't order him to remove it.

He hoped if they were followed, the London Night Court had waylaid whatever werecreatures were assigned tonight. Patrick didn't think they'd have to worry too much about the London god pack until they turned down a street and the overwhelming recognition of werecreature coursed through his magic.

"I thought you said the London Night Court was going to keep werecreatures off our six?" Patrick asked, staring at the men and women fanned out on the sidewalk as the SUVs slowed to a stop.

"The London god pack is handling security for tonight," Carmen said.

"Fucking hell." Patrick pulled out his phone to send a warning text message on the group chat to the rest of his pack. "What's their perimeter?"

"Why do you think I would know that when we aren't in charge of this auction?"

"They won't be able to smell anything through Nadine's shields. Everyone should be safe in the car," Spencer said.

"Safe is relative," Patrick muttered.

Carmen retrieved a compact out of her Gucci clutch and checked her makeup. "Leave your phones. Electronics aren't allowed inside for buyers, only the auction staff."

"You couldn't have told us that *before* we left the hotel?" Patrick added that warning to his message, sent the text off, and then turned off his phone. Spencer did the same. "You better have someone guarding your vehicles."

Patrick took down the silence ward with a silent command, and the dull chatter of voices beyond the vehicle filtered back in. A tall figure came around and opened the side door. Einar extended his hand to Carmen, helping her out of the vehicle. The silk dress she wore was slit all the way to her hips on both sides. Her black stilettos were knife-sharp at the tip, but Patrick thought he might be the only one who noticed that detail.

Patrick and Spencer exited the SUV, and Patrick nearly tripped over Fatima, who wound through their legs the second he got feet on the ground. He bit back a curse, glaring down at her. Her ocelot form hadn't changed, and everyone around them didn't so much as glance her way. He wondered what they saw, if they even noticed her at all. Patrick knew she could appear however she liked to people, as most spirits could.

The werecreatures standing on the sidewalk drew closer before freezing when Lucien finally exited the lead vehicle. Patrick had thought he'd dress up a little nicer for the auction, but Lucien had stuck with his ripped jeans, T-shirt, and leather jacket pierced through with metal spikes. It was his reputation that would carry him through the doors, and that's what mattered most.

Patrick glanced at Spencer, who stared at Lucien and very obviously licked his lips. Patrick sidled closer and subtly stepped on Spencer's foot, shooting him a pointed look. He couldn't voice the warning to not fuck the vampire because of all the prying ears around them, but he thought he got his point across when Spencer rolled his eyes.

Lucien slung his arm over Carmen's shoulders and reeled her in close before curling his finger at Spencer. "Come here."

Spencer went, because they had roles to play, but he didn't seem to mind the possessive way Lucien touched him or the kiss the master vampire gave him. Patrick tried not to gag, then Fatima swatted at Lucien's foot, forcing them to break apart.

Lucien stared down at the psychopomp before squeezing Spencer's ass. "I don't know why I indulge you that beast."

Spencer laughed a little nervously but didn't say anything, playing up his role just fine. The trio walked toward the main entrance of the Smithfield Market. Einar fell into step beside Patrick, several other vampires appearing around them. No other human servants were joining them tonight.

The three SUVs they'd traveled in drove off, clearing the street for the next arrival. The area of London they were in didn't have any active nightlife, and the street they were on had only light traffic.

The magic wrapped around the long building of Smithfield Market scraped against Patrick's shields, the strength in its making speaking of power he wasn't sure he could break even if he tapped a ley line. The place closed early on Sundays, and he had little hope the security guards tasked with patrolling the area would make it out alive tonight.

Black market auctions were usually not held so out in the open, but considering the number of buyers involved, a larger space had to be acquired. The magic hiding the auction from prying eyes was proof of the auctioneer's power, or at least his ability to pay for it. Considering the London god pack had been roped in as preternatural security told Patrick that Rossiter and Cressida were probably still just as friendly as they had been in the photograph he'd seen at Winfield House.

They reached the entrance to Smithfield Market where the metal gates were winched up. God pack werecreatures handled security while a fae with the look of the Unseelie Court took everyone's invitation.

Patrick refused to be worried about the glamour they wore—it had been set by Brigid, a goddess who sat far above the fae standing at the entrance. If she couldn't hide them against her own kind, then the world was worse off than he thought.

"Invitation?" the fae asked.

Lucien removed the invitation from his inner jacket pocket, handing it over. The fae took it with creepily long fingers, unfolding the magicked paper to read its contents.

"Lucien." The fae looked up, taking them all in with a sweeping glance. "And your Night Court, I presume?"

"Where I go, they go," Lucien said.

The fae studied him for a long moment before looking each of them in the eye for several seconds, her gaze lingering on everyone equally. Patrick tried not to hold his breath, keeping his heartbeat steady beneath the scrutiny.

"No weapons. No artifacts. No magic. No electronics. All hostilities will be held to a temporary truce."

Carmen smiled widely. "Those are the rules."

"Abide by them."

"As required."

Carmen could play word games with the fae well enough. She'd had a few centuries to try her hand at it. The fae couldn't deny them entrance, and Smithfield Market wasn't a home. Hospitality couldn't be forced upon anyone who entered, as there was no threshold laid down around its foundation.

Fire sparked at the tips of the fae's long fingers, catching at the invitation. It burned to ash in seconds, breaking the magic written across it. The remnants of the paper fell to the sidewalk, and the fae gestured toward the entrance.

"Enter freely," she said.

Patrick noticed she said nothing about their options to leave.

Lucien led the way beneath the winched-up gates and into the foggy darkness stretched across the wide entrance. It reminded Patrick of the veil, even though he knew it was only someone's magic they were passing through. The searching spell clawed its way down his body but found nothing, the dagger's magic keeping it hidden.

When they stepped free of the magic, they found themselves in a brightly lit corridor with a high ceiling. The table to their left contained bagged electronics people forgot to leave behind or thought they could hide. To the right was a table almost over-flowing with weapons that ranged from pistols to a sword and everything in between. Most held magic within them, small-scale artifacts that had been confiscated.

The werecreature who blocked their way forward held out his hand. "Your weapons."

No one in their group moved to divest themselves of weapons. Fatima sat beside Spencer's feet and calmly washed her face with one paw.

"We have none," Lucien said disdainfully. "Get out of my way."

Patrick very much doubted that, and the feeling must have been shared by the werecreature, who unsubtly sniffed at them. Whatever he was hoping to find, he didn't. Scowling, the werecreature looked over at a teenager who sat on a folding chair off to the side, hands clasped in her lap, wavy hair falling over both her shoulders.

Recognition hummed through Patrick's magic beneath his shields—the feel of a witch. Her gaze swept over them, eyes flick-ering with an inner light, before she nodded.

"No weapons," she announced.

The werecreature reluctantly stepped aside, clearing their way to the Auction of Curiosities and Exceptional Items.

 them with a smile at the entrance to the left wing of Smithfield Market. "Welcome, buyers."

Her bloodred hair matched her nail polish and lipstick, and while she didn't physically look like your typical fae, she felt like it to Patrick's magic. She stood beside a small table that held a stack of small leather-bound notepads and pens. She handed one of each to Lucien—who promptly passed them to Carmen—before gesturing at the crowded wing behind her.

"The auction begins in an hour. Until then, please browse the items up for sale. Not all are being displayed."

Smithfield Market was filled with buyers from all walks of life that lived in the shadows of the preternatural world or skirted its edge. From what Patrick could see, people didn't mingle so much as give each other wide berths. They stuck to their own groups—human, vampire, fae, magic users, and more—making small talk when they had to. Mostly, everyone browsed the items on offer for the auction.

The small alcoves that filled either side of the wing Rossiter had commandeered to display the auction catalogue usually showed off artwork and sold souvenirs during the day. Tonight, the individual metal security gates were nowhere to be seen. Each counter was draped in black velvet, with a single item of interest held up for prospective buyers to see behind magical shields. Buyers asked questions, making notes in the small leather-bound notebook they'd been issued.

Patrick wanted to go look for the Morrígan's staff, but the second he took a half step away from Lucien's Night Court, Einar grabbed him by the elbow with bruising fingers.

"Stay," the tall vampire hissed at him in a low voice.

Patrick's first instinct was to argue, but he bit his tongue against the urge. He had a role to play, and he had to remember that adoration of Lucien's Night Court would get them further than murder.

They were at the auction for one item only, but Lucien made a show of being interested in every object they passed in their meandering walk through the market wing. A scimitar from the ninth century whose gold hilt was inlaid with jewels came with a metal tassel that connected to a thurible. The thurible had been added later, on a different continent according to the written out history pinned to the velvet drape. The small holes in the incense burner had been filled in to trap the djinn said to reside in its golden depths.

"Three wishes to its new owner," the auction aide said with a wide smile, holding the scimitar in one hand and the thurible in the other. "Guaranteed wealth if you so desire."

Carmen made a show of writing down the auction number of the scimitar, but nothing else that Patrick could see. He noticed more that wherever Lucien's curiosity took them, the people nearby paid as much attention to Lucien as they did the items up for sale.

A cluster of Middle Eastern men in white robes and keffiyehs were having a rapid-fire conversation in Arabic in front of a display housing a shimmery Konrul egg, according to its auction history. Patrick didn't speak Arabic, and what bits of the language he used to know while in the Mage Corps had fallen by the wayside.

The youngest man with a neatly trimmed, thick black beard peeled away from his group and approached Lucien. He looked to be in his midthirties, with brown eyes and a smile that wasn't friendly.

"Lucien," the man said, greeting the master vampire like an old friend. "I hear you have finally left the Gulf states for American cities."

Lucien smiled, fangs pricking his lips. "Don't believe all the rumors you hear in your country, Kalid. Half are spun by your subordinates, and we both know the lies you tell."

Patrick didn't get any hint of magic off Kalid, nor any hint of recognition beyond mundane human. He seemed to be exactly what he appeared as—a wealthy businessman looking to buy rare, collectible magical items. Though if he was on a first-name basis with Lucien, his business dealings were less aboveboard than his public persona indicated.

"What brings you to the auction?"

"What do you think?"

Kalid's attention shifted to Carmen, gaze undressing her from head to toe. "I think Carmen still has expensive tastes."

Carmen laughed throatily, the hint of sexual pheromones drifting away from her not enough to incapacitate. Patrick was just glad he had his shields up.

"I *do* have expensive tastes," Carmen purred, extending her hand to Kalid. "You still can't afford me, but I do love that you try."

Kalid took her hand in his and kissed the back of it, fingers caressing her wrist. "A man can hope."

Carmen slid free of Lucien's hold to kiss Kalid full on the mouth, putting on a show for everyone to see. Lucien let her, watching them both with shrewd black eyes. As dedicated as they were to each other and the business empire they kept building, Patrick knew Carmen needed to feed on more than just one undead vampire and some willing human servants.

"If you're open to doing business afterwards, you know the avenues to reach us," Carmen said after she broke the kiss.

Carmen went to cuddle up to Lucien again, who smirked at Kalid before walking away. The rest of the Night Court followed, with Patrick and Spencer ending up in the middle of a circle of vampires. Fatima had disappeared, probably scouting ahead. Playing their roles of human servants meant they were overlooked by the people in power walking the length of the market wing. It also meant they were restricted in where they could go, which wasn't helpful.

"See anything you like?" Spencer asked innocently enough as they walked past another display.

The cursed gold necklace draped over velvet made Patrick pick up the pace a little. "Not yet."

There were close to thirty objects up for sale tonight, but as they neared the end of the market wing and its many displays, Patrick had yet to get eyes on the Morrígan's staff. He chewed his bottom lip, hoping the months of intelligence gathering that had brought them here hadn't been wrong.

As they neared the end of the wing, something caught his attention out of the corner of his eye. Patrick turned his head, staring at the bright golden thread a beautiful woman was weaving from a drop spindle.

She sat on a tall stool, her white gown like starshine in a night sky and as nebulous as moonlight. Her white-blonde hair fell straight to her hips, so thick it looked as if it should weigh her head down. But she held herself tall and proud, shoulders thrown back, staring right at Patrick with eyes the color of a freshwater lake never touched by man—deep and fathomless and filled with endless shadows.

She smiled, pale pink lips quirking at the corners as she

dropped the spindle once again, fingers coaxing the golden thread straight and true. The pile of coarse thread resembled a cloud of gold on her lap and it glittered brightly beneath the lights.

Patrick couldn't look away. All of his hair stood on end, the taste of ozone thick on his tongue.

"Well met, Patrick," the goddess said, her voice echoing as if from a great distance.

Time seemed frozen around them, the clusters of buyers caught midstep, midword. Spencer was a rigid statue beside him, gaze unseeing. Patrick swallowed thickly before easing around his friend and sidling between two vampires to get to the display.

"Who are you?" he asked.

"A cousin of the Norns."

He couldn't hide his flinch at the realization one of the Fates sat before him, weaving a future he knew wasn't a sure thing. "I don't know your name."

"You may call me Srecha."

An old god, from an old religion whose worshippers had mostly faded into history long ago. Those who remembered the Slavic pantheon were few and far between these days. The Fates in all their multitudes had chosen their sides in this fight. Patrick just wasn't sure whose side Srecha was on, especially since she had faces for both.

"What do you want?" he asked.

Srecha added more of the raw material to the thread she was spinning, fingers smoothing out the thickness of the strand. "I want what my cousins want. What we all desire in this day and age. An end to mortal arrogance."

"If you mean Ethan, I've already got my marching orders."

"Your paths will cross eventually."

"They already have. More than enough times for my liking."

Srecha smiled slightly, hands gliding over the golden thread she'd spun. She twisted her fingers around it, raising it to her mouth as the spindle came to rest against her chest. She cut it with teeth that glittered like diamonds, severing the thread in two. The golden strands fluttered between her hands, and she unwound the end of it from the spindle. What remained was an unfinished thread, cut sharply at one end, tufted slightly at the other.

"Prayers are our livelihood. Some of us forget they should be given freely," Srecha said. "Give me your hand."

Patrick made a fist, not wanting to give her anything, but he found himself obeying anyway. Leaning over the counter draped in velvet, he extended his arm toward Fate, and she took his hand with an implacable grip he'd never been able to break.

"We gods are never truly forgotten as long as one person speaks our name and remembers us." Srecha traced the lines on his palm with cold fingers, the golden thread tickling his skin. "Memory can be long-lived, so long as it *lives*."

"Is that what you want?"

Srecha smiled, and Patrick could see eternity in her eyes. "We live because you mortals do not forget. We are not gone when our names fall from your lips. Take my blessing and remember us when it matters."

Patrick blinked, and before his eyes fully closed, her face changed. A flicker of the light maybe, or a trick of the mind, but Srecha's beautiful face aged a lifetime in an instant, becoming wrinkled and old, with bloodshot eyes and crooked teeth.

The thread burned white-hot against his palm, and Patrick yanked his hand free of the goddess' grip, taking a step back. As soon as contact was broken, his ears popped, and everyone started moving again. The display area he stood in front of was empty.

Patrick blinked at where Srecha had once sat, spinning a future only Fate could weave, the only warm spot on his body the line where her golden thread had touched his skin. When he looked at his palm, the skin in that area was an angry red color, and it hurt like a burn.

"Hey," Spencer said, slinging an arm over his shoulders. "There you are. The auction is going to start in ten minutes."

Patrick jerked his head around, noticing that the auction staff in the nearby display areas were beginning to pack up their items in warded boxes. Lucien and Carmen were a few meters away, staring at him expectantly. He didn't think he'd been taken beyond the veil, but the goddess had done *something* to shift everyone's attention and sense of time so their conversation could happen.

Spencer hauled him around, and Patrick went. "You wandered off. You know Lucien doesn't like that."

Patrick curled his fingers over the burn on his palm. "Sorry. I got distracted."

They stepped back inside the circle of vampires. Carmen raised an eyebrow at him in a silent question, but Patrick only shook his head. His conversations with the gods weren't something they needed to know about.

"Let's find our seats," Lucien said.

As they moved with the crowd out of the wing, a distinctive laugh Patrick remembered from the challenge ring in Farningham reached his ears. He craned his head around, gaze skimming over the crowd, until he saw the riot of blonde curls belonging to Cressida.

"Oh," Spencer said in a mild voice that belied the way he grabbed Patrick's hand that throbbed with the burn and held on tight enough to hurt. "That's not good."

"What's not good?" Carmen asked.

"Bad seafood for dinner. I need to use the toilet."

Spencer hauled Patrick out of the circle of vampires, who let them go, though Einar followed after them to keep up appearances. Lucien wasn't known for letting his human servants out of sight alone when surrounded by potential enemies.

The toilets were located in the cross-corridor where they'd come in. Spencer didn't let go until they were in the men's room. Einar followed them inside, leaning against the door to keep anyone else out. Fatima passed through the door right between

Einar's legs, tail lashing in displeasure as she went to Spencer's side.

"No magic," Patrick warned.

Spencer ran a hand through his hair. "Fatima can keep people from listening in without triggering the spell hiding the building."

Patrick looked down at Fatima. The psychopomp yawned and licked her sharp teeth, golden eyes half-lidded. "If you're sure."

"When you said the god pack alpha werewolf had a demon in her soul, I thought that would be an easy break to do," Spencer said in a low voice. "Easy isn't happening."

"Why not?"

"Because that's not just any demon. It's powerful and it's *old*, and the only ones I've ever seen like that in the mortal world usually belong to the ruling class of the hell everyone's most familiar with these days."

"Have you ever exorcised a demon like that from a soul?"

Spencer grimaced. "Once. It didn't go well."

"For the demon?"

"For me."

"But you exorcised it, right?"

Spencer drew in a deep breath and let it out in an explosive sigh. "Yes."

"Okay." Patrick dragged his hand down his face, sucking air through his teeth. "And the London god pack is handling security for the fucking auction. I don't like what that implies."

"Is she the one who fucked Rossiter?"

"Yeah." Patrick looked over his shoulder and met Einar's gaze. "I'm sure there's some kind of code word or phrase you guys hashed out for something like this?"

"We aren't new to bad business deals," Einar said. "We're going back to Lucien."

Fatima yawned again and twitched her tail. Spencer leaned down to scratch between her ears. "We're clear."

They left the toilets, Einar leading the way back to the others.

Lucien studied them with narrowed black eyes as they approached.

"Are you done?" Lucien asked.

"Carmen should've worn the sapphires," Einar said blandly. "The human servants agree."

Lucien's expression didn't change—no one's did—but Patrick knew the warning had been received.

"Sapphires don't match my eyes," Carmen replied.

"They match mine," Spencer muttered.

Patrick made a mental note to remind Spencer later that Lucien was the enemy, despite being their ally tonight, and that fucking the enemy was not allowed.

Lucien turned on his heels. "Move."

They followed his lead to the opposite wing, where white folding chairs had been set up in multiple rows. Each chair carried a folded name card on its seat, indicating which invited group it belonged to. Lucien's was at the very front, his name the only one written out, while all the other cards merely listed *Guest of Lucien*. On Lucien's seat was a small plastic sign with a number on it that would be used to indicate his interest on items up for sale.

Carmen always sat on Lucien's right, but Patrick made sure to take the seat on the other side. Their group took up two rows in a small cluster. While they were in the front, they were farther from the center aisle and the podium on the temporary stage, but closer to the side aisle and some of the werecreatures acting as security.

The seats in the row opposite theirs were eventually taken by a group led by a man whose magic made Patrick's stomach temporarily roil. He tried not to be obvious about staring, but it was impossible not to look and match that face to the memory of the one he'd seen in the WSA briefing.

Ilya Nazarov was tall and broad-shouldered, with slicked back dirty-blond hair and a face hollowed out from magic. His fingers and thumbs were adorned with gold rings that burned with black magic to Patrick's senses, though the gold chain necklaces he wore seemed plain enough. The people with him took their seats, but their attention never left Ilya as the necromancer sauntered over to Lucien with an arrogance Patrick wanted to punch off his face.

"I've heard much about you, Lucien," Ilya said with a smile. His Russian accent wasn't as thick as Patrick expected it to be, most likely a byproduct of his under-the-radar travels.

Lucien didn't acknowledge Ilya for half a minute. When he finally tipped his head back, the pause was a calculated dig of disrespect that Ilya couldn't miss. "Did I say you could talk to me?"

Ilya's smile never wavered. "I am the Patriarch of Souls for the Orthodox Church of the Dead. I talk to whoever I want."

Lucien looked him up and down with obvious disdain. "If I had wanted an introduction, it would have happened."

"I think our desires might align. If you are staying in Europe beyond the auction, perhaps we can meet. I'm sure there's favorable business to be had between my Church and your Night Court."

"I'm not interested in your preaching, necromancer."

"Our god could save you."

Lucien leaned forward, menace in every line of his body. "I don't need saving."

Ilya stared at him for a few seconds before casually shrugging off Lucien's refusal. "Everyone needs saving. Even the undead."

Lucien said nothing to that, merely stared Ilya down until the necromancer left. Patrick watched the necromancer walk back to his seat and lean in to whisper with one of his fellow worshippers. Patrick wished he could've got a picture of the man. He hoped CCTV cameras were working outside the building, but even if they were, he didn't know if the WSA would share any information after they realized they'd been deliberately misinformed about the auction date.

Patrick looked around at everyone seated for the auction, wondering which of the present buyers belonged to the Dominion Sect. Not knowing was worrisome. He didn't see Ethan or Zachary

Myers, but if those two were remaining Stateside, they'd have sent someone else in their stead.

A flurry of movement at the back near the cross-corridor caught his eye. Patrick watched as Dillon Rossiter started down the center aisle, trailed by several auction aides carrying items of interest. Rossiter was dressed in a flashy dove gray business suit, collar open, and a royal purple silk scarf wrapped around his neck rather than a tie.

In person, Rossiter gave off an aura of cold confidence that didn't speak of the Seelie Court. Patrick tried not to hunch down in his seat as Rossiter took the stage, pressing his thumb against the filigree ring on his middle finger. He hoped Brigid's magic would be enough.

Werecreatures staggered themselves down the side aisle and in front of the stage, though only Cressida was allowed on the stage itself. She stood near the stairs, off to the side and out of the way of the auction aides busy displaying the first item up for bid. Cressida scanned the crowd, and Patrick hoped they didn't stand out in the front row.

The fae in the white corset who had greeted them climbed up to the stage and tottered over to the small table situated near the podium where Rossiter stood. She sat in the chair there and opened up a leather-bound tome.

Rossiter leaned his weight against the podium and adjusted the microphone, smiling widely at the crowd. "Welcome to the Auction of Curiosities and Exceptional Items. I hope all of you have managed to ascertain which object is your heart's desire. Be advised that I have some items up for bid which were held back from the viewing hour. Don't forget to save some of your money for those."

Rossiter gestured for his aides to come forward. A woman held aloft a golden birdcage with a fledgling phoenix inside it, flickers of fire burning at the tips of its tail feathers. It looked small and depressed, hiding its face and beak beneath one trembling wing.

"We'll start with Lot 809137, a baby phoenix found in the Carpathian Mountains. Bidding shall begin at one million pounds sterling," Rossiter said. "Do I have one million?"

His approach wasn't rapid-fire, but he kept the momentum moving, coaxing a bid price out of a buyer that would've made even Marek raise an eyebrow. The fledgling phoenix was moved offstage, the buyer's number written down in the record-keeping book, and the next item was brought up.

Rossiter kept things moving, raking in an amount of money in one hour that most people wouldn't see in ten lifetimes. Patrick noticed the necromancer, like Lucien, didn't bid on anything that had come up for auction so far—not until the Morrígan's staff was carried onto the stage.

It took two aides to carry a long, heavy iron box onto the stage and set it down on the display table there. The woman who had been showing off items had exchanged her white cotton gloves for steel gauntlets this time around. The wards on the iron box glowed when Rossiter hissed out a set of command triggers in no language found on Earth, keeping clear of the box.

Patrick leaned forward when the woman lifted the Morrígan's staff free of its confinement. He wasn't the only one. Even through his shields Patrick could sense the deep, primordial power emanating from the staff. It set his teeth on edge.

The Morrígan's staff looked exactly like the picture General Reed had shown Patrick last summer. The wooden staff was long, with a tip shod in iron and the dull quartz crystal at the head surrounded by twisted Celtic knotwork depicting leaves, ravens, and three phases of the moon linked together.

The aide was careful to keep the staff at arm's length from her body, ensuring the iron tip pointed away from Rossiter. Iron would always be deadly to the fae, and Patrick thought it odd that the weapon of a Celtic war goddess would be made with some. Maybe it was supposed to be a deterrent to thieves, but that hadn't helped much since it had gone missing decades ago.

"I did mention items that had not been put up for show," Rossiter said with a wide smile as he angled his body toward the staff. "This is one such item. Made for the hands of a goddess, filled with magic that can be yours for a price, the staff is a work of priceless art perfect for any discerning collector. I'll start the bidding at ten million pounds sterling."

Lucien raised his number, looking almost bored. "Fifteen million."

Ilya quickly lifted his own number. "Twenty million."

"Thirty million," someone behind them shouted.

"Forty million," Lucien countered.

Ilya's voice rang out again. "Fifty million."

The price kept rising, and Patrick internally winced. Whatever number the staff sold at was going to be astronomical, and when Congress found out, he knew it wasn't going to be pretty.

The shouts of bid amounts tapered off after a few minutes until it was only Lucien and Ilya calling out their bids. When it reached five hundred million pounds sterling, with no signs of stopping, Patrick thought he was going to crack a tooth from stress.

Turned out Rossiter was ready to do it for him.

"That is more than I actually thought anyone would be willing to pay," Rossiter said in between bids, momentarily putting a stop to the one-upmanship going on. "Interesting to know this is the only item you both came here for."

"I have half a billion pounds sterling more to spend," Lucien said, staring Rossiter down. "Keep going."

Rossiter smiled in a way that stretched his lips nearly to the sides of his head, like someone had cut through flesh and elongated his mouth. "No, I don't think so. I think this is one item I'll keep."

The werecreatures surrounding the buyers moved, going in for the kill.

Einar shoved Patrick backward, causing his folding chair to tip over. The only reason he didn't crack his head on the ground was because Spencer caught him. Patrick flailed for a couple of seconds before Spencer hauled them both to their feet amidst the melee that had sprung up around them, spurred by the London god pack's surprise brutal attack on the auction buyers.

"*Motherfucker*," Spencer snarled, a dark green mageglobe burning into existence by his shoulder. Fatima yowled at his feet, guarding his six, tail lashing back and forth.

Einar had put himself between Cressida and Lucien, but going toe-to-toe against a werecreature carrying a demon in her soul was a good way for Einar to end up permanently dead. Carmen had pulled her wooden telescoping aconite rod from *somewhere*— Patrick didn't want to think about where she'd hidden it—and had put her back to Lucien's.

"Exorcise the fucking demon," Patrick snapped as he yanked his dagger free from its sheath.

White heavenly fire burned around the matte-black blade, drawing both Cressida's and Rossiter's attention. Rossiter reacted first, yanking the scarf free from his neck to reveal an ugly, rotten line encircling his throat. The smell of gangrenous flesh hit the air, and Patrick almost gagged.

The screams of people dying around them intermingled with the howls of werecreatures, flickering bursts of magic as people defended themselves, and the yells of people urging their compatriots to run.

But there was no running from what Rossiter was, or the alliance he'd formed with the demon riding Cressida's soul.

Rossiter leaped from the stage into the crowd, landing somewhere behind Patrick. He thought the fae had miscalculated the distance, but when Patrick spun around, he realized that wasn't true.

Rossiter slammed a man in a white robe to the ground with brutal strength. Kalid's terrified face stared back at Patrick for just a moment. Then Rossiter punched a fist into Kalid's back, and the man screamed, the sound cutting off with a gurgle when the fae tore Kalid's spine out of his body in one gruesome pull.

The line of vertebrae ripped free, taking the skull with it, eyes still in their sockets hanging by thin nerves. Kalid's skin sheared free from the force of the pull, and what was left of his body fell to the floor, his white robe turned red. Rossiter snapped the spine like a whip as he turned, spraying the undulating crowd of fighters and dead people with blood. Then he reached up with his free hand to grip his hair and *pull*.

Rotten skin stretched and tore, peeling apart like rancid fruit. Bone cracked and broke as Rossiter removed his head from his body, holding it aloft in his hand, smiling nightmarishly wide as blood stained his suit. Sickly yellow magic slithered down the human spine he carried, covering every inch of stolen bone.

"I will see you into a grave," Rossiter said as he strode forward, stepping on the dead.

16

"WHAT THE *FUCK* IS THAT?" SPENCER YELLED, TOSSING A CHAIR OUT of his way.

"The Dullahan," Patrick replied.

"Fuck that shit. Give me the dead over creepy-ass fae any day of the week."

Patrick wrenched open the soulbond, pouring his magic through the connection to reach deep below London for the ley lines running beneath the ancient city. They burned like a live wire to his senses as he manipulated the wild magic into the shape of half a dozen mageglobes.

Jono would know something was wrong, but Patrick didn't know if Nadine would be strong enough to get through the magic wrapped around Smithfield Market. He couldn't worry about that right now, because they needed to get the staff. Retrieving it was going to be a difficult task to do while fighting off werecreatures, a Dullahan, and the banshee the records-keeping fae turned out to be.

The banshee's face was nothing like the one she'd worn while greeting them at the entrance. It was grotesque, misshapen, with slate-gray eyes that had no pupils and a too-large mouth. She attacked the frightened aide holding the staff and sent the weapon skidding across the stage, intent on ripping free the steel gauntlets from the woman's hands. From the way the woman screamed, it sounded as if the banshee had ripped off her hands with them.

Patrick surged forward, intent on retrieving the staff before anyone else could, but didn't get far. The banshee threw back her head and *screamed*, the preternatural sound high-pitched and agonizing.

Patrick jerked, his entire body vibrating from the wail that seemed to make the air shimmer around them. Then a dark blur slammed into Patrick with what could've been bone-breaking force if he didn't expand his personal shields to keep claws from ripping into his skin. He hit the floor with a grunt, skidding a few feet before slamming into a pile of tipped-over chairs.

Wolf-bright blue eyes glared down at him as sharp fangs bit at his shields, causing sparks to ripple through the air. Patrick didn't have much space to move, but it was more than enough to twist his right hand so his dagger pointed upward. He slammed it through his shield into the werewolf's belly with a grunt. The blade cut deep, sinking into flesh with burning ease.

The werewolf howled at a pitch that rivaled the banshee's wail before staggering off the dagger and away from Patrick. Blood gave shape to his personal shields for a second before he was on his feet again. Movement through the air forced Patrick to jump aside from the crashing hit of the Dullahan's whip.

Kalid's skull slammed into the spot where Patrick had stood, Rossiter's magic keeping the bone intact. It had lost the eyes, and bits of brain were forced out of the eye sockets from the impact. Patrick ducked under the reverse whip strike, going to one knee and flinging a mageglobe at Rossiter. The Dullahan knocked his magic aside, the explosion of raw magic ripping through the air between them.

Patrick sought to use that brief respite to get to the stage but found his way blocked by Cressida, fingers dripping with blood he hoped didn't belong to any of Lucien's vampires. Patrick would never hear the end of it if that were the case.

"Spencer!" Patrick yelled, pointing his dagger at Cressida and thrusting his other hand with a mageglobe spinning at his fingertips toward Rossiter. "A little help here!"

"Not much without your pack, are you, Patrick?" Cressida growled. "I know it's you beneath that face you're wearing."

"And I know you have a demon riding your soul."

Cressida's smile got wider, flashing her fangs, but the smug superiority vanished from her face when Fatima landed in between her and Patrick. The psychopomp yowled at her, a chill emanating from the ocelot-shaped spirit guide that made Patrick shiver.

"Watch my six," Spencer demanded as he dodged around one of Lucien's vampires to reach them. "This is going to take all my attention."

Beyond Cressida, the banshee had quit wailing and was being protected from Lucien's Night Court by several werecreatures. When Patrick tossed a mageglobe in their direction, a foreign one came out of nowhere to crash into his before it reached his target. Both exploded in midair, the sound deafening in the enclosed area.

Patrick's head snapped around. Ilya stood within the protective circle of his followers, arms outstretched, ochre-colored magic glittering at his fingertips. Their eyes met across the fight-filled corridor, and Patrick gripped his dagger tighter.

The werecreatures got the banshee off the stage with preternatural speed under cover of magic and dragged her into the midst of the fighting all around them. Patrick's attention drifted for only a second, but it was long enough for Ilya to disappear with the help of magic.

Patrick's stomach twisted. If Ilya got to it first, they were fucked.

If the Dominion Sect representatives got to it first, *everyone* was fucked.

The Morrígan's staff was still in the banshee's possession, and they needed to steal it back. The only problem was Patrick refused to leave Spencer to fend for himself in the middle of a life-or-death fight against a high-ranked demon from hell. The gods would probably denounce his decision, but Patrick wasn't going to turn his back on one of the few people he considered a friend.

He'd lost enough over the years.

"Fucking shit," Patrick snarled, standing shoulder to shoulder with Spencer as he turned his attention to Rossiter. "Someone get that goddamn staff!"

Rossiter cracked the bone whip again, a cackling laugh escaping his too-wide mouth. His severed neck kept spilling blood down his suit, staining the fabric in a macabre way, while his head swung back and forth in his hand like some horrific lantern.

Patrick expanded his shields to surround himself and Spencer, tapping the ley line through the soulbond to power it. Spencer's dark green magic haloed his entire body, swirls of power that twisted between him and Fatima as he raised his hands toward Cressida, a single mageglobe burning between them.

"I cast you out from the mortal plane, demon," Spencer said in the face of Cressida's wordless, furious snarl as she lunged for them.

Patrick glanced over his shoulder in time to see Cressida caught in midair by brightly swirling lines of magic that twisted into the shape of a fiery pentagon. Her arms, legs, and head were wrenched toward each of the five points as three concentric circles expanded outward to contain her. The circles started to spin as Fatima got to all four paws, gray mist twisting around her.

Then a wave of power crashed through the area, and all Patrick could smell was sulfur as the demon in Cressida fought against Spencer's magic with a strength that shook the ground.

"You have no power over me," the demon raged, using Cressida's mouth to speak.

Her body twisted in the binding spell Spencer held her in, skin bulging as if she were going to shift forms but couldn't. Spencer squared his shoulders, and Patrick could sense how his soul *opened* in a way that made Patrick not want to be near him.

Spencer felt like death—empty and cold—even as he channeled magic through his soul.

"I cast you out," Spencer commanded. His words came out harsh and shredded, magic spinning around himself and where Cressida floated in the air with enough power Patrick's hair stood on end.

Flashes of black magic skittered over Cressida's body, and the demon screamed. Patrick's attention was wrenched away from Spencer's attempt to carve a demon out of a human soul by the crash of the Dullahan's bone whip against his shields. The hit vibrated through his magic all the way to his soul, and Patrick swore, readjusting his grip on his dagger.

His shields wavered, fae magic slicing into them over and over again with each strike of the bone whip. Rossiter's head was still clenched in his left hand, mouth gaping wide and eyes staring right at Patrick. Around them, the auction buyers were still fighting for their lives, but the London god pack was getting pushed onto the defensive. The buyers had retaliated with what innate magic some of them had to save their own lives and, like Carmen, smuggled weaponry.

Then the dead rose.

"Uh, Spencer," Patrick said, staring past Rossiter at where broken and viciously clawed bodies were jerkily getting to their feet.

Spencer ignored him. Cressida's screams were guttural in a way that spoke of something else being channeled through her. The sound mingled with the banshee's scream somewhere in that melee, and Patrick's ears rang painfully from the noise.

"Spencer, there are motherfucking zombies walking around!"

The other man ignored him, all of Spencer's focus on trying to exorcise the demon from Cressida's soul. Spencer's jaw was clenched together so hard the tendons in his neck stood out, body rigid as he fought against a demon from hell. His entire focus was on breaking apart Cressida's soul, and he had no attention to spare for the fight around them.

He normally never blocked out the world like this, and that worried Patrick. Right now, Spencer's focus and power were both a strength and a liability, but Patrick wasn't going to leave his side.

"Lucien!" Patrick yelled. "Where's the fucking staff?"

He didn't get an answer. He didn't know where Lucien was, but Patrick hoped the bloodsucking bastard was keeping his side of the bargain.

Patrick spun up a mageglobe, filled it with a strike spell, and pushed it through his shields straight at Rossiter's chest. The Dullahan was thrown back by the force of the explosion, slamming into a pile of folding chairs. He skidded over the floor and crashed into the metal security gate covering a display area. Patrick hoped he was dead, but the sickly magic lining the bone whip never faded, which spoke of shields saving the headless bastard.

Then what was left of Kalid stumbled toward them, body bent over at the hips, robe more red than white, the loose flesh of his face dragging against the floor with every step the zombie took. Behind him came more of the walking dead, but Patrick didn't know where the fuck the necromancer was. As much as he wanted to do a wide strike spell, that would damage Smithfield Market more than they could afford, and it would put Lucien's Night Court at risk.

Patrick added another layer to his shields as the zombies converged, powered by the souls of the dead, not deterred by magic in the least. Without shields, they'd tear a man to pieces in minutes, their strength backed by black magic. Fighting zombies was almost like fighting a hydra—you cut down one, but it never stayed dead, and everyone who died was fair game to be raised.

Bodies, skeletons, it didn't matter. The souls of the dead could animate flesh as well as bones.

Patrick raised his dagger and poured magic into another mageglobe, readying himself to step through his shields and fight them off. He never got the chance.

Hellish power crashed through Smithfield Market with a ferocity that cracked Patrick's shields, drove Spencer to his knees, and knocked everyone else—whether they were dead or alive—to the ground. The spells surrounding the building *shattered*—and Jono's furious howl echoed through the air.

Patrick slapped another layer over his wavering shields, drawing more magic from the ley line below through the soulbond. He ignored the zombies getting back to their feet or leg stumps, more concerned about Spencer, who looked so pale the skin on his face seemed translucent.

"*Spencer,*" Patrick bit out, kneeling to wrap an arm around his friend's shoulders and offer support.

"I cast you *out,*" Spencer said, eyes wide and unseeing and filled with an inner cloudiness Patrick didn't like.

Fatima exploded in light, wispy gray fog filling their immediate area, merging with Spencer's magic. The pentagram and concentric circle pulsed like a quasar star, so bright it made Patrick's eyes water. A coldness that reminded Patrick of walking through the veil expanded around them, but it wasn't enough to stop the zombies.

It certainly wasn't enough to stop Jono.

He came racing around the corner, larger than every other werecreature still standing, and went for the nearest werewolf, taking them down to the ground and tearing out their throat. Sage was a streak of orange and black behind him, her guttural roar causing more than one werecreature to flee the fight.

Patrick got to his feet as Nadine rounded the corner, half a dozen violet mageglobes trailing in her wake, followed by Wade. She and Patrick locked eyes over the crowd.

"I'll cover him," Nadine shouted, pointing at Spencer.

Violet magic rose up around the two of them in a shield more solid than any Patrick could ever make. A gap lingered long enough for Patrick to slip through before sealing shut behind him, keeping Spencer and Fatima safe.

Relatively speaking.

The banshee screamed again before the sound choked off with a gurgle. Patrick nearly tripped over a folding chair in his haste to get eyes on the fae while trying to stay out of reach of Rossiter's bone whip. The Dullahan was back on his feet, not fazed in the least by the handful of zombies between them.

Patrick twisted out of reach of a zombie walking on its knees, legs having been ripped off, but not its arms. He slammed his dagger through its throat all the way to the hilt. The zombie jerked, spasming on the blade as heavenly magic ravaged what was left of its body. Patrick kicked it in the chest to shove it off his dagger. The zombie fell to the ground and didn't rise again, the necromancy that had called the spirit forth and the black magic that let it walk cut by his dagger.

Spencer could do it quicker, and in larger numbers, but he was still busy trying to pry the demon from Cressida's soul.

A furry blur streaked toward him but abruptly changed direction when Carmen appeared beside him, the wooden aconite rod in her hand. The poison it carried in its shape was strong enough to hurt a werecreature, but not to kill it. That's what the Ka-Bar in her other hand was for.

"Isn't that Lucien's?" Patrick asked.

Carmen shifted her grip, holding the Ka-Bar behind the raised rod. "Not anymore."

"Did he get the staff?"

"No."

"Asshole had *one* job."

Carmen said something rude in Italian that he ignored. Patrick spun on his feet, scanning the area for any signs of the banshee.

Amidst the fighting, he caught sight of a body crumpled on the ground near half a dozen tipped-over chairs. He left Carmen to deal with the werewolf and headed toward the banshee.

A zombie lunged at him, broken jaw hanging low over a slashed-open throat, the one behind it still bleeding even though it was dead. Patrick slammed a mageglobe filled with raw magic into the zombies to clear his way forward. Blood and flesh splattered across his shields as he ran, leaping over a couple of tipped-over chairs.

He landed near the banshee, and even before Patrick made it to her side, he knew she was dead. A short sword he'd seen on display earlier for the auction stuck out from the center of her chest. Her eyes were sightless—until they weren't. The banshee suddenly blinked, and the dead looked back at Patrick.

Steel-gauntleted hands curled like claws as her spine arched, limbs jerking as black magic filled her corpse. Her body twisted and jerked, snapping to her feet with a grotesque twist. The sword shifted in her chest, white outfit stained crimson from the mortal wound.

Patrick conjured up a mageglobe but hesitated to cast a spell into it. He didn't know what kind of artifact that short sword was or how it would react to magic. Then the zombie opened her mouth, and newly dead or not, necromancy could still bring a fae's power to life.

She never got the chance to scream.

Dragon fire washed over her with such force her entire body was consumed by it. Patrick threw up his arm to cover his face, the heat vicious even through his shields. He turned his head in time to see Wade cough out a fireball to clear his lungs. Red scales pushed through the skin of his face, neck, and arms, his eyes golden, cut through with reptilian pupils, but otherwise human.

"Zombies are *gross*," Wade said.

Patrick groaned. "Then don't *eat* them. They aren't food!"

"I didn't eat one! They tried to eat me!"

"Zombies don't eat people. They just want to kill you so their master can raise you." Patrick wrapped a shield around the zombie banshee burning to a crisp, not wanting to spread the fire to any other part of the building. "Have you seen the Morrígan's staff?"

"No, I—"

Wade cut himself off, eyes going wide. Then he grabbed Patrick by the arm and yanked him to the side. Patrick's feet left the ground with the force of the pull, the bones in his elbow joint grinding together beneath Wade's grip. The pain was better than having the Dullahan's bone whip slam down against him. Even with his shields, he'd have felt that hit.

Kalid's skull and spine had yet to break, fortified by Rossiter's magic. The bone whip cut through the air again, crashing against the shield Patrick raised between them. Rossiter stalked forward, holding his head high to see as he cracked the whip again.

Jono vaulted over two zombies and landed in between them, massive jaws snapping down on Rossiter's head. It burst like a ripe melon, blood and brain exploding out from between Jono's teeth. Patrick didn't know how he got through Rossiter's shields until he saw the white fire burning in Jono's eyes.

Not Jono—Fenrir.

The Dullahan collapsed, the bone whip splitting apart, vertebrae clattering to the floor. Fenrir crunched Rossiter's skull into so many pieces using Jono's teeth. Then he spat it out, blood coating his fangs.

"*Ew,*" Wade gagged. "That can't taste good."

"You eat demons," Patrick said, looking past Jono at Cressida.

"As a last resort!"

The roiling hellish magic pouring out of Cressida's body fought against Spencer's. She was still trapped in his spell, tendrils of his magic twisting through her flesh and seeking to sever the demon from her soul. Nadine had fought her way to his side, standing outside the shield and doing her best to cut down the zombies and what few werecreatures remained.

That was the problem with the walking dead in a fight like this. When someone died, they could easily be raised and thrust back into the fight, or wandering souls were captured to fill someone else's body or bones. By Patrick's count, there were less zombies than there had been after the auction turned into a bloodbath, and the newly dead were staying dead.

He didn't see Ilya or his followers.

Maybe it was too much to hope the fucker was a body on the ground.

"Has *anyone* seen the goddamn staff?" Patrick shouted.

No one answered him, and he had the sinking feeling someone had run off with it during the chaos of the ambush. Before panic could really set in, Cressida screamed, the sound shrill and ugly before growing deep and furious. A roar filled the wing of Smithfield Market, reminding Patrick of a waterfall thundering over the side of a cliff.

Spencer's magic exploded around Cressida like a star gone nova, but it wasn't bright enough to block out the swirling darkness that wrenched itself free of her body. The shapeless shadow streaked away from her like smoke, and the inhuman deepness of her voice shaded back to its normal tone.

"*Andras!*" Cressida screamed, sounding scared and mournful in a way Patrick didn't expect. "Don't leave me!"

Spencer's magic folded around her, bearing Cressida's limp body to the ground. The god pack alpha no longer fought the magical bindings holding her in place, face wet with tears, more in shock than anything else. What werecreatures remained in Smithfield Market fled, not a single one of them attempting to save their alpha.

Spencer didn't look like he was in any condition to put to rest the handful of zombies left, but Lucien's Night Court were handling that threat just fine. Patrick did a quick head count, coming up with the same number of vampires as when they'd arrived. His pack was still standing, too many buyers were dead, and those who had survived had already fled the scene or were in the process of doing so.

Patrick let them go. No point in chasing after them when their entire reason for coming to London wasn't anywhere to be found.

"Fuck," Patrick ground out. "*Fuck*."

Nadine drew down her shields, hauling Spencer to his feet. He was white-faced, eyes like holes in his head, but at least he was conscious. Fatima stalked forward to sit on Cressida's chest, staring down at her with eyes filled with veil mist in their depths. Cressida jerked before going limp, head lolling from unconsciousness.

"We need to get out of here," Nadine said, violet light playing over her face from her mageglobe.

Jono stepped closer to Patrick, his eyes gone back to their normal wolf-bright blue. Sage stood in the midst of broken chairs and bodies while Lucien and his Night Court went about ensuring no one on the ground was left alive.

"What about the authorities?" Patrick asked.

"I'll call Gael, but we aren't staying here. The United States government can't be caught red-handed executing a mission behind an ally's back inside their borders."

Patrick wanted to punch something. "We can't go to the hotel like this."

Nadine hauled Spencer with her. "We'll go to Lucien's."

"None of you are welcome," Lucien called out irritably.

"Tough shit."

Jono went to where Cressida lay and grabbed her shoulder with his teeth. Fatima latched her claws into Cressida's chest, refusing to move, the psychopomp's strangely colored eyes riveted on the werewolf's slack face. Jono dragged her toward the exit, not careful in the least.

Patrick cast a slew of look-away wards, letting his magic spin around all of them as they fled Smithfield Market, the Morrígan's staff having slipped through their fingers, nowhere to be found.

17

"I think she's waking up," Wade said.

Órlaith, seated in the front passenger seat, didn't bother looking over her shoulder at their temporary prisoner. "Cressida is not waking up."

"She twitched."

"She's unconscious, Wade," Jono said, keeping both hands on the steering wheel. "Eat your chip butty."

"I'll eat my chip butty because I *like* it, not because you told me to."

Jono glanced at the rearview mirror in time to see Wade take a large bite out of the road trip snack he'd insisted on bringing along, still side-eyeing Cressida. Sage sat in the back seat between Cressida and Wade, hands clasped in her lap and appearing serene. Jono couldn't smell her, not with the fae pendant she wore, but she hadn't been thrilled about delivering Cressida back to her pack rather than the police or the WSA.

Cressida sat slumped against the side door, unconscious from whatever spell Órlaith had cast on her when the Summer Lady arrived that morning. Cressida's hands were bound behind her back with a set of metal cuffs Órlaith had set with a binding spell that would prevent her from shifting and keep her preternatural strength in check.

Cressida's shoulder and clothes were a bloody mess from Jono's teeth, though the wound itself was long since healed. She was pale, her blonde curls a tangled mess. She seemed to have aged over the course of hours, face ravaged by the loss of the demon she had carried in her soul. Jono didn't know if that was a byproduct of possession or not. He'd meant to ask Spencer, but they'd left the mage asleep on Lucien's sofa with Fatima curled on his chest, still recuperating from his efforts at Smithfield Market.

Last night had been a shitshow. They'd lost the Morrígan's staff and didn't know who'd run off with it. After holing up at Lucien's flat to clean up and change clothes, Patrick and Nadine had been summoned to the WSA headquarters in the middle of the night. Jono didn't envy them having to explain their actions and face the consequences of lying to their country's allies.

Lucien had grudgingly let them stay at his flat until Órlaith showed up midmorning. Cressida had been a handful until the Summer Lady arrived. Jono had used that time to contact the London god pack. Finley hadn't been thrilled when Jono demanded a meeting after announcing Cressida was his pack's prisoner. Finley had promised a fight when all Jono wanted was a chat, which was why Órlaith was coming along and Wade had been given full permission to shift mass if things went tits up.

They might not have had any mages with them for this meeting, but Órlaith was a demi-goddess in her own right, and she let that fact be known when they pulled into the long drive of the country house in Farningham. Jono could smell the werecreatures in the home and on the grounds, but all their righteous anger was suddenly drowned out by the wave of power that rippled away from Órlaith as she got out of the car.

She smelled like a mix of summer rain and green things Jono had no name for and wouldn't recognize if he hadn't crossed the veil into Tír na nÓg last December. Órlaith exuded otherworldly power that stilled Finley's feet at the threshold to the home, the god pack alpha watching her the way prey eyed a predator.

"Wolf," Órlaith said coolly. "I come as an ally to the New York City god pack. You will stay your hand, or I will take this land of yours for the fae on their behalf."

Jono got out of the car, as did Wade and Sage, but he was the one who pulled Cressida from the back seat. He didn't bother being gentle, letting her body fall heavily to the ground. He scanned the crowd of werecreatures, gaze lingering on Bryson only a couple of seconds longer before focusing all his attention on Finley.

Órlaith was a tall, fierce defense that kept Finley rooted where he stood. The rest of the London god pack took their cue from their alpha and didn't move. Jono met Finley's furious gaze with his own.

"We'll do this in your challenge ring," Jono said.

"Come back to take what you think is yours?" Finley spat out.

Jono smiled nastily. "I don't want your sodding pack. I have one of my own. I just know better than to cross your home's threshold."

Órlaith led the way, with Sage taking up the rear as Jono dragged Cressida around the home and to the back field that pushed up against the reserve. By the time they got there, the London god pack had filled the space around the challenge ring, all eyes on them. Jono weathered their attention easily, keeping his focus on Finley.

The other alpha's expression was a grim mask where he stood on the edge of the challenge ring, his pack arrayed around him. It was far more people than had been present the other night, and many of them looked ready for a fight.

Órlaith came to a stop on the grass some meters away from the edge of the challenge ring. Jono slowed to a halt beside her. Sage and Wade lined up beside him, but there was still enough space between them for Jono to swing Cressida around and toss her to the ground between their two sides.

"Wake up," Órlaith commanded.

Cressida jerked, body heaving against the ground. She gasped for air, hands clenching into fists behind her back as she fought the metal cuffs that kept her trapped in human form. She rolled from her side onto her back, eyes flicking back and forth as she took in her predicament. Órlaith calmly stepped forward to slam her foot down onto Cressida's chest, pinning the woman to the ground like one would pin a bug.

"You *cunt*," Cressida gasped out.

"Rude," Wade retorted. "She's a princess."

Órlaith looked at Jono, her riot of red-orange hair falling in thick waves past her hips, eyes calm in her too-beautiful face. "Speak your truth. I will keep this one in her place."

Jono's gaze slid back to Finley, the other man scowling so hard Jono could see nearly all his teeth. "We've come in peace, with no desire for your territory. All we want is a word."

"You come with the fae, dragging my pack's co-leader after you like a slave. That isn't *peace*, Jonothon," Finley sneered.

"Way I see it, you haven't had peace in years. Not since Cressida came down from the north." Jono looked at Bryson, seeing the way the other man held himself so stiffly, the same way too many others in the pack did so. "You never questioned where she came from."

"It's not our way. You know that. Pack is who you are, not what you were."

"Maybe it should be. Maybe you should've wondered why Cressida's first act after joining your pack was to challenge Jessamine."

"Jess—" Finley's voice didn't crack, but Jono knew it would've if the other man had spoken her full name. "—accepted the challenge. And she lost. Pack law gave her rank to Cressida, as tradition dictated."

"And every year since, Cressida has run your people through the rank of dire, killing them off one by one. But only those she considered a problem or a threat, am I right? People loyal to Jessamine. Those who knew pack law and tried to use it against her. Anyone who would get in her way of breaking down the London god pack."

"Your *point?*" Finley growled, rankled by Jono's words.

Jono would've pitied him if he cared enough to—but he didn't. "The other god pack in New York sent hunters against mine earlier this year."

"Not our problem."

"The hunters belong to the Krossed Knights, and you know hunters willingly carry demons in their souls." Jono looked down at where Cressida lay on the ground, glaring up at him. "Just like Cressida here."

Cressida rasped out a laugh. "Do I smell like I have a demon in my soul?"

"You called him Andras last night, and cried for it like you were dying when we tore the bastard out of you."

The rage spilling off Cressida was matched only by the bleak grief that filled her scent, making Jono's nose twitch. Finley's gaze snapped to Cressida, who wouldn't look at him, all her attention reserved for Jono.

"I don't—" she began.

Órlaith twisted her fingers in a sharp motion. Cressida's mouth snapped shut, neck arching from the pull of magic. "You will not lie, wolf. Speak your truth, or I will pull it from your mind."

Finley's gaze flickered back to Jono. "Just wanted a friendly chat, yeah? I don't call this friendly."

"The Summer Lady agreed to accompany us as a favor," Jono said.

"To force lies out of Cressida's mouth?"

Órlaith straightened her fingers, and her magic left Cressida's body. Cressida panted for air, chest rising and falling beneath

Órlaith's boot. Jono caught Sage's eye and nodded at her. Sage wandered away to pace around the challenge ring.

"Last night we were at Smithfield Market for reasons that don't concern you. Cressida and some of your pack were there, acting as security for fae of the Unseelie Court," Sage said calmly. "If you want corroborated truth, we'll give it to you."

She singled out seven people in the gathered pack, finding them by scent even though she didn't know their names. Finley tracked her movements when he could, meeting her gaze when Sage finally returned to Jono's side.

"Those members of your pack were with Cressida last night. Do you want to hear what they have to say?" Jono asked.

Finley's jaw worked. "My pack doesn't obey you."

"They don't seem to obey you much either, mate."

Finley charged forward at the insult, only to be brought up short by the fireball Wade belched in his direction. The heat of dragon fire singed Finley's clothes, forcing the other man back. Wade coughed beneath everyone's wide-eyed stares, smoke curling out of his nose. He patted his stomach with a scaly red hand, eyes metallic gold with slit-black pupils in a face whose features weren't quite human.

"'Scuse you," Wade said. "Jono told me I couldn't eat any of you, but the chip butty wasn't enough and I'm starting to get hungry again."

He'd stopped hiding his true aura; Jono could sense the change emanating from Wade without even looking. Wade could and did pass as human, hiding his aura beneath shields General Reed had taught him to build. Jono always forgot how dangerous Wade could come off, because dragons were *rare*, no matter what shape they took. Despite Wade's lean teenage body, he came across as an apex predator to Jono's hindbrain right then.

Finley couldn't miss that. *No one* in the London god pack could miss it.

Jono focused his attention on Cressida and the prideful hate in her eyes, remembering how willing she'd been to let a demon own her soul.

"You're a hunter, aren't you?" Jono asked.

Cressida's lips curled into a mocking smile before she laughed, fighting for breath against Órlaith's weight pinning her down.

"Come closer and find out, you pissant monster," she snarled. "I'll cut you down like all the other animals over the years who were too worthless to live."

She must have known there was no way out of this—not with Órlaith forcing her to stay still while Jono used words to strip away what hid the real her. Hate was a festering thing, a poison most people never realized was there even as it seeped into their lives. But the people who were targets of that hate knew how to recognize it, and Jono had spent months hunting and being hunted in New York City by people who would only ever see him as a monster.

He couldn't imagine a Krossed Knight would willingly infect themselves with the werevirus, but it seemed whatever hunter group Cressida belonged to had found her agreeable.

The demon had as well.

"*Cressida*," Finley ground out, staring at her as if he didn't know her and the rot she'd let seep into the London god pack underneath his nose.

She turned her head to look at Finley, bared her teeth, and laughed in his face. "I had plans, you know. To bury your bones where you buried your love and piss on them."

If Órlaith hadn't been standing in the way, Jono thought Finley would've ripped out Cressida's organs one by one.

He still might, after they left.

"Is this what your kind hopes to do in New York?" Jono asked.

Cressida bared her teeth at him. "London needs to be cleansed of the monsters that think they belong here. That's what Andras promised me. Promised *us*. It won't be the only city we'll cleanse."

Jono clenched his teeth and shook his head. The damage Cressida had caused was more than enough to wound the London god pack. The cracks she'd forced open between its members and the packs beneath them wouldn't be fixed with her death.

Some of that toxicity had been there back when Jono had lived here, an outsider looking in, but this was far worse. He was still that outsider, because despite the crisis the London god pack was hurtling toward, it wasn't his problem. It *couldn't* be his problem.

This wasn't his pack, had never *been* his pack, and never would be. Its damage wasn't his responsibility to fix.

London wasn't his to save.

"The cuffs will keep her from shifting. Do with her what you like," Jono said into the tense silence that had fallen over the challenge ring.

Órlaith removed her foot from Cressida's chest at his words, stepping back. Cressida continued to lie there, panting for breath and staring up at the sky, lips peeled back from her teeth in a rictus of a smile.

Cressida would die today. How long it took was anyone's guess. Jono knew she would face what was coming with the righteous belief of her people that they were better than those who weren't like them, no matter the werevirus running through her veins.

Jono led the way back to the car, keeping his hearing dialed down low. It didn't stop him from hearing Cressida's first painful cry that trailed off into a breathless laugh.

Sometimes the worst monsters were the human ones.

JONO STEPPED inside Lucien's Hyde Park flat in time to see Spencer stare mournfully at a mug he had tipped upside down.

"Coffee, no," Spencer whined. "Why are you empty?"

"You look better," Sage said.

"I'd feel better with more coffee."

They'd dropped Órlaith off at the fae embassy before returning here rather than the hotel. Jono doubted the London god pack was trying to watch their every move anymore, but he couldn't be sure about the WSA. He didn't smell Patrick or Nadine in the flat, which meant they were still handling the crisis with their foreign counterparts. Jono hadn't received a text or call from Patrick as of yet.

They'd need to feed Wade soon, if his grumblings on the drive back to London had been anything to go by. Supper was two hours away, but Jono didn't think Wade would last.

"Where's Lucien?" Jono asked.

Spencer set the mug down and hiked the blanket higher over his shoulders. Fatima jumped onto the sofa and headbutted her way onto his lap. Spencer pet her absentmindedly.

"I don't know. Sleeping? It's still daylight out. I woke up an hour ago and had to figure out the coffee machine on my own. It was like something NASA invented as a joke for us poor people who don't understand science while half-asleep."

"Should've made tea."

"If I wanted to drink leaves and flowers, I'd have Fatima fetch me some from the park across the street." Spencer yawned widely, then winced. "Think there's any Advil around here?"

Victoria Alvarez would've come in handy right about then. The witch, who was a nurse allied with their god pack, had a deft hand for potions. As it was, Lucien didn't keep potions around, and Spencer's best course of action when they'd arrived last night had been sleep.

Jono eyed the mage. The tightness in Spencer's jaw and around his eyes spoke of a headache he hadn't slept off. Jono knew the signs of when a mage had overextended themselves and wished he could help the other man out.

"I doubt Lucien has any paracetamol. He doesn't seem the sort to need it," Jono said.

Spencer leaned back on the sofa and propped his socked foot up on the coffee table. "I'll live. How'd returning the prisoner go?"

"They were gutting her as we left," Sage said in the same tone someone would use to say *pass the butter* at a meal.

"Sounds cathartic."

Jono watched Wade slink out of the living room through the door that led to the kitchen. He wished Wade luck finding anything edible in a master vampire's home.

"Care to chat about that demon?" Jono asked.

Spencer ran a hand over Fatima's back, gaze shuttered. "We'll wait for Patrick and Nadine to get back."

They'd needed answers last night after the auction, but Spencer hadn't been up for the sort of conversation they all needed to have. It seemed they would still have to wait.

Lucien's Night Court slept the day away, their human servants acting as guards. Naheed popped in to check on Jono and the others only once, a silent figure in the doorway before slipping away again.

Wade was threatening to chew a hole in the wall by the time Patrick and Nadine made it back to Lucien's flat. Jono smelled the takeaway before he saw the pair, unable to sniff them out due to shields.

Carmen and Lucien were both awake by then, even if the rest of his Night Court were still sleeping. The sun hadn't set yet, so the rest wouldn't be up for the conversation everyone was about to have.

"Do I smell Chinese food?" Wade said loudly, jackknifing to a sitting position on the floor.

"You're using a plate and fork, not your fingers," Jono warned as the front door opened.

"I'll pour an entire box in my mouth, I don't care. I'm *hungry*."

"Didn't you feed him?" Patrick asked as he and Nadine came inside.

"Twice. Once each way there and back to Farningham," Jono said. "He ate chip butties each time."

"Should've packed a trunkful of snacks."

Patrick looked tired and irritable, weighed down by the six bags of bulging takeaway he carried. Nadine carried just as many because it took a lot of food to feed their group. The pair headed toward the kitchen, and Jono got up to follow them. Wade was sticking his nose into the bags by the time Jono made it to the kitchen, dancing from one foot to the other in his excitement to eat.

"Aw yeah, double order of shrimp fried rice," Wade said happily.

"You're sharing," Sage said.

Wade clutched a box to his chest and gave her a scandalized look. "But there's two! Which means one is all mine."

Patrick reached over to pry the box out of his hands. "Sharing means you don't eat all the food by yourself."

Wade shoved a spring roll into his mouth and chewed sulkily.

"If you've led the British government to my home, I'll murder you right here," Lucien said as he draped himself over Carmen's back, staring at Patrick with half-lidded eyes and an expression on his face that wasn't welcoming at all.

"The fuck you will," Jono told him.

Lucien sneered at his protest, but Nadine headed off a fight with a steely eyed glare directed at the both of them. "We made sure the WSA had no names for our CIs and that we lost whatever tail they set on us after we left their headquarters."

"How did it go?" Sage asked.

Patrick popped open a box full of pot stickers and stabbed one the way he'd stab the enemy. "Not good."

"We've got orders to be out of the country by tomorrow evening," Nadine said.

"What about the Morrígan's staff?" Jono asked.

"CCTV captured Ilya Nazarov leaving London via St. Pancras International early this morning. The only luggage he had on him was a case long enough to hold the staff," Patrick said flatly.

"How did he make it through Customs?"

"Must've used magic to scramble the computers in the controlled areas, but CCTV got partials of his face on a couple of feeds after the fact. The system red flagged him too late for us to do anything about it. He took the Eurostar south. Our French counterparts checked the train at Calais, but he wasn't on board."

"Do you still think he's going to Paris?"

Patrick passed the box of pot stickers to Wade, who promptly dumped what was left on his plate that was already piled high with Chinese food. "It's the most likely scenario. The Orthodox Church of the Dead has a strong foothold in that city. Intelligence indicates that's where Ilya operates out of."

"Did you tell the WSA about where you think Ilya is going?" Sage asked.

"No. It's a fucking diplomatic mess right now, which is why Nadine and I were told to leave the country. I'll leave it to them to put two and two together."

"Do they expect you to go back to the United States?"

Nadine scooped up some sesame chicken and dumped it over her fried rice. "The WSA knows I work out of Paris. It won't seem out of the ordinary if Patrick comes with me. They don't have jurisdiction in France."

"What about Sage and Wade? Does the WSA know about them from CCTV?" Jono asked.

Nadine shook her head. "I made sure all security cameras were scrambled when we went in and out of Smithfield Market."

"Could've shown up elsewhere."

"Which is why we all need to get out of England." Patrick pointed his fork at Lucien. "Goes double for you."

"My bargain with your government was restricted to London. It said nothing about Paris," Lucien said flatly.

"You bargained to retrieve the staff for us, so you're going to Paris. Call up your private jet or whatever, but you're going."

"It'll cost you."

"We already paid you."

"I realize we have a staff problem and a necromancer problem, but we also have a demon problem. Let's not forget that," Spencer said as he half-heartedly tried to scrape what remained of the Sichuan chicken onto his plate. "If hunters and demons end up working with the Dominion Sect, we're all fucked."

Patrick grimaced. "We're already fucked."

"Andras." Jono stole the fried rice box out of Wade's hand, ignoring the teen's squawk of protest. "Who was that demon?"

"A Great Marquis of Hell." Spencer slumped against the kitchen island, still looking like he could've slept another twelve hours. "I hate trying to separate the upper echelons of demons from their hosts. Gives me such a fucking migraine."

Patrick paused with a forkful of rice halfway to his mouth. "The demon was that high up?"

"High enough for my head to feel like it wanted to fall off like the headless fae we fought."

"Does that mean we're going to have to deal with angels at some point?"

Spencer winced. "For the sake of my head and soul, let's hope not."

"Demons have a rigid hierarchy?" Jono asked.

Patrick finished the motion of getting the fork to his mouth, talking after he chewed. "They're part of some of the widest-spread religions. There's some truth in the stories and myths about demons, the same way there's truth about gods."

"Demons worked with Ethan during the Thirty-Day War. What makes you think he won't call on them again?" Lucien asked derisively.

Jono didn't like the bleakness that settled on Patrick's, Nadine's, and Spencer's faces.

Spencer rubbed at his eyes, his food momentarily forgotten. "The Dominion Sect called forth lesser demons during that war."

"Didn't think soultakers rated as lesser," Jono said.

"There were exceptions. But if Ethan strikes a bargain with Andras or another higher-ranked demon, it'll be bad."

"Worse than the Thirty-Day War?"

"Ethan summoned demons back then, he didn't bargain with them. He already has some alliances with different gods of hell. I'm guessing he hasn't touched their godheads because he needs their help against the gods of the heavens. If he makes a deal with demons from hell, what happened in Cairo will look like a weekend party." Spencer looked over at Patrick. "Am I right?"

Patrick nodded jerkily but didn't say a word.

"Throw in the Morrígan's staff and no one will be able to escape the hell Ethan wants to make of Earth," Nadine said morosely.

Jono swallowed hard. "So what now?"

"Rossiter was working with Cressida, but I don't think either were in contact with Ilya or the Dominion Sect. Rossiter wasn't favoring any particular buyer over the other until the staff came up for bid," Patrick said.

"Then all hell broke loose," Wade snickered.

Sage rolled her eyes. "You're not funny."

Wade stuck his tongue out at her before shoveling another forkful of chow mein into his mouth.

Patrick pinched his nose, and Jono wanted to reach across the kitchen island to pull his hand away. "We need to stop Ilya from using the staff or handing it off to the god he worships. I don't know if Ethan has a bargain with Peklabog, but it wouldn't surprise me if he does. If he doesn't, he's going to try to make one. Which is why we're *all* going to Paris."

"You don't even know where to start looking," Carmen said with a faint curl of her lip.

Patrick dropped his hand away from his face, rubbing at the red mark there on his palm. Jono frowned. He'd noticed it last night before Patrick had left with Nadine to deal with the fallout of the auction, but had thought Patrick would've got it healed at the WSA.

"Summer solstice is happening soon. I don't think it's a matter of looking so much as they won't be able to hide whatever they hope to do."

Jono grimaced. "We've shit luck with solstices and equinoxes."

"Guess we'll have to work on that."

"Don't take that as a challenge."

London had been a bloody mess. Jono had a sinking feeling Paris would be worse.

18

GETTING THROUGH CUSTOMS AT THE PARIS CHARLES DE GAULLE Airport on a Tuesday morning was a headache Patrick hoped not to repeat anytime soon. The scrutiny over his dagger took far longer than it had in London, and by the time his paperwork was cleared and his passport stamped, he'd been held up for almost an hour. At least when Patrick finally made it to the others at baggage claim, all their luggage had been retrieved.

Wade was eating his way through a box of Jaffa Cakes and looking like he needed to be fed again. Everyone else just looked tired.

"Are you still okay with us staying with you?" Patrick asked Nadine as he approached. "Or did you want us to find a hotel?"

"I don't like the idea of us being separated," Jono said, his eyes hidden behind dark sunglasses.

"It would be better if you stayed with me. I have room, and neither of our agencies will think much of you bunking at my home. Considering the potential property damage this case might have, it'll be one less bill to pay," Nadine said.

"I'm never the one who blows holes through buildings," Patrick grumbled.

"Your entire case history with the SOA says otherwise." Nadine grabbed the handle of her luggage and turned around. "Come on. Let's get a taxi. I don't feel like taking the train in, and the Ministry of Magical Affairs is expecting us in three hours."

"No rental car?" Wade asked as he pried free another Jaffa Cake. The smell of orange and chocolate made Patrick weirdly hungry.

"I've only the permit for my car. It's too much of a hassle otherwise to find parking where I live. You can take a taxi or the Metro to get around."

Nadine tactfully didn't mention why they'd have to travel around. Patrick wasn't looking forward to dealing with the Paris god pack, not after the state they'd left the London god pack in. Rumors spread quick through the werecreature community, and less than twenty-four hours was more than enough time for packs in position of power to know something was wrong with a foreign counterpart.

People talked. Always. Reputation mattered, and the London god pack's was in the gutter at this point, the same way Estelle and Youssef's was. Resentful people made things worse. At the heart of the problem was a selfishness demons had exploited in different ways. Sin was impossible to get rid of completely, which meant demons would have their pick of souls to choose from. Patrick only hoped no more werecreatures turned up with a demon riding their soul.

They followed the signs to the taxi stand outside. Patrick's French had never been the best, and he'd lost the knack for it over the years. Nadine was the one who gave the taxi attendant her address for the two taxis being waved forward. Jono and Wade handled all the luggage while the rest of them climbed into the vehicles. Jono slid in next to Patrick, buckling up as the driver pulled forward.

"Where does Nadine live?" Jono asked.

Patrick pulled at the seatbelt strap to settle it over his shoulder. "In the 8th arrondissement on the Right Bank. Her parents worked for the State Department, and she spent a lot of years in France. The apartment was theirs, but they deeded it to her before retiring to Nice."

He'd been her guest only a couple of times since his discharge from the Mage Corps. Their schedules rarely lined up, and getting time off was difficult when the difference between taking a case or walking away could mean someone's life.

The drive into central Paris was choked with morning traffic. Patrick was glad he wasn't ultimately responsible for the fare cost when they finally turned down the street Nadine lived on. No trees lined the densely packed buildings, and cars were parked on only one side of the street. The taxis pulled to a stop in front of a set of green double doors. They got out, dragging their luggage across the sidewalk to the building's entrance.

Nadine tapped in her passcode on the tiny security panel, buzzing them in. Her building thankfully had a small elevator, so even though it took them two trips with all the luggage, no one had to use the stairs.

"I have three rooms, but one is my office. Sage can sleep with me, the rest of you can sort yourselves out in the living room and guest room," Nadine said as she led the way inside a sunny fourth-floor apartment that was stuffy from being locked up for the last week or so.

The threshold wrapped around the home pulsed gently against Patrick's shields but welcomed them readily enough. The small credenza Nadine used for hospitality was empty of food and drink, but he knew she wouldn't ask it of them.

The furniture and décor hadn't changed much. The open-plan design meant the dining room and living room overlooked the street. Tall, wide windows opened out into tiny balconies that someone could stand on, but the view wasn't much to look at.

Nadine left her luggage by the couch to go unlock and open all the windows, letting a soft breeze waft through the home and clear out the musty air.

"Dibs on the guest bedroom," Wade said.

"No," Jono said. "You're sleeping out here."

"Dibs on the couch," Spencer said swiftly.

Wade scowled. "I want the couch!"

Spencer very pointedly went to sit on the couch, the look on his face practically daring Wade to evict him. Patrick could've told his friend that Wade was a thief, and that Spencer's claim on the couch wouldn't last long, but he thought the fight might be entertaining, so he kept quiet.

Patrick waved at Jono to follow him, knowing the way to the guest bedroom even though he hadn't been there in over a year and a half. It was small, but the bed was big enough for both of them. Patrick sat on it, sinking into its softness, and watched as Jono set about unpacking their things into the closet and dresser.

"Leave my suit out. I'll need to change before heading over to the ministry," Patrick said.

Jono nodded, leaving the garment bag on the bed for him instead of hanging it in the closet. Patrick would get dressed in thirty minutes. Right now, he wanted to rest. He wouldn't get much time for that in the coming days.

When Jono finished, he came over and extended his hand to Patrick. "Come on. Let's get back out there."

Patrick allowed himself to be pulled off the bed with easy strength, tipping into Jono's embrace. He took a moment to steal a kiss from Jono, enjoying being held close and safe. As pissed off as Patrick was about the near miss in London with the Morrígan's staff, Jono calmed him in ways he never wanted to let go.

"I hear Wade complaining about being hungry," Jono muttered against Patrick's mouth.

"There's a boulangerie a street over. I'll give him some euros and he can go eat his weight in bread," Patrick said.

"Careful, love. He might eat all the boulangeries out of baguettes, and the last time there was a bread shortage here, it started a revolution."

"A starving Wade is worse."

Jono chuckled, allowing himself to be pulled out of the room. Patrick didn't let go of his hand as they retreated back to the living room where everyone else was lounging. Sage had pulled out her MacBook and was currently catching up on email. Wade had two Jaffa Cake boxes in his lap and was methodically eating his way through them. Patrick wasn't looking forward to the day they got back to New York and Wade realized those weren't available in any store in Manhattan.

Spencer was sprawled on the couch still with Fatima in his lap. The ocelot-shaped psychopomp had her nose tucked into his neck and sounded like she was snoring. Which was weird. Patrick didn't think spirit guides needed to sleep.

Nadine had rustled up a tray of champagne glasses, a bottle of champagne, and a pitcher of orange juice. Patrick wasn't a fan of mimosas, but he wasn't about to say no to alcohol, not after the last couple of days. She cast a silence ward that muffled the noise of Paris beyond the open windows before putting together the drinks.

"Do you think the French will be willing to share intelligence on Ilya?" Spencer asked, scratching behind Fatima's ears.

"We have a meeting soon. We'll see what comes of it," Nadine said.

International relations weren't Patrick's strong suit, for obvious reasons. It was Nadine and Spencer's line of work more than his.

"Are you going to ask them about the Orthodox Church of the Dead?" Sage asked, eyes on her laptop.

"We're going to have to, even if they won't believe in Peklabog." Patrick drew Jono over to the love seat that no one else had claimed, getting comfortable in it. "We have a necromancer who is in possession of the Morrígan's staff and spends his time worshipping a god of the Slavic underworld. If they're going to use it, they'll use it here."

"Why?" Wade asked around a mouthful of Jaffa Cake.

"Paris has a lot of dead."

"You mean graveyards?"

Patrick nodded. "In a way."

Jono sighed heavily, reaching up to rub his face in a tired motion, jostling Patrick a little. "Oh, bloody hell. The Catacombs."

Spencer's hand stilled on Fatima's back as he turned his head to look at them, expression troubled. "A necromancer can animate bones, but you still need spirits to fill them. The new or recently dead would be easier to raise. There are, what? Six million dead in the Catacombs? Even a necromancer who is a mage can't raise that many."

"A god can," Patrick said. "So can the staff."

Spencer shook his head, looking defeated. "That's going to be a goddamn nightmare."

Patrick rubbed at the tender red line burned into his left palm. His muscles kept cramping, and it didn't feel like it was starting to heal, even with the potion Nadine had poured down his throat at the WSA before they were given their marching orders. He stopped only when Jono reached over to pull his hands apart.

"When did this happen?" Jono asked.

"Before the fight started at Smithfield Market." Patrick stretched out his fingers, frowning down at the angry-looking skin. "I met one of the Fates while we were walking around viewing the items up for sale."

Spencer straightened up on the couch, staring at him. "Is that where you went when I turned around and you weren't with us?"

"You couldn't have mentioned this *sooner*?" Nadine said exasperatedly before downing her entire mimosa.

"When? Srecha manipulated everyone around me during the auction, I couldn't exactly talk about her while we were there, and we've been stuck defending ourselves to the WSA. I couldn't risk anyone knowing," Patrick said, trying not to feel defensive about his choices. "And it's not something Lucien needs to know."

Jono wrapped an arm around his shoulders, tugging him closer. Patrick leaned into his warmth. "What did the Fates have to say this time?"

"Srecha talked about being remembered. Called this her blessing." Patrick lifted his hand so everyone could see the red mark there. "Your guess is as good as mine about what she really meant by that."

Nadine pursed her lips. "The gods have given you enough cryptic gifts, don't you think?"

"I'd give the fucking thing *back* if I could and it didn't mean chopping off my hand. My dagger and the Greek coins were enough."

"What about me?" Jono asked lightly, rubbing his hand up and down Patrick's arm.

"What about you?" Patrick turned his head to stare at Jono, raising an eyebrow. "You aren't going anywhere. I'll give you up over my dead body."

Spencer winced. "We're fighting a necromancer. Let's not tempt the gods."

"Too late," Wade said. "Patrick does that all the time."

"Eat your snacks," Patrick told him.

"I want French snacks. I saw little colored cookies with cream like an Oreo on the way out of the airport. I want some of those."

Jono snorted. "I'll take your stomach for a walk in a bit. Let's get Pat and Nadine out the door first."

Patrick groaned, not really wanting to move. "I hate suits."

Nadine pushed herself to her feet, running her fingers through her hair. "We do need to get going. I'll leave the silence ward up. Jono, let me give you my spare set of keys."

Patrick left Jono's side even though he really didn't want to. He managed to get to his feet, but that was as far as he went. Jono grabbed his wrist, keeping him in one spot. Patrick turned to look at him.

"Be safe," Jono said, bringing Patrick's hand to his lips to kiss his own sort of blessing over the one already burned into his skin. "I love you."

Patrick framed Jono's face with his fingers. "I'll come back."

He could feel Jono's smile against his palm, those wolf-bright eyes looking up at him. "I know."

It was a promise Patrick intended to always keep, no matter what.

He left the living room for the guest bedroom, getting dressed in his suit in record time. Patrick was in the middle of looping his tie around his neck when Jono entered the bedroom, letting the door click shut quietly behind him.

"Going to feed Wade?" Patrick asked.

Jono reached for the tie, sliding it out of Patrick's hand. He turned so Jono had room to work with, enjoying the feel of Jono's hands brushing against his body.

"We'll feed him. Sage is communicating with the Paris god pack's dire. We'll have to meet with them, and Sage thinks they'll want to meet today," Jono said, eyes on the silk he was deftly knotting around Patrick's throat.

Patrick bit his lip as Jono straightened his collar. "I should be there for that meeting."

Jono's gaze flickered up to meet his. "You need to focus on the government side of the mission."

"Our pack is more important than my job."

Jono blinked at him, but Patrick wasn't about to take those words back. Warm fingers slid up his throat to stroke over his jaw, cupping his chin. Jono drew him into a kiss that made Patrick dream about getting undressed and messing up the bedsheets.

"You staying safe is important, and your job helps with that," Jono murmured against his mouth. "So don't get fired."

"I'd get a vacation if that happened."

Jono laughed, pulling back but not going far. "We'll make it to Maui one day, love."

"Promise?"

Jono tugged on his tie, voice rumbling in his chest when he spoke. "Promise."

Patrick stole another quick kiss before extricating himself from Jono's arms. They left the bedroom, and he wasn't surprised to see Nadine waiting for him in the living room, dressed in a pristine white pantsuit and scarlet high heels that matched her lipstick. She looked like she could've been walking a runway rather than preparing to do battle with a foreign intelligence and magic agency.

"Ready?" Nadine asked as she tossed Jono a set of keys that he easily caught.

Patrick nodded and followed her out of the apartment. Sound popped back into his ears once they crossed through the silence ward. They left the building, and Nadine led him a block over to where she paid a monthly fee, covered by the PIA, to park her car. It was a black two-door Audi that had scratches over one rear wheel from claws rather than keys. Patrick didn't ask what had caused it. They got in, and Nadine started the engine, pulling out of the tiny space.

"How long do you think this emergency meeting will go?" Patrick asked as they got on the road.

The French Ministry of Magical Affairs was located at the Quai d'Orsay. Luckily, the drive wouldn't take too long since it was near the Seine. While it wasn't within the same arrondissement as Nadine's apartment, it was still close as opposed to being clear across the city.

"However long it needs to take." Nadine shifted gears as they came up on a red light, sunglasses perched on her nose. "We should probably report in."

Patrick sighed as he smacked his hand against the roof of the car, setting a silence ward into place before pulling out his phone. "All right."

The time difference between Paris and Washington, DC, meant he wasn't waking Setsuna up, but she still sounded pissed off when she answered the phone.

"We're in contact with INTERPOL," Setsuna said in lieu of a greeting. "They'll be present at the meeting you're scheduled to attend."

"Any hits on Nazarov?" Patrick asked.

"Not since London."

Patrick leaned his head back against the seat. "He'll be coming to Paris if he's not here already."

"How certain are you?"

"If Nazarov has been worshipping out of Paris, then his god is here."

"The French government will need something more concrete than a myth."

"That's all I have."

It should've been enough, but the old myths weren't the predominant religions these days. Science and magic and religion might coexist, but believing in the old gods was a step too far for most people. The ones who worshipped the gods whose lives had fallen by the wayside were few and far between compared to the billions who worshipped in churches and mosques and temples across the world.

Patrick curled his fingers around the mark on his palm, Srecha's blessing burning deep as he thought about Ashanti and the altar he hadn't prayed before in over a week.

"The auction was where this should have ended, Patrick," Setsuna said.

"The auction was a means to an end. This whole fucking mess won't stop until Ethan is dead, or I am. You know that," he bit out.

Setsuna's breathing was sharp and staticky across the line. "We don't win this fight if you're dead."

"I'm well aware of that."

"Then find the staff. Director Franklin has sent senior agents to meet you and Mulroney at the ministry. They've been informed of the auction, but not what artifact we were after. They'll take lead on the negotiations with France."

Patrick's jaw twitched. "Understood."

There wasn't much more they needed to discuss, so he wasn't surprised when Setsuna ended the call. Patrick put his phone away, glaring out the windshield.

"If you'd gone after the staff, you would've left Spencer vulnerable," Nadine said quietly. "I'm glad you didn't."

Patrick drew in a sharp breath and let it out slow. "Me too."

The gods could demand the impossible of him because they owned his soul, but that didn't mean he'd drag his friends down with him. The Morrígan's staff was still missing, but Spencer was alive and safe.

Patrick would never regret that.

THE METRO TRAIN ROLLED INTO ANVERS STATION, FACES FLASHING by on the platform. Jono stood, gesturing for Sage and Wade to follow him to the nearest exit. A few people were already positioned in front of the door, darting out the moment they opened.

They stepped out between the barricades on either side of the door on the platform, sliding past commuters waiting to board. Jono spotted the blue-and-white *Sortie* sign over everyone's head and veered in that direction. Sage and Wade stuck close until they reached the surface, where they came up on an island between the streets.

The buildings that surrounded them were much like the ones they'd left behind in Nadine's neighborhood. Densely packed apartment buildings lined the street, with shops taking up space at the ground level.

They'd left Nadine's because Sage had worked out a meeting with the Paris god pack's dire, and it was happening today after all. Jono had texted Patrick an update, but he hadn't gotten a response yet.

Sage stared at her mobile, moving her thumb to shift the map on the screen. "We cross here and take that street over there up the hill. We have twenty minutes until we meet Gaspard and Mireille. Most likely they're already there."

Jono nodded. "Let's go."

They could easily make it up to the meeting point at Square Louise-Michel near Sacré-Cœur in that time frame, except Wade got distracted first by a boulangerie, then a crêperie, and finally a gelato shop.

"Wade," Jono said through gritted teeth as the teenager hiked his bag of croissants higher in his arm and tried to fit as big of a bite of his Nutella crêpe as he could into his mouth.

"Let me finish this so I can get gelato," Wade managed to somehow get out around the food making his cheeks bulge.

Sage opened up her sleek Chanel wallet purse, pulled out a twenty-euro bill, and tucked it into Wade's front pocket. "Meet us at the top. Don't dawdle."

Wade beamed at her from beneath the red felt beret he'd convinced Jono to buy him at a little souvenir shop near the Metro stop at the bottom of the hill. "You're the best."

"We should stay together," Jono said.

Sage hooked her hand around his elbow and pulled with a preternatural strength that forced Jono to move his feet. "He'll be fine. Besides, we may need backup. At the very least, a warning."

She was probably right.

"When you come find us, be obnoxious about it," Jono called over his shoulder. The order wouldn't make sense to anyone around them, but Wade nodded his understanding, lips smeared with Nutella.

They left Wade to feed himself, joining the summer crowd of people that filled the street and the park up ahead. Jono's nostrils flared at the scent of so many people packed in together but he didn't dial down his senses. He caught the scent of more than a few werecreatures in the crowd and tried not to bare his teeth. Jono didn't appreciate being surrounded, but he didn't think the Paris god pack would be one to start a fight in a public space, especially in their city.

Rather than choose a restaurant or a home, Rami, the Paris god pack's dire, had instructed them to meet at the park. The open space provided very few, if any, spots to get cornered in, and the number of mundane humans would make most people think twice about initiating a fight. That was never a guarantee though, so Jono kept his guard up.

Montmartre was both a hill and a neighborhood, and its crown jewel was the basilica that sat atop it. Sacré-Cœur's white façade stood out against the blue sky as they took the steps that bisected the park up to the top. Its turreted roofs were atypical of most churches in the city, but the panoramic views of Paris its court-yards provided were unparalleled.

"Up there," Sage said, pointing at the next terrace level.

Amidst the tourists milling around on their climb up to Sacré-Cœur and the best view in Paris, a cluster of men and women had taken over a bench. A gentle breeze brought their pack scent to Jono a second later, thick and heady, but without the underlying fear and unease that had permeated the London god pack.

The werecreatures in the crowd who followed their climb up the steps kept their distance. That didn't stop Jono's skin from prickling with all the eyes on them as he and Sage approached the Paris god pack. While he could understand their precaution, Jono didn't like being surrounded.

Jono and Sage stood shoulder to shoulder on their approach to the group on the bench. The midafternoon sun beat down on them, providing a clear panoramic view of Paris stretched out around them. Only a few puffy white clouds floated across the sky, making for an idyllic backdrop to heavy negotiations.

"*Bonjour*, Jonothon," Gaspard Renaud said where he lounged on the bench, one arm draped over a lovely brunette woman, who flashed sharp teeth at them.

"Hello, Gaspard," Jono replied, eyeing the blond Frenchman and his companion. "Mireille. I appreciate the courtesy."

"I would expect the alpha of the New York City god pack to sound American. You don't," Mireille Chastain said. Tall and slim, stylishly dressed, she was quintessentially Parisian and would have been welcomed anywhere if her eyes weren't the same shade as Jono's behind her Dior sunglasses.

"Ex-pat. New York City is my home now, and has been for years."

Mireille puffed on her cigarette and blew smoke out her nose. "Interesting. You smell like truth, but you'll forgive us if we don't quite believe you. The London god pack has been, how do you say, *troublesome* lately. We would not put it past them to send you here with lies on your tongue."

She spoke quietly, but Jono could hear her just fine. The rest of her pack were enforcing distance between their alphas and the tourists to keep the conversation as private as possible in such open space.

"If you're talking about Cressida, she's dead," Jono said.

Mireille's hand stilled, cigarette hovering in front of her lips. Gaspard's hand tightened ever so slightly on her shoulder, staring at them through his sunglasses.

"She was a hunter with a demon riding her soul, sent to infiltrate the London god pack and damage it from the inside out. Finley executed her," Sage said calmly before anyone could lunge at them. "Call him if you doubt us."

"Rami," Gaspard said, the order in his dire's name and nothing else.

A lean man of Middle Eastern descent slipped away from the bench, already tapping away at his mobile. Jono didn't bother listening in on whatever conversation the man would have.

"Why should we believe you had nothing to do with such a terrible breach in protocol?" Mireille said.

"Because we have our own territory back in New York. We

didn't want Finley's, and we don't want yours. We're only here to ask for pass-through rights, nothing more," Jono said.

"I find it odd you're the only one of your pack who is present." Mireille eyed Sage contemplatively. "My dire said yours was a woman, but humans aren't pack."

"I'm human enough," Sage demurred, not removing her necklace.

"I trust Sage with my pack and my life. She's my dire, so treat her as such," Jono said.

Gaspard smiled thinly. "I always knew America did things backward."

Jono said nothing to that, content to wait out the silence that settled over everyone. Rami came back a couple of minutes later, face expressionless as he leaned over the bench to whisper his report in rapid French to Gaspard and Mireille. Jono didn't understand it, but the way the alphas went absolutely still had him tensing, readying for a fight.

Before anyone could make a move, Gaspard and Mireille's heads snapped to the side, along with everyone else's in their pack. Jono followed their stares, squinting against the sun. He didn't see anything out of the ordinary. Then the breeze shifted and he was suddenly bowled over with the acrid, fiery scent of a dragon.

A figure darted through the crowd below, taking the steps up to them two at a time and racing down the path. Wade must have eaten the gelato and the crêpe, but he was still working his way through the bag of croissants and bread judging by the half-eaten croissant in his hand when he came running up. The red felt beret sat askew on his head, but he hadn't lost it yet.

"Jono! These are *so good*. Why don't they taste like this in New York?" Wade asked as he approached, flaky crumbs standing out on his shirt.

While Jono couldn't see Wade's aura, his scent was unique and triggered Jono's instincts the way few things did these days, even with Fenrir howling through his soul. Dragons were the sort of apex predators that made werecreatures want to turn tail and run. The werecreatures around them might not know what Wade was, but the Paris god pack knew he was a *threat*.

Except Jono had walked in on Wade sprawled out on their sofa at home too many times to count, covered in crumbs and snack wrappers as he heckled at sports on the television or played video games. He and Patrick had argued with the teen over school, homework, and remembering to stay safe. Wade was ridiculous and loud and *pack*, and Jono would never be scared of the fledgling.

"Because the French do croissants better. You're a mess, Wade. Finish that one, then save the rest for later," Jono said.

Wade stuffed the rest of the croissant into his mouth, chewing rapidly as he stared down the Paris god pack. "Hi. I'm with them."

Mireille's voice came out slightly strangled. "What is he?"

Jono smirked. "Pack."

Gaspard never took his eyes off Wade, recognizing the biggest threat in the park despite Wade's teenage form. "Rami tells me his London contact corroborates your news. Cressida is dead."

"Does this guy think I ate her?" Wade asked. He made a disgusted noise before pointedly pulling out a *pain au chocolat* from his bag and ripping off the corner with sharp teeth. "I didn't eat her."

Mireille dropped her cigarette to the ground and ran the sole of her strappy sandal over it to crush it out. "This is not a conversation we should have here."

Jono could've told them that when they requested the initial meeting, but it wasn't his place to tell another god pack how to go about their business. "We just want pass-through rights."

"And while we don't believe the London god pack sent you, I'm thirsty and would like a drink."

It wasn't a yes, but it wasn't a no to his request. The nonanswer was frustrating, but it was what Jono had expected after the two checked in with London.

Gaspard got to his feet and helped Mireille to hers. "You and your pack will have dinner with us tonight at our home near la pelouse de Reuilly."

"There's four of us. My co-leader had other business to attend to today."

"Come by our home in five hours. You will abide by hospitality."

Jono nodded. "We'll be there."

Gaspard rattled off an address that Sage tapped into a file on her phone for later. Jono let the Paris god pack leave first. The second they vacated the bench, Wade threw himself onto it and stuck his face into the bag, humming to himself as he picked out his next snack. The prickly presence he exuded abruptly diminished, his scent returning to that of a normal human's as he dragged all that he was back behind the shields Reed had taught him to build.

"That went better than I thought. They didn't outright deny us entry," Sage said once the Paris god pack was out of earshot.

Jono sighed. "They still might."

"There doesn't seem to be any love lost between them and the London god pack. Makes me wonder what international pack relations have been like since Cressida joined them."

"Bloody awful would be my guess."

Wade lifted his head and stuck his arm in the bag, coming up with an almond croissant. "Can we eat dinner before their dinner?"

Jono eyed him. "You want two dinners?"

"They're eating late. I can't wait that long."

"You just ate two crêpes, who knows how much gelato, and that entire bag was full before you made it up the hill." Jono shook his head. "Must be growing pains."

"No, I think it's his normal appetite," Sage mused.

Jono sat beside Wade and pulled out his mobile to text Patrick the update. They had time to rest there for a bit and let Wade finish his food before they headed back to Nadine's.

The sound of wings flapping through the air and the distinctive *caw* of ravens and crows made Jono look up at the sky. Overhead, dozens and dozens of the corvids momentarily blocked out the sun as they flew over Sacré-Cœur and the park, their cries ringing in Jono's ears. People looked up at the sky and pointed at their passage, the birds dark spots against an endless blue.

Jono watched them fly, unease washing through him.

"YOU'VE GOT another pack who wants protection," Emma said into his ear.

Jono hummed thoughtfully as the taxi drove through the 12th arrondissement to their destination. "Which one?"

"The Davenport pack."

Jono's eyebrows crept upward. "Really?"

"Their alpha seemed annoyed you were out of town, but she's willing to wait for you to return and pass judgment on her."

"I doubt I'll find her lacking."

Some of the packs who came to them asking for protection were denied such support because their underlying loyalties remained with Estelle and Youssef, despite their claimed change of heart. Fenrir was one hell of a lie detector, and Jono never questioned his patron's final decisions.

If Fenrir accepted the Davenport's request, then that would effectively cede half of Brooklyn to them. The Davenport pack was *big*, not a huge supporter of Estelle and Youssef, and had always been on good terms with the Tempest pack. Their alpha was married to a federal judge and was herself a partner in a venture capitalist firm. She'd leaned hard into her local ties to make it difficult for Estelle and Youssef to retaliate against her pack, but those connections only went so far.

"That's what I told her," Emma said cheerfully enough.

"How are things otherwise?"

"The Queens Night Court unearthed a small group of hunters hiding out in a motel. They dumped the remains in front of the PCB."

Jono winced. "I don't think Casale would've liked that."

"He didn't, judging by the news conference. None of the packs have been attacked yet, but I ordered everyone to stick close to their territories until you're back."

"Good idea."

"When *are* you coming back?"

Jono glanced over at where Patrick sat between him and Wade in the taxi's back seat. "I don't know."

"Did you find what you were looking for?"

"No. We're in Paris now."

"I won't ask what you're doing there. Just stay safe."

"We'll try."

Jono ended the call after a couple more minutes of bland conversation. Patrick glanced at him when he put the mobile away, looking tired.

"How are things back home?" Patrick asked.

"Fine."

Patrick nodded, taking him at his word.

No one spoke for the rest of the drive to the Paris god pack's home territory, though the taxi driver's stench of fear and pounding heartbeat made Jono roll down the window. The man sped away so fast after dropping them off in front of the building the taxi's tires squealed.

Jono removed his sunglasses and let Sage pack them away in her purse. He no longer needed to hide his eyes since they were eating here and not going out. The Paris god pack's home consisted of an entire ring of connected buildings on a single block that formed multiple apartments. The property was right across the street from Bois de Vincennes, and their pack scent saturated the area.

"That park would be nice to stretch our legs for a run if we were here under better circumstances," Sage said as they headed for the front door.

"Yeah," Jono agreed.

The door opened before they reached it, Rami standing in their way. He eyed them distrustfully and said something in French Jono couldn't understand, but the annoyed wave for them to come inside was easy enough to parse.

They stepped inside a small foyer, crossing the threshold. Rami gestured at the credenza set beneath a large oval mirror hanging on the wall. A bottle of red wine, four glasses, and half a baguette were lined up neatly on the wooden top there.

"Be welcome," Rami said in heavily accented English as he tore off pieces of the bread and passed them out.

They ate the bread, drank the mouthful of wine, and the uneasiness Jono had felt upon entering faded away once hospitality was given and accepted. Beside him, Patrick winced.

"Pat?" Jono asked, immediately on guard.

Patrick shook his head and rolled his shoulders. "Nothing. It's fine. Just some prickly magic."

Jono took him at his word, mindful of Rami's narrow-eyed contemplation. Then he gestured for them to follow him.

Like the property Estelle and Youssef claimed as their territory and the one in Farningham, the multitude of connected buildings here had history pressed into their walls. Thankfully, they wouldn't have to spend however long surrounded by the scent. Rami cut through the level they were on, leading them to a pair of french glass doors in the rear of the building that opened into an inner courtyard.

The lushness of trees and blooming flowers overrode the pack scent, clearing Jono's lungs. The warm night air was like a soft blanket around them as they approached a long table set with plates, food dishes, and a dozen bottles of wine. All but five seats were taken, and those were located near the head of the table where Mireille and Gaspard sat. Rami claimed the empty seat to Gaspard's right. Jono and Patrick took the seats by Rami while Sage and Wade sat beside Mireille.

It was a better second meeting than the one they'd had with the London god pack by far, but Jono still didn't trust it would go easy.

"*Bonsoir.*" Mireille raised her wineglass at them, the smile on her face one of cool welcome. "You've left London quite a mess."

"Wasn't our mess to begin with." Jono gestured at his pack. "You met Sage and Wade at Sacré-Cœur. I'd like to introduce you to Patrick, our co-leader."

"Hey," Patrick said, gaze sweeping the table. He was still in the suit he'd worn to his meeting, dagger secured to his belt at his lower back.

Gaspard blinked lazily at them. "America certainly does things backward by allowing magic users into packs."

Jono shouldn't have been surprised they'd done their due diligence, though he wondered who in the London god pack had told them. "We'll abide by hospitality."

"Good." Mireille's gaze slid toward Wade before returning to him. "We have decided you may have pass-through rights to our city, but keep out of our politics."

"Might be a little hard to do," Patrick said evenly. "I understand your preternatural community here has a missing-person problem. And by person, I mean a lot."

The news had been surprising for all of a moment to Jono when Patrick and Nadine had returned from their long meeting with their French counterparts earlier in the evening. But then, considering the sacrifices Ethan always needed to power his spells, it seemed likely Ilya would need the same. Murder was overlooked in certain communities more than others.

Authorities didn't care as much for those with a preternatural bent as they did mundane humans, and that held true no matter the country. Jono had lived it in two where he experienced that sort of discrimination, and now it seemed he could add France to the mix. Distrust between government authority and communities built by those who weren't always welcomed in society rarely faded away.

Jono met Mireille's gaze over her wineglass and stayed sat. "We're in Paris hunting a necromancer. Perhaps you've heard of him. Bloke calls himself the Patriarch of Souls to the Orthodox Church of the Dead."

The pack scent drifting on the night air became sharp with bitter fear. Jono took a sip of wine to clear the taste of it from the back of his throat.

"Since when do wolves hunt necromancers?" Gaspard asked.

"I'm not a wolf," Sage said as she delicately cut into the steak she'd served herself. She didn't state *what* she was and let their curiosity live a little longer.

"It's my job," Patrick said simply. "To take cases like these."

Gaspard snorted. "You are not French. This is not your concern."

"I'm still pack, and it's a threat to mine. So." Patrick reached for the platter of steaks and speared one with his fork, bringing it to his plate. "The French Ministry of Magical Affairs has their own reports, but they won't contain everything. You're the alphas of the Paris god pack. Whatever rumors are running through this city about a threat like that, I'm betting you know some of the underlying truth."

"We aren't here for your territory. All we're asking for is a bit of help," Jono said.

Silence settled over the dinner party for a long few minutes. Jono focused on eating, taking his time like everyone else because the French never rushed when it came to food. Only Wade was eating as if he didn't know when his next meal would be, but Jono didn't tell him to slow down.

"People have gone missing from the packs under our protection. We have not been able to track the one doing the murdering,"

Gaspard finally said when the meat was half-gone on all the platters and the roasted potatoes had disappeared into Wade's stomach.

"So you've found bodies?" Patrick asked.

"No." Gaspard's mouth twisted. "But we know that when our kind goes missing like this, in such numbers, we will not get them back."

"What about your city's graveyards? The Catacombs? Any disturbances there?"

Mireille shattered her wineglass with her grip. She stared at the wine spreading over the wooden tabletop and the glass shards clinging to her wet fingers. "*Merde.*"

Gaspard plucked the cloth napkin off his lap and used it to wipe her hand clean. When he finished, he pressed his lips to her palm for a lingering kiss. Mireille graced him with a smile that spoke of fondness without the cruelty Jono always saw in Estelle.

Mireille looked across the table at them, wolf-bright eyes practically glowing in the low light. "The Catacombs have been closed since winter. The government will not confirm it, but there is *something* that lives within the Mines of Paris. Even the cataphiles will no longer venture below. We've banned all packs from going near the known entrances."

Jono shared a *look* with Patrick, having a whole, silent conversation with his lover in the span of seconds.

Patrick put down his knife. "We need to get into the Catacombs."

20

"THEY SAID MEET HER HERE AT 1700," PATRICK SAID, SQUINTING down the street. It was still light out, sunset hours away at this time of the year. "She's late."

"By two minutes. Give it a little longer," Jono said.

Patrick scowled, wanting to be on the move already. They'd been in Paris two days, summer solstice was tomorrow, and they still had no new leads. Getting the French Ministry of Magical Affairs to take the situation seriously when the United States couldn't mention the Morrígan's staff had resulted in a log jam of bureaucracy that had resulted in not much getting done outside meetings.

Nadine and Patrick had been relegated to the sidelines in those meetings. The senior agents Director Franklin had assigned to the case were the ones handling communications with their French counterparts. The French government knew Ilya was a problem and a threat, but they didn't think he was in Paris. No one knew where the necromancer was, and that meant manpower to take him into custody was grounded until solid intelligence came through on a location.

By then, Patrick knew it would be too late.

Which was why he and his pack were standing on a corner outside a smoke shop in the hazy border between the 13th and 14th arrondissements, waiting for their contact to arrive.

During dinner last night, Gaspard and Mireille had promised to send them someone who could get them underground. The Paris god pack had refused to help beyond that, putting the safety of their packs over everything else. Patrick had thought that was shortsighted seeing as how the entire city was in danger, but he knew better than to argue.

When they'd received the call that morning for an early evening meeting, Patrick had wanted to argue for *sooner*. Time was running out like grains of sand in an hourglass, but their contact had been adamant about when and where she would meet them, and they'd been forced to agree to it. Considering the access they were after was illegal, Patrick could understand why their guide would want to meet at a later hour than midday, but it wasn't easy to wait when he knew a threat was coming.

Patrick had spent most of Wednesday in one long meeting after another, understanding only some of what was said and relying on Nadine to act as his translator. When they'd finally left, no closer to convincing the Ministry of Magical Affairs to act now with little evidence, he and Nadine had split their duties for the mission.

Lucien had grudgingly followed them to Paris, his promise to Ashanti about keeping Patrick alive the only reason he'd gone. Nadine and Spencer were meeting with Lucien tonight after sunset at his Paris home to see if the master vampire could get any information out of the Night Courts in Paris. They all had a long night ahead, and the tightness in Patrick's shoulders wasn't close to easing.

A slim woman crossed the street on the next red light, heading in their direction. She was dressed all in black, wore sturdy work boots, and carried a backpack. Her light brown hair was tied back in a sleek ponytail, and her makeup was minimal. The only accessory she wore was a pendant hanging around her throat carved from moonstone in the shape of a snake twisted into the infinity symbol.

"Jonothon?" she asked cautiously in a thick French accent. "Patrick?"

"That's us," Patrick said.

She beamed at them, looking impossibly young. "*Bonsoir*. I am Lisette. I was told by the *loup-garou* you needed access to the network?"

Patrick cupped his hand against his thigh, conjuring up a tiny mageglobe. He filled it with a silence ward, creating a bubble of quiet around them on the street. Lisette startled at the sudden absence of sound, hands rising to her ears.

"It's a silence ward," Patrick said.

"Ah. Good. We can speak freely then, *oui?*" At Patrick's nod, her expression lost some of its cheerfulness. "The network is not safe. Were you not warned?"

"We understand it's not safe, but we still need to go down there," Jono said.

Lisette bit her bottom lip. "I can only take one of you."

"We all go," Sage said.

Lisette shook her head. "You are new to the network, and I can't promise you safety. One, only. That is what I told the *loup-garou*."

"Whatever lives in the Catacombs right now is a threat no matter how many people you bring down there," Patrick said.

"I know the way. You do not." Lisette made an agitated cutting motion with her hand. "One person, or we do not go."

Patrick sighed and looked at Jono. "I'll go."

Jono blew out a breath. "You don't know what's down there."

"Exactly. Which means I'm the one most capable of dealing with it. Space will be tight in the mines. Shifting might not be an option."

Zombies or drekavacs or Peklabog himself—no matter the

monster or god, Patrick's magic and dagger were far more versatile to handle such a threat. His pack could only shift, and that had the threatening possibility of producing a cave-in, bringing city blocks down around their ears. Patrick could shield, but he couldn't shield against something like that and hold it for hours on end. He wasn't Nadine.

Jono stared at him, jaw working, eyes hidden behind his sunglasses despite the late hour. The sun was low in the sky, but not low enough for the sky to go dark in the east. This close to summer solstice and Patrick knew the sky would take its sweet time to show the stars.

Patrick stepped closer, putting his hand over Jono's heart. His skin, burned from Srecha's blessing, scraped against the soft fabric. He looked up at Jono, searching his face. "I'm going below. I need you to stay up here. I need you to follow me. You know how."

Like he had last summer when Patrick had traded himself for a werecreature's life, a plaything between gods before a trickster dragged him through the veil, high on shine and one breath away from death's touch. Jono had found him when Patrick couldn't even find his thoughts at the time.

Patrick trusted Jono to find him through anything except the veil. That was a barrier that made it almost impossible to track each other, but Patrick wouldn't be going through the veil below.

He hoped.

Jono reached up and flattened his hand over Patrick's. "I don't like it."

Patrick shrugged, saying nothing to that. Jono's dislike wasn't going to stop him from doing his job—it couldn't. Too much was at stake for them to wait and do nothing. They'd chased the Morrígan's staff across two continents already. They needed to find it, and soon, before Ethan bargained with Ilya or murdered the necromancer outright to get his hands on it.

He didn't want to think what would happen to Hannah and her unborn child if that came to pass.

"I still need to go." Patrick rose up to brush his lips over Jono's. "I'll come back."

He still couldn't bring himself to say what he felt in his heart—not yet—not with Ethan still out there. Patrick had learned hard lessons young about losing those you cared about, and the scars on his chest couldn't match the ones in his memories. The only way this familial dispute and war of beliefs would end was with one of them dead.

Patrick wanted to spare Jono what pain he could in the face of an uncertain future.

He stepped back and turned to face Lisette. "I'll go."

Lisette nodded. "Follow me."

Jono, Sage, and Wade stayed close as Lisette led them down unfamiliar streets. It wasn't long until they were forced to separate as Patrick followed Lisette through a rusted door in a wall with the words *Interdit d'entrer* painted over it.

Patrick looked over his shoulder only once, seeing his pack watching worriedly before the door swung shut between them.

Lisette led him through the narrow space between buildings, through a hole in a fence, until they reached a railway line. Patrick's boots crunched over gravel between the tracks as they walked toward the brick archway of a tunnel hunkered between towering apartment blocks.

Patrick could sense the protective wards that ran the length of the Metro and rail lines before they reached the entrance, pooling in that opening. Layers of old magic saturated the area, twisted and anchored to the tracks themselves before stretching into the tunnel walls.

They paused there, long enough for Lisette to pull two sets of chest-high green waders out of her backpack, along with a head-lamp. She passed a set of waders to Patrick, who yanked them on over his boots and jeans, shrugging his arms through the shoulder straps. He hitched the belt tighter so they would fit better, wrinkling his nose at the musty smell of old water and mold coming from them. Lisette did the same, donning the headlamp.

"This way," she said, gesturing for him to follow.

Magic glimmered at the edge of Patrick's vision as they walked into shadows so deep even light from the emergency bulbs could barely penetrate it. Since Lisette didn't turn on her headlamp yet or ask Patrick to light the way, he swallowed his offer of casting some witchlights to see by.

"What do you think is causing people to go missing down here?" Patrick asked quietly as they walked.

"Paris below has always been a different world. What the government believes is the problem could be anything. During World War Two, the Nazis tried to break the Resistance with ghouls and hellhounds. We fought back with magic and ghosts. Some say none of either side ever left the quarries."

"You cataphiles aren't the only ones who come down here. Have you run into any other groups?"

Lisette made a vaguely annoyed sound. "Only cataflics, as always. They use magic and concrete to seal the entrances, but Paris belongs to all its citizens, aboveground and below."

Patrick frowned, thinking of Ilya and the Orthodox Church of the Dead who called Paris home after being forced from Odessa and the catacombs there. "No one else?"

"There are only bones down here, *mon ami*. All they do is sleep."

He very much doubted that.

They walked, the tracks staying level until they started to rise on a slow incline. That's when Lisette turned on her headlamp, the shine of it making Patrick flinch at the brightness. She drifted to one side of the tunnel, pointing at a hole in the ground with three layers of concentric circles dug around it and filled in with colorful pebbles.

"We'll go through here," Lisette said.

Patrick eyed the hole warily, sensing how the subway's protective wards warped around the way underground. The wards weren't broken but had been forcibly shunted aside to allow the hole to exist. That made the wards less stable over time and capable of breaking when people could least afford it, allowing for creatures at the edge of the preternatural world to slip through.

"Take the lead for now, and I'll tell you what direction we'll need to take once we're underground," Patrick said.

"How will you know?"

Patrick shrugged, not wanting to get into the specifics about his damaged magic. "Trust me. I'll know."

Lisette dropped down into darkness feet first, and Patrick could only follow. The landing jarred his knees, and he winced. He couldn't see beyond where Lisette's headlamp pointed, and he needed more light than that. Patrick pushed magic out of his soul, flicking witchlights off his fingertips to light the dark around him.

The limestone walls on either side of the tunnel they found themselves in were filled with graffiti—words and pictures and tags he couldn't decipher. Sigils of spells and wards were spray-painted on the walls near the ceiling, but their magic had long since faded away. He knew their shapes though, and what they had been set down for—protection against all manner of things.

Lisette wasted no time in pitching herself down the tunnels, and since she was heading in the direction where the hellish taint was stronger, he let her go. Patrick stayed close on her heels, the route down twisting tunnels dry for a long while until it wasn't. The dirt beneath his feet eventually turned to mud, then to water, and Patrick was glad for the waders she'd shoved into his hands aboveground.

The water got deeper and deeper until it hit his chest. The cold seeped through the waders and his clothes, making him shiver. The only thing that kept him warm was the soulbond, the tie to Jono a comforting link between them. Patrick could vaguely feel where Jono was above, but not knowing the Paris streets, he couldn't begin to figure out their location on a map.

They kept walking until the water receded, but the smell stuck in Patrick's nose. He kept his shields up, leaning into his magic and the damage in his soul that let him track the demons and monsters that called the shadows home.

The taint of hell was thick around them, making Patrick grind his teeth. They passed junctions that split off into dark tunnels his magic had no interest in following. Lisette sometimes looked over her shoulder at him for clarification, and he'd motion which way they needed to go. The saturation of black magic and hellish taint was strongest in a particular direction, and when Lisette would've turned right at one junction sometime later, Patrick tapped her on the shoulder and pointed left.

"Can we go that way?" he asked.

Lisette frowned, her headlamp casting strange shadows on her face. She swung her waterproof backpack around and opened it up, pulling out a thick stack of folded-up, plastic-lined paper. She swiftly flipped her way through it, finally stopping on a square filled with silvery-gray lines that were washed out by her headlamp. Beneath them were lines of various colors depicting areas and notes in French that Patrick couldn't read.

"We are here, *oui?*" Lisette tapped a faded junction with a fingertip before following the line leftward. "We can go this way, but it is tight."

Patrick studied the section of the map depicting the underground network, tracing a route that shot off in the direction his magic was tugging him toward. The problem was he didn't know what he was looking for.

If Ilya was using the Catacombs as a place for his people to pray to their god, then he'd need room for his sermons and their moments of worship; space for an altar and all that entailed. He tried not to think of Santa Muerte and her altar draped in marigold beneath New York City. The similarities drawn out of need were difficult to ignore though.

Patrick tapped at a large square that seemed a viable spot and hopefully still where his magic was taking him. He wouldn't know until they got farther into the tunnels. The hellish taint was everywhere, and even the water in the extra bottle Lisette had brought for him wasn't enough to wash the foul taste away.

"What's this?"

Lisette looked at where he pointed and hummed softly. "The Salle du Drapeau. It is a large chamber, one where parties are sometimes held."

"Can you get us there?"

Lisette folded up the map. "*Oui*. It is a long way though. No easy exits."

She sounded a little uncertain, and a little scared. So far they hadn't come across anything out of the ordinary, or anyone else for that matter. Not having an exit strategy wasn't great, but Patrick couldn't walk away from this.

"I'll keep you safe," he promised.

Lisette gave him a brittle smile before tucking the map into her backpack. She settled its weight on her shoulders before turning down the leftward tunnel and started walking.

They walked for hours.

Hunched over, upright, sometimes even crawling—they kept moving. The cold and the dark surrounded them, headlamp and witchlights providing the only illumination. From time to time Patrick thought he heard movement in the tunnels they left behind, and they'd wait while he scanned the area using his magic, coming up empty of a threat each time.

It didn't make him feel better.

However many hours later, they came upon a set of old stone stairs and descended deeper between levels. Patrick's ears popped on the way down, the air getting colder and the hellish taint getting stronger.

Lisette slowed at one point, pointing at a tiny space Patrick thought was a shadow until it revealed itself to be a narrow passage in the wall, only a couple of feet wide.

"We'll go through here to the Bone Well," she said.

What dead were buried below had been mostly hidden behind the limestone walls they'd passed through, bones few and far between in the tunnels. That changed once Patrick dragged himself through the narrow passage, finding himself in a space on the other side where a tall wall was filled to the edges with bones.

The witchlights floated upward, revealing numerous skulls, ribs, spines, arms and leg bones embedded in the wall itself, the structure bulging from the mass grave. The space was thick with bodies slowly pushing free of their resting place.

As Patrick pulled himself out of the hole, his hands brushed against fallen bone gathered on the floor. He straightened slowly, breathing musty air and tasting dust on his tongue, trying not to think about where that dust came from.

Lisette tugged on his arm. "This way."

They kept walking, the passageways filled with bones and a trail of hellish taint that only grew stronger the closer they got to its origination point.

Then the noises started.

And Patrick's magic sparked a warning.

Scratches on stone, the echo of quick footsteps, and the sound of heavy, monstrous breathing drifted their way. Lisette froze, face draining of all color as her breath came in rapid puffs. Patrick touched her arm, conjuring up a small mageglobe, the pale blue light casting them in an eerie glow where they were half-hunched in a tunnel.

"How much further to the Salle du Drapeau?" he asked. Lisette didn't answer, and the feel of hell pressed closer through Patrick's magic. "Lisette!"

She let out a shuddering gasp, hands shaking. She clenched the straps of her backpack to keep them still. "We're close, but the way in is very tight."

"We need to go." Patrick grabbed her hand and pulled her forward, even though he didn't know the way. "Tell me where we need to go."

He had to drag her along after him, her feet not wanting to work, the ceiling slanting low as they kicked bones aside with their feet. Patrick's heart was pounding double time even as they ran, the light from his magic and her headlamp bouncing around them.

Then something *screamed* behind them, the sound glass-sharp and echoing through the dark with the same ferocity he remembered on London streets.

Drekavacs.

The demonic-looking zombies threw themselves around the corner, crawling on the floor and walls and ceiling of the tunnel, moving shadows that smelled like rotten death. Their eyes reflected the light in a hideous way as they scuttled closer through the dark.

The ceiling dipped, forcing Patrick and Lisette lower, stunting their forward momentum. Patrick raised a shield between them and the drekavacs as he and Lisette were forced to their knees by the confines of the tunnel. His palms scraped against the cold ground as he pushed Lisette forward, trying to see around her in the dark ahead while hell nipped at their feet.

The tunnel was a dead end.

"*Motherfucker*," Patrick ground out.

Lisette squirmed in the tight space, twisting free of her backpack and kicking it aside. "There's a way through!"

Patrick couldn't see what she was talking about until she shoved herself headfirst into a tiny opening that was maybe a little taller than twelve inches if he was lucky. Lisette pushed her way deeper using her toes, the panicked sound of her breathing echoing beneath the screams of the drekavacs.

Patrick did not want to go into that space.

He had no choice but to follow.

As Lisette's feet disappeared, Patrick crawled after her, sliding flat with his arms outstretched, the ceiling so close he had to turn his head to the side, stone scraping against his cheek. He breathed out, a puff of cold air that left his mouth dry, magic the only thing keeping the drekavacs from tearing them to pieces as they desperately inched their way forward through the impossibly narrow shaft.

And then they didn't even have that.

The spell that ripped through the tunnel crashed into Patrick's shields with enough force to crack them, pain lancing through his head. The walls around them vibrated in a way that made him freeze, lungs gone tight. Stone dust fell onto his face, and he breathed it in, trying not to choke on it.

They were going to be crushed.

Then Lisette's voice reached him, high and thin from panic. "Just the late-night trains. We're beneath Gare Montparnasse."

"Sure, just the trains," Patrick muttered under his breath as they dragged themselves forward by their fingertips and toes while the drekavacs clawed against his thinned-out shields behind them. "Not like I need my heart or anything."

The stone walls got impossibly closer, and Patrick swallowed against the tightening in his chest and *kept going*.

The only time he stopped clawing himself forward was when his shields broke.

The spell came out of nowhere, powered by an immortal's strength, tearing through his focus like a bomb. His mageglobe sputtered out, plunging them into darkness, Lisette's body blocking the shine of her headlamp.

Then the drekavacs *screamed*, and Patrick didn't know which way was up as his head spun, nausea from the backlash twisting his gut.

He could hear the dead clawing at the stone, wriggling through the space beyond his feet, and the thought of getting torn to shreds while trapped underground got Patrick moving through the pain. He reformed his mageglobe and dragged his shields back up. His bones ached from the weight of them as he pieced them back together, leaning into the soulbond to do so, drawing magic from a ley line far below.

Half a second later, a drekavac slammed into his shaky barrier, screaming loud enough to make Patrick's ears pop. Patrick was ready for the next hit, bracing himself for the blow. The walls vibrated around them again, and he wasn't sure it was the trains that time.

Lisette moaned, high and frightened, but she kept moving, kept dragging herself forward through the dark. Patrick followed her, listening as the stone creaked all around them while the drekavacs screamed like a nightmare behind them, forcing himself to breathe through the taste of hell.

Patrick didn't know who had summoned the drekavacs, but he'd be unsurprised if it was Ilya. The necromancer could be anywhere in the Catacombs. Patrick only hoped Ilya wasn't ahead of them, where the black magic roiled against his senses like crude oil in water—a poisonous, tainted mess.

He could sense the drekavacs clawing at his shields, desperately trying to break through. Patrick willed his shields as strong as they would go, painting over the cracks with magic. The anchors in his bones that Persephone had reset last summer hadn't been damaged, but his head throbbed from the attack. The stone his breath blew against was so close he could feel the chill of it.

Another couple of inches, another rolling hit of magic, and then the ceiling above started to slant away from his body. Patrick's lungs expanded the same way the tunnel started to. He breathed in dust, then air, fingers clawing at the ground as he dragged himself forward, following Lisette's kicking feet.

The ceiling bent higher, and Lisette pushed herself to her knees, able to crawl. Another foot, and Patrick could do the same. Patrick's breath came sickly fast, and he wished he could cast a spell of some sort, knowing the only magic he could use down here would be defensive wards, or he'd risk bringing down the stone and graves above them, burying them alive.

He could hear Lisette crying as she continued forward with a speed that probably skinned her knees and shredded her palms.

Patrick's weren't much better. But he could breathe again, and soon they were both hunched over and running down a jagged tunnel. Then the ceiling angled upward and they were running upright, cutting through the dark.

The drekavacs never stopped screaming.

The damage to Patrick's shields made his nerves burn, but he kept them up as Lisette scrambled her way through twisting tunnels by memory alone. The dry floor beneath their feet began to turn damp, then muddy, the tunnel they were heading into partially flooded.

Lisette barreled into the water with a trembling cry, running toward a corridor Patrick hoped they wouldn't die in. Water splashed over his chest as he followed in her wake, the tunnel rising ahead to a dry path that led to a rectangle opening carved into stone. Patrick reached out and grabbed Lisette by the arm. Her scream was nearly as loud as the drekavacs, and she swung around to hit him before she saw his face and remembered he was there.

"Sorry," Patrick said, pulling her to the side. "Let me go first. Stay close."

He raised a shield between them and the entrance, pouring raw magic into a mageglobe that he sent hurtling through the opening. It wasn't giving off enough light to push back the darkness entirely, but the glimpses Patrick got when they entered made him wish he could pretend he never saw what was hidden in the Salle du Drapeau.

Bone cracked beneath their boots, no matter where they stepped. The smell of bodies left to rot in a damp grave filled the air, making Patrick gag. Lisette moaned, her breath coming shallow and panicky.

Witchlights spilled from Patrick's fingertips, the bright white illumination glittering like stars as the sparks rose into the air. The space had a high ceiling, and a tricolor flag was painted on the large far wall, giving the room its name.

Against that wall was an altar made out of bones stacked on top of each other, layers of femurs rising between three layers of skulls. The skulls that made the topmost layer had all been smashed open on the top, dark from old blood, the altar covered in it. Stretched out on top was a man whose throat had been carved open all the way to his navel, his guts spilling out down the altar.

Around them, filling the rest of the space, were piles and piles of bodies not yet eroded into bones.

Sacrifices.

"*Fuck*," Patrick breathed out, staring at Peklabog's altar.

He didn't think much of Lisette moving behind him—not until the rounded joint of a femur slammed against the side of his head and the witchlights high above smeared through the dark like shooting stars.

21

Patrick's concentration broke, but at least it wasn't his skull.

His shields far down the tunnels collapsed, and he knew what was coming. The witchlights all around them sputtered and nearly died from the pain in his head, blackness eating at the edges of his vision.

"I pray to our god in the Orthodox Church of the Dead, and you'll be our next sacrifice," Lisette bit out.

Lisette no longer looked fearful, only murderous as she swung the femur bone down like an axe. Patrick rolled out of its way and kicked out hard with his foot, catching her in the knee. The crunch was bone getting broken and jammed into an angle the joint was never meant to go. Lisette screamed in agony, dropping the femur and falling to the ground with a sob.

Patrick got an elbow underneath him, yanked his dagger free, and retracted his shield to cover only himself. It left Lisette beyond the safety it provided as the drekavacs hurled themselves into the Salle du Drapeau.

"Je vénère votre Dieu!" Lisette yelled, holding out one arm toward them in a pleading manner.

The drekavacs never stopped coming. Lisette never stopped screaming until one ripped out her throat with its teeth.

There went any hope of getting answers.

The rest of the demonic zombies threw themselves on his shield, clawing and biting at his magic. Their screams made Patrick's ears ring as he struggled to hold up his shields through the throbbing ache in his skull and the nausea twisting up his stomach.

The soulbond pulled tight in his chest, but Patrick paid it no mind, forcing himself to focus on the problem at hand. Something wet trickled down the side of his face, but he ignored it. Shoving himself to his knees, Patrick flipped the dagger around in his hand, readjusting his grip.

His shields were thin, pulsing in time with his heartbeat. But they stayed up, powered by external magic when his own kept slipping away from him like his thoughts.

Head wounds were a fucking *bitch* to deal with.

Patrick lunged, stabbing the closest drekavac straight through his shield, tearing into its torso. The scream it let out was furious for a single second before what magic animated it bled away beneath heavenly white fire. Patrick yanked his dagger free and withdrew his arm back behind his shield before it could get bitten off by sharp teeth.

"This will not do."

The raspy voice came from behind him, dry like bone. Patrick froze, breathing harshly through the pain in his head. He conjured up a mageglobe, filling it with raw magic despite the way it made the nerves in the back of his eyes burn.

The drekavacs wrenched themselves away from his shield, skittering backward, low to the ground, all the while screaming furiously. The shadows were pushed away by a dull light flickering to life behind him. Patrick slowly twisted around, still holding his dagger, and watched the altar *move.*

Bones shivered and jumped, rising up on their ends to roll around each other as the altar broke apart. Every eye socket in every skull glowed with a dim orange light. The body lying atop it slipped through bone, falling to the stone below as the altar reshaped itself into something else.

The long bones and skulls adhered to each other in the shape of a tall, narrow column that resembled a mortar if one squinted hard enough. The bones shifted and spun until they settled into their final shape, supporting a shadowy figure that slowly coalesced into an old, haggard crone who took her place on top of the floating mortar.

Shadows played across her heavily wrinkled face, mouth and large nose both misshapen to a monstrous degree, but her eyes were clear and sharp in the light from the skulls. Her long white hair fell around her face in a tangled mess, knees pressed to her chest, dirt-stained fingers gripping the knobby ends of thigh bones beneath her.

The crone smiled, revealing iron teeth that reminded him of Ashanti. "Perhaps I should give you task, *da?*"

She gripped the air in front of her, and a wooden pestle appeared between her crooked fingers. The crone whacked the pestle against the mortar, and her strange mode of transportation floated closer. The drekavacs skittered over the bodies and bones surrounding Patrick, keeping their distance from the crone.

The spark of ozone in the air was familiar, if dulled. The crone was immortal, but not a god. Still a myth prayed to life through stories though.

Still a problem.

"Pattycakes here already has a task, Baba Yaga," a gratingly familiar voice said from behind Patrick. "Persephone won't appreciate you trying to give him another."

"Bah." Baba Yaga floated toward the drekavacs, keen eyes riveted on her prey. "What else mortals good for?"

The drekavacs screamed a warning Baba Yaga didn't heed. Patrick looked over his shoulder in time to see her wield her pestle with brutally precise strikes at the walking dead. Each hit broke bone and split dead flesh, leaving the drekavacs writhing on the stone floor. Several retreated through the low entrance and back into the dark.

Baba Yaga speared one of the drekavacs with her pestle and lifted the body. She cackled softly before ripping out chunks of flesh with her teeth, swallowing the bites whole.

Patrick blinked, and when he opened his eyes again, Hermes was leaning over him, staring at him through his shields.

"You know, if you wanted to lie in a grave so badly, you could've done it back in New York," Hermes said around a smirk.

"Fuck you," Patrick said, the words making his skull vibrate. He swallowed against the bile creeping up his throat.

Hermes laughed. "Think your wolf might not like that."

The god still reached through Patrick's shields like they didn't exist, framing his face with warm hands. Patrick tried to jerk away, but Hermes' grip was like a vise, even if the brush of his lips across Patrick's forehead was cool.

Magic washed through him, electrically sharp, stealing the pain away in his head. It felt less like a benediction and more like a grudgingly given gift. Patrick batted Hermes' hands away and got to his feet once his head stopped spinning. His shields sank back beneath his skin, an afterthought of protection he no longer needed to fuel with a ley line.

The soulbond thrummed between him and Jono. Patrick separated himself from the ley line below, magic running out of him and through Jono's soul, draining away. He stared over Hermes' shoulder as Baba Yaga turned to face them, the skulls in her bone mortar still glowing.

"Shall we depart?" Hermes asked her.

Baba Yaga snorted, tapping her gore-covered pestle against a row of skulls in her mortar. She had dead flesh stuck between her teeth. "My way is not your way."

"It is tonight."

Baba Yaga floated closer, bringing with her the scent of death that permeated the bones which once formed Peklabog's altar. She tapped the mortar again. "Hold fast."

Hermes grabbed onto the mortar, and Patrick could only do the same. The bones ground together as they rose to the ceiling, his feet lifting off the ground. Layers of the mortar broke off to slide over Patrick's body. He flinched against the bloodied bones, tilting his head back to watch as they formed a circle on the ceiling. The stone crumbled, and he quickly leaned his head forward again, squeezing his eyes shut as dust and stone rained down around them.

They floated higher. Patrick cracked open one eye, watching the floor of the Salle du Drapeau fall away from his feet. Then the bones that had carved their way through stone and earth and the bare edges of the veil filled in the hole. When Patrick let go of the mortar, he landed on the dark hardwood floor of a shop.

Lights flickered on in dozens of small lanterns hanging from the ceiling, revealing shelves filled with candles, soaps, and bottles of neatly labeled potions. The windows were made of frosted glass, with no name written across it. The register on the counter was an electronic tablet setup with a wireless card reader. It looked weirdly out of place.

It smelled like herbs and oils, medicinal beneath a layer of perfume that made Patrick want to sneeze. Patrick rubbed his nose before yanking at the belt attached to his waders, stripping out of the disgusting things. He kicked them underneath the nearest table.

Baba Yaga's mortar shrank to fit the space, but she still didn't leave it. Her mortar settled to the ground, the bones of it grinding together. Something long and thin whipped through the air from the other side of the room. The broom smacked into her free hand, and she busied herself with sweeping up the dust of their passage.

Hermes bent over a table and poked at some of the items there. "I see you are still in business."

"Potion selling always good." Baba Yaga spun her broom lightning-quick to smack it across the back of Hermes' hands. "Is not for touch."

Hermes yanked his hands away from the table and glared at her as she floated past. "What drew you down to the Catacombs?"

Baba Yaga rapped the pestle against the mortar. "Very little forest these days to tempt lost travelers. One must eat."

"The dead?" Patrick asked, failing to keep the disgust out of his voice. He could've done without watching her eat a corpse.

Baba Yaga ignored him, busying herself with sorting the extra bone from the mortar on an empty table in the rear of the shop.

Patrick pressed a hand to his chest as the soulbond drew sharp and tight. Jono was a distant presence he could sense drawing closer with every breath he took.

Find me.

The answering tug in his soul eased the tension in Patrick's shoulders, but not by much.

"So." Hermes wandered away from the table and back to Patrick. "I hear you lost the Morrígan's staff."

"We didn't *lose* it," Patrick snapped.

"You were in the same location and never got your hands on it."

"Doesn't mean we lost it."

Patrick was not going to admit defeat to Hermes, even if—yes, *technically*—they might have lost track of the staff. And now it was in the hands of a necromancer and a god who had no right to it.

"Ilya is in possession of the staff. He'll give it to Peklabog if he hasn't done so already," Patrick said.

Hermes rolled his eyes. "And whose fault is that?"

"It's been out of the Morrígan's hands for what? Over a century? Don't blame me because you gods lost it first."

"It wouldn't be a problem if your family hadn't done such damage over the years."

"I'm doing what you want."

"Not well enough."

Patrick raked a hand through his hair, shaking loose stone dust he'd carried with him out of the Catacombs. "Peklabog had an altar down there before Baba Yaga dismantled it. He's been accepting sacrifices."

"He's been keeping bodies and souls," Hermes corrected.

Patrick linked his hands behind his neck and stared up at the ceiling. "The staff isn't his."

"Doesn't mean he won't try to force it to accept him."

"How?"

"One must use artifact to own," Baba Yaga said as she floated back over to them on her mortar.

"It's not part of his myth."

Hermes tilted his head, gold-brown eyes becoming half-lidded. "Do you really think that matters when your father is busy creating his own?"

Myths had a core of truth, and while the stories sometimes changed, Patrick didn't think they could change *that* much. The Morrígan was a goddess of war and fate, and the dead were her purview as much as Peklabog's in a way. But the staff belonged to her, and Patrick didn't believe the goddess would let anyone keep what was rightfully hers.

Not without a fight.

"If Ethan wants it, he'll bargain with Peklabog for it. Or he'll just take it."

Someone banged rapidly on the front door to the apothecary shop. The soulbond settled in Patrick's soul the way it always did when Jono was nearby, and Patrick let out a sigh of relief.

The door to the shop swung open on its own. Jono, Sage and Wade hurried inside, and the door shut behind them with a quiet click. Jono scowled at Hermes before muscling his way between the god and Patrick. Warm hands framed Patrick's face and tilted his head up. The motion dislodged more stone dust, and he sneezed.

"What the bloody fuck happened?" Jono asked.

"The cataphile was one of Peklabog's worshippers. Either that, or the Paris god pack was fucking with us," Patrick said.

Hermes raised his hand, Lisette's blood-spattered necklace hanging from one finger. Patrick was surprised it was still in one piece. "She was his worshipper. This is one of his emblems."

"I'll call their dire when we get back to Nadine's," Sage said, practically biting out the words.

Jono stroked his thumbs over Patrick's cheeks, studying him. "I felt your panic."

Patrick winced. "Sorry. Drekavacs cornered us in the Catacombs. I was limited in the spells I could use. Didn't want to risk bringing a street down on top of me."

"Were you hurt?"

"Lisette got the drop on me. Whacked me upside the head with a leg bone. Baba Yaga got me out of there, and Hermes got rid of the concussion."

Hermes smirked at Jono. "Need him in fighting form."

"Fuck off," Jono growled.

Wade, who'd been wandering the shop unsupervised and probably had pockets filled with potions at this rate, sidled back over to them. "Is there a bakery nearby? I smelled bread on the street."

Patrick frowned. "What time is it?"

"Close to five in the morning," Sage said.

Patrick blinked, staring up into Jono's eyes. "Summer solstice."

Jono nodded grimly and let him go. "What now?"

Patrick looked around at his pack and realized there was only one thing they could do. "We fight."

"Peklabog will not be easy adversary," Baba Yaga said as she floated back over to them, whacking Wade across the knuckles with her broom. "Is not yours."

Wade yanked his hand away from a display of potions in shiny crystal bottles. "Ow! I was only looking."

Baba Yaga snorted, looking down on them from the height of her mortar made out of stolen bones. "Church filled Catacombs with prayers. Dead will rise. Soon."

"Are you sure?" Patrick asked.

"Think I not know dead?"

"That's not what I meant. If Ilya is starting the spell now, then we're out of time to warn people."

Baba Yaga shrugged. "Can still fight. Have Srecha's blessing, *da*? Do not waste."

Patrick's left hand twitched, the line of heat across his palm still sore from dragging himself through tight tunnels. "What's that supposed to mean?"

Baba Yaga let the end of her pestle hit the floor, leaning forward to balance her weight on the other end. She stared at him with eyes the color of freshly turned earth, a hunger in them that made Patrick want to reach for his dagger.

"Mortals can't hold staff without proper magic. Magic you not have."

"You mean my affinity for combat magic won't be enough?"

"Think I hunger, mortal? Staff aches with it. Use what Srecha give you, but can use only once."

"Like a wish?" Sage asked.

Baba Yaga straightened up, humming thoughtfully as the mortar swayed a little in the air. "The staff wants. You must want more."

"Who would've thought you'd be so helpful without running poor Pattycakes through a plethora of tasks?" Hermes drawled.

Baba Yaga shot him an irritated look. "I know his place."

"It's good you know yours."

Hermes disappeared through the veil, getting the last word in because he was a dick like that. Patrick rolled his eyes.

"Thank you for your help in the Catacombs," Patrick said,

because Baba Yaga wasn't the fae, and it was only polite to acknowledge the immortal's help since she hadn't tried to eat him.

Mostly.

"Take thief out of my shop," she grumbled.

"I'm not a thief," Wade protested from behind a different display of potions, hands moving suspiciously.

"Funny how she didn't specify who and you still spoke up," Jono said.

Wade scowled at them and headed for the door. "I'm getting some bread. All the bread. And I'm not sharing."

Jono stroked his hand down Patrick's arm, linking their fingers together, and tugged him toward the door. "Come on. We have a fight to prepare for."

Patrick rubbed at one eye, trying to get the dust out as he followed after Jono, not looking forward to the day ahead.

22

JONO WOULD HAVE MUCH RATHER HAD A LIE-IN WITH PATRICK THAT morning after a shitty night chasing him through Paris rather than going their separate ways because of politics. Unfortunately, that hadn't been an option.

"Your contact was a traitor," Jono said flatly.

Mireille blinked at him over her closed laptop on the dining room table. "So your dire accused over the phone."

"So my co-leader had to deal with in the fucking Catacombs *alone*."

"You knew the risk. I am sorry for your loss—"

"What loss? I never said Patrick was dead."

Mireille hesitated, but Jono couldn't smell fear on her, just confusion. "He went below."

"Patrick is a mage. He got out of there just fine." Jono's jaw twitched. "No thanks to you."

"There was no deceit in our actions. You asked for a guide. We reached out to the most well-known group of cataphiles that reside in Paris to get you one. We've helped them find lost members in the past, before the Catacombs closed. They owed us, and we asked that they send you someone who was familiar with the tunnels." Mireille shook her head, never looking away from Jono. "We didn't know of the guide's allegiance."

She smelled like truth and nothing else—no magic, no lies. Mireille's scent was clean in a way Estelle's never was and Cressida's hadn't been. Fenrir only confirmed her stance with an indifferent growl that echoed in the back of Jono's mind.

Not a threat, the god said.

That didn't make the Paris god pack allies.

"That's a shit apology," Jono said.

Mireille's wolf-bright blue eyes narrowed. "We have nothing to apologize for."

"Are we correct in assuming only the Orthodox Church of the Dead have been roaming the Catacombs lately?" Sage asked, steering the conversation away from an argument.

She'd made Rami uncomfortable when they'd arrived at the Paris god pack's home that morning, having left her fae necklace at Nadine's. Sage clearly gave off the scent of a werecreature, just not any kind the Paris god pack were used to crossing.

"We informed you of that the other night," Gaspard said as he entered the dining room, sipping at some red wine.

Rami found a different spot along the wall to stand guard, keeping both his alphas within reach. The handful of other god pack members tasked to protect them didn't move.

"So you are confirming you've given up parts of your Paris territory to the enemy."

Sage's calm words made both Gaspard and Mireille bristle.

"We admit no such thing," Mireille snapped.

Jono stared them down. "You've known about the missing and the murdered and haven't ventured into the Catacombs to fight to get them back. Sounds to me like you gave up territory."

Gaspard set his wineglass on the table so he wouldn't break it, anger suffusing his scent. "You don't know anything about our situation. The French government doesn't care about dead werecreatures. Trying to search for them only resulted in more of us dying."

"They're going to care about dead *people* at some point today if the Orthodox Church of the Dead manages to resurrect every last body buried in Paris."

Mireille sniffed derisively. "That is an impossible feat."

"Ilya Nazarov is a necromancer who worships a god that guides souls. He has a weapon now that will only amplify his power. The dead won't care *what* you are when they rise. They'll still try to kill you for their master."

"Gods don't exist," Gaspard said.

Jono glanced at Sage, but neither said anything to that statement. Belief was subjective, and it was an argument they didn't have time for today.

"Magic does, and Ilya's kind will decimate Paris. You should warn your packs to be on alert."

"We believe the Dominion Sect is also involved. We're not sure if they're allied with Ilya's church, but they're both a threat. If you have any alliances with magic users, you may want to warn them as well," Sage said.

Gaspard and Mireille shared an unreadable look. Eventually Gaspard blew out a heavy breath and sat on the chair beside hers.

"You are not what we expected from the English," Gaspard said.

Jono frowned. "I'm not—"

"You are New York City's god pack alpha, *oui*, we know. We see that now. We hear your warnings as well." Gaspard looked over his shoulder at one of the god pack members standing near the door. "Maxime. Is Helene working today?"

The man nodded and said something in French Jono couldn't follow.

Gaspard faced forward again, meeting Jono's gaze. "Helene is Maxime's wife. She is a policewoman and will be on duty at the Arc de Triomphe today. She can tell you some of what they know is going on in the streets."

"Patrick has been dealing with your government already. He's with them right now," Jono said.

Mireille shrugged. "Politicians do not like disclosing the truth, and bureaucracy means nothing will get done quickly. The police are the eyes and ears of Paris. They may not be kind to our community, but they know and understand the threats better than politicians in their gilded seats."

Sage slipped her mobile out of her purse and checked the time. "At this hour, the tourists will be out in force. We should get going. It'll take time for a taxi to get here."

"Maxime can drive you. It will be quicker," Gaspard said.

"Thank you."

Jono didn't say anything, too annoyed with the Paris god pack to mean any thanks he'd give them. Noon was behind them, and Jono had been up for over twenty-four hours at this rate. He wasn't capable of patience right now.

Jono and Sage followed Maxime out of the building to his car parked on the street. The sun was bright in a clear blue sky, morning heat filling the air. He wondered if Patrick and Nadine were making better progress than they were.

The drive to the Arc de Triomphe was made in silence. Sage spent that time on her mobile, relaying what they'd learned to the rest of the pack.

"Wade is asking if he can leave for lunch," Sage said.

"He's not allowed to leave until we get back to the flat," Jono said, staring out the window at the passing buildings.

They'd left Wade and Spencer in Nadine's flat because no one was getting left alone today. Between everything that needed to get done, Jono felt incredibly shorthanded and outnumbered.

Sometime later they reached the Louvre, the long gray buildings on the left abruptly turning into the Jardin des Tuileries. The stretch of greenery was filled with people, tourists and locals alike taking advantage of a warm summer day. Maxim drove through a maze of traffic, past a grand fountain, and eventually turned onto the Avenue des Champs-Élysées. Jono stared ahead, the wide avenue lined by trees and shops on both sides, crowded with people.

The Arc de Triomphe came into view, rising over the traffic. They'd almost reached the roundabout when Maxime pulled over to the side of the road in a bus stop.

"I will let Helene know you are here," Maxime said, looking at his mobile rather than at them.

"What does she look like?" Sage asked.

He hummed, minimizing his text to show off the home screen and the picture of a woman that was the background. Jono memorized her face before following Sage out of the car.

"*Merci*," Jono said.

Maxime didn't say anything in response, merely drove off before anyone started honking at him. They hurried onto the sidewalk, Sage leading the way to the pedestrian tunnel that would take them under the famous roundabout to the center island. They moved easily through the crowd in the tunnel, bypassing the lines of people waiting to buy tickets from the kiosks to get to the top of the Arc de Triomphe.

Human and not-so-human scents hit Jono's nose, but none smelled threatening. That could've changed if he hadn't been wearing his sunglasses to hide his eyes. God pack alpha werecreatures weren't liked on the best of days, and he didn't much care to deal with a frightened public, especially one that might not understand what he had to say.

"There we go," Sage muttered as they came upon the stairs leading up to the center island.

They took the steps up at an easy pace, packed in on all sides by tourists eager to see the famous monument. They arrived aboveground in the center of the roundabout, the Arc de Triomphe rising above them. The island itself was crowded with people, the ever-moving traffic in the roundabout surrounding filled with the noise of engines, horns, and squealing brakes.

Jono dialed up his senses as he looked around, standing taller than most of the people around them. He could see two separate Police Nationale vans parked on either side of the Arc de Triomphe. The police themselves wandered the area, along with men and women in military uniforms, the lot of them a heavily armed security presence that tourists gave a wide berth to.

He remembered what Maxime smelled like, and it took only one circuit of the island to find Helene. He recognized her face and the underlying faint scent of Maxime she carried with her. She seemed to be scanning the area, as if looking for them. Her gaze drifted past them before refocusing on them as they approached her.

"*Bonjour,*" Sage said with a friendly smile. "Are you Helene?"

"*Oui,*" Helene said.

"Maxime sent us. Is it possible to speak with you for a few minutes?"

Her partner said something in French that caused anger to cut through her scent, though it never showed on her face. Helene ignored him before gesturing for them to follow her, putting distance between them and the other police, but not her duty to guard the monument.

"Maxime said you had some questions. I'll answer what I can, but I don't know how much help I can be," Helene said in a thick French accent. "I was demoted last year when word got out I was engaged to Maxime."

Jono had a vague idea what sort of insult her partner must have said to make her angry. "I'm sorry."

She shrugged. "What is it you need?"

"Can you tell us if the police have done anything to prevent the Orthodox Church of the Dead from operating in Paris?" Sage asked.

Helene frowned. "You are asking about the Catacomb rumors?"

"We know you have missing and dead people, most of them from the preternatural world, but I'm sure there's some mundane humans thrown in there as well. Your government wouldn't have closed them off for so long if it was only werecreatures going missing."

"The Orthodox Church of the Dead is not welcome in Paris, but hunting down the perpetrators has not been a top priority."

"Because it was only werecreatures who were dying at first?" Jono guessed.

"*Oui.* Some magic users as well, but the covens and families they came from had no political power. They were mostly from immigrant communities in the surrounding arrondissements. Only when some cataphiles and tourists went missing is when the government closed the Catacombs."

"You never found any of the missing?"

"*Non.*"

Jono remembered how Patrick had described the underground room filled with bodies and wondered if the police had even tried looking for the missing, or if they thought they could use the rumors to seal off the Catacombs to illegal entry for good.

"Mireille and Gaspard said they banned all the packs from Catacomb entrances. Do you know where those are?" Sage asked.

Helene shrugged. "I don't know the locations, but they are everywhere in Paris. Hidden doors, manhole covers, holes in the Metro tunnels are mostly how the cataphiles get below."

"None you know of that the police have been monitoring more closely as of late?"

"I don't know. I am sorry."

Jono opened his mouth to tell her not to apologize when a deep, sonorous hum cut through the air. It sounded like a distant roar, making the nerves in his teeth ache. Helene gripped her rifle and called out to her partner, hurrying away from them.

"What the hell *is* that?" Sage asked, turning quickly on her feet to get eyes on their area.

"I don't know, but it can't be good," Jono said.

Everyone around them had stopped taking pictures and were

now looking around in equal confusion. Some people had their mobiles up to record, but the general ease of the crowd was rapidly fading as the hum kept going, never rising or falling, remaining a continuous sound that buzzed in Jono's ears.

Over the tops of the trees and roofs of buildings surrounding the roundabout, Jono could just make out the very top of the Eiffel Tower in the distance.

It glowed a sickly, malevolent ochre color.

Jono pulled out his mobile and dialed Patrick, who picked up almost immediately.

"Tell me you're back at Nadine's apartment," Patrick said.

"Finished that chat with the Paris god pack. Went to the Arc de Triomphe to speak to a policewoman married to one of their members. Got interrupted by that bloody noise. You should know the Eiffel Tower is covered in magic," Jono said.

"*Fuck*. We need to regroup. Head back to Nadine's apartment. INTERPOL got a hit on Zachary Myers last night. He's in Paris."

"Ethan?"

"No hits, but we can't rule out his presence."

Some of the police pushed through the crowd, heading toward the stairs that led to the tunnel, shouting orders in French and English. The crowd wasn't moving very quickly, not yet starting to panic.

That changed when magic rolled like a wave across Paris, pushing outward from the Eiffel Tower.

The force of it bent the air like a mirage, pushing through buildings, trees, and people as if they didn't exist. Jono grabbed Sage by the shoulder and braced them both against something they couldn't outrun. The hit was like getting shocked by static electricity all over his body, making every single nerve in his body burn as if he were going to shift.

Then it was gone, rolling past them out to the edge of the city. The scent that lingered in the air in its wake smelled more like rotten garbage than the air after a thunderstorm.

Cars slammed into each other in the roundabout as they careened to a hard stop, their engines suddenly gone dead all at once. When Jono looked at his mobile, the screen was black. Sage held up her own, a grim slant to her mouth.

"Dead," she said.

Jono tucked his now bricked mobile into his back pocket. "Patrick wants us to meet at the flat."

"I heard. We should—"

A deep, heavy *bang* echoed through the air, coming from the ground under the Arc de Triomphe. Jono looked over at the area directly beneath the monument's arches where ropes outlined the memorial inlaid on the floor above the Tomb of the Unknown Soldier.

The sound came from the grave.

The police had already turned their attention toward the noise, which hadn't stopped and only gotten louder. Ochre-colored magic flickered to life over the memorial, setting fire to the flowers that surrounded the edge of it.

People screamed, the crowd rushing toward the exit that would take them under the roundabout in a dangerous crush. Jono and Sage stayed put, staring at the grave.

"You smell that?" Sage asked, nostrils flaring.

Jono nodded. "Yeah."

Like garbage that had sat on the curb for weeks, meat gone rotten and moldy in the sun, the foul stench of something *dead* clung to the sluggish breeze.

Magic, and not the good kind.

The covering of the tomb exploded upward. Stone, metal, and dirt flew through the air, giving way. A skeleton dressed in a ragged uniform frayed from over a century of entombment clawed its way out of the grave, magic burning in its eye sockets.

The police yelled a warning Jono couldn't understand before they fired at the skeletal zombie exiting its grave. The bullets didn't stop it, and the zombie lurched forward on old, time-worn leather boots.

"We need to go," Jono said, still staring at the zombie. "That won't be the only sodding zombie we'll have to deal with."

Sage turned on her feet. "No need to tell me twice."

Rather than head for the tunnel entrance where everyone else was pushing and shoving their way down the stairs, Jono and Sage ran for the edge of the concrete island. They threw themselves with preternatural speed into the stopped traffic surrounding the roundabout, racing to the other side.

23

"THIS IS BULLSHIT," PATRICK GROWLED AS HE YANKED THE CAR DOOR shut.

Nadine shoved her key into the ignition of her car and started the engine. "We aren't in our country. We can't force them to listen to us and then do what we want."

"Just because they haven't been able to locate Ilya doesn't mean he's *gone.*"

"The ministry is aware of that."

"And I thought our government was a fucking headache."

Nadine pulled into the street, merging into the traffic that surrounded the Quai d'Orsay. They'd been stuck in emergency meetings at the Ministry of Magical Affairs since early morning after Patrick escaped the Catacombs. Maybe it was the lack of sleep from being awake for over twenty-four hours that was making him short-tempered, but dealing with politics today was more annoying than usual.

They weren't on US soil, and Patrick was acutely aware that he didn't have the political backing or approval to operate how he normally would. If he got in a fight over here it would turn into a huge diplomatic mess he couldn't afford to be in the middle of. Neither would he have Setsuna to cover for him and explain away his actions.

This wasn't like the Thirty-Day War, when countries banded together to fight back against the hells. Patrick wasn't able to act under military orders, and he knew the French government would be incensed if he ruined any of their monuments.

They drove east, heading toward the 8th arrondissement, where the Embassy of the United States was located. The PIA was currently running the Paris portion of the mission behind diplomatic walls, and they had another lunch meeting to attend despite the fact that Patrick wanted to be out hunting. Red tape and the restrictions it came with had never before seemed so terrible.

"With the INTERPOL hit on Zachary, at least we have proof the Dominion Sect is in Paris," Nadine said.

"I don't know if that makes this situation better or worse. It's summer solstice, there's a god of the underworld who guides souls waiting for his priest to deliver him a weapon that doesn't belong to him, and we're considering Ethan's right-hand bastard a good thing?" Patrick rubbed at his eyes with one hand, breathing sharply through his clenched teeth. "I need a drink."

"There's a flask in my glove compartment."

Patrick made a desperate sound in the back of his throat as he yanked open the glove compartment, ignoring the Browning there in favor of the small metal flask that would fit in almost any of Nadine's designer purses.

"Thanks," Patrick muttered right before taking a swallow of good whiskey.

"There are mints in my purse. Chew some before we get to the meeting."

"Work been that stressful for you lately?"

"It's been mostly you."

"That would hurt me if I cared."

Nadine smacked him in the chest, a smile tugging at her lips. "Asshole."

She turned left onto Pont Alexandre III, the low bridge spanning the Seine filled with cars. The golden statues on the pillars bracing each side of the bridge glittered in the sunlight. They were halfway across the span when a deep, sonorous hum ripped through the air, sounding out of place in the buzz of Paris streets.

"What the fuck?" Patrick leaned forward to peer through the windshield, scanning their position on the bridge. "Are you hearing that?"

"Yes. I don't like it," Nadine said, speeding up as much as she could as traffic continued to move across the bridge.

Patrick's phone buzzed in his pocket. He pulled it out, answering immediately after seeing Jono's name flash across the screen. "Tell me you're back at Nadine's apartment."

Jono's voice came across the line, deep and familiar, annoyance coloring his tone. "Finished that chat with the Paris god pack. Went to the Arc de Triomphe to speak to a policewoman married to one of their members. Got interrupted by that bloody noise. You should know the Eiffel Tower is covered in magic."

Patrick twisted around in his seat, rolling down the window so he could stick his head out and get eyes on the horizon. The Eiffel Tower rose in the sky behind them, painted a sickly, familiar ochre color that made cold sweat break out on his skin.

"*Fuck.* We need to regroup. Head back to Nadine's apartment. INTERPOL got a hit on Zachary Myers last night. He's in Paris."

"Ethan?"

"No hits, but we can't rule out his presence."

Before Patrick could say anything else, they reached the other side of the bridge right as the magic surrounding the Eiffel Tower pulsed like a heartbeat before exploding outward.

Nadine's fingers curled over the collar of his suit jacket and yanked him back into the car. He almost cracked his head against the edge of the door, and then Patrick was back inside and Nadine's shield snapped into place around the vehicle.

The wave of magic rolled right over them, sending water from the Seine splashing into the air, curling over the edges of the high walls. The car's engine sputtered and abruptly died. Nadine swore as she slammed on the brakes, expanding her shield outside the frame of the car. The vehicle behind them slammed into her shield rather than the backend of her car.

Patrick stared at his phone and the blank screen it now showed. He tested the power button, but when nothing happened, he opened up the glove compartment, took out the Browning, and left his phone in its spot.

"Phone lines are dead," he said, checking the gun for bullets.

"Going to bet everything electronic in Paris is down. Fucking magical EMP strike. That's a military-grade combat spell, something Ilya doesn't have an affinity for," Nadine said, shoving open her door. She kicked off her high heels and got out of the car.

"Zachary does."

"Give me my fucking gun."

Patrick made sure the safety was on before tossing it to her over the roof. "Is it even legal for you to carry it?"

Nadine dislodged the clip and checked how many bullets she had, before slamming it back into place. "It is now."

"Next time Setsuna sends me out of the country, I'm bringing my tactical pistol."

Nadine took her keys, pried a knife out of her purse, and left everything else in the car. She used the knife to rip slits in her sheath dress on either side of her legs, giving herself more freedom of movement.

Patrick squinted at the Eiffel Tower in the distance and the malevolent magic burning over it, trying to ignore the sick churning in his stomach. "I told Jono to meet us at your apartment."

"Then we'll go there and regroup. We can't fight in business casual, and I have weapons you can borrow."

"How far do we have to run?'

"If we double-time it and don't get waylaid? Maybe fifteen minutes."

Patrick shrugged out of his suit jacket and undid his tie, leaving both on the front passenger seat before slamming the door shut. "Then let's go."

Nadine tossed the knife on the seat, shut the door, and set a ward that would keep the vehicle locked and safe against trespassers. Then they ran, ignoring everyone on the street getting out of their cars or trying to get the vehicles to start. They passed a couple of minor fender benders on the way, but no one seemed hurt.

They dodged around people milling about in the street. More people streamed out of the Grand Palais and Petit Palais on either side of them as they ran.

"How are your feet?" Patrick asked, because the asphalt had to be hot underfoot.

"I have my skin shielded. Keep running," Nadine huffed out.

They reached the Avenue des Champs-Élysées a minute later, the traffic there at a standstill like it was behind them. People stood near cars that wouldn't start, kept gesturing with phones that wouldn't turn on, the agitation in the air clawing at Patrick's nerves.

They dodged between people and cars, the buzz of frantic, worried voices drifting on the breeze. The soulbond tugged sharply in his chest, and he looked to the left, the Arc de Triomphe a distant stone arch against the blue sky. The knowledge that Jono was close by would've made Patrick breathe easier if he had any room to spare in his lungs.

They crossed the wide avenue in a handful of seconds, racing down the street ahead. The open grass on the right gave way to low stone walls with iron fencing on top. Buildings on the left were dark, no lights shining through their windows. People were annoyingly in the way, which was a problem, and then became a *problem* when hellish recognition ripped through Patrick's magic.

Screams echoed from the other side of the wall.

Not all of the noise was human.

Patrick skidded to a halt, facing the thick trees and greenery the wall partially obscured. "Nadine!"

She thudded to a stop, toes flexing against the asphalt, breathing fast. "We need to *keep going!*"

A demonic zombie threw itself over the wall with surprising agility, showing off the blood on its teeth with a snarl. Its form was familiar from London and the Catacombs as the drekavac launched itself at them, screaming all the while.

"Fucking *zombies*," Nadine swore as she raised a shield around them, a single violet mageglobe spinning near her shoulder. "Ilya's raising the dead."

"You think?" Patrick spat out as he conjured up half a dozen mageglobes.

More drekavacs threw themselves over the wall, but not all attempted to attack Patrick and Nadine. More than half went after easier targets—the citizens of and visitors to Paris.

People screamed in terror as the drekavacs chased after them, fleeing down the street between stopped cars. One person tripped and didn't get up, frozen in terror at the death hunting her down. Patrick filled his mageglobes with raw magic and sent them careening through the air, releasing them in the midst of the horde before the zombies reached their prey.

They exploded like bombs, ripping through the drekavacs with brutal intensity. Body parts flew through the air, and a head slammed on top of Nadine's shield, sliding down with a smear of blackness that might've been blood at one point.

Not surrounded by underground walls that could cave in and crush him, in the middle of a citywide emergency, Patrick figured the French government wouldn't mind much if he got a little defensive in an offensive way.

His attack didn't remove all of the drekavacs from the fight. More were flinging themselves over the wall, choosing to go after easier targets than the two mages safe behind near-impenetrable shields.

"Patrick, we need to go," Nadine said harshly.

He knew that, but it was still difficult to accept the retreat. "If Ilya is using the Morrígan's staff, we're going to be fighting zombies all the way to your apartment."

"We're going to be fighting them all the way to the Eiffel Tower, but I'll feel better about doing that with a Carbine in my hands. So let's fucking *go*."

"Who gave you a Carbine?"

"Who do you think?"

At least Lucien was good for something after all.

Patrick hated to turn his back on the drekavacs and the people the demonic zombies were hunting, but he had no choice. They couldn't stand their ground and fight for this one small corner of Paris when the bigger threat was still out there.

Because all around them the dead were rising, and Patrick's side couldn't stop a zombie invasion until Ilya and Peklabog were stopped first.

24

JONO LIFTED THE CAR WITH A SNARL AND HEAVED IT TOWARD THE intersection where a horde of rotten bones animated by lost souls were clawing at a family trapped on top of a vehicle. The car he'd tossed slammed into the zombies, shattering some of them.

The ones left turned glowing skulls their way and started shambling forward.

"Oh, wonderful," Sage sighed irritably. "More zombies."

"We're almost to the flat," Jono grunted.

He could sense Patrick's general location through the soul-bond, the connection wide open between them. The sluice of burning magic from tapping a ley line hadn't yet hit him, which made Jono hopeful Patrick wasn't cornered by the dead.

The streets they'd run through were still filled with people, but the crowds were starting to thin out as the threat became readily apparent. Nothing like the dead clawing their way out of manholes in the middle of the street to make people scream and run for cover. Some people weren't fast enough, and that was the family's problem on top of the car.

Jono squinted against the sunlight, having lost his sunglasses somewhere in the streets behind him on their run from the Arc de Triomphe. "Let's get them out of danger first."

"I don't know where you think there's no danger in Paris right now."

Sage still stayed right by his side as they ran toward the zombie, preternatural speed enabling them to vault over the horde, missing getting caught in bony, clawing hands. Despite being bone stitched together by magic, Jono had seen what damage they could do. He and Sage had passed numerous people who hadn't been quick enough to escape the dead. Their bodies had lain on the street with torn-open guts and gouged-out eyes and throats, magic already crawling over their corpses to make them rise and walk again.

Jono had faced plenty of nightmares in his life, but a never-ending army of the dead was definitely one he could've done without.

They reached the car with the family on it—Sage grabbed the mum and toddler, while Jono went for the dad—and then launched themselves over the remaining zombies. Jono grunted when he landed on the street amidst old broken bones, the man screaming in his ear not helping his concentration any. They set the humans on the ground, and Jono pointed down the street that didn't have any zombies in it at the moment.

"*Run,*" he growled.

He wasn't sure they understood him, but terror was a decent motivator. The three stumbled into a run, and Jono hoped they made it to safety somewhere.

Sage yanked on his arm, dragging Jono forward with bruising strength. "Come on."

They kept running, faster than most others on the street. They passed police trying to protect mundane humans against encroaching zombies amidst stalled cars. Nothing electronic was working, and Jono had a sinking feeling the entire city was affected. It would make communication between groups impossible and provide no easy way to work together and fight the walking dead.

Finally, they turned down the street Nadine's apartment was on. It was empty, with only a handful of cars abandoned and their drivers nowhere to be seen. Jono was thankful no one was around for the few seconds it took them to reach the door. It was unlocked due to the security panel being disabled.

"That's going to be a problem," Jono muttered as he shoved open the door.

"We'll bring something down to barricade it later."

They slipped inside the public foyer, and Jono made sure the door closed firmly behind them. They took the stairs rather than the elevator, because that was a kill box situation if zombies made it past the gate.

Jono pulled out the extra set of keys Nadine had given him once they reached her floor. Even before he opened the door, he knew Wade and Spencer weren't inside, unable to hear any heartbeats or scent them.

"We told him not to leave," Sage said.

"He's grounded when we get back to the States."

Jono locked the door behind them, setting the keys on the small table flush against the wall to his right. He sniffed the air, scenting for any lingering threats, and came up with nothing.

"No way to contact Wade or Spencer. We'll have to wait for them to return," Jono said.

"Here's hoping they're actually together. I wouldn't put it past Wade to have gone out for food with Spencer none the wiser."

Jono was going to have words with Wade about listening after they survived this whole bloody nightmare.

Sage dumped her purse on the coffee table and kicked off her shoes. Jono tossed his mobile to her, and she dropped it in her purse. No use in carrying it around with all signal towers dead across Paris.

A loud, drawn-out yell reached Jono's ears. He met Sage's gaze for a single second before they both lunged toward the windows. Jono opened up the nearest one and looked outside.

Racing around the corner, clutching a bag bulging with bread to his chest, was Wade. Trailing behind him was a horde of drekavacs who screamed louder than Wade.

"Don't eat me!" Wade shouted. "I just wanted lunch!"

Jono didn't think and threw himself off the balcony with a grunt, falling four floors to the ground and not caring about the height. He slammed to the pavement hard enough he felt the impact vibrate up his spine, the cement cracking beneath his feet. Sage landed beside him, neither of them harmed from the jump.

Wade scrambled on top of a stalled car, yelling his bloody head off as he jumped from one car to the next. A drekavac rebounded off a parked car, twisting through the air after Wade, who lashed out with one leg while shoving a macaron into his mouth. He kicked the zombie in the side of the head while hopping on his other foot. He managed to dent the drekavac's skull but lost his hold on his bag of food. It went flying—bread, croissants, and brightly colored macarons spilled through the air before tumbling to the ground.

Wade made a noise that was more pissed-off shriek than frightened scream. "*No*! My passionfruit macarons!"

"Wade!" Jono yelled, already moving. "Leave the food and get your bloody arse over here!"

"But my macarons! And my bread! That was my after-lunch snack!"

A high-pitched growl cut through the air from behind them. Jono looked over his shoulder in time to see Fatima vaulting from the bonnet of one car to another, eyes grayed-out in her small face. She was a tawny-and-black blur as she raced toward the drekavacs. Behind her came Spencer, a dark green mageglobe orbiting his body in tight circles as he ran.

A coldness cut through the air, reminding Jono of Smithfield Market back in London. Fatima landed on the roof of a car and went still, all four paws braced wide. Spencer thrust one arm forward, sending his mageglobe streaking through the air at the drekavacs. The zombies screamed, the sound making Jono want to dial down his hearing.

Spencer's magic smelled cleaner than Patrick's, but it still made Jono's skin crawl. He watched as the mageglobe exploded like a mini-supernova, magic cutting through the drekavacs. Every last one of the demonic zombies went rigid before collapsing on the street. Ghostly fog drifted up from their bodies, twisting through the air.

Fatima yowled again, tail lashing as each individual spirit flew toward her. She opened her small mouth, jaw dropping wider than an ocelot would be capable of in the wild, and ate the spirits whole.

"Sorry, I took a nap and woke up when that damn spell rolled over Paris and saw that Wade was gone. I went looking for him, but then, you know, zombies," Spencer said as he lowered his hands.

"That spell seemed a bit quicker than your casting in London," Sage said.

"I can put the dead to rest in my sleep. Exorcising a Great Marquis of Hell is a different headache entirely."

"Wade!" Jono shouted. "Get over here."

Wade scrambled away from the bodies in the street, gold eyes wide as he looked at Jono. "All I wanted was one of those croak mister sandwiches!"

"We *told* you not to leave the flat, and this is exactly why."

Wade scowled, the gold fading from his eyes now that these particular zombies were no longer a threat. Jono hooked a hand over his shoulder and gently pushed him toward the front door.

Fatima licked her teeth and twisted around. She launched herself at Spencer, who caught her easily enough, murmuring softly to her. She head butted him before wriggling until he put her on the ground.

"Let's get inside," Sage said.

They were filing back through the front entrance of the building when the soulbond tugged sharply in Jono's chest. Awareness washed through him, and he paused in the doorway, leaning back out so he could look down the street.

Sage paused at the bottom of the stairs. "Jono?"

"Patrick is nearby," he said.

Spencer urged Wade upstairs, but Sage stayed where she was, waiting with Jono. Less than a minute later, two figures rounded the corner at the end of the street. He could hear their hearts beating fast and their labored breathing, but both Patrick and Nadine appeared to be uninjured.

"Fucking *zombies*," Patrick gasped once he was within arm's reach.

Jono reeled him in for a hug, breathing in the smell of sweat and anger that surrounded Patrick. When Jono pressed a kiss to his temple, sweat-dampened hair tickled his nose.

"Inside," Jono rumbled.

"Communication is dead across Paris," Nadine said, breathing heavily as she slipped past them, heading for the stairs.

Jono urged Patrick after her and yanked the door shut. They took the stairs two at a time up to Nadine's floor. Spencer stood at the door, holding it open, a mageglobe burning in his free hand. They all hurried into the flat. The second the door closed, Nadine strengthened her threshold to a level that made Jono's teeth ache from close proximity.

"What's the plan?" Jono asked.

"Ilya is using the staff to raise all the dead in Paris," Patrick said.

"And the Eiffel Tower?"

"It's amplifying his spells. The first one knocked out electricity for the entire city, but it wasn't his. We think it was Zachary's."

"There goes any hope of coordination between first responder groups, or getting a warning out," Spencer said.

"The zombies are warning enough."

Nadine twisted her arms behind her back to unzip her dress,

sliding it off with a full-body wriggle. "I got a crate of weapons from Lucien the other night. There's a Carbine for each of us and some body armor. Let's gear up and get on the street. It's not going to be easy getting to the Left Bank."

Patrick and Spencer followed Nadine out of the living room, off to get ready.

Sage looked at Jono, already kicking off her shoes. "We'll shift once we're on the street."

"What about me?" Wade asked. "Don't tell me to stay here. I'm not gonna listen."

"We know," Jono said dryly. "You already proved that."

Wade scowled and crossed his arms over his chest. "Do I shift?"

"Paris already has millions of zombies clawing out of their graves. The last thing the city needs right now is a dragon."

"So no shifting mass?"

"Stay human. Blow fire. Don't shift unless Patrick gives you the go-ahead. You don't need to become a target."

Wade nodded. "Right. Crispify the zombies."

"And don't eat them."

"Don't—hey!"

Wade's affronted squawk had Jono laughing, despite the situation. He left Sage to remind Wade what he could and couldn't do in a fight and went in search of Patrick.

Jono found him in the guest bedroom, having stripped out of his sweaty suit in favor of dark jeans and a cotton T-shirt, combat boots laced tight. Jono watched Patrick strap on the Kevlar vest with practiced ease.

"We're going to be an odd lot running about. Will the police target us?" Jono asked.

"Maybe, but it can't be helped. Nadine will do most of the talking for us if we need to get past any police barriers," Patrick said.

"And if they don't let us through?"

Patrick looked up from adjusting the last strap, rotating his shoulders against the weight of the vest. "We go through anyway."

"It's daylight out, and will be for at least nine more hours. Do you think the Night Courts will help when the sun goes down?"

"Lucien will know to join the fight if it's still ongoing. The others in Paris?" Patrick shrugged his ambivalence about that. "What about the werecreature community?"

Jono grimaced. "I don't know."

Patrick blew out a breath, fingers ghosting over the hilt of the dagger strapped to his right thigh. He stared at his left hand and the line of reddened flesh stretched over his palm, Srecha's blessing stark against his skin.

"If we get the staff, we can stop them."

Jono reached for him, pulling Patrick into a fierce, hard kiss that tasted a lot like desperation. "You aren't fighting alone."

Patrick twisted his fingers around the fabric of Jono's shirt. "I know, but I think I might be the only one who can touch the staff."

"Couldn't Spencer? It's closer to his kind of magic, yeah?"

Patrick shook his head. "Srecha gave me her blessing for a reason."

Jono kissed him again, quick and bruising, breathing in the bitter scent of him. "Bloody stubborn self-sacrificing arsehole."

"You love me anyway."

"I do."

He pulled back, and Patrick managed a tight, brittle smile, but his green eyes were clear, gaze steady when he looked at Jono.

"I know you won't leave me," Patrick said, sounding so sure, so insistent, that Jono could only kiss him again.

"Never." Jono sealed that promise with a biting kiss that Patrick never pulled back from. "I'll fight by your side, and when I'm not there, I'll find you. Always."

Patrick pulled back with a soft gasp, brushing his lips over the edge of Jono's jaw. "Then let's go fight."

Jono followed Patrick out of the guest bedroom and to

Nadine's, where she and Spencer had already claimed a Carbine for themselves, extra ammunition clipped to the front of their Kevlar vests.

Nadine nodded at the weapon laid out on her bed. "That one is yours."

"You give the best presents," Patrick said.

"Wasn't me who procured it."

"Yeah, we all know Lucien has a weapons stash in every country."

Jono eyed the mages, how they were kitted out in similar dark clothing and Kevlar vests. Knee and elbow guards and hard helmets were in a crate at the end of the bed, and they all strapped them on, pulling on fingerless gloves. As far as body armor went, it was makeshift, but it would have to do on short notice.

At least Patrick finally had a rifle. While it wasn't his pistol, maybe he'd stop whinging now.

Nadine hooked the strap connected to her rifle to her vest. "Ready."

"Ready," the other two echoed.

They left the bedroom for the living room where Sage and Wade patiently waited. Sage noted their weapons before her gaze skipped to Jono. "Shall we leave our clothes here and shift outside?"

Jono nodded, and they both set about stripping off their clothes. No one cared that they were nude, and neither he nor Sage were body shy.

They left the flat as a group, with Nadine locking the door behind them and sending a pulse of magic through the threshold with a flick of her fingers. They took the stairs down to the ground floor and emerged onto the street in bright, early afternoon sunlight. Nadine set a shield over the door, sealing it shut.

Jono didn't waste any time shifting forms, and neither did Sage. His body twisted, bones breaking while skin split as he shifted from human to wolf. The agony of the shift lasted only for a second before his pain receptors turned off. Colors bled into different shades, the world tilting on its axis as everything human about his body became wolf.

Everything but his mind and soul, and the patron god that resided deep inside him.

Fenrir rose up through the depths of his soul, a powerful presence that pressed against the back of Jono's mind. He shook his massive wolf head to settle his vision, Fenrir clawing at his awareness.

Patrick looked at Jono, jaw tight, smelling of grim determination and a hint of fear for the fight ahead. "Ready?"

Jono growled deep in his throat, the sound echoed by Sage's low snarl. Beneath the sound was the ghost of Fenrir's voice in the back of his mind, sharp like teeth.

Let's hunt.

They started down the street, the scent of death growing in the air as high above, the cries of ravens and crows drifted on the summer wind.

25

PATRICK FORMED A MAGEGLOBE, FILLED IT WITH A SHOCK-WAVE spell, and lobbed it at the horde of zombies about to overrun a group of police and more than a dozen civilians standing their ground at the obelisk in the Place de la Concorde. Whatever witch they had with them was barely holding up a shield, her magic flickering from lack of strength.

When the mageglobe exploded, the shock wave that followed slammed through the zombies, pushing them through the air and over the street, away from the boxed in police and civilians. Some got severed on abandoned cars, leaving limbs crawling about. With clear line of sight achieved, Nadine was able to raise a shield around the group to give them some breathing room.

Jono and Sage veered right, racing toward where a police unit had set up a barrier near the building to their right. Rather than weave through cars, the pair played hopscotch with the vehicles, their weight crushing the roofs. It still got them close to the fresher-looking zombies coming out of the Jardins des Champs-Élysées.

Violet magic followed Jono and Sage in their push forward—Nadine keeping them covered in case of any friendly fire incident from the police. Patrick hefted his rifle up higher, digging the butt against his shoulder.

"You're up, Dead Boy," Patrick said.

"I don't know how many times I've had to tell you Hellraisers I'm not dead, Razzle Dazzle," Spencer said.

"Stop arguing and clear us some space," Nadine said, attention split between the two groups she was protecting.

Spencer jumped onto a car, climbing onto the roof. Fatima joined him, twining between his legs to sit between his feet. Her tail lashed against his ankles as Spencer conjured up two mageglobes, the summer heat fading around him.

Patrick shifted on his feet, moving so he could watch their six. Nadine's shield around them was a protection no zombie could get through, but they still needed to know what threats were coming at them.

Spencer thrust one arm toward the small group near the obelisk and the other toward the park. His dark green mageglobes streaked through the air like heat-seeking missiles, exploding amidst the zombies. Bones and bodies went rigid, the malevolent magic sustaining them fading away as Spencer ripped the wandering souls out of the physical bodies. They hovered above the motionless dead like sticky fog, moving like nothing else in nature.

Fatima launched herself off the car, fog drifting around her small body. She opened her mouth wide, and the cold got a little worse. Patrick watched as the souls were drawn to her across the square, getting sucked in like a whirlpool, pulled by Spencer's magic. His magic guided them home to rest, Fatima the transition point between the living world and the place beyond the veil where the souls should've never been disturbed.

The psychopomp's form flickered, like a computer glitch, jaws snapping shut on the final bit of soul slipping past her teeth. Fatima stretched before giving herself a shake and looking back at Spencer. She made a small questioning sound Patrick couldn't parse.

"Who's a good girl?" Wade cooed, walking up to the car and holding out his arms to her.

Fatima chirped proudly before jumping into his arms. Wade cuddled her happily while Spencer only shook his head.

"You're spoiling her. She has four feet and can walk on her own," Spencer said as he jumped off the car.

"But I like carrying her." Wade scratched behind Fatima's ears, not bothered in the least by the fact she'd eaten at least a hundred souls just now. "She deserves to be spoiled."

Spencer shook his head, finally giving up on the argument he'd been having with Wade since they left Nadine's apartment.

"Let's pull those people back while we have the chance," Nadine said, lowering the shield around them.

Jono and Sage were standing guard some distance away from the police by the building, facing the park to give a warning at the first sight of the next wave of zombies. Patrick was under no illusions this horde was the only one in the area.

It had taken them five hours to make it from Nadine's apartment to the square, each street put behind them a hard-fought battle. It hadn't been a direct push, not with the amount of dead in the streets, people needing rescuing, and themselves needing to conserve their energy. The path had been winding and brutal. They'd lost Wade inside a boulangerie for half a block a couple of hours ago before anyone realized he wasn't with them. He'd come away from that excursion with half a dozen premade sandwiches and a declaration of "I'm not dying hungry."

"You're not dying, period," Patrick had retorted.

Lunch had been eaten on the run—fuel for their magic and to stop Wade from complaining—as they followed the makeshift lines of defense popping up on the Paris streets. From police to the army, locals and tourists alike, those with magic were standing their ground alongside some from the preternatural world. Pockets of safety were being defended against the walking dead, but Patrick didn't know how long they would last. People needed to sleep, and communication was still down.

Summer solstice was the longest day of the year. They still had four hours of daylight left, and they weren't anywhere close to the Eiffel Tower. The spell Ilya had cast wasn't close to peaking yet, which made Patrick wonder if Peklabog had been given the Morrígan's staff, or if the necromancer had kept it for himself.

Neither option was a good one.

Patrick weaved his way through the abandoned cars, keeping watch on their six as Nadine led the way across the square to the obelisk. She made a hole in her shield covering the small monument for them to step through before talking in rapid French with the nearest police officer.

Patrick made his way to the group of civilians, several of whom were standing over a teenaged girl who sat on the ground. She was holding on to her knees, head hanging down, breathing raggedly.

"Wade, give me one of your cookies," Patrick said as he lowered his rifle.

"But they're *my* cookies!" Wade protested, still holding Fatima.

"*Wade.*"

The teen grumbled as he put Fatima down and stuck his hand into his pocket, coming up with a folded napkin. Inside was a broken palmier, but the sweet was still edible. He grudgingly passed it to Patrick, who took it and knelt in front of the teenaged witch.

"Here." He offered her the palmier, and the sugary scent got her to lift her head. "Eat this."

"*Danke,*" she muttered.

She took a piece and popped it into her mouth. The second it touched her tongue, she yanked the napkin out of Patrick's hand, stuffing the rest of the cookie into her mouth and chewing fast. The sugary pick-me-up would give her a quick burst of strength, enough to get her feet back under her.

Patrick looked over his shoulder. "Nadine?"

She turned away from the handful of police officers and approached him. "Let's get them across the square. Some of the police are hunkering down in the buildings there. They have a sorceress who is warding all entrances and windows. They're using it to house civilians who can't make it home behind thresholds."

"Sounds like a plan." Patrick extended his hand to the teenaged witch and helped her to her feet. "Come on, let's get you guys to safety."

The second the words were out of his mouth, Jono howled a warning. Patrick snapped his head around, getting eyes on the zombies breaking free of the tree line across the way. They moved faster than the skeletons they'd just cleared, bloodied and newly dead, raised by magic. Between them cut a couple of darker, more demonic looking drekavacs.

"Oh, this feels like Cairo all over again," Spencer mused, already raising both hands and conjuring up another set of mageglobes. "Could've done without reliving that time."

"There aren't any soultakers," Patrick pointed out.

"Fuck, man. Don't tempt fate."

Considering the Fates had been the ones to keep prodding Patrick down this road, he thought it was a little late for that.

Jono and Sage surged across the square, blurred figures that twisted between cars as they charged the drekavacs. Movement out of the corner of his eye had Patrick looking left, squinting against the sunlight at the zombies coming from the direction of the bridge.

Patrick raised his rifle, conjuring up half a dozen mageglobes as he tapped a ley line through the soulbond. "We got incoming."

Spencer nudged Fatima with his foot and pointed at the park. "Go."

The psychopomp yowled before running off, trailing Spencer's magic behind her, fog breaking in the air. Patrick reached out and grabbed Spencer by the back of his tactical vest, hauling the other mage with him as Nadine and the police corralled the civilians huddling around the obelisk and got them moving.

"Think Wade would share any more of his cookies?" Spencer muttered, not fighting Patrick's pull as he was dragged between cars, just like old times.

"Yes," Patrick said, lying through his teeth.

"Uh, *no*," Wade protested.

Spencer kept conjuring, but his tone turned pleading. "I need a pick-me-up."

"That sounds like a you problem and not a problem for my cookies."

"Both of you, shut up. Spencer, focus on the zombies," Patrick snapped.

Spencer snagged a mageglobe in one hand before throwing it toward the zombies coming from the bridge. "I *am*."

Even as he spoke, Spencer's magic ripped through the zombies they could see, separating the souls that animated bones and flesh. Patrick could sense the tearing as Spencer pulled the souls free, sending them to rest with Fatima to guide them. The twisting fog they created moved swiftly toward the psychopomp, who swallowed them whole.

But the zombies kept coming.

Jono and Sage stayed within the square, not chasing the zombies into the park. The zombies on the bridge coming from the Left Bank were skeletons filled with souls, bones that hadn't seen the light of day in centuries suddenly called back to life.

"Shit," Spencer swore as he stumbled over someone's discarded bag.

Patrick kept him on his feet, hauling the other man along toward the police barrier. "No luck?"

"They just keep *coming*."

He sounded aggravated. Hours of already breaking souls free nonstop were starting to catch up with him. Even with the ability to tap a ley line, mages weren't inexhaustible. It still took concentration and power to do what Spencer did, and that wore on a person's strength. Patrick knew Spencer needed a breather, so when they ushered everyone behind Nadine's shield and the dragged-together cars in front of the building at the corner of the square, Patrick shoved Spencer down on the steps.

"Sit. Call Fatima back and take a break," Patrick said.

Spencer scowled, nose scrunching up in distaste at that order. "I'm fine."

"We need to stagger the use of your magic or you'll be no good to us when we finally reach the Eiffel Tower. I have an idea that should get us across the bridge without needing to break souls this time around."

"Is this one of your ideas that Gerard always said gave him a heart attack?"

"You think you're funny, but you're not."

"So it *is* one of those ideas."

Patrick ignored him. Nadine was talking in rapid French to several police officers, hopefully getting updates. Communication was still impossible with dead electronics across the city. Coordination was dangerously hit-or-miss.

Zombies broke through the tree line again, staggering toward them. Patrick's mouth twisted as he took in their state—fresh bodies of the newly raised dead. The skeleton zombies and drekavacs Ilya had raised were hunting and killing Paris citizens for fresher bodies. Some of the souls animating the dead were from sacrifices, others from being killed, but the sheer number of zombies crawling out of the ground meant the Morrígan's staff was more dangerous than any of them had thought.

"Jono!" Patrick yelled. "Sage! Fall back!"

Their snarls were confirmation they'd heard him, but they were in danger of being cut off in seconds as the zombies surged to cut them off. Patrick jumped onto the hood of a car, conjured up a mageglobe, and filled it with another shock-wave ward. He threw it at the zombies closest to their location, letting magic tear through the bodies.

The dead were blown backward, some bodies ripped apart from the force of the spell. It cleared a small area of the square, but Patrick could see more zombies moving in the park, the new group threatening to box in Jono and Sage.

"Jono!"

Patrick moved forward, calling up his magic even as he raised his rifle. Before he could pull the trigger, a multitude of howls ripped through the air. Patrick removed his finger from the trigger as a snarling group of werewolves raced around the far corner by the park. They hurtled themselves at the zombies, fangs and claws viciously tearing through bodies.

Jono and Sage took the opportunity to pull back, vaulting over parked cars to put distance between themselves and the zombies. Patrick waited until they had almost reached his position before flinging his mageglobes at the latest wave of zombies. The blast of raw magic erupted in the scrum, turning the bodies into miniscule pieces of bone and meat.

The other werecreatures retreated to their position at the building. As soon as they were close enough, Nadine expanded her shield over them, her magic giving the world a faintly violet cast to it. Patrick pulled back to the clear space behind the barrier of cars. Jono and Sage followed after him, along with a brown werewolf half the size of Jono. All three crouched nearby, but only Jono and the other werewolf shifted.

The grinding sound of bones breaking and reforming made Patrick wince. He never looked away from the twisting bodies of fur that became skin, limbs settling from wolf to human. Jono shook his head to clear it, remaining crouched on one knee, naked and streaked with blood that wasn't all his.

The woman who knelt on the other side of Sage had skin so dark it looked glossy in the sunlight. Her hair was twisted into Bantu knots, and her dark brown eyes were locked on Jono. She said something in rapid French that made Jono shake his head.

"Sorry, don't speak French," he said.

"You are not with our god pack," the woman said in heavily accented French.

"Passing through."

"What caused this?"

"Bloke with a god complex. We're trying to get to the Eiffel Tower."

She gave him a troubled look. "That way lies certain death. My pack and I had to swim across the Seine for safety. The Left Bank is overrun with zombies."

Patrick looked across the square and the smudge of swarming zombies he could see beyond the obelisk where the Pont de la Concorde started. "So is the Right Bank. Nowhere in Paris will be safe until we take down the one responsible for all this. If you keep trying to run, you'll be overwhelmed, and the last thing any of us need is a zombie werewolf."

"We tried to help people to safety but the zombies were too much."

"That's probably going to happen on this side of the Seine. You can keep pushing through to your homes and risk getting boxed in and killed, or get behind the shields here in this building," Patrick said.

The woman glanced at Jono, her full lips twisting. "Paris is our home. Hiding will not save it."

"Everyone is without communications all across the city. If you're willing to fight, do you think you and your pack could run relays between police headquarters on Île de la Cité and the Ministry of Magical Affairs?" Nadine asked.

The woman blinked before her expression hardened. "*Oui.* There are fifteen of us in my pack."

"I'll pull one of the police officers from their duties here, and they can act as a liaison once we get you to the Ministry."

It was a risky endeavor, but connecting two major groups of first responders would be helpful in the long run. Patrick met Jono's gaze and gave him a nod.

"I have a plan to get across the bridge," Patrick said.

Jono sighed, resting both hands on the ground. "Will the bridge survive?"

"See, that's what I'm talking about," Spencer called out from behind them.

Patrick rolled his eyes. "Oh, fuck you both. Let's get moving."

Jono and the woman shifted back into their animal forms, Jono towering over her slimmer bulk. Patrick looked around until he spied Wade standing behind a car and stuffing his face with the last of his cookies.

"Wade, I'm going to need you to stay with me up front," Patrick said.

Wade rushed over, dragging the back of his hand across his mouth. It didn't do much but smear cookie crumbs across his cheek. "Yeah?"

Patrick reached out and tugged him close, looking Wade in the eyes. "We're going to push forward as much as we can. When I tell you to, I want you to firebomb the zombies without shifting. Can you do that?"

Wade hesitated a moment before squaring his shoulders and nodding determinedly. "Yeah, I can do it."

Patrick clapped him on the shoulder. "Great. I'll be right by your side. Just do what I say, when I say it, and don't get distracted."

"Okay. No distractions."

Wade dug one last smushed cookie from his pocket, shoved it in his mouth, and chewed. He looked a little wide-eyed and worried, but not overly frightened, which was all Patrick could hope for in the situation.

Less than a minute later they moved out, Nadine dropping her shield as the last officer hustled inside the building. Patrick sensed the sorceress' magic rise over the entrance, and he wished her all the best in keeping everyone safe.

The lone police officer who'd volunteered to come with them stuck close. Nadine scrambled on top of a car to get a better view of the square. Patrick joined her, scanning the area. Zombies were coming from the east and west, pouring out of the two parks on either side of the square. They looked newly dead compared to the dense movement of old skeletons lurching across the bridge south of them.

Nadine clapped her hands together, and the tiny mageglobe trapped between her palms exploded outward like ball lightning gone nova. A domed shield formed around them, moving quickly over the square. It split down the middle, two walls peeling back to momentarily block the zombies coming from the parks, buying their group time.

"Let's go," Patrick called out.

They ran toward the bridge, the group of werecreatures they'd brought into the fold keeping pace but giving them a wide berth to work in, which was fine by Patrick.

"Plan?" Nadine asked as she slid across a hood rather than waste seconds detouring around the car.

"Fire."

"That's not going to stop enough zombies to make a difference. The souls will still be wandering and get put back into the dead."

"Can't have a zombie without a body."

She shot him an exasperated look. "This is why you get banned from cities."

"I don't get banned. It's just suggested I never return."

Nadine rolled her eyes and gestured expansively with her free hand at their current situation. Patrick opted to ignore her silent opinion of the way he interpreted things.

Patrick stuck his free hand behind him and wiggled his fingers. A second later, Wade latched on, and Patrick pulled the teenager along with him. Fatima bounded ahead of them, trailing a coldness the sun couldn't cut through.

They passed the obelisk, growing ever closer to the dense wall of walking skeletons that waited up ahead. The eerie magic that enslaved souls to animate bones made Patrick squint against the glow hazing the air around the dead.

As he watched, the horde of zombies started to expand, rising up as they climbed each other to block the bridge, a wall of bones that reminded him of that shiver-inducing space in the Catacombs.

"Patrick?" Spencer called out harshly.

Patrick kept running, keeping hold of Wade. "Hold your magic. Everyone, stay close."

The horde of zombies grew, clawing on top of each other in a rising wave of the dead that blocked out the far side of the bridge. Some skeletons couldn't hold on and tumbled over the edge into the Seine. The mass of skeletons in front pushed outward like a leading trough, a multitude of old, bony fingers reaching for them as countless skulls with glowing eye sockets kept them in sight.

Patrick yanked Wade closer, skidding to a stop. He let go of Wade's hand, settling his own in between the teenager's shoulder blades in a supportive touch.

"*Now!*" Patrick snarled.

Fire could break most spells, but even magefire wasn't strong enough to burn thousands of skeletons to ash and leave stolen souls without their anchor.

Dragon fire was.

Wade sucked in a deep breath and let it out with a roar that sounded as if it came from a body larger than the skinny teenager vibrating beneath Patrick's touch. Fire erupted from Wade's mouth, bursting forth with such intensity Patrick had to let go of his Carbine and throw up his other arm to protect his face from the heat.

The wave of zombie skeletons collapsed beneath dragon fire, limbs clawing at each other for a safety they would never find. Bone blackened in seconds, getting charred down to ash with every breath of flame Wade let out.

He was warm beneath Patrick's touch, red scales pushing up through the skin on the back of his neck and on his arms. It took Wade less than a minute to clear the bridge of that group of zombies, but Patrick knew more would soon take their place.

"Move, move!" he shouted.

Patrick pushed Wade forward, catching him under the arm when Wade stumbled over a bone that missed getting burned to ash. He kicked it aside, then swore in surprise when a dark shape dove from the air to catch the tibia up in sharp talons.

The sun was dipping down toward the horizon but still bright in the sky. Its light was suddenly blotted out by the hundreds of crows and ravens that descended on Pont de la Concorde, picking at any bits of bone left. Patrick's heart was beating double time as they ran across the bridge, boots sliding on the ash that covered it. His face reflected back at him in countless black eyes that watched them, the shadow of someone else's visage overlaid on his own in their shiny depths.

Wade coughed out smoke, eyes squeezed shut as he heaved for air. Patrick never let him go, hauling him forward with a firm hand.

"Good job," Patrick said. "You totally get a cookie when this is all over."

Wade choked out a laugh that smelled like fire and sulfur, golden eyes with their reptilian slitted black pupils blinking rapidly. "*Cookies*. Plural."

"As many as you can eat."

When they made it across the Seine to the Left Bank, Patrick's skin prickled with the awareness of too many eyes on them. The ravens and crows weren't the only ones watching their push into central Paris.

The Morrígan watched as well through the countless eyes of her winged specters, and Patrick knew nothing good would ever come of gaining the attention of a war goddess.

26

The City of Lights had gone dark.

The sun was passing over the horizon, half-set, and the blue of the sky had deepened to something darker. In the east, where the sky was darkest, stars were slowly becoming visible. The sun and the beacon of sinister magic the Eiffel Tower had become were the only points of brightness in the city.

Well, aside from the souls animating millions of skeleton bodies, magic glittering between rib bones and in countless eye sockets, fresh zombies, and the barrage of offensive magic courtesy of Dominion Sect mercenary magic users.

"Incoming!" Patrick yelled.

The flurry of mageglobes that arced through the air from the west carried military-grade spells within them. Patrick conjured up a set of his own, thrusting an arm upward and guiding them through Nadine's shield.

The strike spell he'd filled them with must have been the same as the ones aimed at their position. When they collided, the resulting explosion in the air was less fireworks and more nuclear, lighting up the night sky with magic. It provided a flash of illumination, enough light for Patrick to check that yeah, the sea of zombies blocking their way on the Boulevard de la Tour-Maubourg hadn't decreased.

It wasn't the only explosion going on in Paris. Pockets of resistance set up by magic users and those in the preternatural world were still coming to the city's defense, working hand in hand with the police when they could. French resistance was alive and well against the dead.

Two hours ago they'd managed to catch a breather at the Ministry of Magical Affairs, if one could call being interrogated for thirty minutes a breather. Their French counterparts had finally wanted to listen to what they had to say now that Paris was overrun by zombies. The PIA's warnings had come too little too late to stop Ilya from raising the dead, but that didn't mean they could stop fighting.

They'd had to come clean about Spencer and his kind of magic though. Whereas before the French government might have thrown a fit about having a foreign mage with an affinity for the dead and a kind of necromantic magic inside their borders, this time they'd only been grateful.

But Spencer was just one mage against millions of dead, and he could only do so much. In retrospect, it wasn't anything like the Thirty-Day War. The dead had never overrun Cairo like this. Spencer was flagging but still fighting, though the number of dead he could put to rest at one time had slowly decreased over the course of the day.

They'd been routed from Place Joffre and were now boxed in on either side of the Boulevard de la Tour-Maubourg by zombies. Spencer was focusing on their forward position, but it was like trying to move the ocean. The waves of zombies kept coming.

At least it wasn't just Patrick's pack, Nadine, and Spencer fighting. The ministry had asked for volunteers to aid them on their push to the Eiffel Tower, and they'd come away with twenty magic users to help them, though only one was a mage.

It still wasn't enough.

"We need to clear a path," Nadine said, staring at the zombies clawing at her shield a few meters ahead of them.

"What do you think we've been trying to do?" Spencer snapped tiredly.

"I know, I know, but this isn't *working*. The fucking Dominion Sect knows our position, and they're rerouting the zombies to keep us in one spot, hoping to overwhelm us."

"At this rate, it's less hoping and more succeeding," Patrick said.

Nadine shot him an exasperated look. "Not helping."

Patrick tossed another set of mageglobes filled with strike spells at the next volley of incoming attack spells. "Now that's a lie. I'm a great help."

The spells crashed together and lit up the sky again. Time was he wouldn't have been able to keep up a sustained counterattack like this, not after the Thirty-Day War and the wounds he'd walked away from it with. Jono sidled closer and Patrick dug his hand into thick fur, leaning against him for a brief moment. The soulbond hummed between them, a depth of magic at his fingertips he was grateful for.

Jono and Sage had been forced behind the shield once they all got boxed in, and both were itching to fight. Patrick was reluctant to let Wade shift mass into his dragon form, not wanting French officials to know the truth about what he was. Wade was willing, Patrick knew that, but it was one thing to let him breathe fire in front of werecreatures, quite another to do it in front of representatives of a foreign government. He knew, as the minutes ticked down to midnight, they might not have a choice.

Right now, the only option they had was to keep fighting.

So that's what they did.

However long later, when the sun had finally fully set, the Eiffel Tower became a warning beacon against the night sky, ochre-colored magic flickering like fire on the massive monument. The only light that didn't come from their magic burned in the skulls of skeleton zombies, the dead piling up around Nadine's shield.

The French magic users were tossing spells ahead and behind them, trying to clear a path, but the zombies were too numerous. Any dead that got blown up were immediately replaced by more bodies. Patrick couldn't help them; all his attention was on incoming aerial attacks. As the only combat mage with offensive magic capabilities, it was his job to keep those attacks at bay if at all possible.

"Oh, that can't be good," Spencer said from behind him.

Patrick never took his eyes off the sky. "What can't be good?"

Nadine yelled something in French, and the echo of explosions to the rear of them faded as the magic users with them focused their efforts on the front. Patrick tore his gaze away from the night sky, eyes going wide at what was coming toward them.

Walking over the sea of zombies was a glowing white taxidermized horse carrying a short rider on its back. The zombie was nothing but bone beneath a ragged uniform whose colors had faded from centuries of internment. The bicorn hat worn sideways sat limply on the zombie's skull, doing nothing to hide the fiery magic burning in its eye sockets. The zombie rider and horse were too far back for any of the magic users' spells to get a clean hit. Everyone still tried, but the zombies kept coming.

"Is that…Napoleon's horse?" Patrick asked in disbelief. "Is that *Napoleon*?"

"His body, yeah, maybe," Nadine said, throwing up another layer into her shield. "We're right next to Les Invalides."

"First zombies, now zombie horses. What's next? Kings and queens? Will we get cake for our efforts when this is all over?"

"Marie Antoinette isn't buried in Paris."

"I want cake," Wade piped up.

Spencer thrust his arm forward, sending a mageglobe toward the horse and its rider. He broke the souls free of the bodies, but even as the horse lurched and lost its footing on top of the zombies filling the street, the swirl of another soul sank into its form, reanimating the body. Another soul settled in its rider, and the two zombies walked once more.

"The staff is pulling too many fucking souls out from beyond the veil. I keep breaking them, but more keep filling the bodies left behind," Spencer growled.

Mageglobes streaked through the sky again, carrying attack spells from the direction of the Eiffel Tower. Patrick turned his attention back to the threat coming from above and drew magic from the ley line below through Jono's soul to power them. He sent his counterattack into the sky, working to neutralize the threat.

"We need to—" he began.

Patrick was cut off by the distant *booms* of a type of weapon he recognized from his time in the Mage Corps and not one he expected to hear in the center of Paris.

The rockets cutting through the air originated from the domed roof of Les Invalides to their left. Patrick reacted instantly, ready to protect their position, before he realized the rockets weren't aimed at their group but at the mass of zombies directly in front of them.

Half a dozen rockets slammed into the Boulevard de la Tour-Maubourg, blowing apart countless zombies and abandoned cars, eradicating the dead, including Napoleon and his horse.

"That's it. The French are never going to forgive us now," Nadine muttered.

What space the rockets gained them wouldn't last long, but Nadine still used the reprieve to push her shields forward the way an ice ship broke through sea ice in the Arctic. She gained them more ground one meter at a time, the same way she'd done during the Thirty-Day War.

The Eiffel Tower was so close, but still so far.

"I don't know who that was, but anyone want to tell them that won't stop the zombies?" Spencer said, using the lull to break as many souls free as he could and put them to rest. Fatima paced the leading edge of Nadine's shield, drawing the souls into herself to guide them back beyond the veil.

Patrick crunched his way over bone, relying on Jono to take point and clear the way, ensuring the handful of zombies still intact enough to be a problem were torn to pieces by sharp teeth.

A second volley of rockets cleared the area between them and Les Invalides. Nadine didn't hesitate and cut her shield sideways through the mess of bones the rockets had left behind, forming a narrow shielded tunnel.

Patrick was countering another volley of attack spells—too many for him to clear alone—when Nadine swore savagely in both English and French. The push of her magic was a pressure against his personal shields, but he couldn't turn to look at what had caught her attention.

"Brace!" he yelled.

Patrick caught most of the attack spells midair, magic exploding above their location. Four got through, despite his best efforts.

The spells crashed against Nadine's shield with enough force that Patrick felt the impact vibrate through her magic into the ground. Light exploded overhead, violet-colored waves rippling through the barrier between them and certain death. Nadine's expression of rigid concentration didn't change as she expanded her shields outward, holding back the attack with little more than an annoyed flick of one hand.

Her rapid push outward to provide their sudden backup with cover hadn't been clean though, and more than a few zombies were now inside their defenses. Jono and Sage left Patrick's side to take down the zombies—joined by Lucien and his Night Court.

"I hope you brought me one of those rocket launchers," Patrick shouted.

"You don't need one," Lucien retorted, ripping a skull off a zombie and crushing it in one hand. The soul left in the body flickered until Spencer broke it free.

Carmen, dressed all in black with no glamour to hide what she was, hefted an actual honest-to-gods sword and cleanly decapitated a fresh-looking zombie with a single swing. Sage crushed the head in her massive jaws, and Spencer broke apart every last soul in the zombies inside the shield. Fatima swallowed them whole, drawing them to the other side.

"How did you even find us?" Patrick asked.

"Your magic isn't subtle when you're throwing combat spells around," Lucien said.

Patrick opened his mouth to argue, then thought better of it. He swallowed dryly, wishing he had some water. Looking around at their position—surrounded by zombies that kept relentlessly coming—he knew getting through millions of them was an impossible feat.

The Catacombs were the resting place of more than six million dead, to say nothing of the aboveground graveyards in Paris, church crypts, and monuments that doubled as tombs. The only way to stop the dead was to get the Morrígan's staff. They couldn't do that stuck where they were.

"How did you get here?" Patrick asked, looking at Lucien.

The master vampire peeled his lips back in an annoyed snarl. "Rooftops. The streets were impassible."

"Any other Night Courts going to join the fight?"

Lucien shrugged. "They'll protect their territory first."

"Of course they will."

"They'll still fight, just not here," Carmen said.

Lucien set the grenade launcher on the ground and took a moment to reload. "We can't eat the dead, remember? The Night Courts here want Paris returned to the humans as much as you do."

The French ministry magic users eyed Lucien and his vampires with more than a little trepidation, but at least no one attempted to challenge their presence. Patrick really didn't want to have to explain his relationship with Lucien to foreign allies, and he knew this would get back to people who weren't Setsuna. Before anyone could start asking questions, the earth trembled in a way Patrick didn't like.

"Please tell me that's more zombies and not an earthquake," Spencer said as he scooped up Fatima into his arms.

"Look," Wade said, yanking on Patrick's arm to turn him around.

Patrick stared at where Wade pointed, right hand bypassing his rifle and straying to his dagger. The manhole cover behind them in the street between two abandoned cars vibrated in place for a few seconds before exploding upward, shattering from the force of its expulsion. Patrick expanded his personal shields to cover Wade, ensuring the teenager wasn't hit by any stray shrapnel.

Every single magic user had a spell ready at their fingertips when a wooden pestle thrust itself up out of the dark hole and knocked against its edges to force it wider. The earth obeyed the silent command, and the hole expanded with a grating crunch.

"Hold fire!" Patrick yelled.

Nadine repeated the order in French as the sewer entrance finished expanding, providing more than enough room for Baba Yaga to rise up from below on her floating mortar made of bones. The skulls that decorated it still glowed like they had in the Catacombs, but at least none of them moved as if they carried souls within them. Her face was just as ugly as Patrick remembered though.

Someone—on the French side of the group, not the vampire side—retched loudly.

Baba Yaga banged the pestle against bone in an absentminded way, staring at the zombies clawing against Nadine's shield. "Is not good for business."

"Oh, you think?" Patrick couldn't help but ask.

Baba Yaga looked down her large nose at him, mouth twisting disdainfully. "Below is empty. Will take you through."

Spencer whistled. "Well, shit. The bastard emptied the Catacombs."

Jono settled by Patrick's side, growling softly. Patrick didn't think twice about clenching his fingers around Jono's fur. He remembered the map Lisette had pulled out of her backpack, knew how twisted and convoluted the Catacombs were.

"There's no direct route from here to the Eiffel Tower," he said.

"Will make way as far as can go," Baba Yaga retorted.

"Not through the veil. There's only what? Two hours left before midnight? It's still summer solstice. We go through the veil and we risk Ilya completing whatever spell he's trying to finalize tonight. We can't afford to lose time like that."

"Think I not know risk?" The mortar drifted closer to the ground so she could lean forward, resting the pestle against the asphalt. "Dead are Peklabog domain. Earth? Mine. Will make way."

She banged the pestle against the ground for emphasis, cracking the asphalt. Patrick stared at the crack in the earth before sharing a long look with Jono, who only chuffed at him, incapable of human speech with a wolf's mouth.

"What the hell?" Patrick said. "We're fighting with Lucien. She can't be any worse."

The piece of bone that slammed into his hard helmet had Patrick looking over his shoulder, scowling at Lucien, who raised both middle fingers at him rather than rip out his throat. War always did make strange bedfellows.

"We don't have a choice. Staying here is a losing battle," Nadine said tiredly.

The fight at the foot of the Eiffel Tower wasn't going to be much better, but it would be *there*, and that was all that mattered.

"Let's go," Patrick said.

Baba Yaga led the way, floating backward until her mortar hovered over the manhole. She descended into the sewer in one smooth motion, the hole enlarging in a way that made asphalt crack.

Nadine pointed at her shield. "I'll go last. I'll draw my magic down after everyone is below."

"The dead will keep coming," Spencer warned as he carried Fatima with him to the hole.

Patrick conjured up a mageglobe, filling it with a raw magic that was little more than a grenade without a pin and a command trigger in the back of his mind. "I'll buy us some time."

Nadine nodded, then raised her voice to give the order to the French magic users. The group didn't hesitate before following Spencer into the sewer. Lucien and his Night Court went next, dropping down into the dark one at a time. Then it was Sage's turn, followed by Wade, but Jono waited for Patrick.

Patrick gripped his fur, sparing a second to lean over and brush his lips across the tip of one ear. "Go. I'll be right behind you."

Jono blinked at him with bright blue eyes streaked through with white. Patrick wondered how much longer it would be until Fenrir joined the fight.

Patrick watched Jono slide underground before crouching by the edge and staring into the dark. Far, far down below he could make out the pinpricks of witchlights. He didn't think sewers went that deep, but there was only one way to find out.

Patrick threw himself into the hole and skidded down a steeply slanted hill of cold earth to the bottom. Jono was there to stop him from tumbling any farther, a solid wall of muscle that didn't move an inch. Patrick got to his feet, the chill below drying the sweat on his skin from the long hours fighting in the sun.

Then Nadine came sliding down, body glimmering in violet magic as she pulled her shields down behind her. Beyond her, the lit-up skulls of zombies appeared in the dark, and he could hear the clattering of bone.

"They're coming!" Nadine shouted.

She hit the bottom and pitched into his arms. Patrick hauled her up, and she went racing after the others, following Baba Yaga. Patrick took up the rearguard, sliding into the tunnel Baba Yaga had made and releasing his mageglobe behind him. The blast of raw magic brought down the earth above, the cave-in flattening the zombies hunting them.

In the dark tunnel beneath Paris that spun and grated like bones twisting in a joint from an immortal's magic, Patrick and the others ran from one hopeless fight to another.

Baba Yaga stepped off her mortar as the earth trembled around them and split upward. The bones of its making rearranged themselves into a dome and pushed against the dirt falling down around them. The slant of earth was just as steep as their way in.

Nadine pushed her way to the front and went first, a single violet mageglobe lighting the way, her shield a pressure in the air Patrick could almost touch. Everyone else followed after her, with Patrick taking up the rearguard.

He paused at the bottom, long enough to look Baba Yaga in the eye. "Peklabog will know you helped us."

Baba Yaga smacked her pestle lightly against the back of his calves. "Is not problem. Am remembered more than him."

Patrick took Baba Yaga at her word and climbed out of the tunnel straight into a hellish fight.

27

Spencer offered his hand, and Patrick took it, getting hauled out of the hole Baba Yaga had carved right in the center of the Champs de Mars. Nadine's shield held strong between them and the horde of zombies that blanketed the park in front of the Eiffel Tower. What zombies that had been trapped inside her shield with them had been taken care of by Spencer judging by the lifeless bodies and skeletons strewn under everyone's feet.

Patrick looked over Spencer's shoulder at where the Eiffel Tower stretched to the sky, lit up by magic rather than its normal evening light show. The area was saturated in so much black magic that it was all Patrick could sense, all he could taste in the back of his throat.

"There is no way we're getting through all of the dead that stand between us and where Ilya is," Spencer said grimly.

Patrick nodded, knowing Spencer had reached the limits of what his magic could do. With no weapon of the gods and a monument to amplify his magic like Ilya, they were left with a measly amount of power, no matter their ability to tap the ley lines fed by the nexus under Paris.

"We have to hope if we get the staff and break his spell that will stop the zombies," Patrick said.

"We need to get to the fucker to do that," Nadine said, arms outstretched above her as she poured magic into her shields. "How do you expect us to clear a path to him and whoever is protecting him if we're buried under zombies?"

Patrick looked at the dead massing beyond her shield and trying to climb it, searching for a way in. Then he looked back at their ragtag group of fighters who couldn't do much fighting stuck behind her shield. They needed to clear a path to Ilya, but there was probably hundreds of thousands of zombies between them and the Patriarch of Souls. Fighting piecemeal wasn't going to work.

Patrick stared up at the Eiffel Tower and the magic surrounding it, fingers tightening on his Carbine. Then he unclipped the rifle from his vest, disengaged the magazine, and passed it over to Nadine.

"It's half-empty," he told her. "Take it."

Nadine took it and clipped it to the front of her vest. "Plan?"

"Expand the shield. We're going to need the room."

Nadine didn't argue, merely cupped her hands together above her head before wrenching them apart. Her shield pushed back against the dead, zombies falling over each other and getting trampled as she fought to get them space. Patrick curled his fingers at Wade, and the teenager hurried over.

"You want me to breathe fire again?" Wade asked.

"Yes, but first I want you to shift mass," Patrick said.

Wade glanced uneasily at the French magic users before squaring his shoulders. "All right."

Patrick gripped Wade's shoulder, giving him a comforting squeeze. "Listen to me. I'm not going to let anyone come after you when this is over. If any government tries to put a claim on you, I'll stonewall them until Lucien can get you home safely. He's good at crossing borders unnoticed."

"Do you think the government here will do that? Try to keep me?"

"No one is keeping you, Wade. Not if I have anything to say about it. But greedy people do stupid shit all the time, and I want you to know that you're pack and we'll do whatever it takes to keep you safe."

Some of the tightness in his body eased beneath Patrick's grip, and the blinding smile Wade gave him strangely didn't seem out of place while surrounded by the dead.

"I know you will. Why do you think I wanted to stay with you and not go with General Reed last summer?"

Patrick couldn't help but smile back. "After you shift, get high and burn the fuck out of the zombies between us and Ilya. We'll make sure no spells knock you out of the sky. After that, burn whatever you can reach. Be careful of anyone on the ground fighting for our side."

As a dragon, Wade was immune to mortal magic. While getting hit by a barrage of spells might not hurt him, it could knock him out of the sky due to the sheer number of attacks the Orthodox Church of the Dead and the Dominion Sect might throw at him. It would be Patrick's job to keep him safe.

"I bet they'd think twice about throwing anything at me if I was on the Eiffel Tower," Wade said.

Patrick let him go with one last comforting smack on the shoulder. "Don't break it. France will never forgive the United States if you knock it over."

"Well, if it gets broken, then I'll just keep it."

"You aren't keeping another country's national monument."

Wade heaved out a put upon sigh. "*Fine.*"

"Nadine," Patrick called out. "Wade is going to shift. He'll need room to fly out."

"I can't shield him," Nadine warned.

"You won't need to. Just tell everyone else we're going to need to block any spells aimed at him."

"If I reduce my shield to half height, the zombies will climb over."

"I'll keep them at bay until Wade is in the air," Spencer said.

Nadine turned her head and called out orders to the French magic users. Jono herded Patrick as far from Wade as they could get while Sage did the same for Nadine. Patrick tossed the body of his rifle aside and unsheathed his dagger. The matte-black blade flared up white with heavenly fire. The same sort of light began to burn through Jono's eyes, washing out the familiar blue for something otherworldly.

Patrick scowled down at Fenrir. "Don't let Jono get hurt."

"*Don't waste your blessing,*" Fenrir said, voice deep and cracking, sounding the way the dead did when Patrick walked over broken bones.

Patrick readied a dozen mageglobes before looking over at where Wade stood in the center of the space Nadine had carved out for them. Wade looked him in the eye and nodded.

Shiny red scales pushed through his skin in a rippling wave. His brown eyes turned gold, pupils elongating into slits. Pressure in the air *shifted*, and the mass of Wade's dragon body he somehow kept contained in an earthly form came into existence. Wade's human body shimmered, stretching into a larger one that grew and grew and *grew*.

He stretched out his sinuous neck and powerful tail, snaking both over everyone's heads. His wings cut through the air and scraped against the edges of Nadine's shield as he tried to flap them. Wade's wedge-shaped head angled down, one huge eye blinking at Patrick as he puffed out a hint of smoke between teeth that were half Patrick's height.

"Now, Nadine!" Patrick yelled.

Her shield split above them, opening up to the sky. It shrank to half height, and Wade wasted no time in flinging himself into the sky, wings flapping hard enough that Patrick was pushed to his knees by the downdraft.

Zombies spilled over the sides of Nadine's shield, but every single body that fell quit moving before they hit the ground, Spencer's magic breaking the souls free and putting them to rest. As soon as Wade was clear, Nadine snapped her shield back together again and layered it as thick as she could, knowing what was coming next.

Magic cut through the air, aiming for Wade, but Patrick sent a volley of strike spells through Nadine's shield to intercept them. His magic wasn't the only one defending Wade, as the French magic users hit back as well.

Wade gained altitude with a fierce roar, spitting a fireball at a spell that managed to slip past. The magic was broken and incinerated, never getting close to do any harm. He soared toward the Eiffel Tower, banking wide around the monument to dodge a flurry of attack spells, half of which exploded harmlessly in the air thanks to Patrick and the others.

Patrick watched Wade turn on a wingtip, bringing him closer to the Eiffel Tower. The ochre-colored magic covering every last inch of iron didn't seem to affect Wade when he landed on the monument. Wings flapping for balance, Wade curled his talons around the metal beams, one wing stretched all the way up toward the top of the tower, the other half folded against his back.

He thrust his head forward toward the park below and roared loud enough to be heard across Paris. The dragon fire that exploded from his mouth could probably be seen from Sacré-Cœur.

Nadine's shields went opaque in defense of the ferocious heat of Wade's dragon fire that rained down on the massed walking dead that stood between them and the Eiffel Tower. Patrick sweated from the heat even through Nadine's defensive magic. He could see layers shear off from her shield, only to be replaced by more as she held steady.

The smell of fire and sulfur burned away the stench of the dead. It took maybe just over a minute for Wade to clear the way, and Nadine didn't waste any time once he finished and banked his fire. She split her shield down the middle and reshaped it into a defensive U-shaped wall. It left the charred park that had become a battlefield clear for them to fight in.

The fencing that separated the grass from the pathway had melted beneath Wade's dragon fire, giving them a clear shot forward. Squinting through the eerie light emanating from the Eiffel Tower, Patrick could sense a riot of black magic forming.

"*Move!*" Patrick yelled.

Patrick ran forward, Spencer keeping pace with him as Fenrir raced ahead in Jono's body. Fatima was a tawny streak against the ground as she scouted ahead, the cold trailing in her wake a brief respite from the lingering heat.

Wade kept spitting fire outside Nadine's shields at zombies when he wasn't trying to fry the magic users at the base of the Eiffel Tower. He scuttled over the monument to remain a moving target, shaking off the handful of spells directed his way. Most spells were now being aimed at Patrick's group, and he got busy neutralizing as many as he could.

Running toward oncoming fire was always a risk, and some spells got through, exploding on the ruined ground between them. Patrick ripped his personal shields out of his skin, strengthened them, and kept running, dagger burning bright in his right hand while Srecha's blessing burned in his left.

Spells crashed to the ground around him, three out of two dozen he hadn't been quick enough to neutralize. The explosions sent him crashing to the ground, sliding through ash, tasting the dead on his tongue.

Patrick shoved himself to his feet and kept going.

Another burst of dragon flame aimed at the base of the Eiffel Tower bought them time, a handful of seconds to cover ground without being bombarded by magic. It got them closer, but not close enough.

Then the dead started clawing their way out of the earth.

A bony hand burst through ash to grab his ankle, yanking so hard Patrick felt something *snap*. Pain shot through his leg, and Patrick kept his mouth shut on a yell when he slammed to the ground. More hands burst through the earth, clawing at him, seeking to hold him down. He sank his dagger into the earth, and white heavenly fire burned a circle around him. The zombies around him turned to ash.

He got one elbow beneath him before Spencer was there, helping him to his feet. "No lying down on the job, Razzle Dazzle."

"Shut up, Dead Boy," Patrick grunted.

He put weight on his foot because he had to, pain throbbing through the joint. It didn't feel like a full break, but it definitely wasn't comfortable. He forced himself into a run, clenching his teeth against the pain.

Up ahead, through the flash of fire and magic and the dead clawing free of the ground, Patrick could see Ilya standing beneath the Eiffel Tower on the pavilion there. The high fencing that surrounded the Eiffel Tower had been melted beneath Wade's attack, but the Orthodox Church of the Dead refused to be snuffed out.

"I'll clear you a way through," Spencer said.

Dark green magic burned over the ground like wildfire. The zombies pushing their way through shuddered as the souls animating the corpses were ripped free and put to rest. The bony hands, skulls, and rib cages stuck out like creepy garden decorations. Fatima guided the spirits home, a cold transition point between the living and the dead.

Patrick hurled himself over red-hot, half-melted metal, landing on the other side with a pained grunt. The spell careening toward him would've been strong enough to pitch him back against the metal if not for Fenrir catching the mageglobe in Jono's powerful jaws. The spell was crushed between his teeth, magic sputtering to nothing beneath the god's power.

Patrick shoved himself to his feet, sweat sliding down the back of his neck and forehead, staring at the circle of worshippers that surrounded Ilya up ahead. Some still stood, others had collapsed on the ground, but whatever shield they'd held up against Wade's attack had finally broken.

He didn't see Zachary or any other magic users who might've been affiliated with the Dominion Sect. Either they'd cut and run, or would strike soon when Patrick's side least expected it.

Hellish power seeped out of the concentric circles that expanded away from where Ilya stood at the center, holding the Morrígan's staff. The pulse of magic touched each leg of the Eiffel Tower, and the hum of the staff's power made Patrick want to run.

Beneath the sound of Wade's roars, the heavy tread of the dead, and the hissing explosion of magic all around them came the furious shrieks of ravens and crows and the thunder of thousands of beating wings.

Fenrir looked at him through Jono's eyes, white fire burning where blue once existed. *"Break it."*

This spell wasn't a tear in the veil, wasn't ripping a hole to a forgotten hell, but there was only one way to end it. Fenrir turned to savage the nearest worshipper with vicious teeth, ignoring the screams that asked for mercy.

Patrick could've told them gods never offered mercy.

He pitched himself forward into the spaces between the concentric circles, gritting his teeth against the hellish magic seeking to suck his own dry. He kept his eyes on Ilya, the necromancer looking right at him over the top of the Morrígan's staff the necromancer held in iron gauntlets.

The quartz crystal trapped beneath the carved knotwork shone like a star, white fire that pulsed in time to the magic burning around his dagger's matte-black blade.

Patrick raised his dagger against the crashing wave of necromantic magic that erupted from the staff, carving a way through it with the only weapon he had. Every step he took between the concentric circles of magic was taken against a hurricane force that should've thrown him out of the spellcasting, and would have if not for his dagger.

One weapon of the gods against another should've been even odds, but Patrick knew war was anything but predictable.

Fenrir tore through the followers anchoring the spellcasting with a brutal ferocity that only left blood and bodies behind. Every death lessened the force trying to drive Patrick into the hands of the dead behind him. His left ankle kept wanting to buckle whenever he put weight on it, but he refused to go to his knees.

This altar wasn't one he would ever pray at.

"Where is he!" Patrick shouted over the roar of magic and the supernatural wind spinning around them. "Where is Peklabog!"

Ilya's face was washed out by the light coming from the Morrígan's staff, the quartz crystal a white hole of magic that threatened to blind Patrick.

"I was made to serve a god," Ilya snarled, his voice carrying on the wind.

"Fuck your god! I was made for war."

Patrick crossed the inner circle, stumbling into the center of the spell. The icy coldness that suffused him made his breath puff out in a pale cloud.

It glittered like a soul.

The tug in his chest was like a hook behind his ribs, catching and pulling with inhuman strength. There wasn't anything he could see, nothing for him to cut with his dagger. In the distance, Fenrir howled a warning he couldn't listen to.

Chilled down to his bones, the only warmth Patrick could feel was the line of heat across his left palm, Srecha's blessing a kiss of fate he'd never wanted.

Ilya raised the Morrígan's staff over his head before slamming it down to the ground. Magic exploded away from it in a wave of power that rolled over Patrick like a tsunami. The only reason he didn't drown was due to the hole his dagger carved through it as he planted his feet and refused to move.

The necromantic magic flowed up the four legs of the Eiffel Tower, powering the dead. Patrick's soul peeled apart at the edges, the Morrígan's staff eating away at what didn't belong to it. The soulbond tightened somewhere deep inside his chest, an anchor bracketed by Persephone's soul debt carved deeper than the tie that linked him to Hannah.

One step, then another, both arms stretched out in front of him, the dagger providing a shield and the blessing a promise.

Ilya screamed a wordless challenge as ravens and crows flew beneath the arched legs of the Eiffel Tower, cawing their defiance.

Patrick's arms shook, his soul bleeding free at the edges of his aura, and there was a hunger in his gut that didn't belong to him. Ilya raised the staff again, bringing it down like an axe on his enemy.

Patrick caught it in his left hand, Srecha's blessing burning like a brand. The first contact with that notched wood ripped a scream from his lips that shredded his throat until all he tasted was blood.

Mortal flesh was never meant to touch a weapon like this.

Patrick gripped the head of the staff despite the agony, fingers curling between the carved knotwork of the raven, skin burning from the bright magic emanating from the quartz crystal.

Magic exploded around them, white-hot and catastrophically dangerous, not meant for mortals to touch. Death wasn't Patrick's affinity, wasn't his kind of magic. It wasn't his to own or control.

Please.

The word rattled through Patrick's mind, the only command— the only prayer—he could stitch together in the face of a hunger that threatened to swallow him whole.

What lived in the Morrígan's staff—sentience of a sort, but nowhere close to human—burrowed deep into his brain, into his soul, carving him up like a vivisection done without anesthesia as it searched for what he wanted most.

Forgiveness.

Absolution.

Resurrection of the dead and gone of past mistakes.

Patrick couldn't see Ilya's face through the sun-bright burn of death magic that sought his soul. He was only aware of a cold that threatened to freeze him from the inside out as the staff unwound *regret* and *guilt* and *want* from the depths of memory.

He thought of bone and blood and iron teeth stretched in a smile, the feel of ash beneath his fingernails, and a hideous desert heat of a hell Ethan never finished calling to Earth.

He thought of demon's claws in his chest, his sister's screams, and his mother's sightless eyes staring at him from the darkest corner of his mind as Macaria lost her freedom.

A foreign awareness washed through him, distant and vast like the ocean, threatening to swallow him whole.

Choose.

Patrick had bled for many gods over the years, but he'd only ever prayed to one.

And in the presence of gods and monsters and weapons of war, what was one man's prayers worth?

Nothing, he knew.

Srecha's blessing, however, was worth everything.

Black dots ate through the brightness, melding together into a hazy distant figure Patrick had seen in a nightmare once—a woman wearing a hooded cloak made with a thousand black feathers, pale-skinned and starved-thin. She was nothing but a shadow in that light, but she still reached for him with fingers stained red with blood, grave dirt on her feet and the promise of death on her lips.

Only it wasn't his mother's face staring back at him this time, but that of a goddess.

And her staff—it *hungered*.

Made of iron and earth, notched with the memory of the brittle dead, the Morrígan's staff required a sacrifice for its power.

It always had.

Patrick squeezed his eyes shut, and when he opened them

again, all he saw was Ilya's face contorted in fury, stripped of the mantle that he'd carried as the Patriarch of Souls for the Orthodox Church of the Dead. Patrick knew the staff could raise the dead from a battlefield and graves, but the amount of zombies in Paris seemed astronomical. To guide that many spirits from beyond to earthly anchors required a godly touch.

"You fed it Peklabog," Patrick said through numb lips, tasting blood on his teeth.

The man on the Salle du Drapeau's altar in the Catacombs had been no man after all.

"I've been promised a different way," Ilya spat out. "I'll pray to another."

Patrick pressed the dagger edge against the base of the raven's feet on the staff, and the prayers in its making cut through the wood as if it were made of nothing.

The raven broke free with a snap that could've caused an avalanche. Patrick curled his fingers tight around it, never letting go.

He left Srecha's blessing behind—payment for the prayer the staff drew out of his soul.

Please, Patrick thought once more in the messy static of his mind as his soul ripped wider, tearing from his bones, barely knowing what he was asking for.

Praying for.

Magic exploded from the Morrígan's staff, a shriek he couldn't hear, only feel cutting through his skull. The force sent them flying apart. Patrick fell to the ground, the broken-off wooden raven clenched in one hand as the spell powering the summoning of the dead broke apart around him.

He didn't see where Ilya went.

Looking up at the underside of the Eiffel Tower, Patrick watched the magic lighting it up fade into darkness. Then the only thing he could see was Jono's wolf-bright blue eyes in a human face as the soulbond pulled tight between them, smoothing down the frayed edges of his battered soul with a permanency that made him choke.

"Patrick!" Jono said, sounding faraway to Patrick's ears.

The hand framing his face burned, but it took Patrick several seconds to realize it was because he was so cold. His fingers spasmed, releasing his dagger and the piece of the Morrígan's staff he'd managed to steal back in a moment he wasn't sure was real.

Jono's face faded into shadow as the magic that had sustained the dead walking through Paris was siphoned away, leaving the city in darkness and the bones of its past falling lifeless to the ground.

Above them, a murder of crows and an unkindness of ravens blotted out the vastness of the Eiffel Tower against the starry sky, their grievance echoing like bells at the midnight hour, calling an end to summer solstice.

War does not rest.

And oh, how she was fury born.

28

Jono scrubbed a hand over his face and sighed, staring tiredly at the electric kettle and willing the water to boil faster. The power in the 8th arrondissement had finally been turned back on, and he'd been dying for a cuppa for days already. He pressed a hand to his chest, absently drumming his fingers against his collarbone. Three days since summer solstice and everything was still a bloody mess, but at least Nadine had tea.

Despite it being Sunday, Patrick and Nadine were meeting with the French government alongside several senior PIA agents and the United States Ambassador to France. To say what had happened in Paris was an international shitstorm was putting it mildly.

The PIA's warnings to their counterpart were seen as too little too late in the aftermath. France had known about Ilya and the Orthodox Church of the Dead being in Paris. What they hadn't known about was the dangerous artifact the United States had refused to warn them about. Keeping the Morrígan's staff a secret was still a priority, but it made placating allies difficult when governments refused to be honest with each other.

All Jono cared about was that his passport wasn't flagged and he'd still be able to fly home tomorrow with Sage and Wade. Patrick, unfortunately, was still required in Paris for political reasons. He'd been the one to break the spell, and French officials were alternating between being grateful and being angry.

If Jono could carry Patrick onto the plane home, he would.

"Is that coffee?" Spencer asked as he stumbled blearily into the kitchen. "Please tell me it's coffee."

"Sorry, mate. Just tea. I can make you a cuppa if you like," Jono said.

Spencer groaned and set about digging through Nadine's cupboards. "Urgh. You Brits and your tea."

Jono didn't take offense, having come to the conclusion that Spencer lacked coherency until he'd drunk at least half a pot of coffee after waking up. Spencer still managed to get his coffee brewed even with his eyes half-closed.

The kettle started to bubble and steam in earnest. When it clicked off, Jono poured the hot water into his mug and let it steep for a few minutes, watching Spencer stumble about the kitchen and holding up all sorts of different food for Fatima to choose from after the psychopomp strolled in and started yowling. She eventually decided on half a stale loaf of bread, running out of the kitchen with it in her mouth.

"You know she's going to get crumbs everywhere, right?" Jono said.

Spencer let the kitchen island hold up his weight as he drank his coffee. "Nadine won't mind."

Jono very much doubted that. "When do you leave?"

"Tonight. Director Franklin wants me back in DC for debriefing tomorrow."

"But not Patrick?"

Spencer shrugged. "French officials are apparently making noise about our government bringing me into their country without approval. Franklin wants me back before they try to arrest me."

Jono stared at him through the steam of his tea. "You and your magic were the main bloody reason we got to the Eiffel Tower in time to stop Ilya."

"True. Which is probably why the French government didn't arrest me once they found out about my magic. Necromancy is illegal for a reason, as you just experienced."

"You aren't a necromancer."

"Close enough by most legal standards."

Jono took a sip of his tea and grimaced. "Sorry."

"Eh, could be worse. I could've been born an *actual* necromancer and been put to death as soon as my magic manifested itself."

Spencer spoke about being executed the way some people spoke about what they might order for dinner—musing and unconcerned in a way.

"Thanks for coming when Patrick asked."

Spencer looked at him from across the kitchen island, blue eyes clear and sharp when a moment ago he'd seemed half-asleep. "Patrick's my friend. I might not have been a Hellraiser, but I still fought with him when our missions crossed, and he's one of the few people who didn't flinch when he first met me. Having magic like mine doesn't earn me many friends. I like to keep the ones I got."

"Smart."

"Yeah." Spencer sipped at his coffee, squinting at Jono. "Which is why I'm going to tell you what I'm going to tell him once he gets back from being interrogated. Whatever that staff did to him when he touched it, it made your soulbond permanent."

Jono ran his tongue against the back of his teeth, thinking of that moment beneath the Eiffel Tower and the way his soul had been twisted so tight he'd thought his ribs would break in protest. "Thought it already was?"

"Soulbonds can be severed. When I first arrived and saw your souls, the bond wasn't tangled as deep as it is now. And when I say deep, I mean *deep*." Spencer paused, grimacing. "I know the gods set it. I think, at this point, they'd be the only ones who could undo it."

"We aren't going to ask them for any favors."

"Good plan."

"I'll tell Patrick. No need for your goodbye to end with news like that."

"Bad?"

Jono shook his head. "We both don't mind the soulbond. We don't want it removed."

"So, good news, then?"

"Good enough."

Jono's ears picked up on quiet footsteps, and then Sage padded into the kitchen on bare feet, mobile pressed to her ear and looking right at him.

"Hold please," she said in a crisp voice before muting the call. "Rami says Mireille and Gaspard want to speak with you."

Jono gulped down another burning swallow of tea. "On your mobile or mine?"

"I have them standing by."

"I'm ready."

Sage got back on the line, and a couple of seconds later, she handed her mobile to him. Jono pressed it to his ear and leaned against the kitchen counter, staring out the open window at the sunlight outside .

"Yeah?" he said, too tired to be polite.

"*Bonjour*, Jonothon. One of the packs under our protection said you gave them aid during the zombie incursion. That you brought them to the ministry so they could continue to help the city with support," Mireille said after only a brief pause, sounding as if she was on speaker.

"We did."

"She said you did not stay there but moved on."

"Someone had to get rid of your zombie problem."

"You fought for our territory," Gaspard said.

"Your territory was caught in the middle. If this had happened in any other city, we would've been there fighting the bastards." He didn't give any more information than that because it wasn't their business. Jono took another sip of his tea. "I meant what I said at our first meeting. We weren't here for your territory, only pass-through rights, and we leave tomorrow."

The silence echoed on their side for a few seconds before Gaspard spoke up. "We know there are two god packs vying for New York City. We will acknowledge yours and inform our European contemporaries that your god pack has sole claim to the territory. Expect to receive some calls in the future."

Jono's eyebrows crept upward while Sage crossed her arms over her chest and got a very pleased look on her face. "That's unexpected."

"You aren't the London god pack. Your…pack members may be atypical, but we can't say they aren't useful."

"When next you are in Paris, call ahead. We will welcome you at our table if it remains ours," Mireille said.

"We'll ring you," Jono promised.

"Have a safe flight home."

The call ended and Jono handed the mobile back to Sage. "Seems we're getting international backing now."

"Good. We can shove it down Estelle and Youssef's throats when we get home," she said.

Jono grimaced. They needed the support, but after learning what they had about hunters and demons in London, he wasn't sure what they would return to in New York City. He didn't know if Estelle and Youssef were willing to do what Cressida had and accept demons into their souls—or if they would be the only ones.

An entire god pack of werecreatures sharing their souls with demons wasn't going to be easy to defeat if those two went down that road.

"We'll see how things go."

Sage reached up to settle her fingertips against the side of his throat, pressing against his pulse. "One step at a time."

Jono touched his own wrist to her throat, pressing the pack scent into her skin. Sage hummed happily, their quiet moment interrupted when Wade came into the kitchen carrying Fatima like a furry baby.

"No one told me we had any bread left," Wade complained.

Fatima stopped chewing on the baguette and held it up to him between her paws. Wade gave her an adoring look before taking the offered bite.

"First pegasi and now psychopomps. Maybe we should get him a dog," Sage mused.

Jono winced. "Please don't give him any ideas."

Wade narrowed his eyes at them. "Hey! I'd be a great pet owner!"

"The state of your apartment and latest hoard says otherwise."

"What's his hoard?" Spencer asked.

"Nothing," Wade muttered.

"Right now? Lucky cat figurines," Jono said.

"They're *mine*."

Spencer snorted into his coffee. "You just said your hoard was nothing, and now it's something?"

Wade reached out lightning-quick to grab Spencer's coffee cup before darting out of hand-smacking range. "Fatima and I are going to enjoy our bread and coffee on the balcony. None of you are invited."

"Hey!" Spencer called after him. "That's mine! They're *both* mine!"

"I can't hear you over how loudly Fatima is purring because she likes me best," Wade singsonged.

Spencer stared after him for a moment before turning to give Jono an incredulous look.

Jono just shrugged. "Dragons, mate. What can you do but feed them?"

JONO FOUND Patrick lying on their bed in the guest bedroom after supper, staring at the ceiling. The sun was low on the horizon, already hidden behind the surrounding buildings. Jono went to the windows overlooking the flat's balcony and gently closed the curtains, shutting out the lit-up skyline of Paris.

Electricity was up and running for the entire city now, but the stench of death still hung on the air. Millions of bones and bodies were piled up on the streets, but the general consensus from officials was that millions more were *missing*. The United States government was of the opinion Ilya had somehow managed to flee with the Morrígan's staff *and* an army of the undead.

Honestly, it was the stuff nightmares were made of.

That still left Paris having to deal with reinterning its dead, a process their pack wasn't going to stick around and watch.

"You didn't eat much," Jono said, coming to stand at the foot of the bed.

Patrick didn't move, didn't even look at him. "I wasn't hungry."

He was still in the suit he'd worn for work, a charcoal-gray one this time. His dagger and sheath had been removed, and both now hung off the headboard. Jono gently undid the laces of Patrick's oxfords before slipping off his shoes and socks.

Jono dug his thumb against the arch of Patrick's right foot, feeling the muscle there twitch from the pressure. Patrick had left the Eiffel Tower limping, but someone at the ministry had healed whatever had been wrong with his ankle.

"You haven't eaten much at all lately."

Patrick blinked, those green eyes finally looking at him. "I eat."

"Wade has finished off your plate for every meal you've taken with us."

"Everything tastes like ash." Patrick lifted a hand to stare at his fingers. "Everything *feels* like ash."

Jono sighed, letting go of Patrick's foot in favor of putting his knee on the bed so he could undo Patrick's belt. "You keep saying that."

Patrick dropped his hand to his chest, fingers slipping between two buttons of his dress shirt to touch scar tissue. "Because it's true."

"Why?"

Patrick drew in a breath that sounded like hissing air, but didn't speak. Jono grabbed his hands and pulled him into a sitting position. Patrick didn't fight him, sitting quietly while Jono removed his suit jacket, undid his tie, and unbuttoned his dress shirt. He tossed everything aside, knowing Patrick wouldn't care about wrinkles.

Jono ran his hands over lightly freckled shoulders, fingers brushing over the top of the scars bisecting Patrick's chest. His heartbeat wasn't as steady as his breathing.

"Tell me," Jono urged quietly.

Patrick opened his mouth, then closed it, still not speaking. Jono waited him out, and it took long enough he managed to rid Patrick of his pants and underwear. Jono, still dressed, crawled on top of Patrick's naked body, straddling him. He leaned down for a kiss, drawing the words out with a gentle touch of his lips.

"I keep getting flashes of a desert," Patrick said, not staring at Jono, but *through* him, at something only he could see. "But they don't feel like my memories."

"Cairo?" Jono asked, kissing the corner of his mouth.

"No." Patrick drew in a breath, finally focusing on Jono. "Maybe."

Jono blinked down at him, propping himself up on one elbow. He trailed the fingers of his other hand down Patrick's chest, tracing the scars there. "You've had nightmares every night since summer solstice."

Every time he'd woken up thrashing, breathing hard, never seeing Jono until seconds later, it made Jono want to dream it all for him, to spare him whatever horrors lived in his mind.

Patrick swallowed, the sound a soft click in his throat. "The staff…it wanted something from me in exchange for holding it."

Jono reached for Patrick's left hand, running fingers over healed, smooth skin, the burn there gone since breaking off a piece of the staff. "Srecha's blessing?"

"Her blessing was a conduit. The staff would've torn me apart without it. Without you."

Jono started to kiss his way down Patrick's throat, following the beat of his pulse to his heart. "Spencer says the soulbond is permanent now."

"I know."

He didn't sound angry about that news, or surprised. Jono nipped his teeth at Patrick's left nipple, enticing a soft gasp from him. "I told him you wouldn't mind."

"I don't."

"Good. Neither do I." Jono drifted lower, kissing his way down Patrick's body one centimeter at a time. "You're stuck with me."

"You have it backward."

"Shut your gob and let me make you feel better."

Patrick huffed out a laugh, some of the stress bleeding from his scent. "Okay."

Jono slid off the bed, letting his knees hit the floor. He tugged Patrick closer until his legs hung over Jono's shoulders, heels digging into his back. Patrick propped himself up on his elbows, staring at Jono with a heated look in his eyes. Jono never looked away when he ducked his head to lick a slow stripe up Patrick's cock.

Patrick's breath hitched in his throat, heartbeat picking up out of pleasure rather than the lingering fear of the unknown. The change in his scent was subtle, but growing, and Jono preferred passion over pain any day.

He wrapped his lips around the head of Patrick's cock, sucking at it, enjoying the heady, musky taste that hit his tongue. Patrick groaned softly, tipping his head back when Jono took more of him into his mouth. His hands clenched at the duvet as Jono swallowed him down in a slow glide, taking his time.

The weight of Patrick's cock in his mouth was familiar and wanted, a growing thickness that Jono worshipped while on his knees. Tension filled Patrick's body, legs tightening over Jono's shoulders. Jono undid his own trousers, freeing his half-hard cock to stroke it, indulging his own desire.

"Jono," Patrick breathed out, hips coming off the bed as he thrust lightly into Jono's mouth.

He drew Patrick deeper, encouraging him not to stop with a hum that made Patrick swear. The sound of his heartbeat in Jono's ears, the deepening scent of desire that filled his nose, the soul-bond twisting tight between them all said *home* without either of them saying anything at all.

Jono drew out their pleasure with slow strokes, ceaseless wet heat, and hard swallows until it ended with Patrick coming down his throat on a ragged moan, both hands tangled in Jono's hair. Jono came five strokes later, still sucking on Patrick's cock until they were both finished.

When he finally pulled his mouth away, Patrick was lying flat on the bed, trying to catch his breath, lazily running his fingers through Jono's hair. Jono turned his head to press a sticky kiss to the inside of Patrick's left thigh before getting off his knees. He undressed in seconds, using his shirt to wipe himself clean. Then Jono hauled Patrick farther onto the bed, holding him close in the fading sunlight.

The shadows had grown deeper before Patrick finally spoke.

"I think it took a memory." Patrick sighed, pressing his face against Jono's chest. "A prayer. Twisted it into *something*."

Jono thought about what the Morrígan's staff was, what it had done in Paris, and the cost that came with praying to gods.

How all it took was one person's faith to keep them alive for eternity.

"It's not your kind of magic."

"I don't think it mattered with Srecha's blessing burned into my skin."

Jono buried his nose in Patrick's hair and dug his fingers into Patrick's hip, wishing he could keep him safe. "No matter what happens, you know I love you."

"I know," Patrick said after a moment, a promise in the second of silence that had come before.

Jono closed his eyes and never let go.

29

* * *

Patrick stood in front of Setsuna's altar in her DC home, staring at the fine coating of sand strewn over the bone and shallow dish there.

He swallowed very, very carefully so as not to puke.

"You'll need to return here next week," Setsuna said from behind him where she sat on the couch. "Congress will have questions. I have it on good authority subpoenas will be issued if you don't."

"Closed-door session?" Patrick asked.

"I've been told the president will require it."

"Guess I can't say no."

He turned away from the altar in favor of the wet bar, pouring himself a nearly full glass of whiskey. Setsuna only arched an eyebrow when she took in the amount, but said nothing about how he chose to self-medicate tonight. His flight had already been delayed, and he was waiting out the extra hours at Setsuna's home.

A week and a half since summer solstice, and Patrick had spent only half that time on US soil. It'd been ten long days of meetings with government officials in two different countries, and his ability to be diplomatic had died well before he even made it back to Washington, DC. Dealing with the aftermath of a zombie invasion in a foreign city caused by a weapon only a handful of people in power knew belonged to a god was the stuff of political nightmares.

Patrick was better at making fires rather than putting them out, and Paris was only further proof of that.

The attack had made international news once Paris' electric grid was back up and running again. While no video existed of the walking dead wreaking havoc on the populace, the number of dead bodies Paris was still grappling with how to bury was proof enough. Photos and video of the Eiffel Tower burning with black magic had been captured by people living in outlier suburbs, but none of them showcased the horror of that day.

Some had even caught blurry, distant shots of a dragon hanging off the monument and flying through the air. At least no one in the French government was disclosing Wade's identity.

The *how* and *why* of it all was getting twisted by the powers-that-be. Blame was being laid at the feet of Ilya Nazarov and the Orthodox Church of the Dead, the latter of which was being labeled a terrorist group by multiple countries.

Patrick was pretty damn certain the Morrígan's staff had eaten Peklabog in exchange for raising the dead on a mass scale. He didn't know if the god could return how Odin had. Patrick had broken the staff after all, and maybe that would free Peklabog's godhead. Patrick didn't know. He could only hope that because the staff was broken, it wouldn't be capable of wielding its full power anymore, but who the hell knew when it came to gods and their weapons.

The carved raven was packed at the bottom of his suitcase. Patrick had reported back to Setsuna, Franklin, and Reed that he'd broken the staff, but not that he'd *kept* part of it. He didn't know what he was going to do with it, but he knew he didn't trust any government on Earth to keep it safe.

Patrick carried his whiskey with him to the couch and sat beside Setsuna, not looking at her. He drank it in burning mouthfuls until half of it was gone before he spoke.

"Ilya said he got a better offer than the one Peklabog gave him," Patrick said.

"So you said in your report. Your assertion he was speaking about Ethan and the Dominion Sect is one we're looking into. Those two groups don't have much of a history with each other though."

"They will now. Zachary was in Europe. I think Ethan sent him to make a deal with Ilya after London."

"We'll find out one way or another eventually."

Patrick tipped the glass a little, watching the whiskey creep toward the rim. "The staff nearly ripped my soul out. It would have if I wasn't soulbound. Ilya couldn't even touch the damn thing. He wore gauntlets while using it."

"He still used it."

"Ethan *can't*. I proved that in Paris."

"I fail to see how that is a negative." Patrick took another long swallow of whiskey, eyes watering from the burn. Setsuna reached over and took the glass from him, setting it on the table. "Patrick. Call your ride and go home."

He had a flight waiting to take him back to New York City, where his pack was waiting for him. What was done was done, and yet—

And yet.

Patrick licked his lips free of whiskey. "Ethan still got what he wanted."

A possible ally that could summon an undead army and was no stranger to worshipping a god on a grand scale, along with the power of resurrection and all the horror that implied.

"The fight isn't over," Setsuna said quietly.

Patrick tapped his fingers against his knee, one at a time, until he stopped on five. "We're in July already. Hannah will be five months pregnant."

Setsuna sighed and pushed herself to her feet without her cane. "As I said. The fight isn't over."

Patrick finished his whiskey and called for a ride to the airport.

HOURS LATER, Patrick finally stepped through the front door of his apartment in Chelsea with a tired sigh after too long a time away. The smell of lasagna for a late-night dinner made his stomach growl until he spotted Wade on the couch.

"Tell me you're not cooking," Patrick said.

"He's not cooking," Sage called from the kitchen.

"Oh, thank fuck."

"I can cook," Wade retorted, not looking away from the television.

"You eat better than you cook."

Wade smirked. "You're not wrong."

Patrick moved aside so Jono could come in with his suitcase, taking it into the bedroom. He shut the front door and locked it out of habit.

"Dinner will be ready in about ten minutes," Sage said, coming out from the kitchen to give Patrick a tight hug. "I'm glad you're home."

Patrick hugged her back. "Me too."

He'd hated being gone, hated sleeping alone. Nightmares had plagued him in his sleep and while awake for a week straight until they abruptly stopped. Patrick was looking forward to sleeping in his bed with Jono and not dreaming.

He should've known his homecoming wouldn't be that easy.

They were seated around the table, dinner half-finished, when someone knocked on the front door. The threshold wrapped around the apartment didn't register whoever was out there as a threat, but Patrick still froze in his chair.

"Are we expecting anyone tonight?" Patrick asked. It was closing in on 2300, and the only thing he had wanted to do after they finished dinner was *sleep*.

Jono got to his feet. "No."

Patrick followed Jono to the door, hand straying to his dagger's hilt. When Jono opened it, he couldn't say he was surprised to see Einar standing on the landing. He was just more surprised it wasn't Lucien or Carmen.

"Finally back in the country?" Patrick asked.

Einar stared at him with such intensity that Jono actually stepped between them.

"What do you want?" Jono demanded.

Patrick edged around Jono so he could see Einar. The vampire's gaze tracked him and no one else.

"Lucien wants to see you," Einar said.

"It's *late*. Tell him the government isn't backing out of the bargain they made with him. He's got even more freedom now to be a fucking troublesome asshole. He doesn't need to see me to confirm that," Patrick said.

Einar never crossed the threshold—he'd never been invited to, and the building's front door was technically public property, just not theirs—but he lifted his hand, and the sand that poured free of his fingers fell into the apartment as fine and light as ash.

Patrick stared at it, a chill coursing through his body so fast it caused his teeth to clack together. The only sound he could hear was the dull roar of his heartbeat in his ears.

"Patrick?"

Jono's voice, his touch, pulled Patrick back to awareness. He barely recognized his own when he spoke. "There was sand on all the altars."

On Setsuna's, on their own, on every pack's in their territory.

When Jono had called about it days ago, Patrick had told him to leave it alone.

The call had come, he realized, the same day the nightmares had stopped.

Einar never blinked. "*She* wants to see you."

Patrick didn't remember leaving the apartment. He didn't remember the drive to Ginnungagap.

He only came back to himself when they stood in front of the door to the club, tongue numb, his hand held in Jono's tight grip, while the smell of ozone drifted on the hot summer breeze.

"Patrick," Jono said, staring at him with concerned eyes. "What's going on? This doesn't feel right."

Maybe it didn't for him, but for Patrick, it felt like waking up from a years-long nightmare.

Einar had opened the door, looking at him expectantly. Patrick pulled free of Jono and walked inside, hearing the sounds of active shelling and attack spells hitting the front lines beneath his ragged breathing. Every other blink brought a flash of desert sand across his sight, war-damaged city walls that flickered over the solid ones holding up Ginnungagap's roof.

They came into a club filled with Lucien's Night Court and the promise of prayers answered by the power of resurrection Patrick had held in one hand with a goddess' blessing, just for a moment.

A figure turned away from Lucien: short and predatorily lean, with midnight-black skin and an aura leaking from the godhead she carried that burned Patrick's eyes like the sun. The colorful skirt of her woven strapless gown shifted around muscular legs that ended in bone hooks sheathed in iron caps. Gold bands encircled her upper arms and wrists, bright against her dark skin, but it held nothing to the shine of life in her black eyes and the smile that stole across her face, revealing jagged iron teeth sharpened into fangs.

Patrick opened his mouth, the words clawing their way out of his throat like knives. "There was nothing left of you."

"Oh, child," Ashanti said. "Have you forgotten all I taught you? Prayers aren't *nothing*. They are a weapon, just like you. The desert cradled the dust of me, as it always has in my history. My body was never gone, only waiting on faith to rebuild it. I was born of ash long ago, and I have died of ash many times, and I will always rise."

~~~

Patrick and Jono's adventure continues in *An Echo In The Sorrow*.

Don't miss out on sneak peeks, exciting news, and more! Sign up for Hailey Turner's newsletter to stay up-to-date on her upcoming books.
~~~

GLOSSARY

Short descriptions of words, acronyms, and phrases used in the story that weren't readily explained in text. Included as well are character names.

Abuku, Setsuna: Witch. Director who oversees and leads the Supernatural Operations Agency.

Academy: K-12 school that teaches magic to practitioners of all affinities and designations. All provide boarding options to students.

Allfather, the: *See* Odin.

Andras: Demon. Ranked as a Great Marquis of Hell. He sows discord in humanity and is in charge of thirty legions of lesser demons.

Ashanti: Immortal. Goddess and mother of all vampires. Takes the shape of an Asanbosam vampire out of West African myths.

Baba Yaga: Immortal. A supernatural being whose story stems from Slavic folklore. She appears as a deformed or ugly old woman who rides a flying mortar, carries a pestle and broom, and traditionally lives deep in the forest in a house perched on chicken legs. She is sometimes depicted as a child-eating monster. She may choose to help or hinder a person drawn into her path.

Bailey, Spencer: Mage. Former combat mage with the Mage Corps, currently a PIA special agent. He is a soulbreaker with the power to put the dead to rest and travels with a psychopomp who takes the form of an ocelot.

Beacot, Sage: Weretiger. A Diné lawyer who works for the fae law firm Gentry & Thyme. Dire to Jono and Patrick's god pack.

Bifröst: A burning rainbow bridge between Midgard and Asgard.

Breckenridge, Gerard (Captain): Immortal. Current identity of Cú Chulainn. *See,* Cú Chulainn.

Brigid: Immortal. Celtic goddess associated with fertility, spring, healing, smithing, and poetry. Spring Queen of the Seelie Court. Daughter of the Dagda and member of the Tuatha Dé Danann.

Brynhildr: Immortal. Leader of the valkyries and a shieldmaiden.

Cailleach Bheur, the: (Pronunciation: KAI-lach burr) Immortal. Goddess and divine hag. Considered a creator deity and Queen of Winter. Has various Irish and Scottish origin stories.

Carmen: Succubus. First known recorded appearance was in Venice, Italy.

Casale, Giovanni: Human. Chief of the NYPD's Preternatural Crimes Bureau.

Catacombs of Paris: Location. *Catacombes des Paris.* A subset of the Mines of Paris, consisting of underground ossuaries that hold the remains of over 6 million dead.

Cataflic: Slightly derogatory term used by cataphiles to describe a group of police and officials tasked with closing up the mines to illegal entry.

Cataphile: Urban explorers who illegally explore the Mines of Paris.

Cernunnos: Immortal. A Celtic god generally known as the "horned god." He has horns on his head and is associated with stags, horned serpents, dogs, bulls, and rats. He is interpreted as the god of animals, nature, fertility, travel, commerce, and bi-directionality.

Citadel: United States military academy for magic users. Located in Maryland. All Academies across the nation feed into the Citadel. Mages get automatic inclusion. All other kinds of magic users need recommendations.

Collins, Patrick: Mage. Former combat mage with the Mage Corps, currently an SOA special agent. Has a tainted soul and crippled magic. Is technically a mage in name only due to a soul wound. Co-leader of the god pack he shares with Jono.

Cú Chulainn: (Pronunciation: ku CULL-ann) Immortal. Celtic god and son of the god Lugh. Member of the Tuatha Dé Danann. Irish warrior. Carries the *Gáe Bulg* in fights. Currently hiding under a mortal identity by the name of Gerard Breckenridge.

Dagda, the: Immortal. Celtic god affiliated with life, death, crops, and seasons. Member and king of the Tuatha Dé Danann. Husband to the Morrígan.

de Vere, Jonothon: God pack werewolf. Originally from London, England, currently resides in New York City. Alpha of a god pack he co-leads with Patrick.

Dire: A rank held only within a god pack. The moniker is taken from the dire wolf but has been shortened to account for different werecreature species. Essentially a rank held by a loyal pack member who helps enforce the alphas' orders.

Dominion Sect: A shadowy terrorist group consisting of mundane humans, rogue magic users, immortals aligned with the hells, and other preternatural creatures intent on destroying the veil between worlds so that hell and its denizens can reign on earth. Some members are attempting to steal godheads in order to ensure their hold on power in the new world they hope to create.

Drekavac: Originates from South Slavic mythology. (Literally, "the screamer") An elongated humanoid undead creature.

Dullahan, the: Lesser fae. A headless fae, usually depicted as a rider on a black horse who carries their own head in one hand and a human spine as a whip in the other.

Espinoza, Wade: Teenaged fledgling fire dragon. Part of Jono and Patrick's god pack.

Fae: Supernatural beings who reside in Tír na nÓg. There are lesser or higher fae depending on their status and species. *See also,* Tuatha Dé Danann.

Fenrir: Immortal. Wolf in the Norse pantheon. Patron to a god pack.

Ginnungagap: Primordial void. Belongs to the Norse myths.

Godhead: Primordial power belonging to immortals that gives them life. The strength of their power can be altered by worship, or lack thereof.

God pack: A pack of werecreatures infected with the god strain of the werevirus. They act as spokespeople for hidden werecreature packs in their territory. They are supported by monetary tithes from the packs under their protection. Very few retain a connection to their animal-god patrons.

Greene, Ethan: Mage. Was a double agent formally employed by the SOA. Is currently a mercenary and allied with the Dominion Sect.

Greene, Hannah: Mage. Currently a vessel. Spiritually deceased.

Hellraisers: A US Department of the Preternatural Special Forces team Patrick once belonged to.

Hermes: Immortal. Greek messenger god and god of trade, thieves, travelers, sports, athletes, border crossings, and guide to the Underworld.

Hernandez, Leon: Werewolf. Partner to Emma Zhang and co-leader of the Tempest pack.

Khan, Youssef: God pack werewolf. Alpha of the New York City god pack.

Krossed Knights: An organization of hunters that formed in the United States centuries ago. An offshoot of European hunter groups that came out of the Crusades.

Ley lines: Metaphysical rivers of powers that drain into nexuses.

Lucien: Master vampire. Was a soldier in William the Conqueror's army before being turned by Ashanti. Currently a weapons and magic trafficker. Is wanted by many governments.

Macaria: Immortal. Greek goddess of the blessed death and Hades' daughter.

Mage: Highest rank of magic users and the only practitioners who can tap external power from ley lines and nexuses.

Mage Corps: Military branch under the purview of the US Department of the Preternatural. Accepts only mages.

Magic: Emanating from and powered by a person's soul. Roughly one-quarter of the world's population has magic. Strength varies, with different titles being bestowed depending on a person's magical reach. Casting is divided into defensive wards and offensive spells.

Medb: (Pronunciation: may-ve) Immortal. Celtic goddess. Queen of Air and Darkness. Ruler of the Unseelie Court. Member of the Tuatha Dé Danann.

Mines of Paris: Location. *Carrières de Paris*. Abandoned subterranean mines found under Paris, France, which are connected by large galleries.

Ministry of Magical Affairs: A French domestic agency that focuses on magical crimes and terrorism in France. (Equivalent to the SOA)

Morrígan: Immortal. Sometimes depicted as an individual Celtic goddess, or more commonly as a triple goddess, of war and fate. She is particularly affiliated with foretelling of death or victory in battle. Often described as a trio of sisters sometimes given the names of Badb, Macha, and Nemain.

Mulroney, Nadine: Mage. Works counterintelligence for the PIA. Is fluent in French and based out of Paris, France.

Nazarov, Ilya: Mage. Necromancer who is the Patriarch of Souls for the Orthodox Church of the Dead.

Necromancer: A magic user who can be of any rank. Their magic has an affinity for the dead, allowing them to raise the dead, control zombies, and manipulate the lingering souls of the deceased. Their kind of magic is heavily restricted in use in the United States and in most countries.

Necromancy: A family of magic that deals with the dead, usually involving blood magic and sacrifices. Predominately illegal or restricted in most countries.

Nexus: Metaphysical lake of power beneath the earth. Usually located in sacred areas or beneath major cities.

Niflheim: Location. A Norse realm.

Night Court: Vampire group that oversees claimed territory. Headed by a single master vampire. Several Night Courts can exist in the same major city.

Norns: Immortals. Norse Fates.

Odin: Immortal. Norse god of wisdom, healing, death, knowledge, battle, and the gallows, and is the titular king of the Æsir.

Órlaith: (Pronunciation: OR-lah) Immortal. Daughter of Ruadán. The Summer Lady of the Seelie Court and heir to Brigid. Cú Chulainn's fiancée within the story.

Orthodox Church of the Dead: Religious cultlike group that worships a god of the underworld and offers prayers and sacrifices to Peklabog.

Patriarch of Souls: The high priest in charge of the Orthodox Church of the Dead. They are almost always a necromancer.

Pegasus: Winged horses favored by valkyries.

Peklabog: Immortal. Slavic god of the underworld who guides the souls of the dead. He is associated with fire, water, snakes, and earthquakes.

Persephone: Immortal. Greek goddess of the Underworld and springtime.

PCB: Preternatural Crimes Bureau. A PCB is usually found only in the police departments of major metropolitan areas in the United States. The PCB in New York City is headed up by a bureau chief. The five detective boroughs within the NYPD all field detectives specializing in preternatural crimes through the PCB. The PCB has jurisdiction throughout the five boroughs and its own detachment of cops that work in homicide, narcotics, major crimes, and CSU. The PCB is one of the least manned departments in the NYPD due to the type of cases it handles.

PIA: Preternatural Intelligence Agency. PIA is a national-level foreign intelligence organization overseen by the Secretary of Defense directly through the USDI. The PIA's intelligence operations extend beyond the zones of combat, and approximately half of its employees serve overseas at hundreds of locations and US Embassies in many countries. The agency specializes in collection and analysis of preternatural-source intelligence, both overt and clandestine, while also handling American military-diplomatic relations abroad. The agency has no law enforcement authority. (Equivalent to CIA)

Psychopomp: Creatures, spirits, angels, or deities that appear in many religions and take many forms. Responsible for guiding newly deceased souls from Earth to the afterlife, whether a heaven or hell. Are used most commonly with necromancy and other magic that has an affinity for souls or the dead.

Reed, Noah (General): Fire dragon. Currently hiding in human form as a three-star Army general who oversees the US Department of the Preternatural.

Santa Muerte: Immortal. *Nuestra Señora de la Santa Muerte* (English translation: Our Lady of Holy Death), commonly shortened and referred to as Santa Muerte. A personification of death associated with healing, protection, and safe passage to the afterlife.

Shields: Ward. Defensive magic used for protection on a large or small scale.

Skellig Islands, the: Location. Irish translation: *Na Scealaga*. Rocky islands in the Atlantic Ocean off the west coast of Ireland.

SOA: Supernatural Operations Agency. SOA is the domestic intelligence and security service of the United States that focuses on magical and preternatural crimes and terrorism. Employs human, preternatural, and magically affiliated people to field positions for domestic defense. (Equivalent to FBI)

Sorcerer/Sorceress: Second-highest rank of magic users and moderately more common than mages but are outnumbered by witches and wizards.

Soulbond: A binding of two or more souls to tie people together for magical needs. Illegal under the laws of all governments.

Spells: Offensive magic.

Srecha: Immortal. Slavic dual goddess of fate who appears as a beautiful woman that spins a golden thread. She bestows positive welfare on chosen recipients. When depicted as misfortune, she is known as Nesrecha and appears as an old woman with bloodshot eyes.

Taylor, Marek: Seer. CEO of PreterWorld, a social media platform geared toward the preternatural and supernatural community. His patrons are the Norns.

Thor: Immortal. Norse god of thunder, lightning, storms, oak trees, strength, the protection of mankind, hallowing, and fertility.

Threshold: Ward. Applied to a hearth and home for protection to keep out negative magic, spirits, and demons.

Tiarnán: Member of the Tuatha Dé Danann. Carries the title Lord of Ivy and Gold.

Tír na nÓg: (Pronunciation: TEER-na-nog) English translation: Land of the Young. A place in the Otherworld past the veil where the Tuatha Dé Danann and lesser fae reside.

Tuatha Dé Danann: (Pronunciation: TOO-ah de-danan) Celtic pantheon of gods. They are considered high-status fae.

US Department of the Preternatural: Employs all manner of magically affiliated and preternatural people for military service. Active duty combat mages are seconded to the Army, Navy, Air Force, and Marines and are required to go through BTC and joint training.

Valkyries: Immortals. A host of female riders who choose who live and die in battle. They guide the dead to either Valhalla or Fólkvangr.

Veil: The metaphysical barrier between Earth/mundane plane and other worlds/dimensions/planes, and versions of hell and heaven derived from myths.

Walker, Estelle: God pack werewolf. Alpha of the New York City god pack.

Wards: Defensive magic.

Warlock: Most common rank of magic users. On par with witches.

Werecreatures: Humans who are infected with the werevirus. Can change form into various animalistic shapes. Werecreatures are either infected later on in life or are born with the disease.

Werevirus: An incurable disease that makes those who are infected change into monstrous beasts. Created by an ancient Roman mage, the werevirus was one of the first recorded instances of magically created biological warfare introduced into society. People are born with the werevirus or become infected through intercourse or blood. Two strains exist: a normal strain and a god strain. The god strain has stronger magical properties which can cause the infected to be susceptible to an immortal patron.

Witch: Most common rank of magic users. On par with warlocks.

WSA: Department for Witchcraft and Supernatural Affairs. A British domestic agency that focuses on magical crimes and terrorism in the United Kingdom. (Equivalent to the SOA)

Yggdrasil: Norse world tree that connects the Nine Realms.

Zhang, Emma: Werewolf. Alpha of the Tempest pack.

Zombie: An undead creature consisting of either a skeleton or fresher corpse. They can only be raised by necromancers. Zombies are powered by black magic and souls pulled from the afterlife beyond the veil.

AUTHOR'S NOTES

This book was a labor of love during a time when real life changed for many of us. I'm thankful my book village could still help me wrangle the words into better shape despite everything going on.

Nora Sakavic, for all her support and friendship and listening to me spaz about moving amidst a pandemic while trying to finish this book.

Leslie Copeland, for being that guiding light when I hit that writing wall and wanted to chuck it out the window, but also for being a wonderful friend.

Lily Morton, for never steering me wrong, for always being there on the other side of the world and the other side of a text message. You've become one of my best friends.

May Archer, who encouraged me so much with this book and cackled in glee rather than horror when I first told her my plans for Paris. Thank you for being such an amazing friend.

Karen Harroch, who was kind enough to read the Paris chapters to ensure I got bits of French culture and Paris locales correct. Thank you so much.

Helen Juliet, who was super sweet and took time out of her

busy writing schedule to ensure the London chapters read like London as opposed to the Moon. Thank you!

Bear, who continues to be an amazing, brilliant friend. I'm so glad you're in my life.

Last but not least: to my readers. Thank you so much for enjoying the worlds I get to write about so that I can write more. All of you are amazing, and I wouldn't get to do this without you.

London and Paris are two of my favorite cities, and I've always wanted to set a story in those locations. I took liberties with foreign police work and agencies in this story. I don't work in either field, I am not English nor French, and I tried my best to blend both into the world I created as best as possible.

I would be thrilled and grateful if you would consider reviewing *On the Wings of War* on Amazon or Goodreads. I appreciate all honest reviews, positive or negative. Reviews definitely help my books get seen, so thank you!

Cover design by AngstyG LLC.
Professional Beta Reading by Leslie Copeland: lcopelandwrites@ gmail.com
Edited by One Love Editing
Proofing by Lori Parks: lp.nerdproblems@gmail.com
Proofing by Jenni Lea at LesCourt Author Services

CONNECT WITH HAILEY

Keep up with my book news by signing up for my newsletter and get the free Soulbound prequel short story *Down A Twisted Path* and several free Metahuman Files short stories while you're at it.

Join the reader group on Facebook: Hailey's Hellions

Visit Hailey's website: www.HaileyTurner.com

Like Hailey's author page

OTHER WORKS BY HAILEY TURNER

M/M Science Fiction Military Romance:

Captain Jamie Callahan, son of a wealthy senator and socialite mother, is a survivor.

Staff Sergeant Kyle Brannigan, a Special Forces operative, is a man with secrets.

Alpha Team, the Metahuman Defense Force's top-ranked field team, is where the two collide and their lives will never be the same.

<u>Metahuman Files</u>

In the Wreckage

In the Ruins

In the Shadows

In The Blood

In The Requiem

In The Solace

<u>A Metahuman Files: Classified Novella</u>

Out of the Ashes

New Horizons

Fire In The Heart

M/M Urban Fantasy

<u>Soulbound</u>

A Ferry of Bones & Gold

All Souls Near & Nigh

A Crown of Iron & Silver

A Vigil in the Mourning

On the Wings of War

An Echo in the Sorrow

A Veiled & Hallowed Eve

<u>Soulbound Universe Standalones</u>

Resurrection Reprise

LGBTQ+ Epic steampunk-inspired fantasy:

Welcome to Maricol, where the land will kill you, kinship turns the gears of war, and burning the dead lest they come back to life is the only way to survive.

<u>Infernal War Saga</u>

The Prince's Poisoned Vow

The Emperor's Bone Palace

<u>Infernal War Saga Novella</u>

An Emporium of Hearts

Contemporary gay romance

Short stories previously published in the Heart2Heart Charity Anthologies.

<u>From the Heart: A Short Story Collection</u>

Audible

All of Hailey Turner's books are available in audiobooks. Visit Audible to discover your next favorite listen.

Hailey Turner Audiobooks

Thanks for reading!

www.ingramcontent.com/pod-product-compliance
Lightning Source LLC
Chambersburg PA
CBHW020336010826
48970CB00012B/1174